IGR

Magical historical fantasy romance

Lavinia Collins

First published in Great Britain and the US in three volumes on Kindle by The Book Folks, 2017.

This paperback edition published in 2018 by The Book Folks.

Typeset in Garamond
Design by Steve French

Available from Amazon.com and other retail outlets

www.thebookfolks.com

ISBN: 978-1-9808-4764-9

For Kay,
As it was in the beginning, and ever shall be.

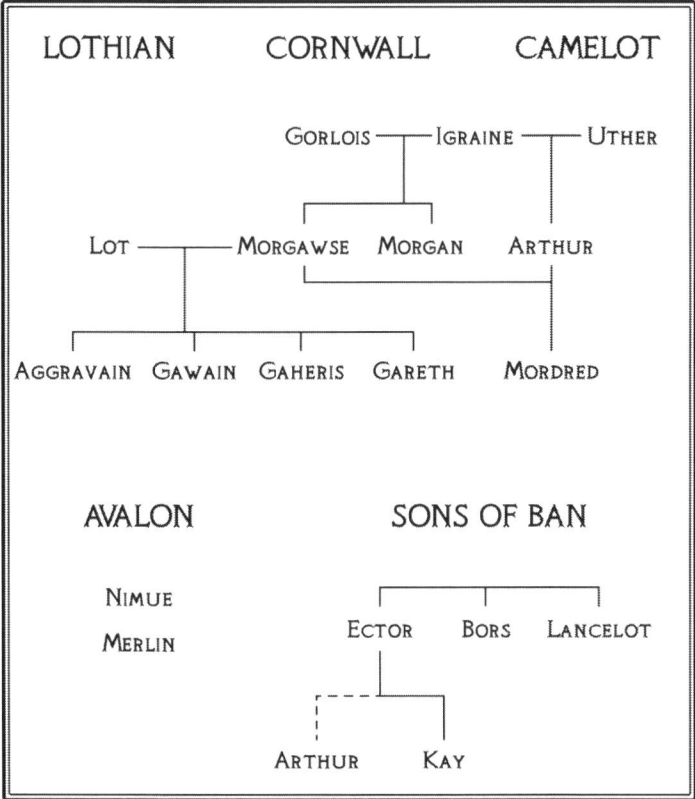

LOTHIAN   CORNWALL   CAMELOT

GORLOIS — IGRAINE — UTHER

LOT — MORGAWSE MORGAN   ARTHUR

AGGRAVAIN GAWAIN GAHERIS GARETH   MORDRED

AVALON   SONS OF BAN

NIMUE

MERLIN   ECTOR   BORS LANCELOT

ARTHUR   KAY

PART I
THE CORNISH
PRINCESS

It befell in the days of Uther Pendragon, when he was king of all England, that there was a mighty duke in Cornwall that held war against him for a long time. And the duke was called the Duke of Tintagil. And so by means King Uther sent for this duke, charging him to bring his wife with him, for she was called a fair lady, and she was surpassing wise, and her name was called Igraine.

Sir Thomas Malory, *Le Morte d'Arthur*

Chapter one

I could hear someone calling my name from far away, from the bottom of the narrow stairs of the south tower, but I pretended I couldn't hear. I wanted another moment alone, to press my forehead against the cool stone of the window and stare out at the waves far below, crashing against the rocks. Even when the sea was calm far out, the waves were white and wild against the dark rock at the foot of the cliff. I didn't want to come down to help my sisters carry the food to the table, or to listen to the men talking about fighting and politics. I wanted to stay there, undisturbed, with nothing between me and the savage beauty of Tintagel.

"Igraine, *Ygerna*, you little grub, come down here!" The shouting grew louder and I sighed, slipping out of the window-seat and back through the curtains into the room. I didn't want to be caught *daydreaming* again. My father would pat me on the head like a child and chuckle as though I were silly. I did not think he would be cross with me, but my sisters would hear, and they would be unkind to me. They would pull my hair and call me spoiled, just like they had done when we were little, only now they were grown, and ought to have been too old for all that. I supposed they were right in some ways, that I was the favourite. I was the youngest, after all, and I had had to be saved from the violent birth that had taken my mother with it by a witch-man who had come from Avalon, just to save me. Fifteen years old and unmarried, too. That was another thing my sisters envied.

"*Igraine!*" It was my oldest sister, Elaine, shouting at me, but as she opened the door, still bellowing, I was running out of it down towards her and she gave a sigh of raw irritation as I bumped into her and her enormous belly.

"It's all very well being in your own little world, Igraine," she scolded, "but sometimes you have to be here with the rest of us. Get your things. We have to ride to London."

"To *London*?" I asked in disbelief. The old Roman town was miles away. The other side of Britain. I did not see what could have been so important that we had to ride all the way to London right when it was time for us to eat. I was hungry. I was annoyed with Elaine for calling me from my thoughts, if it was not to feed me.

"The King of Logrys is dead. We all have to attend the council."

I scrunched up my face in annoyance. I knew I was too old for sulking, but it sounded awful and tedious. Besides, these things all pretended to be civilized at the beginning, and then ended with awful, outright war. I knew how it would be. I had read enough histories to know that it happened the same every single time.

Elaine winced, and put a hand against her stomach. I felt a little less sorry for myself, and little more sorry for her. She would be riding to London heavily pregnant and hungry. I was only hungry.

"Are you alright?" I asked her, gently. She nodded, but she was not. I offered her my arm, and she took it, and I let her lean on me and walk over to the bed. There was an unpleasant-looking clear liquid running down her legs, and I was suddenly sure that she would not be riding with us. I wondered if her husband would stay in Tintagel castle with her. Perhaps they would let me stay.

"Do you want me to stay, Elaine?" I asked her, hopefully. She shook her head. I could see that the thick, gold curls of her hair were already stuck to her forehead with sweat.

"Just tell Máel that I'm not coming."

I nodded, but I didn't want to. Elaine's Irish husband was strange and serious, which ill-suited his little, impish frame. They were a bad match, Elaine having inherited my father's large frame, boisterous temper and heartiness, and her husband so stern and fey. I did not think they liked each other much. This was the first time in six years of marriage that my sister Elaine had been pregnant. I didn't like what that promised for my own future as a bride.

* * *

I ran down the narrow, stone steps into the main hall of the castle. My father was there with my other sister, Enid, and her husband, and Máel. I opened my mouth to say that Elaine was about to have her child, but none of them looked at me as they came in. They were all whispering among themselves. I supposed it was about the King.

After a while, my father noticed me standing there, quiet, and they all turned to look at me.

"Elaine is having her child," I said.

Máel ran off up the stairs. I did not really know why she wanted him there if she disliked him so much, but I said nothing.

"Why do we have to go to London?" I complained.

Enid rolled her eyes. Her husband, Erec – who was a French knight whom she had married hastily, before my father had promised his approval – laughed indulgently at her annoyance, and put his arm around her waist to kiss her on the cheek. She softened a little. I was sure I would have rather had my father's disapproval and Enid's marriage.

"It is up to the wise men of the land to decide what will happen now, since the old King Aurelianus has left no heir. Everyone says that it will be Lot of Lothian, but he is a young man, rash. He has wealth, vast wealth, and armies, but he is only twenty years old. Perhaps not even. We are lucky –" my father glanced around for Máel, and when he was satisfied that he was gone – "that the kings in Tara and Emain Macha have no interest in the throne of Logrys, for there are many who would stand beside them. Perhaps the council would have elected one of Ban's sons, but they will not leave France. Besides, the eldest is also barely a man. Ban himself –" My father made a derisive noise. "Why would he leave France when he can have all of the fourteen-year-old wives he desires there, one after the other? No, I do not know who it will be." He gave another pause, glancing around at all of us, and made a noise in his throat, wary, uncertain. "I have heard it said that Avalon has thrown its might behind Uther Pendragon."

Uther Pendragon. I had heard the name before, but I could not place it.

Behind me, I heard a harsh laugh, and turned around to see Máel standing at the bottom of the stairs, his arms crossed over his narrow chest. He was dressed still in a surcoat of lovely pale blue, sewn through with silver. It was exquisite. If he had not taken it off, then that meant that he had hardly gone to my sister's bedside to hold her hand as she brought his child into the world. I hoped that he had at least called some of the women up there to her. I felt suddenly cold and afraid at the thought of her up there alone.

"Uther Pendragon? So now Avalon gives its support to a half-Roman king, rather than the true blood of the *rightful* peoples of Britain? Men in Emain Macha have been talking for years of the day when Aurelianus has passed and at last none of the British kingdoms will be under the thrall of a Roman king. We need a man of pure blood. Avalon should have already named such a man! Is Avalon grown so weak? So weak, also, that it can only recommend? There was a time – *I* remember a time – when the Lady of Avalon was nothing less than a kingmaker, and now she comes as a suppliant to the council of the King of Logrys to beg that he takes *Uther Pendragon* of all people as his heir? A man of mixed blood. An invader. The lords of Britain won't stand for it."

My father shook his head. "No, Máel. Not Uther Pendragon the father, Uther Pendragon the son."

Máel baulked a little. I had not expected that.

"He is fourteen."

My father shook his head once more. "He is almost twenty."

"He is the witch Merlin's son."

"That is only a rumour, Máel. It is of no matter –"

"It is *not* of no matter." I had not seen Máel shout before, and it frightened me more than I had expected it to from such a small man. "Will Cornwall bow its head to a changeling child of black magic and foreign blood?"

"Who would you have, Máel?" my father demanded, irritably. "Not that upstart Lot, surely? The men north of the Roman Wall are savages, not fit to rule the civilized men of the south –"

Máel's face was turning rather red by now. "He is the only one of noble, ancient blood. Do not overstep yourself – Lot and I are of the same ancient stock. The great line of Gædel Glas and Scota, true rulers of Britain – noble blood of the ancient Greeks and the Pharaohs. Your precious Brutus was, after all, a Trojan, and therefore barely more than a Roman. Some would say those of *his* blood are not fit to rule here. It *will* be a man of the right blood, and the only man is Lot."

"If I hear that nonsense about Greeks and Pharaohs one more time –" My father growled under his breath.

"What did you say to me?" Máel demanded, and the shouting continued. Enid and her husband shrank away. They were always to an extent safely contained in their private world, a little lost in one another. After this, they would go back to France, and I would be alone with my father, or worse with Elaine and Máel. Then the awful thought hit me that this would mean that they would want me to marry someone. My father would want me to do as I wished, but if the new king was a young unmarried man, Máel would want me to be married to him. He was a sharp, careful man with an eye for ambition. That was why he hated old Merlin so much, because he recognised a rival.

* * *

The ride to London was awful. The roads were packed with travellers on horses, all of whom were semi-hysterical with fear at the thought of what would happen to the outlying kingdoms of Britain now the King of Logrys was dead. I wished we could have gone in more comfort, but we went like ordinary travellers. Cornwall was a strange kingdom, I knew from the times I had been to Aurelianus' palace at Winchester, and to Emain Macha to see my sister marry Máel in the court of the King of the Ulaid. It was not that we were poor. We had gold. My father had piles and piles of it, but he sat on it like a dragon and would not spend it. This was the reason that Elaine had gold and jewels, dresses in silk and samite in gorgeous colours, and Enid's clothes were plain and simple. They had only what their husbands could afford to give them.

I was glad that Máel had stayed with Elaine. I thought that it was not a good idea for an angry man to be at a political council. He would have wanted to start a fight. I supposed I would have been less bored.

* * *

As we slowly came nearer to London, I noticed that the knights drew closer to us, and the folk on the road either went armed, or scurrying by without horses. Trouble was coming. I knew that Logrys needed a king if we were all going to be safe from the Saxons and the Romans, but I did not know how those men gathered were ever going to decide.

King Aurelianus' daughter Imogen was there to greet the nobles as we arrived. She was a beautiful, noble lady, middle-aged and childless, but with a proud face and a long, thick rope of red-brown hair. She did not wear her father's crown, though she was covered enough with jewels and fine clothes. I did not see why she could not have been queen. I supposed if she were younger, one of the young kings of Britain would have married her, and that would have been the end of it, but what no one would say was that if some man married her now, she would only create the same problem herself. A queen without a child – who would not bear a child – was only putting off the same old fight for a few years.

"Come into the great hall," she said, waving a hand covered in rings, giving us a gentle smile. But it was strange. Her eyes were unfocussed, fogged a little with white. Was she blind? I found it strange that she was dressed so finely if she was.

I followed my father, and my sister and her husband into the great hall, but I didn't want to go. I wanted to be on my own. I knew what would be expected of me. That I would sit silently while they argued around me, fold my hands neatly in my lap, be a proper young lady.

The hall was already full as we came in, full of bright cloth and loud voices. There was wine too. So they were all going to drink wine while they decided this. That did not seem all that wise to me. I wished that I was old enough that I could ask them to let me speak. They would let Imogen speak, because she was grown old, and because she had no child and she bore her father's voice. She would know his wishes.

As we walked through the hall to the place set for us, I tried to guess who all the kings were. There was a young man, dark and handsome, with a fur cloak over his shoulders that looked altogether too hot for the autumn in Logrys, and I thought I caught a glimpse of the shape of a gryphon's foot on the pommel of his sword. So that was Lot, the new young King of Lothian. I had heard it said that he had an older brother, but that his father had left the kingdom to him because the older brother had gone among the highland tribes and become a savage. I wondered if I would like to become a savage. To be wild, to be free.

Then there were the Welsh princes, each holding his little piece of land. I could not tell which was which. There was one my father's age, grizzled and dark, and a slightly younger man, blond and broad, and two more who looked the same with red hair and bright green eyes, both young; younger than I was. Then there was the party from Avalon. I knew I should not have stared, but I could not help myself. They were so beautiful. The Lady of Avalon sat in their midst, her hair – ash blonde, thick – curled into a twisted plait and lying across her shoulder, her eyes crinkled wise at the edges, a circlet of white gold on her head set with a five-pointed star in bright gems. But most of all, across her skin in lovely swirls like the patterns of the sea, blue-green woad. I wished I could touch her, the flowing hem of her light silk gown, the thick strands of her hair, the patterns on her skin. Beside her sat Merlin the witch, whom I had seen before. He was a strange man, and had been the same for as long as I could remember, with hollow black eyes in a bald head tattooed with the same woad, and nasty skull-like teeth.

Then my eyes met those of the young man sat beside him. I felt suddenly exposed, caught at something I should not be doing, although I knew it was fine enough for me to look at him. He was a strange-looking man, rough, with grey-green eyes that gazed with a steadiness that I could not look away from. He looked away after a moment, but when he raised a hand to push his dull gold hair back off his face, against the inside of his wrist I saw in the blue-green of Avalon's woad the shape of a serpent, coiling around. *Uther Pendragon.* So, *this* was Avalon's choice.

* * *

I had not been wrong about the council. First it was civilised, and men listened to Imogen as she explained that her father King Aurelianus had said to her that he would follow Avalon's judgement and name Pendragon as his heir. First the objections were gentle. Pendragon was no blood relation of Aurelianus, Lot objected, and he and his brothers were cousins. Distant, the Lady of Avalon objected. I wondered why she had chosen him. Perhaps it *was* because he was a changeling child of Merlin's, but I did not think he could be. He did not have the fairy look about him, nor the same Otherworld grace that those from Avalon bore with them. I did not have it in me, but I knew what it was. The Welsh princes began talking about Brutus, objecting that they were the closest descendants of the king who had given the land its name. More shouting. I was glad Máel was not there. I was almost as sick as my father was of hearing him drone on about Scota and Gædel Glas and Greeks and Egyptians. If he and the Scots in the north were such great friends then surely there would have been even one man from the Irish courts here to support Lot.

Then one of the kings stood, a man who identified himself as Leodegrance, King of Carhais and Brittany, in order to declare himself a supporter of the claim of Lot. I noticed that the young wife who sat beside him was dressed in armour, like a man, and had a bow slung across her back. She also had red hair, redder than I had ever seen, and dark where red hair was usually fair. She was beautiful, but strange, with that leather and bronze on her. She did not speak. I wondered what all the queens and wives and mothers and daughters in the room were thinking. I wondered what *I* thought.

"We should put aside arguments of old blood," the Breton King pointed out, with a rather self-satisfied smile. "Otherwise this island of yours would rightfully belong to the giants, or to Albina and her murderous sisters."

Another roar of objections, insults, obscenities which I was sure I should not have heard spoken by such noble men.

"We have spoken. I do believe the wishes of Aurelianus himself and Avalon ought to be sufficient for us to agree." The Lady of Avalon's voice cut through the growing roar of men's voices arguing.

Lot, the bold young king from the north, gave a rough laugh.

"What if we begin to refuse the commands of Avalon? Will you turn us all into newts?"

Some of the men laughed, but there was an uneasy quiet afterwards, and the Lady of Avalon stared hard at Lot. I did not think he was such a handsome young man as when I had first seen him. He looked a little arrogant, over-confident in his youth. I supposed as a new-made king he was revelling in his sudden power. I wondered if I would be the same, if someone made me a king.

"Now Avalon commands we take a king of Roman blood to rule us all from the south, from a palace of Roman ruins? There was once a time when Avalon stood with the kings north of the Roman Wall.

Our lands were the only lands on this island undefeated. Now you want to hand our lands to this Roman?"

"I am three parts Briton," Uther said, quietly. It was the first time he had spoken. Lot laughed, and Uther's expression darkened. "How many parts are you Pict?"

Lot slammed one fist down hard on the table. "I am no Pict. We in Lothian do not carelessly mix our blood with foreigners or savage tribes. Nor do we use that *Roman* word to speak of one of the true peoples of Britain." He turned from Uther to glance about the room. "Stand with me, and see a British king rule the British peoples. A man of ancient blood."

Uther opened his mouth to speak, but the Lady of Avalon rested a gentle hand over his, and he fell quiet.

"You know as well as all these men do that the Pendragon line is ancient, and while not a line as rich in gold as your own, one which has given many sons and daughters to Avalon. True, Uther's mother's father was a Roman, but was Brutus himself not a Roman, descended from Aeneas? You, besides, would have a Britain ruled from north of the Roman Wall, would you not?"

"I would have a Britain ruled by a *true* king, born of true blood."

"You would wrest power from the south, and hoard it for yourself. And if Romans or Saxons come again from the south to our shores, you will be far away, safe behind your wall, and you would not protect us."

There was another uneasy murmur in the room. Many of the men seemed to prefer Lot, but no one would openly speak against Avalon. And the Lady of Avalon seemed to be the only one making any sense. Lothian was the furthest kingdom from Cornwall – I did not see how they would protect us if they had all of the soldiers, and invaders came again. I wished I could have run away, or spoken for myself, but I just sat there as the shouting rose around me, and I wondered what would happen. Why could these men *not* agree? What was so wrong with Uther Pendragon that all the other kings were opposing him? I did not know, I could not know, I just wished the shouting would stop.

Chapter two

Late that night, after my father and my sister and her husband had gone to their rooms to sleep, I sat out in the courtyard of the small, low building we had gathered in for the council. This was not where the old King Aurelianus had lived. His palace was at Winchester, and was full of gold and fine things. We had deliberately called here, to the old Roman fortress town at London, because – I supposed – Imogen had hoped that the young kings of Britain would be less greedy without the sight of her father's great castle and the riches it held. She had been wrong.

As I sat, staring up at the stars overhead, I noticed two figures talking on the other side of the courtyard. They did not look friendly, both standing wary, one with his hand around the arm of the other, as though he was trying to stop him leaving, but they were not fighting. I was curious, but I was also afraid. They were two men, and I was a young woman, out alone at night. I should have been safe enough among nobles, but I knew I ought not to go over. I was only just becoming aware of the danger that I carried around with me now, that would be dangerous until I was safely married. Something I had to protect. It would all *matter* more now. I did not see any of the other kings with a young unmarried daughter, and though my father was not ambitious, my brother-in-law was, and if they could marry me to the King of Logrys, they would do it. I did not want that. I did not like London. It was dense and cramped, and smelled of poverty and sickness. I did not care for Winchester either, and all of the bowing and smiling and chatter that came with a wealthy court. I liked the salty smell of Tintagel castle; I liked the black rocks and the scrubby grass. I liked the quiet. I wanted to marry a man who would live in Tintagel with me, and ask for nothing more than little Cornwall, and be satisfied.

The two men moved further into the courtyard, and I saw it was Lot of Lothian and Uther Pendragon. I shrank back a little into the shadows, but they had seen me already. A strange smile spread across Lot's face, and he called out to me.

"You –" He reached out his hand in a gesture of beckoning. "Come here."

They were noble men, both, and though the castle was sleeping, people would wake if I screamed. I was safer out in the middle of the courtyard. I walked forward. I could feel myself tense with misgivings. These men were meant to be rivals. I wondered what they were talking about down here.

Lot crossed his arms over his chest as I came closer, looking at me with a cold, appraising eye, chewing his lip just a little. I could see him taking in my clothes: the plain, rough silk of the dress, the lack of jewels, my hair just plaited over my shoulder. The women from the other kingdoms had fine hairstyles held in place by nets of gold, or jewelled pins. I knew I looked plain and poor. I didn't mind. So did Tintagel castle, and its vaults were filled with gold.

"What is your name?" he asked. Uther was still quiet, but I could feel him watching me as well, his gaze more steady and unreadable than Lot's.

"Igraine," I told him. "Igraine of Cornwall."

He nodded thoughtfully, then turned back to Uther. "She's a Celt, then. You were right." He turned back to me. "*I* thought you were French."

I crossed my arms, taking a step back from them. I was not sure what they were getting at, wasn't sure I wanted to get involved. I was sick of all the talk of this blood or that blood, this ancestor or that one. Lot had deliberately not said *Briton*. I wished that I had just run away inside. They looked between each other, and Lot spoke again.

"We had a wager."

"About where I was from?" I asked, derisive. They looked like men, but they were boys. I was not sure either of them should have been King.

Lot shook his head. "I wagered Pendragon that I could get you to kiss me, and he told me if I could before he did, then he would support *my* claim to Aurelianus' throne."

I was disgusted. They *were* boys. So, while the rest of the council were anxious over the future of the realm, they were peeking at me and imagining boys' games. Did they think they were clever? I could see why Lot had felt so comfortable making the bet. He was easy and confident where Uther was quiet and sullen; he was handsome in an obvious way where Uther's looks were more rough. Perhaps he had been successful with women before. He was the elder, I guessed, but it could only have been by a little.

"You should be ashamed of yourselves," I said sharply, "to make a game of this."

Lot shrugged. "Is this any more of a game than those men arguing are playing? Who can shout the loudest? Who can get the most other lords to agree with them? We shall make this easier for you. We shall wrestle, and you will kiss the winner."

"I shall *not*," I insisted, but Lot was already unbuttoning his surcoat and pulling it off, throwing it down into the dusty courtyard – even though it was thick brocade and sewn with gold thread – and squaring up to Uther. Uther was wearing a leather jerkin, the clothes of a common soldier rather than the clothes of a nobleman, and he did not offer to take it off. He was broader than Lot, but he did not seem to be trying all that hard; either that or he did not know how to fight in the leisure-manner of the noblemen, and was only used to the sword and the battlefield, because it did not take Lot long to throw him down into the dust. I could see his face darken with anger, but he didn't say anything.

Lot stepped towards me, and I stepped away.

"I'll not do it," I said, stubbornly.

Lot shrugged, and picked up his surcoat, brushing the dust off it. "Perhaps not tonight," he said, "but I can wait."

And he left. I didn't like the sound of his voice. I didn't like the *assumption*.

I glanced at Uther, picking himself up from the dust. He glared at me. I didn't know why. I ought to have been glaring at him. Them with their suggestion of the stupid game. Childish. I just wanted to go home. I turned to leave, and I heard Uther call out behind me, "It's going to be me, Igraine."

I turned around. I opened my mouth to speak again, but he continued.

"They will name me Aurelianus' successor."

I shrugged. "I suppose it still counts for something to have Avalon's favour," I said, evenly. I was not sure if he would make a good king, but there was something solid about him. He did not pretend, as Lot did, to be some fine man.

"It does," he said honestly.

I found myself intrigued. I wanted to know why he had such favour from them. His father had been a great and famous warrior, but was now old. But his father was half-Roman, and Avalon did not always look on them with as much favour as their own people, since they had brought their religion with them, which banned Avalon's magic arts. I wondered if it was true, what Máel had said about him and Merlin.

"Truly, though," I said, carefully, "I have heard it said that you are Merlin's bastard child and that is why Avalon wants you on the throne."

Uther shook his head, pushing the toe of his boot through the dust of the courtyard.

"If you saw my father you would not doubt," he said, with a smile to himself. Then he looked up at me, and when his grey-green eyes caught me again I felt the jump of nerves I resented within me. I ought not to have been shy. "But I did make a bargain with Merlin."

I was not sure if Uther was teasing me.

"What did you promise him?" I asked, softly. He did not look away.

"My first-born son."

He was so serious. I felt a chill go down my spine. An awful promise, especially to a man like Merlin. I thought he was going to laugh, and say he was teasing me, but he didn't. He stared out across the courtyard, deep in thought. I wondered what Merlin wanted with a child.

"What if you never have a child?" I asked.

Uther shrugged. "I'll still be King, and I will be wise enough to name my successor publicly, and in good time."

"Why?"

Uther's eyes narrowed at me, as though he did not understand the question.

"Why would any man want that? Why would it be worth the exchange?"

"Why not? Why should I not want what every other man wants, whether he says so or not? Riches. Power. Each man here would do anything he could to lay his hands on either. Even your father, though he pretends such worldly things are beneath his concern."

I nodded, thoughtful. What a promise to make. I did not think Uther truly understood what he had promised to the witch. I would never have made such a promise. I did not think anything was worth that. But then I thought of my father. If he had made such a promise, he would never have had to give up a child.

Then, while I was deep in thought, Uther grabbed me by the arm and pulled me against him in a rough kiss. I had not kissed a man before, and it took me by surprise. More than anything, I was aware of how he smelled: the leather of his jerkin, the dirt and sweat on his skin. He smelled like an animal, and yet I did not pull away, not for a moment. I felt his hand against my cheek, and then sliding into my hair, pulling me closer, and I let my mouth open with his, and I felt the brush of his tongue. I was lost for a moment, forgetting that I was out in the middle of the courtyard, that he was almost a stranger. I was surprised that I liked the feel of a man's mouth against my own, of a hard body pressed against me.

When he moved away, it took me another moment to collect myself enough to be angry. So, he had only told me the truth about himself to distract me so that he could win his game with Lot. I was angry that I had begun to like him when he was as much of a pathetic boy as Lot. I slapped him once, hard. He gave a strange smile, cocking one eyebrow in amusement. He pressed the back of his hand against the corner of his mouth, where I had caught him, but there was no harm there to feel.

"So, you're still playing your stupid games," I snapped.

"It's not a game, Igraine," he said, seriously, stepping towards me as I stepped back away from him. "The witch Merlin has told me that I shall have you as my wife."

"Well, you shall not. The witch Merlin does not own every man, woman and child in Britain. I shall *not* be your wife. Not now, not ever."

Uther shrugged. "You shall, Igraine. I, too, can wait."

I turned and ran away then, back up to the room that I was set to sleep in. My sister was still awake, though Erec was sleeping, or in any case the bed-curtains were drawn. I was sure she was a little glad that I had not come up to sleep when the rest of them had. She had been angry that Imogen had not had enough rooms for me to have my own, and that I would have to sleep on a pallet in theirs. At least they had had a little peace.

When she caught my eye, I could see that she was grinning, and that she had been looking out of the courtyard window. She, like Elaine, looked like our father – big and hearty and golden-haired. I was the only one, I was told, who resembled our mother: tall, slender, dark-haired. I wished that I looked like them, wished I was bold like them. They would have slapped the pair of them in the face before that stupid game had even begun.

"So…" Enid said, her voice thick with sisterly confidence. I knew what she would want to know. "Little Igraine is old enough to be letting boys kiss her in the courtyard?"

She knelt down beside the little bed as I pulled my overdress over my head and slipped into it with a shrug. I knew why she was pleased. She hoped that I would want to marry him, and that our father would be angry, and that this would mean he was angry with someone other than her.

"He's a brute. He grabbed me," I complained.

Enid smiled more deeply. "Well, you looked to me as though you were enjoying it."

I cast her a dirty look, and turned my back to her to sleep. Still, when I closed my eyes, I could still feel his lips against mine, and I didn't know *how* I felt about it.

Chapter three

The next day, it was clear that the council was not going to agree. The party from Lothian and Orkney left, refusing to support Uther

Pendragon. After that, the Bretons shrugged and decided it was nothing to do with them, and they left. The Welsh princes were affronted that their voice did not seem to be heard, and Imogen was frustrated that her father's choice had not been accepted, and everyone was unsatisfied.

We left before Uther was crowned. I think my father was dissatisfied as well, because he did not say anything. He had not spoken up in favour of anyone, as I had thought he might. The journey back was unpleasant. The news had spread that the council had failed, and for the first time in record, refused to agree, and Avalon had acted against the consensus of the lords of Britain. I thought it had been Merlin more than Avalon. I thought men were afraid of him, because he was strange.

So the roads were full of people, more afraid than they had been before. Worse, Enid kept trying to giggle with me, trying to lead me into conspiracy with her, having imagined in her head something between me and Uther Pendragon. Well, he would marry someone else now. Someone whose father was behind him.

I knew what would happen next. Cornwall would close its borders, put up garrisons, seal off from Logrys. I knew that my father and Aurelianus had been close, had ridden to war together, had been of the same blood. *Blood* – that was the heart of the mess of it all. Men, and their obsession with blood.

* * *

By the time we arrived back at Tintagel, the news had reached Elaine and Máel there. Máel was furious, Elaine too exhausted to care. She had a little baby boy in her arms, so her husband should have been pleased, but it had not softened him. He was angry that my father had not thrown his support in with Lot. He suggested that I should have been offered to Lot as a wife. I did not think I would like Lothian. But my father shook his head, and said that I would not be offered to anyone who had their own land and castle. He wanted me to have Tintagel. My heart leapt. I would never have to leave my home. But that did mean he was thinking of who I would marry.

That night, I lay in my bed staring up at the empty darkness, wondering what would become of Britain. I hoped that it was all fuss about nothing, and that it would settle down, and the other kings would accept Uther. I could not stop worrying about Elaine going back to Ireland, and Enid back to France; I could not stop worrying that I would never see them again. It was lonely in Tintagel without them, even now when they, so much older than I was, had husbands and lands of their own, and things to think about other than their little sister, who was always daydreaming, always missing when she was looked for, always getting away with more than they ever had. I felt an awful childish fear of the world changing. I had the sense that it was about to, and I did not like it.

By the time my sisters left, war had already begun in the north between the armies of Lothian and Uther's army. It was distant, but it still reached us, in the fear in people's hearts, the way they talked. I tried to hide from it, sitting up in my room in the window seat with the curtains drawn, but it was there, like a storm-cloud on the horizon. It also meant that my father was anxious that I be married.

I was sorry for it because I liked the quiet of Tintagel castle, and his declaration that I should be married brought men from all over Britain to the castle. They all wanted Cornwall as an ally for their own lands. I supposed because my father had no sons and my sisters were married and gone, they looked at me and saw my father's castle.

I didn't like the castle being full and noisy. I didn't like having to dress in my mother's old clothes. She had had lovely samite dresses sewn with silver and gold thread, jewels, little ornaments for her hair, and wearing them made me look suddenly like a woman, rather than a girl. I missed my plain dress. I felt as though I was being dressed up and offered around as an enticement for those competing for the castle. I started wearing my hair the way the grown women of Cornwall did, twisted back at the front and pinned, and loose behind. The pin was heavy, and I was aware that it was white gold and set with pearls, and I was afraid of losing it. I didn't like being called down from my room all the time to meet people whose names I instantly forgot.

The first to come were the French. King Ban of France's eldest son came, with a small party of knights. I knew what I was expecting, because I had overheard people talking about Ban. He was an old lecher, they said. I supposed he must be old indeed, because his son was older than I was, and *my* father was old. But the son was not what I was expecting; he had a kind face, and a gentle smile, friendly blue eyes and a sweet French accent to his voice when he spoke. I didn't want to go to France, and I doubted this young man was really intending to stay in Tintagel if he could have his wife in his father's castle, and I was sorry because I liked him as soon as I saw him. He was good-looking, too, with thick, black hair, worn long in the French manner. I did notice, though, that his armour was plated with gold, and looked new. I was not sure that, if Lothian sent someone, he would stand a chance of winning.

A large party came next from Wales, a whole band of boys and men, and those just in-between, all red-haired and loud and boisterous. I could not tell them apart, and they all seemed like children. The Irish did not send anyone, since they already had my sister, and did not need any more of Cornwall's alliance. There was the King of the Vale there, too, though I hoped since he was old and grey in his hair and his beard, that if his son fought and won for him, then I would marry the son. In truth, I did not want to marry any of them.

I wished that it did not have to be decided this way, although I supposed it would not be, really. The tournament was to keep the young men distracted while my father spoke to their fathers, their mothers, their uncles, to determine what was being offered in exchange for me. I hoped that he would ask me, too, what I wanted, although I was not sure any more that I could rely on his fatherly indulgence, now that Britain was at war with itself.

* * *

The day before the tournament, I wandered down to the courtyard, curious to see the men buckling on their armour and preparing for the day. I wondered what they would think when they saw me, or if they would not see me, with Tintagel's turrets looming over me. I walked more carefully than I usually did, conscious of the thin silver bracelets around my wrists, my carefully dressed hair, the expensiveness of the fine samite dress I wore, which was a lovely silver-grey and sewn through with gorgeous patterns of swirls like the women of Avalon wore on their faces. I did not feel beautiful, though. I felt like a child dressed in her mother's clothes.

Down in the corner of the courtyard, I saw the French prince, and deciding that I would make my own investigations into who would make me a good husband, I walked over. He smiled when he saw me, and offered me his hand. When I put my hand in his, he kissed it, and I blushed. He was *very* handsome, and already I was afraid I was making up my mind.

He bowed slightly. "My lady Igraine. It is an honour to be allowed to seek your hand."

I smiled, and he smiled, and I felt for a moment as though there was no one else around us. I was sure I wanted him to win.

* * *

He did not, though. The winner of the day was one of the Welsh knights, young but huge, a head taller than all the other men, and half as broad again. Even though the French prince, who was announced as Ector of Benwick, was a skilled and careful fighter, the huge Welsh boy knocked the sword easily out of his hands. Still, my father was more impressed by the careful chivalry of the loser than the brute force of the winner, and I began to feel hopeful.

* * *

After the meal in the evening, I danced with Ector, leaning into the feel of his hand in mine, and when it brushed against my back, or my arm. I felt full of a bright, excited hope. Would it be this simple – the man I hoped to marry would also be my father's choice? It seemed too good to be true.

"This is a beautiful castle," Ector said gently, as we danced. I smiled.

"I think so, though it cannot be so fine as your father's castle in France."

He smiled to himself, glancing up, not missing the steps of the dance, at the arched and vaulted ceiling over us, the bare beams of it and the deep stone roof that disappeared into the darkness above. We did not have hanging tapestries sewn with gold thread here, or cups and plates of gold like Aurelianus had had at Winchester, nor did we have much fine silk or jewels. I wore almost all that we had. It must have looked strange, and savage and poor compared to the courts of France, which everyone said were finer by far than those of Britain.

"No, it is not so fine," Ector said, his smile deepening, "but it is far more beautiful. Benwick castle is so full of gold and brocade that you feel you are suffocating on it. It is neat and low and square. Tintagel is beautiful. Wild. It looks as though it has grown from the rock, rather than been carved from it. Truly, this is the most beautiful castle I have ever seen."

He met my gaze for a moment, before lifting my hand over my head so that I could turn for the dance. I was glad of the chance to look away. I was sure I was flushed with my wild excitement. He loved Tintagel castle. And he did not love it because its vaults were filled with gold, he loved it for all the reasons that I loved it. By the time I returned to my seat, I felt light and dizzy with excitement. I knew my father would be pleased.

* * *

I did not want to waste any time. I did not want anyone else to ask my father for my hand before Ector could.

I knocked on the heavy door of his study the next day.

"Is that you, little Ygerna?"

He called me by the name he had given me when I was born.

"It's me, Father."

"Come in. A father always has time for his daughters."

I was self-conscious, a little embarrassed. The rickety table my father sat at was strewn with pieces of parchment in Latin and French and some in the rough Cornish they spoke in the towns and villages. News from all around Britain. Little, I imagined, good.

"Sit down, Ygerna."

He moved a pile of parchment from a little chair and I slipped into it. I was glad to be sitting side by side with him at the desk rather than face-to-face. Out of the narrow window ahead of us both I could see the men, far below, saddling their horses and weighing their lances in their hands, ready to compete.

"I think I know who I want, Father," I said.

He nodded beside me.

"Good. That's good. No sense in drawing this out. But tell me one thing – if you could have one wish – one wish in all the world, Ygerna – what would it be?"

I thought about it for a moment.

"To stay in Cornwall. To stay here in Tintagel, and for the kingdom to be peaceful and safe."

My father nodded thoughtfully once more.

"This man you have chosen – can he give those things to you?"

I looked at my father properly then. The skin of his face was slack, his hair all grey and thinned away. I realised with a jolt that this was why he cared so deeply, so suddenly that I should be married. It was not just the wars in Britain. He wanted to be sure that no one could take Tintagel from me after he was gone.

"I think so – I – he likes it here. And he's brave, and strong. I think he can."

My father took my hand between his two old, leathery, ink-stained hands.

"Tell me who."

"It's Prince Ector."

My father closed his eyes and nodded slowly. "Good, Ygerna. Good. That's a very wise choice. A man of great and noble stock. A brave fighter. A man of honour. Good."

He pressed his lips against my temple and I leant against him. I felt like crying, but I didn't. I had always known that this day – the end of my childhood – would have to come.

"I'll send out some letters today, see how things are. I'll be ready, when he asks me."

* * *

I should have waited, I should have been sure, but I was caught up in the possibilities of being a great lady, of being a *wife*, and I thought I was sure. I rushed to Ector, to tell him that he should ask my father. He had said nothing to me, but he had been kind and attentive. He had come here, which surely he would not have done if he did not want me as his wife.

I found him in the stables, and I was glad to find him alone.

"My lady Igraine," he said, giving me his gentle smile as I came in. I felt the pleasant brush of nerves inside me, and I steeled myself. "You look lovely, as always."

I smiled, looking down at my feet, feeling myself blush. I was aware, distantly, that I ought to have been more cynical. I did not know him well. But then, he had loved my home as I had, and he was so kind. Besides, he was handsome. I could not pretend I did not want a handsome husband.

"I have come to tell you, sir," I said, still looking down at my feet, "that it is my wish that you ask my father for us to be married."

He was silent. I did not know what he was thinking, what he was feeling. Was he nervous? Unsure whether my father would say yes? I had expected him to say *something*.

"My father will give his permission, I am sure, if you ask," I added. I wished I could have looked up, looked him in the eye, but I was shy and resentful of that shyness. I wanted to be bold like my sister Enid, who had done whatever she had wanted. Perhaps I should have done what she had done, and run away with him in secret.

"I am honoured, my lady," he said, gently. I looked up to meet his eye and he smiled, but it was less warm and full than it had been before. I told myself he was anxious; I would have liked to have thought so, but I felt uneasy. Did he not want to marry me? But he must have done. Why else would he have come?

"Good," I said, unsure of what else to say. I thought he would be happier, more excited. He had always been so kind and attentive. As though sensing my hesitance, my doubt, he leaned forward and kissed me on the cheek. It was brief, courteous. It was polite. I remembered, suddenly, Uther Pendragon grabbing me and kissing me in London. That had been rude, and unwanted, and somehow so much better, more exciting, than Ector – who I was sure I wanted as my husband – kissing me politely on the cheek.

Chapter four

I left, knowing I ought to have been happy, but feeling heavy and empty in the pit of my stomach. My father would offer me to him, even though he had not won, and we would be married, live here, and I would have what I wanted. But why did I suddenly feel that I did *not* want it? Was it just his nervousness, his awkwardness? But he had *never* been so before. He had been easy and charming, without cares.

I lay awake that night. I couldn't decide if I should go to my father and tell him to refuse. He would think I was a silly child, changing my mind. He would think I hadn't considered my choice properly, and he would not let me choose for myself again. Perhaps *I* was nervous.

Still, I thought that talking to my father would make me feel better, so I slipped from my bed, and wrapped a cloak around myself, and went down the narrow stairs to look for him. The stone was cold against my bare feet, but I was used to it, and it was pleasant enough on that warm summer night. Besides, my heart wouldn't stop beating fast inside me, I felt a little hot and stuffy, and I liked the feel of the cold.

He wasn't in his room, or in the hall. I decided I would go out to the courtyard anyway, since it was lovely to stand on the grass and feel the soft blades of it beneath my feet, and stare up at the stars. It was a clear summer night, and it would give me some peace to be out in it. I thought of the prayers I had learned at school on the shores of Avalon, the ones that no one said now, the ones best in the moonlight for the White Goddess when it was swelling, and the Hanged God when it was fading away. Those seemed like the right kind of prayers for something like this. God and Christ did not seem to care much for the worries of young women who were about to be wed.

But as I came to the edge of the courtyard, I could hear whispering, and I shrunk into the shadows. I could see the shape of a woman, long, gold hair loose down her back, a rough cloak around her shoulders. A peasant, or at any rate someone lowly. But she wasn't one of our servants. There was someone else with her, but they were hidden in the shadow of the castle. I crept closer, led by curiosity.

"Do you wish I had not come?" The girl was whispering, and I saw her hands close around the front of a man's surcoat that glinted with silver thread as it caught the light of the moon, and purple cloth showed between her pale fingers. Her tone was flirtatious, and she pulled the man closer towards her. It was Ector, and I felt my stomach drop. There was another woman. But he looked resistant. Was she someone from his past, who he could not get rid of?

He put his hands over hers, as though he was going to try to pull her hands from his coat, but he did not.

"Viviane, *please*," he said, softly, but when she leaned towards him, he did not seem so resistant at all, and he leant his forehead against hers, and closed his eyes, and sighed. "Viviane, we have talked about this."

She leaned up, and kissed him, pulling him against her. I saw him hesitate, but only for a moment. Then his hands ran down her shoulders, and then her back, and he wrapped his arms around her waist and pulled her tight against him. He had not offered to kiss me like that, though I would have liked it.

Slowly, as though forcing himself, he drew away.

"Viviane, it is for the best if we part. I have made promises – I must be married," he said, but his eyes were closed, and I could see, even from my hiding-place, his chest rising and falling.

She shook her head, taking his face in her hands. I could see that she was a wild, passionate woman entirely unlike me. I felt the hurt of it strike me a little, as I thought it truly must have been my castle that Ector had seen.

"Do you love her?" she demanded, in full voice. Ector shushed her, and she looked annoyed.

"No, Viviane. I love *you*."

She pushed him away then, angry, forcing her voice to a whisper when it was clear that she wanted to shout. "Then you are twice as cruel, Ector, to marry a woman you do not love and to send away one that you do."

"Viviane, you don't understand." He reached out and took her hand, trying to draw her back towards him. His tone was pleading but I did not feel sorry for him. "I cannot take you back to France, to my father. You would hate it. You would have to become someone else. I don't want you to change. I want you to be happy. I want you to be free."

"What about this girl you marry?" she demanded. *Yes*, I thought, *What about her?* "Do you know how women suffer when a man who does not love them marries them? She will know. Women *always* know. Oh, you will be kind, Ector, and you will take care of her, but none of that replaces love. None of that…" She brushed her fingertips against his cheek, then across his lips and he closed his eyes and sighed towards her. She slid a hand into his hair, her fingers closing around the thick, soft waves of it, and drew him close again, her lips so close she could have kissed him. But she held back for a moment. "Nothing is worth as much as love."

She kissed him again, and he slid his arm under her cloak, pulling her against him once more. They kissed for a long time, but I could not look away. At last she pushed him back, and I heard her whisper.

"Run away with me, then we can all be free; you, me, and this poor girl you are all squabbling over."

He looked at her, and I knew it was what he wanted. He had never looked at me the way he looked at her. He was kind, and courteous and friendly, but he *loved* this other woman. If he did not go with her, I would not have him. I did not want a man who would marry me for a castle while in love with someone else.

She leaned up towards him as though she was going to kiss him again, and when he leaned towards her, she moved back, and whispered, "Come with me, Ector. Tonight."

He leaned in once more to kiss her, and she put her fingertips against his lips.

"Say yes, Ector. Run away with me," she whispered.

"Yes," he murmured, kissing her again, running his hands into her long, loose hair. "Yes, Viviane. Yes."

I ran all the way back up to my room and climbed back into bed. In the morning, Ector was gone, and I did not say that I was the only one who knew where he was.

* * *

I felt awful – hot and frustrated and ashamed at my own foolishness. How had I thought that it was wise or sensible of me to ask to marry the first man that I thought was kind to me? I had wanted Ector because he was handsome and kind, but he was already someone else's, and we had been barely more than strangers.

My father was furious. Angry as I was, I tried to stop him writing to Ector's father of how his son had insulted us, leaving in secret. I could not stop him. I was sure that Ector would be punished for it. But then my father put his hand against my cheek, and I looked up at him, and he said gently, "Forget this, my love. Every other man here would give his life for the chance to have you as his wife." And he kissed me on the forehead and I nodded. But I no longer felt the excitement of it. The whole thing seemed awfully like a cattle market, again.

The next day, I watched the tournament without interest. The Welsh giant won once more, but no one seemed to care, since he was the foster-brother of the Welsh princes, rather than a brother of full blood. It was warm in the summer sun, and I was half drifting off to sleep as the knights were unsaddling their horses and pulling off their armour, when a huge shout went up from the gates of the castle, and the hunting horns sounded. That only meant one thing. The arrival of a king. My heart sank, for I knew who it would be. Lot would never have made it all the way down to Cornwall through Uther's lands.

"King Uther," the men were shouting. "The King of Logrys."

We all stood as he rode in – he did not bother to dismount or disarm even as he rode through our gates – with his band of knights. It was aggressive, and it was disrespectful. I could see him at the head of them, his helm thrown off, his coarse gold hair dusty from the ride, his eyes narrowed against the sun. He looked as though he had come here for war. I noticed that the witch Merlin rode with them, his face all but hidden in the cowl of his black robe. I noticed, too, that the Lady of Avalon had not come with them.

My father stood slowly from his seat, leaning heavily on the arm of the chair to steady himself.

"My lord King Uther," he began, his tone prickly, without respect. "To what do we owe this *unexpected* honour?"

Uther jumped down from his horse in the centre of the courtyard. He did not bow to my father. King Aurelianus had always been gracious enough to bow to the other kings of Britain, however small their lands. But Aurelianus had been wise and secure in his power, and he had not needed a young man's cheap intimidations. I wondered where Imogen was now. I hoped that someone was taking care of her.

"No one informed me that the Lady Igraine was to be married."

"Cornwall conducts its own affairs, my lord. We are not a vassal of Logrys." My father was sharp, sharper than he would ever have been with Aurelianus, or even with a young king like Lot. My father *liked* Lot, though I could not see why.

Uther did not seem to notice, but continued as if my father had not spoken.

"You can call an end to this ridiculous display. I will take Igraine as my wife."

Before I could open my mouth to protest, my father was shaking his head.

"I do not give my consent."

"I shall not compete," Uther insisted.

"You are welcome to our hospitality here," my father said, though he did not sound one bit as though he meant it, "to refresh your men and horses, and to compete if you wish, but I cannot consent to give my daughter to a husband who would not remain in Tintagel."

Uther had not looked at me yet, and I was resentful. He thought because Merlin had promised me to him that I was his possession and he did not have to consider my wishes. He was too foolish to realise that he might have persuaded me himself. I had liked the way he had kissed me. I thought he was a little rough, a little arrogant, but I was not sure where a woman found a man to protect her who was not either of those things. Still, I was glad that my father would not consent to marry me to the kind of man who rode through our castle gates demanding me.

Uther nodded in response to my father's offer, and turned to his men, clearly intending to avail himself of my father's generosity immediately. My father leaned over to me and sighed, his voice thick with annoyance, "I wish it were not a sin above others to kill a guest."

Brute though Uther was, I did not understand why my father hated him quite so much.

* * *

The meal that night was tense and unpleasant, and I was eager to leave. As soon as I could, I slipped out into the night air of the courtyard. It was stuffy in the hall, the air filled with the cloying smells of meat, the smoke of the hearth, and the sweaty bodies of knights. Out in the courtyard it was silent and the sky was clear, the pole star glinting above me, and the sliver of the waning moon shining down its faint light. I was relieved to be away. But the relief lasted only a moment, for I heard my name beside me, and Uther was there. He had followed me out. I felt the anger flash within me, but I said nothing. I turned to leave, and he grabbed my arm and pulled me back. When I tried to pull away from him, he grasped me hard by both arms and pushed me against the wall of the courtyard. His grey-green eyes fixed me with their steady look. I couldn't tell if he was aware of how hard he was holding me, that he was hurting me. Already he was bigger, more dense with muscle than he had been from riding in his wars with the heavy armour on his back. I was aware of my own smallness, my slenderness, my weakness.

"I know you are barely more than a child, Igraine," he said, his voice low and level, "but you must try to understand that we are meant for each other."

"That means little to me," I told him haughtily, wriggling against his grip, which he did not loosen, resentful that he had called me a child when I was now sixteen years old. "I don't have to obey Merlin's little fantasises."

Uther leaned closer, pressing his body just lightly against mine. I tensed, but I didn't push him away from me. "Merlin is not some shit-bred travelling purveyor of love-potions or reader of dreams. I have *seen* his magic. It is beyond even what Avalon can dream of."

"Merlin does not own me," I insisted. "And neither do you."

He stared at me, silent for a moment, and I felt his grip on my arms soften as he leaned more of his weight into me, and my breath quickened. His breath brushed my cheek, then his hair, as he leant down towards me. I didn't know what I wanted.

"Truly, Igraine," he said softly, his lips finding my ear, making me shiver, "you would prefer any one of these men to me? *Truly?* Or are these your father's wishes? He dotes on you. Say the word, and he will give you anything you desire. Only say the word. This time tomorrow we could be together – fully together – as man and wife." One of his legs slipped between mine, and I was not sure that I had not yielded to make room for it. My blood felt hot in my veins. His voice dropped to an animal growl. "Do you think I don't feel how you feel right now? Imagine how you could feel if I had you alone."

I blushed. I shocked myself that I could imagine Uther seizing me and kissing me as I had seen Viviane take hold of Ector, and myself yielding with the same sighing surrender. I wondered what it would be like to touch his bare skin, to feel that body pressed against mine stripped of its clothes. Perhaps he was right, and if I were to only ask, I could feel those hands that held me tight now slipping under my dress, feel the heat of his mouth all over my body. I drew in a tense breath, wet my lips as though I were going to try to speak, but I did not know what I thought I would say. I didn't want to leave my home. I knew I should have refused him. He drew back, met my gaze, looked as though he was thinking about kissing me again. I knew I ought to object, but I hesitated.

"I think you are upsetting the lady, my lord." A voice came from across the courtyard, and Uther turned over his shoulder, letting go of me. It was the Welsh giant, standing the other side of the courtyard. He had a drawn sword in his hand, but he held it casually, or seemed to. Uther bristled, but he had weighed the size of the man walking towards us and did not draw his own sword, but stepped back from me.

He turned back to me, for a moment, and said, "Think hard about what I have said, Igraine. It will be now, or it will be some other time, but it *will* be."

And he left.

The Welsh giant walked tentatively over towards me. I was catching my breath. I was dizzy. I took his face in my hands, steading myself as I felt one wary, respectful hand rest at my waist. He was young, not much older than I was, and his face was kind and warm. He was freckled heavily across the bridge of his nose and his hair, even in the half-light, was an obvious bright orange-red.

"Are you alright, my lady?" he asked me, kindly. I felt hot all over my skin, wild, confused. I needed to know if Uther was the only man who could make me feel what I had felt just then – that whole-body weakness, that heat – so I kissed him, fiercely. I heard him give a murmur of surprise, but his hands slipped around my waist, and certainly what I had from him was much more than Ector's dutiful kiss on the cheek. When I drew back from him at last, he was wild-eyed and struggling to catch his breath, his mouth pink from the force of my kiss. Without a word, I turned and disappeared back into the hall, if anything even more confused than I had been before.

Chapter five

The whole thing had been a disaster. Uther Pendragon left, frustrated, the day after he came, and no one seemed to have any attention for the tournament. My father was too angry about being insulted by King Ban and then King Uther to make a decision, and the men who had come were growing frustrated.

There was one advantage to all of this. I was left alone. Tintagel did not have many servants, and since my father was a widower there were no ladies to attend to the mistress of the castle, so I could read in my room in peace and quiet. I looked out of the window, down the at courtyard below. The men were growing listless, and the summer was dragging towards its end, towards the rains of autumn. They would not stay that long. I wondered if it would happen. But it *had* to happen. I would not end up like Imogen.

* * *

One day, when I was sitting in my room, relishing some precious time alone for reading, there was a soft knock at my door, and I was surprised to find that it was the huge Welsh man who had chased

Uther away from me. He had a book in his hands, as well. Remembering my reckless kiss, I blushed.

"I hope you will forgive my intrusion, Lady Igraine, but I have brought you a gift. I was told that you liked to read, so I have brought you a book from my own country. It is the tale of brave Pwyll. It is a good tale, my lady," he added, as though keen to convince me to read it. I stood from the window seat and put down what I was reading to take it from him. Our hands brushed as I took hold of the book, and I looked up to meet his gaze. His eyes were a bright, beautiful blue. I had not noticed before. I remembered the heat of his mouth. I didn't yet know if I had enjoyed the kiss for his sake, or for Uther's. I looked away.

It was awkward; I embarrassed, he obviously hopeful. And he had good reason to be. I wondered if he was ambitious.

"What is your name?" I asked him.

"Gorlois," he said. It did not sound like a Welsh name to me.

I opened the book and glanced at the pages.

"This is in Gælic. I can't read this," I said gently, looking up at him.

He took the book from my hands and turned through the pages until it was past half way through.

"I have had it written into English for you," he said, and I leaned over to see that he had. "But I hope that one day you will learn the Gælic, because the tale is even more beautiful in its own language."

I took the book back, and closed it, and held it to my chest, crossing my arms over it, looking up at him.

"This is a very kind gift. Why have you brought me this?"

He coloured. He was thinking about that wild kiss, as well.

Slowly, the book still hugged to my chest with one arm, I stepped closer, reached up, and brushed the coarse orange hair back from his brow. I thought about what I had said to my father. Even if Gorlois was an ambitious man, Cornwall and Tintagel would be all he could hope for. A cousin of princes. A man with no castle of his own. He closed his eyes, resting his cheek against my hand. His breath was hot, and quick. He wasn't thinking, as I was, about what this was worth to him, or about others he might consider. I had seen a man look like that before. The man I had been supposed to marry, in the arms of someone else.

I brushed my fingers under his chin, and turned his face to mine.

"Kiss me," I whispered.

Slowly, tentatively, he took my face in his huge hands and pressed his lips softly against mine. I felt heat, but of a different kind. In the pit of my stomach, comforting rather than dizzying, slower, less wild. But I felt it.

* * *

Gently, without drawing away from the kiss, Gorlois lifted the book from my hands and tossed it onto my bed where it landed softly. He wrapped his arms around my waist and drew me closer. He was so huge, so much larger than all the other men, but he was so gentle, so careful. I had not expected it. His lips were soft and inviting against mine, his touch soft, delicate almost, as though he was aware of my smallness and afraid he would break me. By the time he drew away from me, I was breathless, and so was he.

I took hold of one of the buttons on his tunic – a thing of simple cloth, the attire of an ordinary soldier – to pull him back to me, and he closed a hand over mine.

"I should speak with your father." His lips rested against my forehead. All I could think of was skin against skin, and his hands slipping my dress off at the shoulders, the moonlight in the courtyard.

I nodded. If this was how Enid had felt, then I did not think she was such a fool anymore. He pulled me to him once more for one brief, burning kiss. I did not think I could bear the wait to become a wife.

* * *

The next day my father called me in to see him, to tell me that the King of Rheged castle's foster brother had asked his permission to marry me. I knew that must be Gorlois, and I knew my father was only considering because he had won in the tournament so effortlessly. I knew how I had felt. But there was more than that to consider. First, there was Uther, who I did not dislike as much as everyone else did – but I *did* dislike Merlin, and I feared Uther's careless promise to him. *I* would not give up my first-born son, and I did not want to live in fear of Merlin taking a child from me. Then, there was my foolishness with Ector. I didn't want a man who was so handsome and charming that he left me two steps behind, too charming to tell the truth, that he was in love with someone else, too polite to be honest. Gorlois was a *sensible* choice. I didn't feel the ground shift under my feet when I looked at him, as I had with Ector, but he was strong and brave and tall. I didn't feel confused when I was around him with the potent mix of anger, resentment and intrigue I felt when I was alone with Uther. I had liked his kiss, and I had felt everything I hoped to in it. He was kind, and he was steady, and he had won against men of nobler blood. He would not be ambitious, because Tintagel was more than he would ever have dreamed he could possess. He would not be hungry for more. Uther would always be hungry for more. I did not think Gorlois would lie to me. I did not think that he had falsified his affections. If he had, he would have brought me something other than a book.

So I said yes, and the other men left, and Gorlois stayed. I was aware, as I sat in the window-seat of my bedroom that I was about to become a woman in the most irreversible way possible. My childhood bedroom would not be my bedroom, and I would spend the rest of my life sleeping beside Gorlois in the main bedroom of the castle. My father had left it behind when my mother died. I would be the lady of Tintagel, and it would belong to me, and I would belong to it. The rest of my life was decided, then. It was a strange thought; comforting, yet terrifying.

* * *

The preparations for the wedding were swift, and simple. I preferred it that way. If I had married Ector or Uther it would have been a wedding for a queen, many days, many tournaments and feasts, and I was already tired from the tournament that had found me a husband. It was quiet, and it was modest, and that was better for me. I was a little shy, still. I had carried my shyness through from my childhood years, losing little pieces of it as I went, and though it had almost gone, I was still relieved that I was spared the public ceremony of a queen's wedding.

The date was set for early autumn. The King of Gore came to join his sons and foster sons, and he brought gold and men to pledge to us, as a sign of his allegiance with Cornwall, and – I suspected – his gratitude that the huge foster-son he had raised had found somewhere else to go and would not (as it seemed to me he had the strength in him to do) wrest Rheged castle from his foster-brothers. Erec and Enid came, too, all the way back over from France. I was pleased to see them, but when Enid greeted me with a kiss on the cheek she whispered, her wicked voice tinkling with glee, "I thought it would be your wedding to *Uther Pendragon* that I was called here for, little sister."

Elaine did not come, because her child was small and sickly. I was glad that Máel had not offered to come on his own. I was sorry that Elaine would not be there. I missed her. She was somewhere between Enid and me, and we had more in common. I was quiet and careful and serious, Enid was wild and impulsive and romantic, and between us, Elaine, the eldest of us, had found a kind of happy pragmatism that suited her. I wanted, too, her warnings, her advice for what I should do the night after I was married. She, too, was married to a stranger. Enid had run away with her husband, and I was sure I would get advice flavoured by fantasy, and recklessness.

* * *

On the morning of the day I was to be married, I sat at my window-seat brushing out my hair, and it struck me that I had spent the last night in my own bed, gazed out of this window at the sheer, rocky walls of Tintagel below in easy, lazy habit for the last time. If I wanted to look out at the cliffs and the sea from just this spot, I would have to wander back here, to plan it.

Enid came in as I was twisting back my hair, and pinning it. She had something in her hand, a wreath of white flowers, but she didn't give it to me. She set it down on the little table, and sat beside me on the window seat. I was surprised to see that she looked nervous, though I did not know what she could have been nervous about. *I* was the one that ought to have looked nervous.

"Igraine," she said gently, taking my hand and folding it between both of hers. She paused then, when I expected her to speak, her soft grey eyes – the same as mine, as our mother's – fixed on my hand in hers. She sighed. "Igraine, I miss our mother often, but it is at times like this that I miss her the most. She would have known what to say. Even Elaine would know better than I what would reassure you now. It was easy for me. I was in love. I hope you find that with your husband, Igraine, for I am told that for some it grows out of long years of marriage to be as full of those who were in love before they wed."

I nodded.

"How do you know? I mean – how do you know the difference between when you love someone, and when you just want to –"

I flushed, but Enid did too, and it shocked me.

"Oh, Igraine. What a question."

There was an uncomfortable silence between us.

"You knew with Erec, didn't you?"

Enid laughed again, but more softly this time, staring down at her hands on mine.

"Oh, I knew. I knew the first moment I saw him. It was as though everything else in the world was very far away. I couldn't hear the birds singing anymore, or feel the wind. There was just Erec. It was here – down here in the courtyard. He sailed over with that funny missionary – what was his name?"

"Ninian."

30

"Yes, Ninian, that's the one. I just saw him and I knew. I knew I would never love anyone else."

Enid wasn't making me feel any better.

She coughed.

"But, Igraine, you don't need to be in love to – I mean, Elaine – at the start she didn't like it very much, but she says you get used to it. Even if you don't like the man all that much, as long as he knows what he's doing –"

I nodded brusquely. I didn't really want to hear anymore. If anything, I felt worse than before.

She leaned forward and kissed me on the forehead. She put her hand lightly against my cheek, and smiled, and it was a motherly smile. She and Elaine were so much older than I was; Enid had been eight years old when I was born, long beyond when my parents had thought they had had their last child, and she and Elaine had taken care of me – though it was Elaine who had been more like a mother.

"You look beautiful, Igraine. Like a grown woman. But still –" She smiled then, and the Enid I recognised was back, fully – "I think every time I look at you I will see you also as you were when you were just a little girl, curled up in that window-seat with a book as big as you are, or just staring out at the waves. I'm glad you get to stay here, Igraine. This place – it belongs to you. You belong to each other."

I kissed her on the cheek and we embraced, tightly.

After she left, I stood before the hammered mirror to try to peer at my reflection. I could see the silver-grey of the fine silk dress that I had chosen for the day, and the darkness of my hair, and somewhere between the glint of the white-gold of my necklace, one of my mother's that I had chosen, so that I would have something of hers about me.

I had not been expecting my father, but he came then, and he took my hands in mine. His skin was wrinkled and papery, and the thought that he was old, and would soon be gone, choked in my throat a little. I knew that that was half of what this was about. He wanted to be sure that when he was gone no one would take our home from us.

"My little Igraine," he said. "You're going to be a wife." He smiled gently, but thoughtfully. "I cannot take a mother's place in this, in the instructions I must give you. I am sure Enid has prepared you a little. Just remember that your husband, too, will be nervous. Trust him not to hurt you, be gentle, be obedient. Remember what this means for you – he will keep you safe."

I nodded, and my father kissed me on the top of the head. Then, he took from his cloak what he had brought for me. I opened my mouth to object when I saw it, but he set it on my head, my mother's white-gold crown set with a large sapphire from the east like a fat drop of rain and sweet bright little pearls. On top of that he placed Enid's wreath of white flowers, and he took my hand, and led me down to the chapel, where they were all waiting.

Chapter six

It was all a blur, the wedding, but I remember one moment clearly. When I walked into the chapel, I barely recognised Gorlois. He was wearing one of the rich surcoats of the family who had raised him, the family of the King of Gore, green and gold, and it took me a moment to realise it was him. I felt my stomach tighten with nerves, with doubt over whether I had made the right choice. But when he caught my eye he smiled, and it was gentle and intimate and easy, and I felt reassured, and I took the hand that he held out to me, and we turned to the priest, and it was done. Or almost done.

Although the wedding was small and modest, there was still a feast afterwards where all the men and women of the castle gathered, and the minstrels played their harps and lutes and people danced. I took my new husband's hand when he offered it, and we stepped out among the dancing people, and I closed my eyes against the music, and felt it all wash through me, all the change, and the doubt, and beneath that the hope and the distant excitement, the daring possibility that I would love my husband as my sister loved hers. I felt his hands against my waist as we danced, and they were strong, and I wanted to lean in to them. I felt his lips brush against my cheek as he held me to him. I felt the youth, the lightness and the wildness of my own body which I always – which I *only* – felt when I was dancing, and it made be bright with hope.

* * *

We left as it began to grow dark. The rest of them, the men and women of the castle, my father, my sister, her husband, the Welshmen from Gore, all stayed and continued to drink the wine, and shout and sing and dance.

I, with my hand in Gorlois' hand, walked up the narrow stone steps, winding around, to the top of the tower, to the room that had been empty since I was born, where I would now live with him as his wife. He was too tall for the little spiral staircase, and had to stoop to walk up without hitting his head, but he did not seem to mind. We were quiet. I did not know what he was thinking, but I was feeling my nerves thrill within me, a dizzying mix of fear and anticipation.

Someone had prepared the room, trimmed the candles, made sure the bed was clean and made properly with the finest covers we had. The sight of the bed made me feel more anxious. Gorlois had been gentle when he had kissed me, but this was something else, and he was so huge, so tall, so broad about the shoulders. He must have weighed twice what I did, and all of that in warrior's bulk. I wondered, suddenly, if he had been to bed with a woman before. He must have done. All the young noblemen had.

Gorlois walked over, and put his arms around my waist, and drew me close, pressing his lips against my forehead.

"You look beautiful, my lovely wife," he murmured, his hand closing around the wreath of white flowers my sister had made for me, and lifting it off my head, "like the White Goddess herself."

"We're not supposed to talk about her anymore," I whispered, teasing. "We just married in a church, in the sight of Christ, after all."

He laughed softly in return, and put a hand against my cheek to turn my face to his and kiss me. His mouth was hot, his touch more urgent than it had been before, but he was still gentle, and when I stepped towards him and pressed myself against him, he stiffened and drew back a little. I felt my heart thud. Perhaps he was only nervous. I closed my hand over one of the buttons of his surcoat, ready to slip it open, but he put his hand over mine.

"Wait –"

"What for?" I murmured, running my hands into his hair, pulling him down towards me, feeling him weaken under my touch. "We're already married."

He groaned deep in his throat as I took his lip softly between my teeth and grasped the fastenings of his coat once more. This time he did not stop me slipping them undone and, with one great hand gently at the back of my neck, the other running up my thigh, he pulled me against him, and we stumbled against the little table that had once been my mother's dressing-stand. I slipped one hand up under the coat, feeling for the heat of his skin through the shirt. He drew away from me slowly, reluctantly, to shrug his surcoat off. I could feel blood rushing all over my body. I could feel my skin aching everywhere he had touched me. Slowly, steadying myself, I lifted the circlet from my hair and set it carefully on the little table. Gorlois folded his coat and threw it over the back of a chair. We turned back to one another. I did not think either of us was sure who would do what next. I felt my nerves tighten. Through the rushing of my blood, I was still aware that we were only just a little bit more than strangers. Was I, truly, going to take my dress off in front of him? And I had not seen a naked man before, not properly.

I reached out a hand to him, and he took it.

"Come," I said, softly, "help me out of my dress."

I turned my back to him, drawing the hair aside. I wanted to lean back into his body where I could feel him behind me, but his hands were careful as he slipped the laces undone. I felt his fingers brush my skin, and I wanted more. It was only when the dress slid from my shoulders and pooled on the floor around me that he stepped forward and leant down to press his lips against my neck. I shivered. I reached for his hand, ready to guide it down to the ache between my legs when he took me by the hips and turned me around to face him.

"Igraine." He kissed me softly. "Before we – I – I want you to know I haven't – there haven't been any other women."

I leant up to him again, and he took me by the shoulders and looked at me seriously.

"I am afraid I might hurt you."

Unbidden and unwelcome came the thought that I would not have been faced with the problem of a wary husband if I had married Uther. Gorlois was kind and gentle, and Uther had been rude. And he *had* hurt me when he had grabbed me in the courtyard.

I put a hand softly against Gorlois' cheek.

"You won't. I'm sure you won't."

He turned and pressed his lips into the palm of my hand. He sighed my name, and I felt the heat deepen at my core, the knowledge that he wanted me. I was about to speak, about to offer some wary words of encouragement, when he picked me up and held me against him. My eager little mouth found his as he carried me three steps across the room and dropped me gently on the bed, falling on top of me, suddenly clumsy with desire. I could feel him fumbling with his breeches as I ran my hands up under the back of his shirt, tasting hot skin and hard, male flesh. As I heard him kick them away, I seized his hand and pulled it up my skirts. Feeling the heat of my readiness, he trembled.

"Are you ready?" he half-gasped.

I nodded breathlessly, and he took me by the hips and sheathed himself deep inside me. I swallowed a small cry, afraid I would make him draw away from me. I wanted to feel his strength, to feel the huge, dangerous size of him. As it was he was gentle; he pressed his lips softly against mine, and stroked my hair with one huge hand. I wanted more, so I wrapped my legs around him and pulled his mouth harder against mine. But as I did, he groaned and sank down limp upon me. It was more brief than I had expected, after all the excitement of waiting, and not long after that Gorlois was asleep, on top of the covers, still in his shirt, and with one arm thrown up over his head. I settled into the hollow of his shoulder, but I didn't feel tired. Every part of my body felt awake and alive with some promising new sensation, and I knew I would not sleep.

* * *

Late into the night, when I had dozed where I lay, the bed curtains and the window-shutters open so that the moonlight streamed in, I was woken by Gorlois stirring beside me.

"Mmm," he murmured, his hand reaching out for me, and his fingers catching under the hem of the skirts of my nightdress. "Last night I had the most wonderful dream. I dreamed that I married a fine lady, and took her to bed."

His eyes opened as I sat up beside him, bright blue in the silver light of the moon, and he reached his hand up to brush through my hair where it fell over my shoulder in a fine curtain. I opened my mouth to say it was still the night, but he put one finger softly against my lips.

"No, no don't wake me, sweet Igraine."

His finger trailed down slowly, tracing the line of my jaw, and then the narrow collarbones, the slight contours of one small breast, to the laces of the underdress I still wore, drawing them slowly open, and slipping inside. I sank down onto him, wrapping my arms around him, pressing myself into his touch. I wriggled out of my loosened dress, and pulled away his shirt, and we wound together, slow and wary, but with pleasurable exploring. It was better now that he was not so clumsy with urgency, that he knew he had not harmed me the first time, and I was more bold – able to enjoy the coarse hair and hard flesh of his huge chest, the taste of his skin, all over. He had the patience for me now, to touch me where I drew him, to wait until I was dizzy and gasping to thrust inside me again. The gentleness that had once been wariness was now somehow both teasing and loving, and my enjoyment that had before been equal parts curiosity and fevered blood grew to the full, wild pleasure I had only dreamt of before, that was delicious and maddening both at once.

* * *

We lay wound together, finally, under the covers as the sun rose and poured cold morning light through the windows that had never been shuttered, and the curtains that had never been closed. I had my head on his stomach, sprawled lazily sideways across the bed, and I could feel the movements of his breath. It was strange, being so close to one who I knew so little. The last time I had shared a bed, it had been with my sisters.

I reached up and brushed my fingers across his chin, which was now rough with stubble.

"You know everything about me," I said softly. "You have seen my home, you have met my father and my sisters. You know what people I come from, but I don't know anything like that about you."

He took my hand in his and pressed his lips against the back of it.

"My grandmother was Olwen the Giant's Daughter, and my grandfather Culwuch was the Giant Killer who completed the giant's impossible tasks to win her hand. Culwuch was the same ancient blood as the Pendragons, who are the blood of Brutus the Conqueror, who gave our land its name, but Olwen my grandmother had the blood of giants in her – giants who Brutus all but chased away. Her hair was red like mine, and my mother always told me that it was because her father the giant used to hold her up in the air, to make her laugh, but one day, because he was so tall, he held her close to the sun, and the fire got into her hair, and made it red. And I have all that in my veins."

I sighed, a little disappointed. "None of that is true, is it?"

He gave a small, sad smile. The morning light picked out the soft, broad lines of his face where I looked up at him. He looked very young for such a big man, but he was older than I was. "No, none of it is true. But it is far, far more interesting than anything I could truly tell you about myself."

"I want the truth," I insisted.

He trailed little kisses down the inside of my wrist, his other hand disappearing back under the covers. I knew that he was hoping that I would lose interest, but when he saw that I would not be distracted by his hand sliding up the inside of my thigh, he sighed in defeat.

"I am all that you know I am, nothing more. A cousin of the Kings of Gore and the lords of Rheged castle. My family have been their squires and knights for centuries. I was an orphan, so I was fostered with the princes, and that has brought me good fortune." He smiled a little at me, and I could not help but smile back. "But truly I am a man of simple family and ordinary knightly blood."

I put my hand against his chest, spreading out my fingers through the rough hair there, feeling the warmth of his skin.

"I don't want any more than that, Gorlois. I only want us to always tell each other the truth. I did not want you as my husband because I thought you had the blood of ancient men and great heroes. I chose you because you brought me the book. Because you were kind."

He nodded, and leaned down and kissed me tenderly. I realised that I still did not, really, know any more about my new husband. I knew his name, and where he was from, but I did not even know how old he was, exactly. I did not know if he had killed a man in battle, or if he dreamed of more than being lord of Tintagel, but I did not ask those things, because I was happy, and falling into the feeling of his lips against mine, and the relief that I did not hate being a wife, and he had not had me alone to be rough or unkind with me. The rest – I would learn that in time. I was pleased to find that, in that moment, I was no longer afraid of the future.

Chapter seven

I stood before the window, brushing through my hair, trying to catch sight of myself in the reflection in the hammered mirror. I wanted to see if there was anything different about me, to see if I had changed on the outside when I had been changed on the inside from maiden to wife. Gorlois was not trying to catch a glimpse of himself. He was pulling on the surcoat he had worn for the wedding, and buttoning it. It was tight across his huge shoulders. Someone else's. Borrowed.

He came up behind me and kissed me on the cheek. I leant my head against his for a moment, and closed my eyes, but then he turned and I followed him and we walked down to the great hall to organise everything that came next. No time for leisure, for savouring. I wished, suddenly, that we were simple people, and marriage were not all about politics. But simple people did not have books, had to work in the fields, and grew diseased, and died of hunger. I was childish to envy them this.

* * *

My father was sitting at the high trestle table with the King of Gore, Ywain and some of his knights, and some of our own from Tintagel. I noticed that Erec had not been invited to join them. My father stood and stepped forward to kiss me on the cheek when I came up to greet him. He didn't say anything, though I had expected him to. I supposed this was strange for him, his last daughter married.

He gestured to Gorlois to invite him to take the place of honour beside him, and Gorlois hesitated, looking to me. I gave him a small, encouraging smile and took his hand, and he sat beside me. I thought he was too anxious about it, his distance from the royal lines of Wales. I supposed he was not close enough to the throne to realise what a small, insignificant kingdom Cornwall was. It was less than half the size of Gore, and no one knew the riches it had because my father never let them show. All it had that anyone knew as precious was Avalon's favour.

"I am sorry to speak so soon of matters of war, when we have just had such a fine celebration," my father began, and I could hear the weariness in his voice. "But it appears that Lot of Lothian is serious about making war with Uther. His troops are in Northumbria. The rumour, too, is that he has married from among the highland tribes, and they are encouraging him in this madness." So much, I thought, for the nobility of unmixed blood. So much for his derision for the Picts. "Uther Pendragon will want Cornwall as vassal-kingdom to Logrys to send fighting men to support his cause." He glanced at Ywain and the Welsh knights. I noticed Ywain's son beside him, a young man, only just more than a boy, with a quiet, thoughtful face and, though shortish, the same broad build as Gorlois. I distinctly remembered my father saying to Uther that we were *not* his vassal. It seemed that had been nothing more than bravado. He did not want to fight Uther. "I am sorry to have to ask for proof of your allegiance so soon."

Ywain nodded. His manner was slow, considered, deliberate. I thought he must have been a good king to his people.

"Gore will send its armies, and the other kingdoms of Wales will follow."

He looked up at Gorlois, and with a sudden chill that went through me, I realised what this was going to mean. He had realised before I had, and taken my hand beneath the table, but I did not feel it. I opened my mouth to protest, but they were already talking about when the time would be set to leave, and who would bring their allegiance to the battle.

I did not want to hear it. I stood, and none of them seemed to notice except Gorlois. I felt as though I had moved outside my body, and was watching myself as I walked out of the hall, up the tight-winding stairs and to my childhood bedroom. It was only when I came inside, and shut the door behind me, leaning back against it, that I realised that I was shaking. As soon as I was properly a bride, I was facing the possibility that I would be a widow. And who would gain anything from that? I had chosen Gorlois with the thought in my mind that my choice would *protect* me from this.

* * *

I sat in the window-seat, staring out. Outside, the rain was beginning to fall, and the clouds were so heavy and dense with it that they seemed to be sinking into the sea. After a while, I heard the sound of the door and I looked up. I did not know why, but I expected it to be Gorlois. It was not. It was Enid, her eyes wild, her gold hair loose around her shoulders. She looked as though she had just run from her own bedroom. I could see the flush against her cheeks.

"They're sending Gorlois to war?" she asked, breathless. I nodded, wrapping my arms around my knees, making room for her beside me. She nodded. "Erec, as well."

She came and sat on the window-seat opposite me, and reached out and took my hand. Very quietly, she said, "All I can think is, perhaps then we will never have a child. Erec and I have been hoping for a child for so long, and if he goes, and he does not return, I will have nothing left of him."

I squeezed her hand. I did not like the way she spoke. It was too adult, too real. She was not normally like this. She was usually laughing, usually careless. It was Elaine who was stern and serious. I did not want to know that unhappiness haunted even Enid and Erec, as they hoped for a child that they would not have.

Suddenly, she took my chin in her hand and turned my face up to hers, fixing me with her fierce grey eyes. I was aware, suddenly, that I was looking into the mother's face I had not known. The grey eyes that were mine, too. The quiet fierceness. Enid was usually so like our father that this caught me by surprise.

"My advice to you, little Igraine, would be go to your husband now, and do not leave him until they tear him away from you. Nothing is more terrifying than the thought of a life alone, and a woman with a child does not *ever* have to be alone."

She was frightening me. I thought of her, married for all these years, no sign of a child, and Elaine's long marriage before she bore her child. I thought of Uther Pendragon, far away in London, telling me he would have me sooner or later.

"Go, Igraine," she said softly; then, as I stared back in blank panic, she shouted, "*Go.*"

I rushed away up to my new room. I stood at the window there, and stared out, but all I could see was the dark, heavy cloud, and the thick rain once more. I thought about Enid. If she was not with Erec now, living out her own advice, that meant that there was no point, that she had her bleeding now, and knew that there would be no child before he was sent away. I stared out into the darkening sky. Perhaps there would be thunder. It felt as if it was going to purge everything away, but it was not. Was it better that I be left, sixteen years old, newly the lady of my castle with an ageing father and a new-born child? What if I did not survive the birth? What if, like Enid, I could not bear a child? And I had tried to be steady, and to be careful. I had turned away a king, and the complex danger I felt there, to choose a man who I thought would be able to protect me. I felt burningly angry at the Lothians. This was all about pride for them. And why did Gorlois have to go? He had responsibilities here now. He had obligations to *me*.

"Igraine…"

I turned around at the sound of my name. I had been so lost in my thoughts that I had not heard Gorlois walk into the room. He stood before me, his surcoat unbuttoned, his shirt open at the neck underneath, showing the skin of his chest, its pale freckles, like gold. He opened his mouth to speak, but he did not say anything. I could see on his face that he did not want to go, that he was sorry, that he had expected it no more than I had. He stepped towards me.

I grasped him by the surcoat and pulled him up against me. I could feel angry tears pricking at the back of my eyes, but I was not going to cry.

"Promise me that you will come back. Promise me that you have not made me your wife only to make me a widow," I said fiercely.

He put his hands gently on my shoulders, but I did not want to be gentle. I could feel the desire to tear, the desperate frustration, tight within me. I wanted to shake him. He was large enough that I could have beaten my fists against his chest, and he would have barely felt it.

"Igraine," he said, sadly, "I cannot promise to live."

"Don't say that," I half-shouted.

He held me tighter, and under his grip I felt my feet lift a little off the floor. I did not think he realised. He had been being so careful with me before, so gentle, for I was so small in comparison with him, but he was upset, and he was forgetting to be.

"Igraine, I must do my duty."

"Part of that duty is to come back to me. Alive," I insisted, still tightening my grip on his coat. I felt the fabric give a little. I could also feel his chest rising and falling hard against me, where we were held tightly together. His eyes looked into mine, bright, bright blue, and I could not read their gaze. I wanted him to promise.

"*Promise*," I whispered.

His hand went into my hair, tangling in a handful of it, tearing it from its little clasp as he pulled me hard against him into a kiss that was rough with a passion that I had not known before from him. It was like the kiss Uther had pulled me into, raw with desire, and no small part of desperation, and I felt my body weaken into his hands in response. He was fast, suddenly, and rough. I pressed my forehead against his, and wound my hands into his hair as he lifted me against the hard stone of the window frame, and I prayed to the gods I had prayed to as a child that he would leave me with some new life inside me, for I knew that they were the gods for that, and if any could help me, it was they.

* * *

The men left before night fell. I stood with Enid in the courtyard even as the rain fell hard around us, watching them as they filed out in their armour, their horses picking their way unsteadily down the little rocky path out of Tintagel. Enid sobbed as she watched them go, but I felt strangely calm. I could still feel my lips burn where Gorlois' mouth had been hard against mine.

Chapter eight

Enid and I slept that night in the same bed – in the bed of my old room where we had used to sleep side by side as children. She cried until she fell asleep, but silently. I held her hand, tight, but she was mourning for something that I was yet to understand. It made me think about Elaine, far away in Ireland, and her child. I wondered if I would ever see it. Ireland, at least, would stay out of Lot's war.

It was quiet in the castle after the men had left. It was just Enid, my father and me, and a few servants and a small garrison of knights. My father's master of arms, Ulfius, who was a youngish yet serious man with a face so sincere it made him look years beyond what he was, paced about the place as though we were still full of knights when all we had left were the old and the weak and the useless. Boys too young to hold the full-sized swords in a single hand. Men who could fight but who would never be knights.

As autumn settled fully around us, I grew sick and so did my father, though my sickness promised life and his, death. I knew it was the end for him, because as the autumn deepened the Lady of Avalon came with some of her women, and they shut themselves in his room; he had been moaning and murmuring with pain before, but when they let me and Enid in, he was quiet, and peacefully sleeping, and we could kiss him on the brow and say goodbye before they took him away to be burned on the pyre. The chaplain wanted him taken to the Cornish mainland to be buried in the ground, but I knew he would have wanted the old ways, and there was besides no earth soft enough to bury him in at Tintagel. We stood with him, Enid and I, the Lady of Avalon and the strange, serious Ulfius, until the stars came out, and the flames died down into ash.

Neither of us cried. He had been old, and the rhythms of life were harsh. The White Goddess and the Hanged God took the old and made it new. If I had a son, I would name it after him, for it would be his life passing out of his body and into the body of my child.

I did not tell Enid. I did not want to break her heart.

* * *

It was only days after that when the Lady of Avalon came to me, and gently took my hand.

"I must take you with me to Camelot, Igraine," she said.

"Why?" I asked. I didn't want to travel. I didn't want to leave my home, didn't want to risk losing my child.

"The lords will gather there for Christmas, and you must attend for Tintagel." She put her hand gently on my stomach, and I knew that she knew, though there was nothing yet to see or feel. "Men will see you, and be reminded that your husband holds Tintagel though your father is gone. You will show by then, and men will remember. I will be with you."

I nodded. She was right.

"Can I bring Enid with me?"

She shook her head, pressing my hand between hers. Her skin, white and threaded with lovely blue-green, looked strange against my own.

"I can only bring you, Igraine. We cannot leave Tintagel without anyone of your blood to guard it."

I nodded in agreement, but I was not happy. I supposed it meant Enid would not begin to see the life growing within me, would not have to watch as I grew what she coveted.

* * *

The journey made my sickness worse, and I was horribly tired all the way, but the Lady of Avalon was quiet, and patient. I didn't want to go to Camelot. I was afraid that Uther Pendragon would be there, even though he was off fighting his war. I didn't want to see him. I was beginning to be happy with Gorlois, in the most tentative way imaginable, and I was afraid that something would shatter that. If anything could, it was Uther Pendragon – one way or another.

* * *

But when we arrived at Camelot, after almost a week on the road, it was empty of lords and knights. It was a city of women. I was surprised to see that it was old, blind Imogen who stood in the courtyard to greet us, Merlin beside her, his blue-painted face half hidden in the shadow of his cowl, but unmissable.

As the Lady of Avalon jumped from her horse before me, Merlin stepped forward to greet her. The way they greeted each other was friendly, if a little formal.

"You look beautiful, Viviane, as always," Merlin said in his unpleasant, rasping voice. *Viviane*, I thought. I remembered where I had heard that name before. She leaned away from him.

"I see you are keeping matters well here at Camelot, Merlin," she replied, prickly. His unpleasant skullish grin spread deeper across his face.

We followed them as they led inside. I was tired from the ride, and felt sick still. I could feel the dust from the road sticking to my skin, and I wished I could have a bath.

I was surprised that Imogen walked so easily in front of us, as though she knew the place so well that it did not matter that all she saw before her was darkness. There was no queen in Camelot, I noticed. No young bride for Uther Pendragon. But Imogen was here, and not in London. He could not have married *her*. She was barren, and ageing. Still, she was Aurelianus' daughter, and there were men around who still questioned Uther's right to be king, who talked about his lowly blood. They called him a soldier with a crown. But although Uther had been no great prince, Gorlois had not been telling silly tales when he said that the Pendragons were ancient blood; that meant more to some people – to Avalon, to the Gaelic peoples of Wales and Ireland – than fathers who had sat on the throne.

Were Imogen and Uther lovers? I couldn't imagine it, although she was a beautiful woman. There was something gentle about her looks, her hair was still thick and glossy, and though her eyes crinkled with lines at the corners she still had the last vestiges of youth about her. I wondered what men would have made of her if she had not been blind, and without a child.

Imogen led us up to a small room set with a long, square table. It was some kind of council chamber; I could tell because there were papers scattered across the desk, and a map, its edges curling, in the middle. Men had left here in a hurry, I supposed, after deciding the course the war would take them on. I thought of Gorlois, fighting beside Uther, and I suddenly had an awful feeling that Uther might try to kill him. But he didn't know – not yet – that I had married Gorlois, and was carrying his child. He would be angry when he learned it. Perhaps Gorlois would tell him, one night while the men were sat around the fire, and Uther would draw his knife and...

I pushed away the thought. I was tired, and the journey had been long, and I was alone and far from everything I knew. I would not help myself by being silly about Uther Pendragon.

I sat down carefully next to Viviane, and she leaned over to whisper in my ear, "Be careful of Merlin, Igraine."

I was surprised because I had thought that she and he were fellows under Avalon's great banner, but it seemed that something more complex existed between them. I nodded, and I could not help unconsciously putting my hand against my stomach, as though to protect myself, although I could feel nothing there yet.

"What news from the north, Merlin?" Viviane asked, and I noticed the way she held him with a sharp, steady stare.

It was not Merlin who answered, but Imogen. "King Uther's troops have pushed the Lothians out of Northumbria. It seems clear that the rest of Britain is against their little rebellion, and will stand with its king."

So, Uther was calling himself King of Britain now, not just King of Logrys. I supposed he was. We had all come as his vassals, after all, to fight for his interests.

"I hear," Imogen continued, and she turned her face to me, although her eyes were fogged with white, and could not have seen me, "that one of the Princes of Rheged castle is Duke of Cornwall now."

I thought Viviane would answer for me, but she did not, and I cleared my throat to speak. "It is so, my lady. My father's death has made it so."

I should have corrected her. *Duke of Cornwall.* Cornwall was still nation enough to have a king. She was being insulting on purpose.

"And your marriage," Imogen insisted.

"Yes, my lady."

"Without the King's permission," Imogen added. Why was Imogen so favourable to Uther that she would question my marriage? My father had not considered it needful, but then he had never had much respect for Uther Pendragon. I was beginning to think I might have been right in my suspicion that Uther had seduced the old king's daughter, though she must have been more than ten years older than him – perhaps even as much as twenty – in order to secure his place on the throne.

I did not know what to say in response. I wasn't going to deny it, because that would have been a lie. The conversation moved on, and I was grateful, but I felt a resentment growing in me towards Imogen, whom I had liked before, that she would push me so about this. It was not her business what I did. I had thought she would hate Uther, for taking the place that would have been hers had she not been born a woman.

The rest of the talk was about the war, about what would happen next if certain moves were made, certain losses sustained. I kept my eyes on the map, imagining the little lines of men moving like ants across it, down the spine of Britain, crawling through the chinks in the wall that separated the lands of the kings of Lothian and Orkney from Logrys, and Gore. How much would it take for Lothian's armies to swarm down across Logrys to Camelot and London and tear everything down? Despite what the others were saying, I was afraid that this was what would happen. I felt as though I was seeing it, right then, in front of me. Black, black little ants rushing all over the smooth, brown parchment of the map, down from the north and over the south until they rushed into the sea and destroyed themselves. I could feel my heart racing inside me, my head spinning. I blinked, but I couldn't get the image out of my mind. I looked up, away from the map, and when I did I caught sight of Imogen, her blank eyes staring at the spot I had been staring at, and fixed there, too, with fear.

* * *

That night, I missed having Enid beside me. Sleeping alone in a bed made for two in a place I did not know was hard, and when I finally fell asleep, I dreamed of the black ants again – that I was following a thread of them down my wall, along the floor, and under the bed. And when I got to under the bed it was thick with them, all heaving over one another in a writhing mass. I tried to scream, but my mouth was dry and stuck together. I coughed and, into the hands that I held to my mouth, spilled more and more of them, as though they were crawling up out of my stomach.

I woke entangled in the sheets and gasping for my breath. It was light outside, so I must have slept long into the morning, for it was fast approaching winter now. A servant had been in and set the fire, for I was too hot. I told myself that that was why I had had such a horrible dream. As soon as I sat up in bed, I was glad to feel nauseous, and rushed to the basin to be sick, and saw with relief that it was not those nasty black ants that came up from inside of me.

* * *

I knew that if I was going to last out my time in Camelot I would have to be wise and sensible, and make a plan. I was the representative of my kingdom now, my husband away at war and my father gone, and it fell to me to make sure that whatever happened to the rest of Britain, Cornwall was safe. I wrote to Enid, asking her how things were in Tintagel. I was sure she wouldn't really know, but she would pass the letter to someone else, one of the knights who could tell me. I thought it was important that we were still training and equipping our men. If Britain fell into war and chaos, I wanted to be able to man the border garrisons and seal Cornwall off from attackers and invaders. I didn't write this in my letter. It was too soon to make my self-interest plain. I felt suddenly strong and brave, and I realised that this was what I had been waiting for, preparing myself for, all this time. I knew that I could keep my kingdom safe. I had married Gorlois to do so, and I would be a careful, strong queen to Cornwall. *Duke*, Imogen had called Gorlois. That *was* an insult, and I should have spoken against it. No, I *wanted* to have spoken against it, but it was not what was wise. She was not married to Uther. She hadn't been wearing a ring. But she behaved as though she was his queen. Perhaps she was just being as careful as I was, making sure that no one could get rid of her. She was a threat to Uther, after all, unless she was with him.

* * *

It got easier, slowly, until Christmas came. I spent my days writing to Cornwall, making plans, and sitting with Viviane and reading. Imogen would sit with us sometimes, too, and listen, although I was never sure if she was concentrating on the words, or staring at me with her blank, sightless eyes. Sometimes I imagined she was staring right at my stomach, which was just beginning to swell beneath my clothes. I could not shake the feeling that some kind of disaster was waiting just around the corner, but I tried not to think about it. I didn't look at the map again, or go into the council rooms, but I did still dream from time to time that I followed a thread of ants around Camelot, and they always led me to somewhere dark and writhing.

I didn't tell Viviane, because I didn't want to know what it meant. She would know if it were some awful portent of the future, and I was not eager to know if disaster was coming. It would do me no good, for I would not prevent it.

Chapter nine

Christmas came, and a small band of men with it. I watched out of the window as they rode into the courtyard. Gorlois was not among them, but Uther was. That meant that he must have commanded my husband to stay with the troops in the freezing north over Christmas, though I could not imagine he did not know I was here. He must have known, by now, that I was married. I was sure Imogen would have had letters written to inform him.

* * *

I would have to be there. I would have to go and greet him, and be a compliant vassal queen. That was what my duties required of me. I hadn't brought fine clothes – we had rushed away. I wanted to hide my pregnant stomach, but I knew that Viviane had encouraged me to come here to show it, to remind people that Cornwall had a King, and possibly also an heir.

I looked through what I had. Apart from travelling clothes and the simple woollen dresses I had been wearing, I had one fine dress, but a summer one made of fine, thin silk. Why hadn't I planned more carefully for this?

I pulled on the dress, which was beautiful soft grey-blue silk sewn with silver thread in the patterns of flowers. It was tight around the bodice, and made the small mound of my stomach look bigger than it was. I wound my hair carefully into a plait, braiding a silver ribbon through it. This was not the fashion of the people of Cornwall, but the women of Logrys sometimes wore their hair that way, and I wanted a little more decoration, a little more protection, when I went before Uther. At least I had a grey fur cloak to clasp around myself, to keep away the cold. Last, I put on my white gold circlet, and drew in a deep breath, and walked down to the courtyard where the men were climbing off their horses.

* * *

As I arrived, Uther was stood paces in front of his men, pulling the leather gauntlets off his hands, breathing out steam in plumes as large as those coming from the horses. His helm was off his head, thrown down beside him, and his face was dirty from the ride, lines of sweat trailing through the plastered dust from the road, and dirt from the armour. His face was tight with angry consternation, and he pulled the gauntlets off with force, throwing them against the ground.

As I looked around the courtyard, I realised why.

"Where is Merlin?" he demanded.

"My lord Uther, I do not know," Imogen replied, flatly. She stood just paces away from him, wrapped in a cloak of white fur flecked with black, the fur cloak that I had seen before on Aurelianus' queen, and beneath flashed a dress of thick, dark-red brocade. She had come to meet Uther dressed like a queen.

"You *do not know*?" Uther growled.

I did not know why he was surprised that Merlin had disappeared, as evanescent as he had always been. Did Uther think that because he was King by Avalon's support that Merlin was his servant?

"I do not," Imogen replied simply.

Uther looked as though he was going to shout again, until his eyes lit on me. He stopped where he stood, and I felt myself lean back warily away from him, and rest a hand on my stomach. I wished that I had not, because that only drew his attention to me further. He stared at me with a level, steady look for a moment, a long moment, and then looked away.

He began speaking to Imogen again, but it was about arrangements for the feast that he wanted tonight, and the Christmas celebrations. I wondered if Uther's people had Christmas games, as I had had them as a child. I did not think I wanted them here, all alone. I looked through the men for Gorlois once more, hoping that I had been mistaken, but he was not there. I felt a jolt of fear pass through me that this meant he was dead, but I did not think that could be so. Someone would have written. Someone would have said.

* * *

I went to the Christmas feast feeling the nerves tight in my chest. This was the moment that Viviane had wanted me to be prepared for. This was the moment in which I had to remind all of the men gathered there that my little kingdom was still strong. There must have been those among them that coveted it, who thought that while Uther was occupied in the north, they might take it. They needed to know that Tintagel had a king in its castle, in name at least, and a queen watching over it, too. I steeled myself for it. It all came down to me, now, and I would do everything in my power to protect my home.

The stench of the great hall hit me as I entered it. They were drinking ale because wine was expensive in winter and we were at war with ourselves, and it smelled stale and unpleasant in the air, as though many men had already been drinking it, and breathing it out. It smelled, too, of the smoke of the hearth fire, and the dirt of the men, and sweat. It did not seem as though many of them had washed since their ride down from the north to carouse with their King at Christmas time. Or, as I heard many of the men in the crowd of knights still call it, *Yule*.

I slipped into the seat for me, thankfully a few seats from Uther and beside Viviane. As I sat down, in the crowd I caught sight of a familiar face, down on the trestle tables with the common soldiers and the low knights. It was Prince Ector, though his golden armour was gone, and he was dressed in an old battered iron breastplate, as though he had stepped in right from the field. Still, it was unmistakably him, his black hair still long, although tied back for the battlefield. I was surprised how well I remembered the way he held himself, the way he moved, the way that he smiled. I had thought I had forgotten him, with everything that had happened. He had dark stubble across his jaw from the fighting; he was dirty with it, but I could not have mistaken him. What had happened? Where was the girl for whom he had run away from everything he had?

I leaned over to Viviane beside me, and asked quietly, "What is Prince Ector of Benwick doing here among the common soldiers?"

Before she could reply, a knight opposite us at the table, some lackey of Uther's, no doubt, answered with a rough, unpleasant laugh that betrayed his enjoyment of the other man's fall, "Not *Prince* Ector any more. And only *Sir* for his valour on the field. They say he lives like a peasant on a little farm out near Glastonbury, and his father has cast him out. They say it is for taking a peasant girl as his wife."

So, he had married her. I wondered if Ector was happy. I felt Uther looking over at us, trying to listen to the conversation, and I kept my face turned away from his.

"I met her," I said softly. "She is a very beautiful woman, very passionate." The knight on the other side of the table was still laughing unpleasantly and nudged the men beside him when I said *passionate*, but I ignored them and leaned closer to Viviane, and whispered, "She is named Viviane as well."

The look that the Lady of Avalon gave me – distant, thoughtful, complex – was enough to tell that it was as I suspected and the girl had *something* to do with her; whether Viviane was the girl's aunt, or her mother, or some kind of patron of her parents, she meant something to her. I did not think it could have been a coincidence. Now I thought of it, I could see something of a resemblance between the Lady of Avalon and the passionate young woman I had caught a glimpse of. Something in the beautiful face, the golden hair. Or perhaps I was imagining it.

* * *

I couldn't eat the food; I felt too nauseous. I did not know whether it was because the child inside me disliked the rich food, or because I could feel Uther watching me, two seats away. I ate slowly, and carefully, and little. I didn't drink the ale. Just the smell of it made my stomach churn. I only listened to the conversations around me, after that. They were about the war, how it was progressing. Uther was winning. That boded well, I supposed, for Gorlois' safety.

When the music for the dancing began, I got up and slipped away. I loved to dance, and I had hoped I might dance a little with Ector, for I had remembered that he was a good dancer, and I thought it would do no harm now, since we were both married to other people, but he seemed to have slipped away before even I did.

* * *

I wanted to go back to my room to be by myself. To read quietly. To think of Gorlois, far away. But then I heard heavy footfalls on the stone corridor behind me, and I felt my body tense. I knew who it would be. I pretended I didn't hear the feet behind me, and hurried a little faster. When I heard him call my name, my stomach tightened with apprehension, but I did not stop.

Uther rushed up fast behind me, grabbed me by the arm, hard, and pulled me aside. I could hear people talking, close by and casual, just servants walking through the corridors, but they were people, and it would be enough. If I screamed they would come. They would not punish Uther, because he was their king, but he would have to let go of me. I tensed against his grip, but he pulled me further with him, round the corner, to a dark little nook in the corridor.

"You are avoiding me, Igraine," he said.

I shook my head. "No, my lord." I was formal, and cold. It was the only protection I had against him. He was the King, and – really – we were strangers. I showed him no disrespect with my formality. Just because Merlin had told him some lie or other did not mean that I was beholden to take to the same sudden intimacy with him that he had with me.

Uther took another step towards me. He was not nearly so tall as Gorlois, only a little taller than I was, but he was broad, and thick with muscle. He was wearing a surcoat of red and gold he had had made for himself, and the gold thread in it shone bright and new, twisting in the shape of a dragon across it. Before, all he had had were plain leather jerkins, and I had seen him only in his dented battle-armour. He was gathering around himself the rich things that a king ought to have. I wondered obliquely if it had been paid for with Imogen's gold. Aurelianus' riches had gone to her, not to Uther. Uther was slowly making himself the king that everyone but Avalon had doubted that he could be. He certainly *looked* like a king now, though he had looked a lot like a boy not long ago when he had been wrestling in the dirt with Lot of Lothian.

"Is it true what the Welsh say, that you are married to Gorlois, and carrying his child?"

His voice was quiet, too intimate. I looked down, away.

"Is that why you did not let him come?"

He put a hand against my cheek, drawing my face up to his, gently for now, so that I could not avoid his piercing stare.

"You have shown me disrespect as your sovereign, Igraine."

"I meant no disrespect, my lord Uther," I said, softly. If he wanted to talk politics, that was a game I could play. "I was obedient only to the wishes of my father."

Uther leaned the weight of his body just a little more towards me. There was still a hand's width of clear space between us, but I could feel the heat of his body, the dangerous gravity of his closeness.

"How is he, then, this overgrown child you have married?"

His look was level, challenging.

"How is he?"

"You know what I mean."

I coloured, indignant. Uther laughed softly, taking another step closer. I was backed as close to the wall as I could, but I could slip past him. If I wanted to. I could feel my heart in my throat as he slipped his hand down from my cheek. It was a caress for the moment, but I felt the strength in his hand, the potential for it to become something else.

"If it were me you had married, you wouldn't blush to speak of it." His voice was very quiet, very intimate. He ran his thumb across my lower lip. I thought about biting it. "We would not yet have left my bed, and I would have had you moaning my name the whole time."

"You must be confusing me with the cheap whores you and your soldiers frequent," I hissed. "Noble ladies don't *moan*."

He seized me hard by the shoulders, drew me against him, and I suppressed a gasp. I turned my face aside as he pressed his lips against my hair to whisper.

"Every woman moans, under the right hands."

If Uther had been any other man, I would not have seen the harm in it. One kiss, one brief moment pressed together, nothing more. No one else would ever have known. It would have been satisfying. But he was not. He was King, and one moment's surrender to him would be Cornwall's surrender into his power. I could govern myself for my kingdom's sake.

"Please, my lord, let me go," I said softly.

He dropped me immediately. My heart was racing, my blood rushing deafeningly in my ears.

Uther took another step back from me, suddenly cold in response to my formal tone.

"How long will you pretend, Igraine, that you feel nothing for me?"

I drew myself up, brushed the loosened strands of hair back from my forehead. Uther spoke again before I could gather myself enough to be firm.

"Are you afraid, Igraine? Is that it? Should I regret my honesty to you, when I told you what I had granted Merlin in return for my throne?"

"You are mistaken, my Lord Uther," I said, moving to push past him. He slammed a hand against the wall beside me, blocking my path. I stared up at him. "I am your obedient vassal, no more, no less. I married the man my father deemed suitable. I had no feelings in the matter. I am the youngest daughter of a poor realm. I never hoped to wed, my Lord Uther. I am a lowly creature and live only in obedience to my father, my husband, my God, and my king."

I made to shove past him, but he was too fast. He pushed me back against the wall, pinning me so hard at the shoulder that I cried out.

"Enough *games*, Igraine," he growled. I wriggled against his grip, but now that he was determined to hold me I was not so confident of my ability to escape.

"You are hurting me, my lord." I knew I sounded frightened. I could feel the tears in the corner of my eyes. I hated feeling weak.

As though surprised that he had hurt me, Uther stepped back, blinking as if against a bright light.

"Igraine…" He rubbed the bridge of his nose between his thumb and forefinger… "My manners are rough – I – it is not my intention to force you into any manner of – I only mean to explain to you – you are putting off the inevitable, and denying what you feel for the sake of a father who is no longer around to prevent –"

He stepped forward again, this time gentle, this time appealing.

"You *don't know* what I feel," I said fiercely, pushing him away from me. I was frightened by him, frightened by myself; desperate to be alone. He glanced over me, detached again, watchful.

"Perhaps I do not," he conceded, his look distant, thoughtful.

I pushed past him, and rushed back to my room. He was so forceful, and unpleasant, and presumptuous. What kind of man was he, to accost a pregnant woman in the corridor of his own castle? I pulled down the shoulder of my dress. In the low light of the stumpy candle that Imogen's stingy housekeeping had allotted me, I could see the red marks of Uther's fingers were already turning purple. I traced them lightly with my own fingers. I could still feel, too, where his fingers had brushed my throat and the skin was burning, but as much as I peered into the hammered mirror, there were no marks there to be seen.

Chapter ten

Although the castle was uncomfortably full, it was still cold. I was anxious about my health, about the child inside me, but when I asked Imogen for more furs for the bed, she shrugged and said she had given them all out, and I could look in the empty rooms – few that there were – for blankets if I wanted them.

At about midday, I weakened and went to look for blankets in the King's tower. The danger of running into Uther seemed less, by then, than the danger posed by the cold. In one of the empty rooms on the ground floor, I did find a promising-looking trunk, made of rough wood. Soldiers' equipment, perhaps, but soldiers had blankets. Rough wool, maybe, but I was cold enough to not be fussy. I knelt down before it, and I pushed the heavy lid of the trunk up hard as I could with the heels of my hands, and it opened. At first, I thought it was just full of rugs and blankets for the winter, but when I pulled out the first one into the light, I saw that it was not a rug, but a cloak made of thick, coarse wool, dark red and very heavy, and beneath was not rugs or cloaks, but what looked like a full set of Roman armour. I folded the cloak up in my arms – it was obviously old, and in places it had been eaten through by the moths – and set it aside. Carefully, as though afraid of disturbing some centurion's ghost, I lifted the breastplate out into the fading afternoon light. For a moment, as I pulled it from the trunk, I thought I saw a little black ant run out from some crevice of it and across the back of my hand, but when I blinked and looked in the full light of the window, it was gone. The breastplate was battered and a little rusted. I pulled it into my lap and rubbed it with my sleeve, rubbing the tarnish from the letters embossed across the chest – letters I recognised – S P Q R. This was no soldier's lorica; this plate had belonged to someone important.

"That's Roman steel."

Uther's voice behind me made me jump, although it was soft and he spoke gently. Still kneeling with the breastplate in my lap, I turned over my shoulder. He stood in the open doorway, leaning against the frame, his arms crossed over his chest. When I turned, he took two easy strides towards me, and leaned down to lift it out of my hands.

"When the Romans came here, our ancestors were fighting with flint spears. Perhaps some of them had bronze, and maybe the Cornish had tin, for all the good it would have done them. The Roman legions were all equipped with iron and steel." He rapped his knuckles smartly against the breastplate. "Light, hard, impervious to the spears and arrows of the native tribes, that were barely more than twigs." He looked up at me then, and met my eye.

"This was my grandfather's armour. I've tried to have our native smiths make something like this, and they can get close, but armour like this isn't even being made in Rome anymore. They've forgotten how. It's something to do with the way the Empire used to smelt the metal ore, or the way the plate is hammered to make it thin and light, but hard enough to resist attacks even at close range. The Empire knew how to equip its soldiers, that's for sure. The British didn't stand a chance. Our people." He crouched down casually beside me, his look thoughtful. "But the Romans are my people, as well." He offered forward one of his wrists, the hand bent back to show the veins beneath the tattooed mark of the serpent there.

"The Roman Empire was built on soldiers. The Welsh, my grandmother's people, my mother's people, they're bards and witches. The Romans were soldiers. Roman blood in British veins. Some men don't like it. Lot of Lothian. Some of my Welsh cousins, in the north. But they like it well enough when I win, when I keep them safe from Saxons and these men calling themselves Romans in the south. They will like it when I keep the Pics and Scots from raiding in their lands. They were not just conquerors, the Romans. Not just –" he said the word with some distaste – "*Christians*. They gave us iron and steel, they gave us smiths and forges to protect ourselves, taught us to build stone houses, castles, walled cities. Taught us to read and write. We forget the past, and we risk forgetting who we are, and believing only those who wish to divide us."

I had never heard him say so much at once. His hands still rested gently on the armour plate, and although his eyes met mine, he seemed far away. I spread out a hand against the breastplate.

"It's beautiful armour," I said softly. I wondered why I had never seen him wear it.

"Roman rule is still within living memory for some," Uther said. "Here in the south. Or at least some say they remember. The Romans were wise enough never to bother trying to rule in the north. We should have kept that wall." His look darkened. "When we got up there, Lot's troops had begun taking it apart, making places they could stream through, reassembling the stone into rudimentary guard-towers. Sometimes I wonder if I, too, ought not to shut them out."

"Britain is better, Britain is stronger, if we are all together," I replied.

His eyes searched my face for a moment as though my words had surprised him, or made very little sense to him, and I wondered for a moment if he was going to try to take hold of me and kiss me again. In this quiet moment, where he had bared something of himself to me, I was not sure if I would protest, but he did not. I had, perhaps, made myself clearer than I had intended to the night before. He sighed, standing up, and set the breastplate back with the rest of the armour in the chest, and covered it with the red cloak, and left. After he was gone, I took the armour out again, and spread it out on the cloak so that I almost had the shape of a man there: the chest, the helmet with its moth-eaten crest, the armoured leather kilt with its brass bosses, the greaves for the calves, and the leather cuffs for the wrists. All old, and empty now. Arranged like that on the floor, I looked down, and I could not imagine Uther in it. I didn't take the cloak; somehow, after that moment of intimacy, it seemed better to be cold.

* * *

Uther and his party of knights did not stay long, thankfully. I sent a letter for Gorlois with one of his knights, but I couldn't write much, because I was sure Uther would read it, and besides I was afraid it would never find its way to him anyway.

I hoped that I would be able to return to Tintagel soon, but the ground was thick with snow and Viviane insisted we wait for spring. Imogen was haughty and hostile, commanding like a queen from Uther's castle now he was gone. People seemed to accept without question that she was the lady of the place. I did not know if she had slept in Uther's bedroom with him when he had come back for

Christmas, only that she slept in the queens' rooms now. I supposed there was no one else to occupy them.

Merlin returned once Uther was gone. He thought I didn't know it was him, but I knew it. I knew it as soon as I saw the dark young man lounging uninvited in the window-seat in my borrowed bedroom that it could be none other than Merlin, even though his loathsome outside was completely transformed. He gave me a broad, bright smile as I stepped into the room, but I crossed my arms over my chest, staring at him narrowly.

"I know who you are," I said.

He laughed softly. "Yes, Igraine, I am sure that you do."

"How long have you been here? King Uther has been searching for you."

"I am sure that he has," Merlin replied.

He sat easy in the seat, one foot against the edge of it, his leg drawn up and his arm balanced lazily against his knee, as though it was his own home. He was dressed in a shirt and breeches with a black wool cloak pinned around his shoulders and, peeping beneath it, a huge, ugly sapphire, shiny as a boil, and bulging like one. That, I had recognised. But, besides, I would not have mistaken him for an ordinary man. I had grown up half-knowing the Otherworld secrets of Avalon, and though I had no gifts myself, I was not so foolish and ignorant that I could not tell those who had them from those who did not. I had, after all, sensed behind the lie of the Giant's Daughter, Gorlois' ancient blood.

"Stop telling him that I will be his wife," I said, taking advantage of Merlin's smug silence.

Merlin laughed softly, getting up lightly from his seat and walking over towards me. I did not back away. I wasn't afraid of him like everyone else was.

"Little Igraine," he sighed. As he came right up to me, he reached out his hand, and I felt his fingers brush against the side of my neck, softly, and I leaned back away from him. "You're already his. All those moments alone, whispering in the corridors, in the courtyards, over dusty old boxes of armour. You don't truly know what you want yet. But you will."

"*I know what I want*," I shouted, suddenly hot with anger. I knew the difference between desire and other wants better than they did. Animals. I knew what I *wanted*. I wanted my husband back from war. I wanted my home to be safe. I didn't want Uther's brutish silences, his rough grasp, his strange promises of a future that was not my choice.

Merlin laughed again, and shrugged. "I am sure that you do," he said, and strode lazily from the room.

It was only after he left, in that beguiling young form of his, that I wondered again about the prickly look the Lady of Avalon had given him, and the girl who was also named Viviane – although I was not sure that the manner in which I pieced it together in my head could have been true. I had seen the girl Viviane quite well, and I was sure that no such creature as Merlin could have made her. She was also too old, since I thought the Lady of Avalon not more than ten years older than me, for it all to make sense. So, all three mysteries could not be neatly knotted together, but that did not mean that there was not some truth in my suspicions. But I did not ask. I thought if I were Viviane, I would not want to talk about it.

* * *

At last the spring came, and I was glad to leave. It was lonely in Camelot, and although Viviane was kind, she was distant and thoughtful, and she did not say very much. When Imogen kissed me on the cheek to say goodbye she lingered as though she was thinking of whispering something to me, but she did not. I felt strangely about Imogen. I certainly thought less of her, for offering herself to Uther as a lover, but I was not sure that I would not have – as she had – done whatever seemed necessary to stay at the heart of a kingdom that was mine. And she was proud, and beautiful, and she did not rule the castle badly. It just seemed like so much less than the daughter of King Aurelianus was worth, to have to offer herself to Uther as a concubine just to keep her place.

I thought about her, as Viviane and I rode away from Camelot side by side. I wondered what it must be like, to have no power where once it had all been promised to you. Aurelianus had raised her to be a queen, and she had had a husband, but he had died, and she had had no living child. I could have come so perilously close to that – to being a tenant in Tintagel when I should have been its mistress. The thought chilled me, and upset me, and I put a hand against my stomach and prayed that it was a little boy inside me, so that even if Gorlois never made it back from war, then we would be safe.

When we finally arrived back at Tintagel, I was dismayed to find that Enid had gone back to France, leaving only a brief note. I supposed that she had been bored and lonely in Tintagel all alone, but I wished that she had been here. Perhaps someone had told her that I was pregnant, and she did not want to see me. She did not seem to have taken good care of the place, either. Too much of the stores had been eaten up and drunk, and the men were not being trained as hard as they should be. In a manner typical of Enid, she had been lax and lazy.

I sat in my old room, in the window-seat, staring at the little white spring flowers pushing up through the scrubby cliff-grass. In Camelot they had had crocuses and primroses growing everywhere. It had been beautiful in its own way, but Tintagel had the bright purple gorse of the cliff-edge, and the little white wildflowers that snaked across the ground, and these were beautiful in the pure way of the wild. Camelot was neat and bright, like the gold coats and the rich jewels they all wore. I felt as though I was one with the wild beauty of Tintagel, its quiet fierceness. It was what it was, and that was beautiful. There was no pretence.

* * *

Viviane stayed until my child was born, right in the bright, beautiful middle of spring. I was glad that she stayed, for I had been delivered into life by one of the women of Avalon, who had saved my life although they had not been able to save my mother's, and I trusted her entirely. I drank the drink she offered me, which made me feel distant from myself, and sleepy. But when I heard the first little cries, all of that faded away, and Viviane handed me my child, and I held her close against my chest. No, I did not care that she was not a boy. She was the most perfect thing I had ever seen, and born with strands of red-gold hair on her head, bright as Gorlois', and what soon grew to be little bright blue eyes like his which blinked against the sun they did not know, and a little mouth that knew I was the source of life. I could not have imagined anything more wonderful than my child.

Viviane wrote to Gorlois, but there was no time to wait for a response, and I named her Morgawse, after my mother. It seemed right. I hoped that he would be pleased when he saw her. She was strong and hearty, and wilful already, screaming for what she wanted, and gurgling with delight at what pleased her. I wished that Enid had stayed. I thought the sight of her niece would have cheered her about her own childlessness, just a little.

* * *

Viviane left once it seemed that Morgawse and I were out of danger. I barely noticed. I could not think of anything else but my little girl.

The end of the summer was beautiful, and I sat with her in my window seat, watching the sun on the waves, and then, as autumn came, the heavy clouds that seemed to touch the sea at the horizon. I didn't send for a wet nurse. I didn't want one, and with my husband far away, there was no need for one.

Autumn passed, and the air grew sharp with cold. Then, at last, after all that time, after I thought that I would be alone all winter, sealed off by ice and snow, Gorlois returned. I heard the tower guards blow the hunting horns for his arrival, the ones they would have sounded for my father, or for me, if I had been born a man.

I stood in the window of the great tower with Morgawse sleeping in my arms, and watched the men ride in through the gates. All helmed and in their armour, they were indistinguishable from one another until Gorlois jumped down from his horse, a head taller than the rest. He *had* come home. *He should have promised*, I thought. It was easy to say that, knowing that he had survived. I hoped that this meant that it was all over, all the war and the fighting.

I saw him rush in, up the tower, running up the stairs in his heavy armour. I heard the plates of it scraping against one another, heard it clanking where his breastplate caught the stone of the walls of the narrow spiral staircase. He must have seen the light of the candle in the room where I stood, because he ran straight up here, and burst through the door.

I turned as he came in, and he pulled the helm off his head, letting it fall with a loud, hollow clatter to the ground. He looked just how I remembered him, but it felt as though it was far longer than the year and four months that had passed since I had seen him. I knew well his broad, kind face, the freckles that were pale with winter but still just visible, the bright blue of his eyes, and yet we had been little more than strangers when he left. I knew him so well from my memories, but did not really know him at all.

"Igraine…" He stepped towards me, and I stepped towards him, offering the little bundle in my arms forwards, turning so that he could look at the face of his child. He pulled off his leather gauntlets, and took her gently from my hands, his eyes fixed on her face. I saw him take in the wonder of it, this little creature made in his image, the big, blue eyes blinking at him, the neat little nose and ears, the soft fine baby strands of red-gold hair, and he smiled. She wriggled in his arms, but not unhappily, and when he reached out a hand to stroke her cheek lightly, she burbled with delight, and reached out her little hands to pull one of his fingers into her mouth, and suck it between her gums. I saw the smile spread deeply across his face, and I was pleased, pleased beyond measure that our daughter was not afraid of him, though she had not known him. She was a brave little creature already, afraid of no one, burbling her nonsense at anyone she saw.

I stepped towards him once more, and laid a hand on his arm. It was only then that I remembered that he was in his armour. I was surprised that Morgawse did not find it strange, the hard, cold shell of the armour over the arms that held her, but she was happy enough.

"Was your journey hard?" I asked him.

He looked up at me, his eyes wide with wonder. "I had forgotten it entirely."

"It is late," I said gently, and he nodded.

I lifted Morgawse gently from his arms, a little protective still, a little jealous, and called for my servant Lethelt to come and take her to her crib. I could see, after the excitement of meeting someone new had perked her up temporarily, that she was struggling to hold her eyes awake.

Lethelt came and took her from my arms, folding the blanket more tightly around her in the quiet, careful way she had.

"And fetch a bath for Gorlois," I told her. "In the bedroom."

She nodded, and left with a little curtsey.

* * *

Suddenly alone, with no child between us to bring us together, Gorlois and I were awkward with each other. Before he had left, we had been fast approaching the intimacy of lovers, as well as that of husband and wife, but now we were stuck between what we had been, and what we now were, which was almost strangers.

I slipped my hand into his without speaking, and led the way up to the bedroom we had shared. I felt the warmth of his skin against mine, I felt the smallness of my little hand in his strong grip, and I closed my eyes against it. It was the bliss of remembering, and I hoped that my memories would not pass away like a dream when I had him back in my arms.

When I pushed open the bedroom door, I saw that the bath was already drawn, and the fire set and lit, and the bed prepared with clean sheets and laid on top with warm furs for the winter, the curtains drawn back. The room looked warm and cosy and inviting, and I was pleased. I didn't want it to be obvious that I had spent the last year sleeping in my childhood bedroom, to avoid sleeping in my marriage bed alone.

Gorlois shut the door behind himself as he followed me into the room, and we stood in the middle of it, face to face, unsure of what would happen next.

He seemed more hesitant than I, but I supposed that I was in my own home, and though he was the lord of the castle, he had been long gone, and had only just been its lord when he left. I stepped towards him, and began to unbuckle the breastplate of his armour. As I lifted it over his head, our eyes met, and he leaned down and pressed his lips softly against mine. I sighed, just a little, at the gentle sweetness of their touch, and I took his face in my hands, and gazed up at him. There was dirt in his hair, on his face, and a little blood on his cheek.

As he pulled the greaves from his arms and his legs, and pulled off his boots, I could see that his shirt beneath was stained with blood. I pulled it over his head, and he winced. Against his side there was a cut that looked a few days old, puckered at the edges and dark with dried blood. When I pressed my fingers lightly against it, he drew his breath in sharply, though he said nothing. He pulled off the woollen breeches he wore under his armour to step into the bath, and as he turned his back to me to step in, the firelight caught the shape of him, the curve of the dense muscles of his body, the power of his huge frame.

When he was in the bath, I knelt beside it, and, dipping my hand into the water, I gently washed the dirt from his face, and ran my wet fingers through his hair. He closed his eyes against my touch, pressing his face into my hand with a kind of desperate relief. He murmured my name under his breath, and as my hand brushed his cheek again, he put one of his hands over it, and turned to press his lips against my hand.

"You've been gone so long," I whispered, though I knew it was not long, not for men at war. I could feel my body remembering his touch, the feel of his lips against my skin. I opened my mouth to say something else, but he had already pulled me into the water with him, and I found that I did not care that I was still in all my clothes. I was not in them for long.

Chapter eleven

With Gorlois returned with news that war had turned to peace and rebellion against Uther had turned to conquering and obedience, my life became steady, and domestic. And happy. Gorlois told me that he had been allowed to return to me when King Lot of Lothian had pledged himself to Uther, and they had turned together on those others who had rebelled, and obliterated them. Uther's conquering meant peace, and peace meant that I had my husband home, and I was glad.

I was busy with the organisation of the castle, and Gorlois with the equipping and training of its garrison with the Welsh knights he had brought with him, and serious Ulfius, as the master of the guard. I would sit in the big window-seat with little Morgawse while she babbled happily. At night, Gorlois and I would eat together, and then we would go to bed; he was always tender and gentle and loving, and I was always glad to have such a husband. That became the pattern of our days, and I was happy. Morgawse was a bright child, always smiling, but somehow too bright, too excited by everything around her to sit still and listen when she was old enough for me to read to her. She wanted to touch everything, to hold everything in her little hands. She laughed at everything new that she saw, and she clapped her hands with joy whenever her father picked her up in his arms, and sang to her in his low, beautiful voice, in his own Gaelic language. He loved her utterly, and wanted her to have whatever she desired. At first, when she was barely more than a baby, running around our bedroom on chubby, unsteady feet, this was little pieces of apple and strawberries in the summer, and to dip her fingers in the honey, and suck them, but as she grew older it was for him to carry her on his shoulders to the top of the battlements, or to sit her on his horse. She was a bold, adventurous girl, and I supposed that she got that from him. She also had his flame-red hair, bright as gold, and his blue, blue eyes, and yet it was my sister Enid that she reminded me of the most. Her ready laugh, but also the recklessness that I could see already in her when she was only four or five years old. She wanted to run everywhere, to try everything. I tried to make Gorlois understand that one day she would have to be taught that she could not crash boldly through her whole life and come out unscathed, but although she often fell and scratched herself, or tore her dresses, or tangled her hair, or hurt herself, Gorlois smiled indulgently, and seemed sure that our little daughter would survive her own boldness. I was not so sure. I had not heard from Enid since I wrote to her to tell her that she had a little niece.

I had heard about Elaine from an insultingly dispassionate Irish messenger. She had died in the birth of her second child, but Máel was pleased enough, for it was another little son.

I hoped for another child. I remembered how much I had loved to play with my sisters when we were all young. I wanted Morgawse to have that. I thought I would worry about her recklessness less if she had siblings, and I could see them take care of one another. Elaine had always looked out for me and Enid. Perhaps it would make Morgawse careful and watchful if she had a little brother or a sister to take care of.

But it did not happen. Gorlois was not worried, for he said over and again that we were both young. But I was. We were often together in the pleasures of our marriage-bed, and Morgawse had been conceived so quickly; I was frightened that something was wrong. I was worried that it would happen again as it had with me and my sisters, and Tintagel having no heir would go to the man who could claim her. I had chosen wisely, and with care. I had chosen a man strong enough, brave enough and good enough to protect me and my castle, to stand by us. I was wary of making that choice for my daughter, and even more wary of letting her make it herself.

By the time that Morgawse was approaching her sixth birthday, I was afraid that there was something amiss with me. I did not ask Gorlois if there had been other women while he was away at war. I knew that was the way of it. I did not ask if Morgawse had bastard half-brothers or sisters far up in the north, because I did not want to know. I knew Gorlois loved me, and that it would not have meant anything, and besides, the thought of it made me sad, and I did not want to put it into words.

We lay in bed one morning, in early spring. It was bright outside, but still cold, and I woke long before Gorlois did, and lay with my head on his chest, worrying that there would be no son of my line to keep my home when I was gone.

When it was full light, Gorlois stirred, and I felt his hand stroke down my hair, and down my back. I snuggled closer against his broad chest, pressing my lips lightly against the skin there.

"Igraine?" he said, and I looked up at him, folding my hands on his chest, and resting my chin on them. "Oh, Igraine, have you been awake worrying?"

I nodded, but I did not want to begin explaining again, did not want to hear him tell me that it would all be alright when I was afraid it would not be. He wrapped his arms around me, and pulled me gently on to him, and into a kiss that was soft and loving.

"Igraine," he said, softly, "we have all the time in the world for another child. And besides," I felt his hands slide down my back, and then down my thighs, drawing me closer on to him, "children are not made by worrying."

It was harder to be anxious with his lips soft against mine, his hands running over my body, and then up into my hair where they tangled and became more passionate, more demanding. The feel of our naked bodies pressed together in the lovely warm, sleepy haze of the morning was enough to make me forget my worries for the moment, but this was a man's solution to a woman's problem and it did not solve it. When it was over, and I rested my head on his chest, and he kissed me tenderly, I was worried once more. How many times had I felt that warm, wet promise of new life between my legs and hoped that it would be *this time*, and how many times had I been disappointed, and frustrated, and upset?

"I am going to go to Avalon," I said quietly.

Gorlois stroked my hair with his huge hand. "Whatever you think is best, my love," he said, and kissed me on the forehead.

* * *

I wrote to Viviane so that she would expect me, and I held Morgawse tight in my arms and kissed her goodbye as she wriggled against it, eager to be free from my motherly embrace and to run around. She thought she was a little boy. I could tell. Sometimes she played with the other little boys, the sons of the knights and the farmers who lived nearby. I had even heard her speaking to them in Cornish, and she had sulked when I scolded her for it. But it was the language of the common people and not proper for a princess. I had asked Gorlois to stop her, because it would only make it harder when she was older, and we had to tell her that she could not play with boys anymore. He tried to tell her not to a few times, but his heart wasn't really in it, and she knew it, and he never scolded her for it.

Gorlois helped me to tie my little bag of things onto the horse's saddle, and took my face in his hands to give me a kiss goodbye.

"Come back soon, Igraine," he said. I nodded, and gave him the brightest smile I could. I did not know what I would do if I went to Avalon and Viviane said that I would never have another child.

I was about to say something else to him when Morgawse at the other end of the courtyard started calling for her father to come and pick her up, and take her up to the battlements. I smiled as I watched him go and lift her up and put her on his shoulders while she kicked her feet with excitement, wrapped her arms around his neck, and rested her chin on top of his head. My father had never been like that with me – he had been loving, but he had always been careful, always anxious and protective – and it was one of the most beautiful things I had ever seen, to see how Gorlois was with our little girl. She was the world to him. She was enough. But I knew the world well enough to know that it would not be enough for the world, not be enough for Tintagel, if she were all the children I would ever have.

* * *

I had been to school in Avalon, long ago, as a little girl. Or rather, I had been to the lake that was its shore, and looked out across it. I had had a woman from Avalon as a teacher, too, when I was little and schooled in a nearby abbey, and I said to people I was schooled in Avalon, because I knew that would make them think I was greater than I was, but I knew nothing of its ways. I would go on to the isle now, to where the witches learned their schooling at the wonderful place where the surface world touched the Otherworld.

I had not dared to ask to come before, but desperation had made me bold. I had not had a right to ask it before. Now, I was sovereign of my realm, small and humble though it was, and Avalon would welcome me. Avalon still gave its favour to Cornwall and Logrys, and some of the kingdoms of Wales, even as it drew them back from Lothian and Orkney who had turned against the old, magic ways.

* * *

Viviane was waiting for me on the shore as I rode up, tired and sore but relieved. I always forgot what a beautiful woman she was because I only remembered the blue-green woad that traced across her face and the skin of her hands, and her arms and her chest. I saw it first, in patterns like the light in summer hitting the surface of the lake, spreading like a web over her white skin. But, as I stepped off my horse and she kissed me on the cheek, I saw everything else. Her kind face, her bright, kind blue-green eyes, and the lovely gold of her plait of hair. She looked as though she was made of the water of the lake, her skin and eyes traced blue, her dress a robe of blue and green silk woven together, like the sea. The common people who lived here and did not understand that there was an isle beyond the mist thought that she *did* live in the lake, and called her the lady of it, and I did not think them foolish for thinking so. If I did not know better, I would have thought so myself.

Viviane took my hand to help me into the little barge that would take us out there, and smiled at me with the gentle auntish way she had as I hugged my cloak around me, and watched my horse disappear through the mist. I felt bad, leaving him on the shore, but Viviane had assured me that there were people to take care of him, that knew he would be there, and would come when we were gone. *Avalon must guard its secrets*, she said. I nodded, not knowing what they were.

* * *

I came through the mist to a place that was beautiful and strange in the same way Tintagel was. It looked like an abbey, but it was carved out of the rugged face of the tor in dark rock. It was harsh, and lovely, and frightening. It was made the same, made to follow the land rather than made against it.

Viviane took me to an empty room that was just like a nun's cell – small, and plain and simple – and told me that was where I would sleep while I stayed. She left before I could ask how long it would take. I had written of what I was coming for in the letter I had sent her, but now I was here I felt nervous to begin asking for it. Viviane was clearly so powerful, so respected here, and this was her space, and steeped in the magic that I barely understood, and I thought it must have been my place to wait, although I did not want to.

* * *

I slept badly alone when I was used to sleeping with Gorlois beside me, and for the first time far from little Morgawse. She would not notice. She was entirely her father's child, and would be overjoyed to have his undivided attention. She would probably beg him to read to her until long after it was dark, and he would let her fall asleep in our big bed. I wished I was there with them, scolding Morgawse for being naughty, and Gorlois for letting her be. Instead, I was alone, on a narrow bed, in a strange place, here to beg for all of our futures.

Chapter twelve

The next day, Viviane came in the morning as I stood in my underdress washing my face with water from the basin that was only just slightly more than freezing. She laughed fondly when she saw me.

"This might look like an abbey, Igraine, but you don't have to live like a nun here. I could have had someone fetch you hot water, or even a bath if you had wanted one."

Shivering, with my wet hair running a trail of cold water down my back, I wished that she could have told me that last night. But I said nothing.

I pulled my woollen overdress on over my underclothes. I hadn't bothered to bring anything fine. It was uncomfortable to ride in fine clothes, and I was afraid of thieves. No one would care how I looked here, and the dress was warm and comfortable in the fresh spring weather. Avalon was, besides, cooler than the world beyond, slightly damp with the breeze that blew through the mists, and always seemed to be chilly, even when the sun shone.

* * *

Viviane showed me round the isle, through the lovely old halls, across the wild tor, then back through the stables where I saw my horse, though I could not imagine how they got him across the lake, and finally to a big library, which smelled of lovely old leather, old ink, and secrets. I breathed it in deeply. I had forgotten how much I missed the smell of old books. I remembered, vividly, the library at the abbey where I had been to school briefly as a girl. It had smelled the same. Comforting, and ancient.

She left me in the library, claiming that she had something important to do. I walked through it, picking books off the shelves, curling up in one of the alcoves in the wall with them, leafing through them. There were wonderful things in them. One of them contained a potion that claimed to have the power to bring a man back to life if administered by the right person, and another described a spell that would change one man into another man, and one that promised relief from boils. There was nothing about a potion that would ensure a child, and I hoped that meant that Viviane had it in her study.

I did not see Viviane again in the evening. One of the girls who was at school there brought me a stew for my dinner, and I ate it in my room, staring out of the window at the lake and the mist, and the dark, craggy rocks. Avalon was truly one of the most beautiful places I had ever seen, but my journey there was already beginning to seem frustrating and pointless. The next day, and the next, I could not find Viviane anywhere, and I got the sense that she was avoiding me.

* * *

I saw her again the day after that, when she came and knocked on my door, greeting me with her usual kind, auntish smile. I wanted to shout at her, to ask her where she had been hiding, why she was making me wait, but I did not. I was too shy, and too aware of her power and her influence. She was greater than a king. Whatever Máel or anyone else said, the Lady of Avalon was still kingmaker in Britain. She had proved that with Uther.

"Igraine," she smiled, "you are looking well. I thought you might like to come and see this wonderful book I have found in the library. I know you like old Gaelic tales, and the librarian has this wonderful red-bound book that I think you would like."

I followed her, but I was annoyed. I had come for help, and she was behaving as though I had come to read. I did not have time for this. I had a little daughter back at home who needed me, to whom I was already longing to return if help could not be found. I was not so desperate for another child that I forgot the child I had. But before we got to the library, we were interrupted by a girl, her face still free from the woad that marked the women who were wise in the magic arts, running up to Viviane.

"My lady," she said, gasping for her breath, "Merlin is at the docks."

She seemed afraid, and I did not blame her, for Merlin was frightening and unpleasant.

I glanced at Viviane, and I saw her face tighten for a moment, before she gave her gentle smile and nodded, and I rushed behind her as she swept off down to the docks. When she greeted Merlin, she kissed him on the cheek and was gracious and welcoming. He came in his usual shape, the shape of the bald-headed man. The skin over his skull was pale, almost translucent, and the woad patterns on it like the traces of veins against it. He was the strangest-looking man I had ever seen. I remembered the handsome shape he had, and I wondered why he did not prefer to go about that way.

* * *

Because Merlin was there, we all dined in the great hall. Viviane invited me to sit beside her. It made me nervous to have such a place of honour. I was aware of the greatness of everyone else there, the powerful magic of Avalon, and my own smallness in comparison to it, even though I was the Queen of Cornwall. I knew enough to understand that the power of Avalon was greater than that. Far greater.

The conversation was dull. Merlin was talking about the war which, it seemed, had dragged on through treaties and tribute once the actual fighting had ended. Lot had surrendered to Uther, and sworn himself into vassalage, and the proud, angry nation of Lothian had retreated into submission, its people resentful but defeated. I could not taste the food. I could not stop thinking about Uther, about when I had seen him at Christmas time, the way he had spoken to me, the way *I* had felt alone with him, the awful temptation. Hadn't that been seven years ago? It still felt so raw. I felt sick and ashamed that I had felt that way now – now that Gorlois had returned and we had had all those years of happy marriage – and unsettled that I still remembered it so clearly. A trunk full of old armour. Uther's smell – leather, and sweat – the steady gaze of his grey-green eyes, and the sound of his voice, low and rough. I ought not to remember.

I wondered what Merlin had come for, but I did not ask. I did not want to stay with him here. I disliked all of his promises to Uther, and I mistrusted his demand for Uther's child.

* * *

If Merlin was staying, then I would go. I was resolved. I asked one of the girls who slept in the room beside mine where Viviane's study was, and I thought I would go and demand that she either give me what I wanted, or tell me I could not have it. I disliked being left waiting, and I disliked Viviane avoiding me.

I rushed there, my courage mustered by my anger, ready to confront her, but as I drew near, I could hear voices inside. As I got closer, I recognised one as hers, and the other as Merlin's unpleasant rasping tones.

"I can't keep having this same argument with you, Merlin," I heard Viviane snap, annoyed. "It is done."

"Why do you pretend that we are enemies now, Viviane?" he asked, "You welcome me here, you seek my counsel, you supported my candidate as King –"

"Merlin," she interrupted him, and I heard anger in her voice, "I do these things because I must, not because I have any lingering affection for you. I allow you to come here because I am not so selfish that for the sake of my anger I will make you knock down Avalon's magical defences to get inside. I supported Uther Pendragon because I knew he would be a good, strong king, as he has been. But I have burned the books of Macrobius that we held in Avalon's library, and I have banned the teaching of your Black Arts on my isle. You came here, you pretended to school with me, side by side, in a shape that was not your own. I know you for a liar, Merlin. Be reminded, be *strongly* reminded, that although I cannot act against you, I *am* your enemy."

"I am not your enemy, Viviane," Merlin said softly; I pressed myself closer against the door. "We want the same things."

"No, Merlin, we do not. I want Avalon to be safe, its knowledge to be safe. I want the world we have made to survive. I want the right man on the throne, who will bring peace and prosperity. That is why I supported Uther Pendragon. You supported him because you have made this pact with him, and you think that he is your creature, and that he will carry out your wishes. And has he done so? It does not seem to me that he has. You have no more power now than you did when Aurelianus was king. And what will you do, Merlin, with Pendragon? What will you do when he is gone? Does he heed you? He shows no sign of producing an heir so that you can continue to control him. He will not take a wife, so you cannot sneak your changeling child into her belly. Do not think that I do not know what you want."

"You have misunderstood my ambitions, Viviane," Merlin insisted, his tone darkening, becoming more threatening. "I have no desire for a child on the throne. How long do you think Avalon will be allowed to continue now all the lesser kings of Britain are Christians? Do you want to have to withdraw from the world, to lose your influence? The world has changed, Viviane. All I want is for us to change with it."

There was a long silence, and I leaned closer, afraid that I would miss what they were saying to one another.

"And I want to see the girl, Viviane. Let me see the girl."

"She is gone, Merlin," Viviane replied coldly. "Disappeared. I do not know where she is."

"You did this to punish me," he said.

"No, Merlin," she sighed, "I did this for her sake. I did not want her to know that she was the product of black magic, and lies."

I slipped away then. I did not know why, but what I had overheard made me feel upset, horribly upset and afraid. I felt dirty, too, all over my skin, as though I had seen something that I knew I had not seen. I had come close to something awful, although I could not quite articulate what it was. I thought of what Viviane had said to Merlin, and of the girl I had caught a glimpse of who bore her name, and the same bright golden hair, but I did not know if the picture I drew in my mind was the truth.

I hoped, deeply, that it was not.

* * *

The next morning, when I woke, there was blood on the sheets, and I cried. I didn't want to. I knew it was stupid, and weak, and that I was young and I had a child already, but I had hoped beyond reason that even coming to Avalon might be enough. But it was not. Once again, no child. Once again, I was afraid for the future of my home.

The door opened as I was rubbing my eyes with the sleeve of my nightdress, pulling myself together, telling myself that I was silly. I jumped back, but it was Viviane, her kind face wrinkling at the eyes with concern.

"Igraine, my dear, what is it?" she asked, but her eyes drifted across the bedsheets, thrown back, and she sighed, reaching out an arm and pulling me against her in an uncharacteristically demonstrative gesture of comfort.

"I suppose I do not need to ask what brought you here, after all," she said, softly.

I shook my head. I wondered if my letter had not reached her after all, but I did not ask. I didn't trust myself to speak. I resented it, too, being so weak over this, when I wanted to be calm, and careful and in control.

"You want another child." She brushed her hand in a comforting, strangely motherly gesture down my cheek, and I nodded. I felt like a child, standing there with her arm around me, being comforted by her. She put her fingers gently under my chin and turned my face up to look at her.

"You will, Igraine. You will have more children. You will have a son. I have seen it," she said with a smile.

"But how can you be sure?" I asked.

She smiled more deeply. "I am sure of more things than you can even dream of, Igraine," she said. She kissed me softly on the cheek and left.

It was strange, and it was not comforting, and when I turned back into the room I was sure I saw her out of the window, walking down towards the little dock. And I felt horribly aware that I was only in my thin nightgown and she – or someone else – had put their arm around me.

* * *

I dreamt that night that I was with Gorlois, and I felt his lips against my neck, and his arms around me, and I sighed with it. But it woke me in the middle of the night, and I opened my eyes onto the darkness, and I felt horribly cold and alone, and wished I had never come to Avalon.

Chapter thirteen

In the morning, I was determined that Viviane would speak to me properly. I thought she was avoiding it, trying to keep me here. I did not know why, or what particular good my presence here would do for her, but she seemed determined to put off giving me what I wanted. If I had not overheard their conversation a few days ago, I would have suspected her and Merlin of trying to keep me here for some plan of theirs. I would have suspected them of trying to keep me there and bringing Uther to meet me. As worried as I was about the future of my kingdom, they must have been about Britain, without its heir.

When I knocked on the door of her study, Viviane called me in, and with a gentle smile, gestured to the little wooden chair that sat empty in the corner. I sat in it, carefully. It reminded me again of being at school, in the abbey. The dark stone of the walls, the dark wooden furniture, the kind, motherly abbess not so different from Viviane. Stern, but forgiving, seeing everyone else as a child, no matter their age. I was long a woman, long a wife. It felt strange to sit in a little wooden chair in a place so like my childhood abbey school.

"So, you have come to hurry me along, Igraine," she said, but her tone was patient and her look was kind.

"Please, Viviane. I want to go home, back to my daughter. Just tell me if there is anything I can do, anything you can give me. I *need* another child."

Viviane nodded patiently, turning from her desk, folding her hands in her lap.

"I can help you, Igraine. There is nothing certain in what I will give you, but it will help. But I will ask something of you in return."

I thought of Uther, and his horrid pact with Merlin, and I opened my mouth to protest, my heart racing inside me.

Viviane put up a hand to quiet me before I had even spoken. "I know about Uther and Merlin and the deal they have made, and I want you to know that I would never ask such a thing of you. All I ask, Igraine, is if the child is born with magic in its blood that you send it to school in Avalon. Only once it is of age, and only to learn. All I require is a promise that any child you have with magic in its blood will school here."

"That is all?"

"That is all," Viviane replied with a nod.

"I do not think that I *can* have a child with magic blood," I said, aware that I should have kept it quiet, for fear of her withdrawing her offer. "I do not have any in me."

"Igraine, my dear, *Gorlois* has it." She seemed surprised that I did not know that his ancient blood was magic, too, and with the same magic as was held in high regard in Avalon, but then she shook her head to herself, thoughtful. "Though I have heard it said that those without it cannot feel it strongly as we do. No, my dear Igraine, it is your husband who carries the blood of the Otherworld folk in his veins. But that doesn't matter. It is a gift, and an honour to be schooled in Avalon. Will you agree to it?"

"I will," I replied. I did not have to think a moment about it. Despite what Merlin had said, Avalon was still powerful, and Christian men cared deeply for its opinion. I did not see how that would change in my lifetime. I would be happy and proud to give a child of mine to Avalon.

As Viviane slipped from her seat to rifle through the jars of potions on her shelf, I wondered once more if there might not have been more truth than I had been willing to believe in Gorlois' fabulous story about his grandmother, the Giant's Daughter. He was larger by far than any other man I had ever seen in my life, and if he had Otherworld blood in him, that made it all seem so much more like the truth. But he had said that he had made it up.

Viviane turned back to me, and pressed a bottle into my hands. It was filled with a dark red liquid, like blood, that looked thick and viscous and unpleasant.

"Drink that, before you go to your husband's bed," she said.

I felt myself blushing, though I knew I had nothing to be embarrassed about.

"Just a little, each time. It tastes disgusting. I'm sorry, there's nothing much I can do about the taste."

I nodded, and cradled the little bottle in my hands. I had what I had come for. Now I only had to pray that it would work.

* * *

I felt a little sad as I said goodbye to Viviane. During our time in Camelot and my stay there, I had grown fond of her. I thought I would be glad to send a child of mine to school with her, although I was not sure how I would explain to Morgawse that she was somehow lacking and unable to go. Gorlois must have known all along that he had not passed that on to his daughter. I could not imagine Morgawse being pleased to be denied anything, but I would deal with it when the time came. Before all of that, I had to make sure I had another child.

I rode back through the night, not wanting to stop, and arrived when the stars were out, and the frost was settling on the grass. I was cold, but I did not feel it.

Someone must have woken Gorlois when they saw me approaching, because he was down in the courtyard to meet me when I rode in, in his shirt and breeches.

He lifted me down from the saddle and wrapped me in his arms. He was still warm from his bed, and huge, and comforting. I put my head against his chest, and he kissed my forehead.

"Igraine," he said, his voice gentle, but concerned, "what were you doing riding through the night?"

"I just wanted to get home, to you, as soon as I could," I replied, and he took my face gently in his hands and kissed me tenderly. I leaned in against him, and felt the bottle I had hung in a little bag around my neck press against my ribs. I felt bold, and hopeful.

"Take me to bed, Gorlois," I whispered. He laughed softly in response.

"Igraine, it's the middle of the night."

"I missed you," I said, winding my fingers into his hair, brushing my lips softly against his nose, and then his lips.

"As my lady wishes," he said with a smile, and picked me up in his arms, and carried me up towards the tower.

"Wait," I whispered, as we approached the door. "I want to be outside."

I had a feeling, a strange, important feeling that Avalon's magic would be more potent under the stars than under any roof made by men.

"Someone might see us."

"Who is awake at this time of night, Gorlois? Only you." I reached up, and trailed my fingertips across his lips, and he closed his eyes. "And me."

He let me slip from his arms as he kissed me, and I took him by the hand and led him round the side of the castle, among the low, sharp rocks of the scrubby land that surrounded us. It was cold, and we breathed out little clouds of mist, but it was beautiful. The sky was clear and the moon was bright and big among the stars. While Gorlois was still trailing behind me, I pulled out the bottle of magic liquid from Avalon, and drank a gulp of it. In my haste, I drank almost half, and it tasted acrid, and iron, and unpleasant like blood, but I felt wild with hope, and I did not worry. For the first time in a long while, I did not worry.

I turned around, and grasping Gorlois by the front of his shirt, pulled him down with me as I sank down to the ground. I was glad of my fur cloak then, for warmth, but glad, too, to feel the brush of the grass against my bare legs below it as Gorlois grasped my skirts in his hands and began to push them back, his mouth pressed against mine in a wild, passionate kiss.

"What has got into you, Igraine?" he murmured at my ear, as I felt his lips against it, and then, lightly, his teeth. But he was enjoying it. I was usually quiet, and reserved and careful.

I did not reply, but I arched my back, pressing myself against him, tangling my fingers into his hair. I felt his hand run up the inside of my leg, and then his fingers go gently inside me, and I gasped softly at the pleasure of his touch. I felt hot already, and eager, and when he felt it, and felt me begin to breathe hard with it against him, he opened his breeches and went inside me, pressing his lips against my neck, holding me tight against him. I moaned softly with delight, and then more as he gripped me hard by the thighs, and he was harder and rougher than he usually was. I liked feeling the huge

74

power and strength of him. He was usually wary. Wary of hurting me, wary of his size and strength. In the wildness of our sudden passion for one another, he had forgotten it, and his kisses were different, too; more demanding. I loved his tender gentleness as much as I loved this wild passion, and I gave myself in equal measure to both, but the bright heat of pleasure was faster on me when we were together like this, and he pressed his mouth against mine to swallow the cry that came from me as it rushed around me, and around him, and afterwards we lay a long time, tangled together, staring up at the stars above us, and I wished on every star I saw that there would be a child.

* * *

Morgan was born in the middle of winter, when the snow around Tintagel was unusually thick. We never normally got snow, so close to the sea, but it was as though the earth itself knew that Morgan was special. It was a perfectly clear night, and the moon shone bright through the window. Viviane was there, and Gorlois – though he should not have been – in his shirt and breeches with his arms crossed over his chest. The birth was difficult and I remembered vividly afterwards the smell of my own blood, Viviane holding my hand and whispering to me, and the taste of some potion she gave me. Not the same as what I had had before, that had turned everything to sleepy softness and light; this one made me hazy, and slow. I remembered, also, the moment when she had wrapped Morgan in a sheet of linen and placed her in my arms. She blinked her eyes open, a blank new-born blue that would grow grey like my own, and little strands of dark hair on her head. She was small and delicate, and I was afraid for her, for she was born early, and she was quiet and barely cried, but she was strong after all, with her own natural determination, and Gorlois' Otherworld blood.

I was afraid that Morgawse would be jealous, but when Gorlois let her in to see her sister early the next morning, she took her gently from my arms and kissed her forehead. Morgan blinked up at her, and yawned her tiny mouth, and Morgawse laughed with delight. I was exhausted, but blissfully happy. It was not a son, but it was another child, another chance, and I was filled with hope that there would be a son one day.

* * *

Viviane was pleased that she would have a pupil in Morgan, and so was I, and as it happened it was she who explained to Morgawse that her sister would one day go to Avalon, and she would not. Morgawse did not seem bothered. She did not like lessons. I had written to the abbey that had schooled me, and they had sent a sweet old nun called Margaret, but Morgawse's favourite game was to try to escape from her tutor and run with the boys in the courtyard. I scolded her, but Gorlois would always smile and pick her up in his arms, where she would giggle and kick her feet with delight, even until she was ten years old.

In Morgan I recognised my own childhood self. She was quiet, and happy to be alone. She liked the books, and even before she could read the words – which she could read long before I could have when I was a child – she would sit staring at the page while Margaret the old nun read. While Morgawse demanded that Lethelt the serving-maid sing her folksongs, Morgan at two-and-a-half years old was trying to figure out the Latin letters on the page that she could not possibly have known, with a strangely adult concentration on her face.

* * *

I could not have been happier with Gorlois and our two daughters in Tintagel, and yet, at the back of my mind I worried still about the future. By the time Morgan was approaching three years old, there was no sign I would have another child. Gorlois refused to worry. I was only twenty-seven years old, he said, and we had all the time in the world. I was not so sure. I had Viviane's potion tucked away at the back of the cupboard among my dresses, but I did not dare to drink the last of it, not until I was desperate.

Chapter fourteen

I sat with Morgan and Morgawse, reading to them from the book Gorlois had brought me when he asked me to be his wife that day in the middle of summer. The sun was bright and streamed through the window where we sat, and shone against the rough waves below us. It was a beautiful day. Morgan sat in my lap, her little hands spread out against the page, staring hard at the letters, following them carefully with her eyes, while Morgawse sat opposite me in the window seat, staring out at the sea, lost in imagining the characters as I read the tales to her. She was beginning to approach womanhood. She was still a child, but her red-gold hair was long and thick and beautiful as it fell across her shoulders. From the summer sun, the pale freckles she had inherited from her father spread across the bridge of her nose and her forehead, gold and pretty. She was still skinny as a child, but her face was gaining some of the sensitivity of a woman; full lips, thick-lashed eyes, bright-blue and flashing with wickedness. That wickedness had been the wildness of a little girl who wished she was a boy, but now it was becoming something else. Morgawse had turned it on the newest knight to come from us, a knight from the Welsh Marches, an orphan whom Gorlois had taken in who reminded him of his own beginnings; a young, handsome man named Brastias, who Morgawse had begun with childish innocence to insist that she would marry. Gorlois had laughed it off, but I had wanted to be serious with her. She would have to marry as I had, to a good man who would protect her. Not to a young handsome man to whom she took a shine. But Brastias, who was fifteen years old and barely more than a boy himself, handled it well enough, ruffling her hair and laughing with her. Certainly, she was a child to him. But she was just old enough to be able to tell which men were handsome, and which were not, and to give her brightest, boldest smile to the handsome ones. She was so like Enid. *So* like her. I wished that Enid had replied to any one of my letters. She would have loved her niece.

As the sun was dipping towards the horizon, Gorlois came in, and Morgawse rushed into her father's arms to be lifted up. She laughed, bright and loud, and kicked her feet up behind her as he hugged her tight.

"Have you all been reading in here?" he asked with a smile.

"We've been reading Pwyll again," I told him.

"Pwyll," Morgan agreed softly, nodding her head with the strange seriousness she had, and looking over the book as though to check I had got it right.

"Ah." Gorlois' smile deepened. "One day, girls, I will read it to you in Gælic. It is much more beautiful in Gælic than in English. Although …" He walked over to kiss me on the cheek and I smiled up at him, "…your mother reads it in English more beautifully than anyone else I have ever heard."

Morgan, seeing her father near, reached up her arms and wound them around his neck as he picked her up. She rested her head on his shoulder, tired and happy, and closed her eyes.

"It is time for you girls to go to bed," Gorlois said, gently. Morgan on his shoulder nodded, but Morgawse protested.

"I'm not tired," she said. "Can you send Brastias to read to me?"

Gorlois laughed. "Not tonight, Morgawse, my love. He has guard duty. Maybe tomorrow."

Morgawse pouted a little but nodded, and took her father's hand as he led them off to bed.

* * *

He returned as I was brushing my hair at the window, took the comb from my hands, and drew back the curtain of my hair to press his lips against my neck. I sighed.

"It has been such a beautiful summer," I said.

He made a murmur of agreement, kissing my ear softly, drawing me back more gently against him.

"It has," he agreed, sliding his arms around me, and his hands up my body, and over my breasts as I leant back against him. One of his hands ran softly up my throat, and his fingers brushed against my lips, and I kissed them softly. I loved the feeling of his arms around me. He was so big, so strong. There was no harm that could come to me with him here. I felt my own smallness, with him, but I didn't mind it. After so many years, his touch was familiar, his kiss, the way he always slipped me out of my clothes and ran his big hands all over me, as though still wondering how he came to marry such a creature; I always felt that I was wonderful to him, and somehow still unexpected, as though, like the first morning, he still expected to wake unwillingly from a dream. I was aware, too, that this was precious, and that we were a rare husband and wife to take such pleasure and find such comfort in one another after ten years and more of marriage. When we came together, it was with the gentle rapture of those who had been lovers a long time, and knew each other's bodies, and whose passion was a part of their deep love. Gorlois was my life, and my safety, and my love, the father of my children and the guardian of my home. I loved him more than I could explain, with all the true, steady love of a wife who wanted for nothing. I loved his touch, his strength, the feel of our bodies as they came together, and we sighed together with it, tangled tight in each other's arms.

It was only when we lay side by side in the bed, I with my head on his chest, he half-propped on the pillows, both staring out the window as the early stars began to peep through the velvety, darkening winter night, that he said, "There was a messenger from Camelot today."

"Oh." I turned to look at him, my heart quickening. He had waited to tell me. He must have been worried.

"It seems that King Uther is making a tour of his border kingdoms, and seeks hospitality at Tintagel. Next week."

"*Next week.*" I sat up, sharply. It was soon, and sudden. I had not seen Uther Pendragon in eleven years. I was not sure how I felt about him coming to my home, when the last time he had come it had been on his horse, in his armour, demanding that I made Merlin's promises good and become his wife. But suddenly, vividly, I also remembered that Christmas long ago, when I had almost let him kiss me, and I felt myself flush a little with half-forgotten shame. "Is that enough time to be ready?"

Gorlois shrugged. "It will have to be. But it will be well enough." He sighed, "The last time I saw Uther Pendragon, I was fighting alongside him. He's a rough brute, alright, but he is one of the finest warriors I have ever seen."

I gave a noncommittal noise of agreement. Gorlois fell asleep long before I did, and though I stared out at the pretty winking stars out of the window, I felt oddly distant from everything around me, and lost.

* * *

Morgawse was feverishly excited that the *King* was coming to Tintagel, and she insisted on sitting at my little dressing table and holding the few jewels I had against her little white throat and giggling at each one. She was just old enough to want to play at being a grown woman. It was still a game to her. It wouldn't be for long. The old nun had told me that there had been spots of blood on the sheets of Morgawse's bed only a few weeks before, and Morgawse had come to me crying, thinking she was going to die. She was only months away from her twelfth birthday, and without a son in Tintagel castle, men would begin to look at her as a valuable bride. She was dangerously close to womanhood to be playing at it, but I did not have the heart to stop her.

* * *

Gorlois was nervous, and spent the day with Ulfius and Brastias checking the knights were ready should there be any trouble, while he also tried to make sure that the preparations for food and drink were being taken care of. I brushed Morgawse's hair, and twisted it back and pinned it with one of my pins. She smiled brightly, and patted it with her hand to check it, knocking some strands loose. It didn't matter. I kissed her on the side of her head.

"Be good tonight, Morgawse," I said gently.

Morgawse scrunched her face up with annoyance.

"I'm always *good*," she insisted.

"Morgawse," I insisted, "this is the King of Britain. Just…"

"I know, Mother," she pouted. I wished that I could make her understand that there was nothing wrong with her, but that she had to be careful.

She slipped off the chair and went to pick Morgan up in her arms. At least Morgan was easy, a little child who could sit with Margaret the nun, happy to be quiet and watchful.

I sat before the mirror, staring at myself. I had not seen Uther Pendragon in so long. I was sure that he would not have forgotten me, but I did not know if I had changed. I peered at my face. The same features: grey eyes, fine, dark hair. Was I beautiful? I couldn't tell. My face had lost the plumpness of youth, and I looked like a grown woman, like the lady of my castle and mother I was. I had nothing to fear facing Uther Pendragon. He was not going to ask me why I was not his wife. Not now. Not after more than ten years.

I slowly brushed through my hair, and twisted the strands at the front, and pinned it back. I wore my finest dress; pale grey silk and silver thread, loose and flowing. It was warm, and it would be warmer in the hall, with the fires, and all the men packed together. Last of all, I put the white gold circlet on my head, and then I took my daughters by the hand, and we walked down to the great hall.

Uther and his men were already there. Gorlois was sitting beside Uther on the trestle table at the head of the great hall where we sat whenever it was one of those rare feast days that we observed in Cornwall. They were deep in some kind of conversation that looked friendly enough. Gorlois sat straddling the bench, resting his elbow against the table, while Uther sat with his back to the table, gazing out across the crowd. Gorlois dwarfed Uther, who was not a small man, and there was something about the casual way that Gorlois sat, and the tense way Uther did, that betrayed that Uther was aware of it. But the knights seemed to be getting on well enough. Brastias was talking with one of Uther's knights, and Ulfius was laughing with some man of Uther's as though they were old friends. I was immensely comforted to see that Merlin was not there.

They did not see me as I approached, and I was glad because it meant that I could hand Morgan to Margaret and kiss Morgawse on the cheek before I went to face Uther. Morgawse was annoyed that she could not speak to the King. She seemed to have the idea that he would be like a king from one of the romance stories she liked so much, but he would not be. She seemed happy enough once she had waved at Brastias and he came over to speak to her. He was as bad as Gorlois for indulging her.

I drew in a deep breath, and steeled myself. I did not know why I was so nervous. So much time had gone by. Surely, I did not have anything to fear anymore. Nothing to be nervous about.

I walked up to Gorlois and laid a hand gently on his shoulder. He looked up at me with a smile, and turned back to Uther.

"My lord Uther, you remember my wife Igraine?"

Uther looked up at me, and his steady gaze went through me like a knife. How had I forgotten that look? How had I thought that years would change Uther Pendragon? He was just the same, from the scruffy dusty-gold hair to the broad, powerful frame, but most of all that look. Steady, serious, penetrating. I felt as though I stood naked before him, and I felt myself flush. Uther inclined his head in the smallest of nods.

"Igraine," he said in greeting.

Gorlois wrapped an arm around my waist, and I turned to him, glad of an excuse to look away from Uther. I put a hand fondly against his cheek. I wanted to feel his touch, I wanted to feel anchored to him.

"Have you eaten, my love?" he asked, gently. I realised that I had not. I had been anxiously preparing, and forgotten. The food was almost gone. "It is good," Gorlois said with a smile.

"I will try some." I went to fetch a plate and get some, but as I moved past Uther, swift as an adder, he darted out a hand and caught me by the wrist. It was quick as a reflex, natural almost, and he dropped my wrist as soon as he caught it, but not before Gorlois saw. There was something strange about the gesture, strangely intimate, strangely proprietorial. I felt his fingers around my wrist after they were gone, burning into my skin, and my heart was racing, and I did not know why. The three of us looked at each other for a tense moment, but then the music began and the men cheered as the dancing started. I felt relief wash over me, and turned away. I picked up a cup of wine from the table, and drank a big gulp. I felt tense and nervous, and I hoped it would take the edge off. It did. By the time I had finished the cup, Brastias was beside me, offering me his hand to dance.

I took it, and out of the corner of my eye, I saw Gorlois smile. He was very fond of Brastias, and Brastias was something of a foster-son to him, so he looked on it with all the sweetness of a father seeing a son dance with his mother. Brastias was a good dancer, polite and lithe. But he was not really interested in dancing. He leaned down to speak softly in my ear as we danced.

"King Uther is not what I expected," he said, glancing at Uther. I could see what he meant. Uther was not wearing the red and gold surcoat he had worn in Camelot, but a plain leather jerkin, soldier's clothes. Brastias was too young to have known Aurelianus, and the jewels and silks of his rich court in London, but he would have heard stories, and Uther was an entirely different kind of king. Gorlois was not richly dressed either, but if one had had to guess who was the King, it would have been Gorlois.

"Don't be deceived," I replied as Brastias lifted my hand over my head so that I could spin around. "He is a very powerful man."

Brastias did not seem convinced. It seemed that he was as disappointed as Morgawse was with the appearance of the King of Britain. I was distracted enough, though, by the pleasant dancing that I loved, to forget my worries for a brief moment. I felt the swift movements of my own body, and the beat of the music through me, and I closed my eyes, and surprised myself when a little laugh escaped me. I wished I had more of an opportunity to dance. I loved it so much.

When I was tired of dancing, I thanked Brastias, and returned to Gorlois. He was still sat with Uther, and seemed deep in conversation, but as I came over, Gorlois took my hand and drew me into his lap. I was self-conscious about letting Uther glimpse the tenderness of our marriage, and I was hesitant when Gorlois kissed me in front of him, even though it was brief and polite. Uther looked as though he was about to speak, when I was suddenly aware of Morgawse standing beside me, her bright blue eyes wide, and fixed on Uther.

"Morgawse," I said gently. "Didn't I tell you to stay with your sister?"

I could see Uther measuring her with his steady gaze. After a moment, he turned to Gorlois.

"Gorlois, is this your daughter?" he asked.

"She is," Gorlois smiled. He was too proud of Morgawse to see the danger. "Come and greet the King, Morgawse," Gorlois encouraged.

Morgawse, to my surprise, for she was usually bold, shrank back closer to her father. Uther leaned forward, resting his elbows on his thighs as though he was measuring her carefully. I felt intensely uncomfortable. If I had been Gorlois, and a huge strong man, I might have stood and demanded that he explain himself. But I was not.

"How old are you, Morgawse?" he asked her. "Thirteen? Fourteen? Old enough to be wed."

I felt my blood run cold. Was that what he wanted now he could not have me?

Gorlois gave an easy laugh that did little to shatter the tension gathering between us. "My lord Uther, she is young for marriage yet.

82

She is a tall girl for her age, but she is eleven years old. But you may ask again in a few years' time."

Morgawse was not tall. Morgawse was little, unusually little for her tall parents, and she looked even smaller and younger than she was now as she shrank further away from Uther and his stare. I felt upset, angry with Uther for frightening my daughter, and I jumped from Gorlois' lap to lead her away.

"Time to go to bed, Morgawse," I said gently. For once she did not protest, and went off obediently with Margaret the nun and her little sister.

I felt awful. I could feel myself shaking, but I had to continue to play the gracious hostess. I poured myself another cup of wine and drank it. I realised that I had still not eaten, but my stomach felt too tight, too nervous. I could see that Gorlois was angry, and holding it in.

I turned to follow them, to escape, but Gorlois put his hand against my hip, and I turned around, back into Uther's gaze. He was not even pretending not to be staring at me by now. He stared right past Gorlois, as though he was not there.

"It has been a long time, Igraine," he said softly.

I wondered what Gorlois was thinking, if he was thinking of when he had chased Uther away from me at the tournament where he had won me as his wife. I wondered what Uther meant, if Uther was thinking of Christmas time, all those years ago. I was thinking about Aurelianus' great courtyard, and I wished that I was not.

I sat down pointedly on Gorlois' lap once more, and affected the best air of casual friendliness I could. Uther was a stranger, a man whom I had not seen in eleven years. He could not possibly have been the same strange, driven man who had dragged himself up from lowly soldier to King, and who had rudely demanded to have me as his wife. He had been King a long time now. He must have grown into someone else. I had.

"I suppose it has, my lord."

I saw him bristle at my formal tone, and I was surprised at how pleased I was to see it. I felt as though I was gaining some ground, making him uncomfortable. He was not to think that he would come here and make my husband and daughter endure his rudeness without his having to endure my insistent politeness.

"You are even more beautiful than I remember you being, Igraine," he said, without taking his eyes from mine. I felt Gorlois' hand against my waist tighten on me a little. I did not know what to say. He was so direct, so intensely sincere.

"What has held you back from taking a wife, my lord?" Gorlois asked, and he was better than I was at sounding casual, conversational. He picked up a piece of bread from the table, dunked it in the gravy left on his plate and bit it, and seemed not to care at all. I reached past him for my cup of wine, and was grateful to have it in my hand.

Uther's eyes stayed on mine, and he was silent for a long time as though he was waiting for me to speak, to confess what he had said to me about Merlin, but he did not, and eventually he shrugged, lifting his cup to his lips.

"I have been too busy for it. The wars were not over when you left them to come home to your lady, Gorlois. No man blamed you for that. But still, there was fighting yet to be done."

Before Gorlois could answer, old Margaret the nun was beside us.

"My lord Gorlois, little Morgawse is begging to see her father. I tried," she glanced between us, and I could see that she was angry with Morgawse, could hear the tension in her voice, "to tell her that you were occupied, but she is in quite a state of hysterics."

"I shall go," I said, standing. I wanted to get away from Uther. Gorlois did not protest.

Chapter fifteen

When I got up to the bedroom that Morgawse shared with Morgan, Morgan was asleep already, curled on her side, neat even in her sleep, and Morgawse was sat up in bed, her arms wrapped around her legs and her chin on them.

"I wanted Father," she complained when she saw me. I supposed she thought I was going to scold her again. I was not.

I sat beside her and stroked her hair until she leaned her head against my shoulder. I knew what it was. Uther had frightened her. I kissed her softly on the forehead.

"Go to sleep, Morgawse," I said. "There is nothing to be afraid of."

"I'm not afraid," she protested sulkily.

"Then that is well, for there is nothing to fear," I said. She nodded against me, and I hugged her tight until I saw her eyes blink heavy, and then fall shut, and she only murmured a little as I let her lie down on the bed.

* * *

When I came back out into the corridor, shutting the door softly behind me, I could hear the sound of men still revelling in the great hall. Uther's men were mainly common soldiers and wanted ale and whores, wanted to shout their own songs rather than dance to the lovely music, wanted to stay awake all night. I thought about going back down. It was what I ought to have done, but I did not.

I thought I would go back to my bedchamber, and sit in the window seat and stare out at the stars, and the light of the moon on the waves below. I was looking forward to the peace and quiet when I turned a corner in the corridor, and Uther Pendragon was standing right there, where the corridor met the spiral staircase, staring out of the narrow window at the sliver of the moon hanging in the sky. He had not seen me, so I turned to go, but he had heard me. I was less quiet, clumsier than I usually was, less lithe on my feet from the wine. I should have eaten.

He called my name, and I turned around, aware that if I ran that was an invitation for him to chase me. I felt my heart begin to race in my chest. I felt suddenly fragile and vulnerable – no, I felt suddenly translucent, as though the moonlight and his steady look were shining through me, leaving me like a gossamer in their glare; bright, but painfully readable. I wished he would look away, or speak.

"It is a beautiful night," he said at last. I did not remember him ever remarking on the beauty of the world around him, but then I supposed I had not heard him speak much at all. "Come closer." He gestured with his hand, and as though caught in a dream, I stepped closer. "Look at the moon."

I stood beside him, and we stared out of the window. He was still dressed in his leather jerkin, still dirty from the ride here. I could smell his sweat, musky, and the sweat of the horse on him. He always seemed strangely half-animal to me; wild, taciturn, impossible to analyse. I glanced down at him beside me, and noticed as I had all those years ago the figure of the dragon tattooed in woad against the inside of his wrist. In the strange, hypnotising light of the crescent moon, and a little hazy with the wine, I reached out and rested my fingertips against it, curious. At my touch, he turned his hand, offering his wrist towards me, and I let my fingers brush down the soft skin of the inside of his wrist. His skin was cool. I was not sure if it was his pulse I could feel racing, or mine.

"Where did you get that mark?" I whispered. In the moment, I had forgotten him frightening Morgawse, I had forgotten Gorlois, I had forgotten Merlin, and the devil's pact they had made. I stared at the figure of the dragon, and all of a sudden I saw a tiny line of black ants running between my fingers, across the spine of the dragon. But I blinked and they were gone. I *had* drunk too much wine. I was remembering bad dreams that I had had while pregnant and a young girl of sixteen.

"I got it in Avalon," he said quietly, and I looked up at him. When our eyes met, I suddenly realised how close we were to one another. If I leaned forward, we would kiss. Why was I thinking about that? He was a rough man, half a savage, whose chief advisor was a witch whose magic had been cast out of Avalon.

"I thought Avalon only gave the woad to witches," I said.

"It was Merlin who gave it to me, and it was in Avalon, but it was not with its Lady's permission," he admitted. My fingertips were still against his wrist.

"It is a part of your pact?" I whispered.

"Igraine." Uther whispered my name, sliding his arm around my waist, drawing me close. He was drunk, but so was I, and, still surprised from having seen him after so long, and feeling so strangely about it, I did not push him away. I let him rest his forehead against mine, I didn't shy back. I closed my eyes. He did not seem interested in answering my question, and spoke as though he was answering a question I had not asked.

"I was a foolish young man when I saw you last, barely more than a boy. I thought the right thing to say, to convince you that you should have me as your husband, was to talk about destiny, and magic, and Merlin's words, when I should have told you the truth. That I love you. That I have loved you since the moment I first saw you, in London. I remember, too, as though it were yesterday, that time we kissed in the courtyard."

His hand was suddenly against my cheek, his breath soft on my lips. I could not quite trace back how we had come to be like this, suddenly so close, so intimate, after eleven years of being strangers. He smelled of the leather of his armour, of the smoke of the hearth-fire in the feasting-hall. I remembered it, too, vividly. I remembered falling into it, though I knew that I should not have wanted it.

"Uther, stop," I said quietly, letting my hand rest against his chest. His shirt was slightly open and I felt the heat of his skin under my fingertips, and the roughness of the strands of coarse, gold hair that caught bright in the moonlight.

I went to move away, but I was a moment too slow with the wine. Or perhaps he had thought that I had meant for him to stop talking, because he kissed me then, and it was a kiss a little rough with passion, so different from the gentleness I knew with Gorlois, but so much like that kiss long ago in the courtyard. My lips remembered it, and my body. I felt as though I was fifteen years old once more. For a moment, I felt my head swim, and my heart thud in my chest. I tore away from it, before I could lose myself in it again, in the feel of his hand at the small of my back, his muscular body pressed against mine. I would not be a betrayer of my husband. Gorlois had given too much to me, been too kind too long for me to even consider giving into the desire that clouded my mind, the strange attraction I felt for Uther. He had waited until I was alone, he had waited until I was *married* to tell me that it was love he wanted me for, not ambition, not to pay Merlin back for his throne. I felt a flash of anger run through me, clearing my mind, and I pushed him back.

"What do you want here, Uther? Did you come here to try to ruin me?"

"Igraine –"

I did not let him finish. He would listen for once, he would understand what he was doing. "After all these years, coming here with the same old demands, that I should be yours. I cannot be, Uther, and you should not ask me for this. I have a husband. I have *children*. Do you even consider what it might mean for them if you demand their mother? I made my choice long ago, Uther. *Give up*."

He planted a hand beside my head, against the stone wall, leaning closer as I leaned back.

"You love me, Igraine," he hissed. "You are just afraid."

When he moved away, and left, I felt shaken inside; hollow, unsteady.

* * *

When I got back to my bedroom, Gorlois was already there, and I rushed into his arms without a word. He did not seem to want to talk either, and I was pleased. It was enough, the feel of his hands running through my hair, pulling it gently loose, his mouth gentle and loving against mine, to shake away the doubt, the unsettling presence of Uther.

He was unsettled by it as well. He must have been, for he was rougher, more insistent than usual. He held me tight, as though he thought I was going to slip away. I welcomed it. I wanted to be sure of my husband, to feel him strong and present, chasing the presence of Uther away from my skin, from my mouth, from my thoughts.

* * *

Uther and his men left the next day. It seemed that he had nothing left to see. No further inspection to make. Gorlois and I stood side by side in the courtyard and watched the men ride away. It was over before it had truly begun. I felt relieved, but I also felt strangely bereft. It had all been so strange and fleeting with Uther. The moonlight. A kiss. The rough way he was in public, and the strange, gentle tone of his confession that he loved me. But he would have to forget that. I loved Gorlois, and we had our daughters. We would have another child, too, I hoped.

But Uther did not leave Cornwall. Word came that he had established a garrison of his own on the border. It was a direct threat to Gorlois. Gorlois shouted with Ulfius and Brastias about it in the council chamber, and I sat quietly with my hands folded, listening, as Brastias – with all of a young man's zeal – swore that he would ride with Gorlois to the death against Uther. Ulfius was more careful, advised sending messengers. Gorlois was furious and trying to hide it.

When Ulfius and Brastias left with instructions to equip messengers and knights to ride to Uther and ask what he wanted, Gorlois rested his head in his hands and fell quiet. When I put my hand on his shoulder, he did not look up at me. We had never dreamed that Tintagel would be threatened like this in our lifetimes. I hoped it was some confusion, but I doubted that it was.

Morgawse did not understand that her father was anxious, and demanded the same games and stories from him as ever. I expected him to be irritated, but those seemed to be the only times in those few weeks that he did not worry about Uther. He would get as lost in the stories as Morgawse did, and I would sit with Morgan on the other side of the room, and she would turn the pages of the book in my lap that I did not see before me. I was caught between fear, and guilt, and sadness. I would have done anything to protect my home from Uther, and he was threatening me, and my husband and my daughters, keeping his soldiers in my land, and yet when I closed my eyes I saw sometimes the moonlight against his face, or I felt him kiss me as he had done in Aurelianus' courtyard. And it made me angry, and sad, that I could not forget it.

* * *

The letter came as the trees were beginning to turn brown and drop their leaves to the ground, and the bracken on the cliffs turned dry and brittle. It felt like the end of something. Uther wanted to meet Gorlois. He wanted us to attend his council. It sounded innocent enough.

"I do not think we should go," I said quietly as Gorlois stared hard at the letter. "He means us some dishonour, else he would not stay in our land without our hospitality."

Gorlois did not answer. Ulfius and Brastias buckled on their armour, and we readied ourselves to go.

* * *

Uther's camp was a few miles away, but the ride was pleasant in the soft early autumn sun. We were called into a low tent, white and blue and with Uther's banner – the blue-green dragon – rippling in the wind above it. Uther stood inside, flanked by knights dressed in full armour. We had come to talk, with Gorlois in the surcoat we had married in, and our men in light armour only for the ride, but Uther's men looked equipped to fight. I noticed, too, Merlin among them once more, hanging at the back, his loathsome face half-shadowed in the cowl of his robe. It boded ill that Uther had Merlin by his side again. I felt my heart began to quicken within me in trepidation.

"Duke Gorlois," Uther greeted him with a curt nod. "I am pleased you came."

Gorlois nodded in return, but did not speak, not for a moment. *Duke Gorlois.* I bristled against that, but said nothing. Gorlois was King of Cornwall in these lands, and Uther knew it. Gorlois glanced to Ulfius, who had grown into his serious looks, and was inhabiting his slow thoughtfulness more deeply than ever as he approached middle age. Gorlois sighed and turned back to Uther.

"I hope you have not called me here, my lord Uther, to offer me the same insults that you did when I offered you *hospitality* in my home."

I realised with a cold feeling that spread through me that something must have been discussed between them when I left to put Morgawse to bed. Why had Gorlois not *warned* me?

"To what are you referring as an *insult*?" Uther replied tersely.

Gorlois glanced at me, and I gave the smallest shake of my head that I could. He did not heed it. There was a long, tense silence in the tent. Gorlois was twice the size of the other men there, but he was not in his armour, and besides, Uther was known throughout the land as a fearsome warrior for good reason. He was ruthless, and brutal when he fought. His men were heavily armed. We had walked into this trap. I was suddenly aware of how I was especially vulnerable. In a light silk dress, with the circlet of Cornwall on my head, I had nothing to defend me other than the promise of retribution from my people. By now I could have had a teenage son, if I had been lucky. With a son made like his father, I would not have had to be afraid of Uther's men.

"Are you referring to my request for Igraine?"

Uther just said it, as though it were normal, as though he had asked Gorlois for knights. Or a horse. I felt my blood run cold. I was glad that Uther did not look at me. I did not know what I felt. Disgusted at him: when I would not grant him what he wanted, he would threaten me and my family. Hollow, nervous, afraid. Empty, as though I were a husk of wheat, and everything that was the essence of me had suddenly blown away from the middle.

"I would not have called it a request, my lord," Gorlois growled. "I would have called it a demand."

I had never seen him so aggressive before. I could see the muscles tensing in his arm, his fist clenched, his jaw set. I was afraid that he was going to leap across the table set between them and smash his fist into Uther's face. I did not want him to. I was afraid that Uther's knights would fall on him and kill him if he did.

"Call it what you like, Gorlois," Uther said wryly. "I have called you here nonetheless to hear your answer."

What about my *answer?* I thought. But I had already given that. I had already told Uther that it was never to be.

"The only honourable answer to such a dishonourable demand is with the sword." Gorlois' voice was dangerously low, and I felt myself tense to run. I did not know what would happen.

Uther banged his fist hard on the table, and the man beside him startled in surprise. He fixed me with a fierce look, and I tensed against it. It was the first time he had looked at me since we arrived, and there was no kindness in it, no appeal, only the demand of a king who would have what he wanted. I would not give it to him.

"Let us put an end to these childish *games*," Uther shouted. Brastias beside me shifted, uneasy, afraid, but Ulfius beside Gorlois was still and calm. "I will have Igraine, Gorlois, with your consent, or without it. It is your choice: surrender or war."

I opened my mouth to object, but Gorlois was already speaking.

"You come to another man's castle, and demand his wife, and expect submission? How can a man like you call himself King? Where is your honour?"

Uther shrugged, pulling on his gauntlets, and picking up his helm. It was a gesture of aggression. He glanced between us, his eyes lingering on mine for a moment longer than on Gorlois.

"Consider it, Gorlois. You have one week."

He turned and left, Merlin sweeping out with him. His knights stood, silent and hostile, to watch us as we turned and walked away.

Chapter sixteen

Gorlois was silent as we rode back, and silent as we entered the castle once more, when the great iron portcullis was lowered for the first time I could remember, sealing out the outside world. It creaked and screeched. It made me think of the gates of hell. In the low-slanting light of the late autumn evening, I could have sworn I saw a line of tiny black ants escaping between its hostile prongs.

* * *

By the time we were alone together, I was angry with him. He closed our bedroom door behind us, and walked over to the window to gaze out at the sun setting into the sea. I stood near the door still, my arms crossed.

"How long were you going to keep this a secret from me?" I demanded. Gorlois did not turn around. Uther had spoken of this to him *weeks* ago. He had known why Uther's troops were camping within our borders. He had *known*. Why had he not *told* me?

"All I keep thinking," Gorlois said, tersely, "is that Pendragon must have some reason to believe that this is what *you* want as well."

"No – Gorlois, what are you saying? Gorlois, why would you think that?"

He turned fully to me then, and I could see a wildness in his bright blue eyes that I had never seen before, and it made me afraid. I was only just learning that my husband was a jealous man. He had hidden it well, all these years.

"I remember how we met, Igraine. Uther Pendragon had you pinned up against the wall, and he was whispering something to you. Men talk, on campaign. When we were newly married and I was away at war, I heard men say that Pendragon still intended to take you as his wife. I had to tell them all that you were already *my* wife. Some men laughed."

I reached out a hand, to try to rest it comfortingly on his cheek, but he brushed it away, still caught up in his anger.

"It seems that a man is never anything more than his birth, and those above him treat him as they please," Gorlois said, looking away from me again.

Very quietly I said, "Uther Pendragon was not born into his great station."

Gorlois turned around and strode towards me so forcefully that I took a step back, surprised.

"Are you *defending* him?" he shouted.

"No, Gorlois, no –"

"I *told* you, I told you *from the start* that all I had to offer was myself." Gorlois was struggling to catch his breath through the force of his emotions, and for the first time I was afraid of him, for the first time I was truly aware of the danger of the huge size of him, the power in his body to destroy as well as to protect, and I had to force myself to stand my ground before him, and meet his gaze. "All I had to offer – all I have still to offer – is my love, and my protection. Igraine – if we cede to him, then there's nothing –"

And all of a sudden, Gorlois choked back his words and stepped back, running his hands through his hair, and I realised that he was not angry, he was *upset*.

"Gorlois," I said gently, stepping forward, lifting his hands away from his face, holding them in mine. "I have wanted for nothing as your wife." I stroked his cheek gently with my thumb, and he leaned down to meet me as I leaned up to kiss him softly. "I love you." I took his face in my hands, and gave him the strongest, bravest look I had. "We will survive this. But we must do what must be done. To protect Morgawse and Morgan. To protect Tintagel."

Gorlois pulled my hands from his face and pushed them back towards me. I stumbled back under the force of it. He had lost his gentleness in the depths of his anger.

"*No*, Igraine. Don't even consider it."

He strode past me, out into the corridor. I could hear him shouting to the men, gathering his knights. I sighed and sat down heavily on the bed, letting myself fall back, staring up at the canopy above. It was dark, dark red, and sewn with dark purple thread. For the first time, I had the thought that it looked like the inside of a body, some horrid organ torn from within. I had thought it was comforting like a womb, but it wasn't. It was raw like a liver, or a heart, opened to the sky above. That was what was coming, if Gorlois did not concede. War. We were a small kingdom. All our secret gold would do us no good against the iron swords of Uther's soldiers.

"Mother." I heard a little voice in the doorway and sat up sharply to see Morgawse standing there in her nightdress. Uther had thought she looked like a woman grown, but she could not, in that moment, have looked more like a child. Her long red-gold hair was loose about her shoulders and she had the sleeve of her nightdress in her mouth, as though she had been chewing it in anxious wakefulness. "What's going on?"

I sat up, and patted the bed beside me, and Morgawse, subdued a little with sleepiness, sat beside me, and rested her head on my shoulder. I stroked her hair, as much for my own comfort as hers. Her hair smelled of wood smoke, and spices. That was because she was always playing in the kitchen, trying to steal apples and honey.

"Nothing for you to worry over, my love," I said gently. Morgawse turned and looked up at me.

"Is Father angry with me?" she asked.

I kissed her forehead. "No, my love," I replied. "He is angry with King Uther." It was half the truth.

Morgawse wrinkled up her face in displeasure. "I didn't like him," she said, snuggling back against my shoulder.

We sat there in a comforting silence until I felt Morgawse leaning more heavily against me, falling asleep, and I stood, ready to pull her to her feet.

"Time to go back to bed," I said.

Morgawse shook her head sulkily.

"Can't I sleep in here? Just tonight?"

I sighed. Ordinarily, I would have let her, but I hoped that Gorlois would come back before I came to sleep. I wanted to make sure he understood that I did not suggest what I did because I would have preferred to be Uther's wife.

"No, Gawse. Your own bed."

She pouted and shuffled her feet. She said something under her breath that sounded suspiciously like *Father would let me*, but I let it go. I did not have the energy to fight her on it, not just then.

* * *

Gorlois did come to bed, but it was late, late into the night, and I was already half asleep. I stirred as he got in beside me, and reached out for me, and took me into his arms. I felt a rush of comfort, and of love. The surety our long years, our long happy life, had given me. He was strong, and safe, and I loved him down to the depths of my bones.

I murmured through my sleepiness, trying to say something kind, something loving. He drew me onto his chest, and kissed my forehead softly. He did not seem to be angry anymore. I leaned up, and kissed him tentatively, and he responded, soft and tender. I sighed closer to him, waking a little more, feeling my body grow bright with desire. I wanted to feel close with him; I wanted to be reminded that there was a place between us that no one could invade, no one could demand.

I slid my hand down his chest, feeling the warm, soft skin, hard muscle beneath, the rough hair of his chest. My hand knew it all so well, and yet all at once I felt the urgent need to savour it. He put his hand over mine as I slid it down his stomach, and drew away from the kiss.

"Not tonight, Igraine," he whispered, and I could not help but feel a little slighted, rejected. I could not help but feel that he was angry with me, and I lay a long time suddenly wildly awake, staring up at the black, empty night air above me that looked horribly like it was writhing, like the writhing of a thousand little black ants all packed in together. And I closed my eyes against it, but I still felt as though they were wriggling against my skin.

* * *

I slept at last. I was afraid that I would have bad dreams, but I did not. Perhaps it was that my desire had been awakened and then rejected by Gorlois, but I dreamed that night that I made love with a man who came up behind me, and brushed his fingers down my neck, light as a kiss, and drew my dress softly down from my shoulders. I felt his fingers brush my lips as my mouth opened with desire for him, and his other hand slid up between my legs. I felt his mouth against my ear, I heard him whisper my name. It was only when he turned me round in his arms, and we fell together onto the bed, that in the dream I saw that it was not Gorlois, but Uther Pendragon. And by then it was too late, for he was already inside me. Besides, I was already wild with desire, and in the dream I wanted it, and I wanted his love. And I woke when the wave of it broke over me, gasping into the empty night, sitting bolt upright in bed besides Gorlois, who slept on, knowing nothing.

* * *

I woke the next morning feeling guilty, and when I tried to comfort us both by wrapping my arms around Gorlois as he stirred in the morning light, he groaned and pushed me away. Either he was still tired, or still angry. I didn't wait to find out.

I wanted to be outside, to feel the breeze, to try to forget the whole awful, sudden mess of it. So recently, before Uther had come, we had been happy. Quietly, perfectly, domestically happy.

I pulled on a plain wool dress for the deepening autumn and climbed up onto the battlements to look out. It all looked normal. Behind me, the sea, grey-blue, glassy, calm, and before me the sheer sides of the castle walls, the narrow walkway that linked us to the mainland, and then beyond, low, scrubby grass and dark stone until the horizon. It was beyond the horizon that Uther's troops waited for us.

I closed my eyes to feel the sea air against my skin. I could taste the salt in the air, familiar. I could not shake the memory of Uther Pendragon, silhouetted against the moonlight in the corridor, and the sudden kiss that had reminded me of being a young girl. That was not the man who had banged his fist on the table to demand me as his wife. One Uther was thoughtful, almost mystical, half like one of the witches of Avalon himself. The other was a brute, a rough soldier who did not care for the suffering of others. One, I feared I was in love with. The other, I hated.

"My lady Igraine." I heard Brastias' voice close by me, and turned around. He had a young man's hesitancy around me. Ulfius was always direct, almost fatherly in his attitude towards me. Brastias was wary of causing offence, careful. I hoped that he would grow out of it.

"What is it, Brastias?" I asked gently, turning to him, shielding my eyes a little from the low morning sun that peeped through the mist. It was white here, and bright with it, high up and on the edge of the sea as we were.

He sighed deeply, shifting on his feet for a moment. He was not ever so nervous when he was letting Morgawse run around the castle, knocking things down and tearing her dress, or spilling cream or honey in her eagerness to eat some treat or other. He was not ever nervous when he was training at swords with the other young knights. He was not even nervous around little Morgan, who somehow seemed to make some of the other men feel nervous in the steady, quiet way she looked at them. I wondered if people had been wary of me in the same way when I had been a child, for I had been the same.

"Brastias," I persisted, growing less patient.

He shuffled on his feet and looked up at me. "Forgive me, my lady, but the men are growing restless. They want to know what Gorlois is planning to do. Uther has already burned some of the border towns, and the people are beginning to fear that nothing will be done. Word is spreading among the common people, lady. Some of the men are saying…" He shuffled on his feet once more, glancing back down at them like a child, and I knew what was coming. I steeled myself for it, drawing myself up to my full height. "Some of the men are saying that peace would be better, and that Gorlois should repudiate you, and give you to Uther."

I nodded, giving him a steady, even look. Did he think that I was afraid? Did he think that I did not care about my country, my people and my castle? Did he think I did not know what must be done? It always surprised me how little men thought women knew. I knew it all. I had seen it all. In a strange moment of calm clarity, I realised that I should have seen this moment coming upon me long, long ago, when Lot had thrown Uther to the ground in Aurelianus' great courtyard, and Uther had stood, and waited for Lot to leave, and seized me and kissed me anyway. He was not a man who stopped at defeat. Perhaps I should have yielded then, but I, too, had been proud, and unwilling to bind myself to a man who was not committed to my land, or my people.

"Perhaps they are right, Brastias."

I could see that he was shocked by my honesty, my calm, but it was time that he stopped being a boy. He behaved like a young man, though he was of age. Time to face the world the blank, dispassionate honesty it demanded.

"Are you not afraid, my lady?" he asked in a whisper.

"Of whom? Of Uther Pendragon? No," I said. "I am not afraid."

Brastias nodded, but the way he did made me wonder if he had not meant something else. Of course I was afraid. It was a stupid question. But I was the lady of my castle, and I would not show fear to one of my knights. I was afraid – terrified – for the sake of my daughters. I wished, painfully, once more that I had had a son. A son who could stay in Tintagel. If Morgawse had been just a few years older, it might not have mattered – if she could have been married to a man who would take care of her, and her home, as Gorlois had protected me.

"What is to be done, my lady?" Brastias asked, gazing up at me warily.

I sighed deeply. It was time for me to do what must be done. I had more to think about than my own desire to keep my domestic happiness intact. I had Morgan and Morgawse to think of, and Tintagel, and the people of Cornwall.

"I will speak to Gorlois, and we will make an end of this," I said. And Brastias nodded, though I was not sure that he understood what I meant.

Chapter seventeen

When I found Gorlois, he was in the great council chamber with Ulfius. He had a map of Cornwall unfurled in front of him. His hair was still ruffled through, as though he had got out of bed only just now, and walked straight here. I felt myself tense as I saw him, for he looked angry already, his finger tracing a line down the map. I knew what that line was. Our border. And as he traced it, he traced another line, closer to Tintagel, as though someone were buckling our border in on us, pushing us further to the corner of our land, towards the sea. *Uther*.

"Gorlois," I said, and he looked up. He had not noticed I was standing in the doorway. He straightened up slowly. He was tense as well. Still angry from last night. It had never been like this between us before. Never tense, never a space of negotiation where we had to work out what the other wanted. I did not like it, but it was necessary. Perhaps I had chosen wrong in choosing a good, strong, honest man. Perhaps I would have been wiser to choose a shrewd politician, but I had thought I had enough strength in me to take that role for myself. If that was the case, I would have to take it now.

"What is it, Igraine?" he asked. I could see he was holding everything back. He wanted to shout, and scream, and smash things. His knuckles were white against the back of the chair he was gripping as he leaned against it; his shoulders were tensed.

I glanced at Ulfius. He was at least not awkward or uncomfortable like Brastias, but he watched it all with a kind of detached disapproval.

"Gorlois, I want to speak to you in private," I said. Ulfius glanced between us, and left without a word. I liked him. He was quiet, sensible and steady. I thought it was probably good for Gorlois to have Ulfius by his side.

"Igraine," Gorlois began, and I could hear in his voice that he was weary, unwilling to talk about it, unwilling to listen to reason. He would listen to me.

"I know that you are upset –"

"*Upset*, Igraine?" he shouted. It shook through me. I had never seen him like this before, never wild with his anger, never beyond the calm gentleness I knew so well in him. I understood at last what made him such a fearsome man on the battlefield. But I did not want him to fight. I wanted him to surrender.

"Gorlois, *please*." I was struggling to keep calm, struggling to keep myself from shouting, losing myself in anger and desperation, because if I did that, then we were all lost. If we wanted our daughters to survive this, if we wanted our land to survive this, we had to approach it calm and detached. I needed to make him understand that. "Please listen to me. We have two options here. The first is that you gather what few soldiers we have and ride to fight Uther." I stepped forward, reaching for the map, and drawing it towards me. He watched me, careful, suspicious. I traced my finger slowly down the line I had seen him draw for Ulfius just now with his own finger, feeling the roughness of the vellum, the smooth lines of the ink. "But Uther is here, already eating into our borders with his troops. These villages –" I brushed my fingers over them, as though I was sweeping them off the map – "have been destroyed; these people, who send us their sons to be knights, and their girls to be servants with the faith in their hearts that we are sworn in return to protect them, have been wiped away by Uther's army. This army will march south –" I brushed my fingers across more of the villages, in a line towards Tintagel, and stopped just before the drawing of my home, tall, and proud and craggy in black ink against the yellowing parchment – "until they reach the gates of Tintagel castle. How many men are dead by this point? How many farms destroyed?" I looked up to meet his eye. His gaze was unreadable, but I was sure I had his attention. "Uther Pendragon is a king made through war. He will not leave us with the resources to survive without surrender if he can help it. He will burn the fields and slaughter the cattle. The men of the towns will defect to him, because he promises them life, and victory. We can only offer them a desperate fight to the death, for the sake of pride."

I was struggling to be calm, because I knew I had to be. The thought of Uther tearing through the lands of my home was like the thought of him driving his sword into me and cutting me to pieces. I had loved this land, and sought to protect it for the last twelve years. I would give myself before I sacrificed it for the sake of my husband's pride. His *jealousy*. I wished I could make Gorlois understand he was being petty without being unkind to him.

Gorlois pulled the map out from under my hand, rolling it, and tying it, and dropping it down on the table once more, where I could not force him to look at the painful truth. He was shaking, the breath coming to him hard.

"I know what you are about to ask me, Igraine, and the answer is still no."

He walked towards the door, and I rushed after him.

"Gorlois, *listen* –"

He strode away from me, but I ran after him. We did not have long before our land was destroyed. We did not have only ourselves to think of. He was not calm; there was no way, no time to impress on him that I loved him, and that this would hurt me as much as it hurt him, yet it would hurt more if he were to be killed by Uther, and

I should never see him again, and our daughters should fall into danger.

"*Gorlois.*" I tried once more, grasping hold of him by the wrist, trying to pull him back towards me. "What will you do, Gorlois? We cannot hide in Tintagel forever while Uther marches further and further towards us."

"No." he turned back to me, and I stopped where I stood, my heart hammering in my chest. His eyes were bright and wild, and I felt my body flood with panic. "We will ride out to meet him. Ulfius is already gathering the men. No man will be expected to die like a coward –"

"Gorlois, *no!*"

He turned away from me once more, and began walking again, and I followed him. I did not realise until we were almost there, that we were walking back to our bedroom. I hated the thought that he would bring this fight there. It was like letting Uther inside, for he was already here between us, closing my husband's ears to the rationality, the truth of what I was saying to him.

"Gorlois, there is a way without danger, where no one will get hurt. Please, Gorlois, *please* –"

Gorlois turned back to me, his look suddenly steady, and set. His hand was on the latch of our bedroom door.

"I do not have anything to offer you besides my protection and my honour, Igraine. Do not ask me to give those up."

We stood for a moment, in silence, staring at one another. It was all so easy for him, so absolute. I wondered if he were even afraid of death. A man his size must think himself invincible, but Uther Pendragon had sold his soul to Merlin the witch, and no amount of brute strength could keep Gorlois alive if he threw himself against Merlin's might.

He pushed on the latch, and the door swung open, and he stepped through. He had drawn the bed curtains when he left in the morning, I had noticed, as though this was the centre of the issue for him, the thought of the sanctity of our marriage-bed, when it was *not*. The issue was our land, and our castle and our daughters, not my body.

I shut the door behind me, and leaned against it, afraid he would leave, would refuse to discuss it.

"You're not even going to consider it?" I asked, sharply.

Gorlois paced before me, into the room, shaking his head.

"No, Igraine."

"Gorlois, please – what about Morgawse and Morgan? What about their safety? I know it's –" My voice cracked as I spoke, and I resented it. I wanted to be strong, and absolute. But I was not. I could not bear the thought that Gorlois would be taken from me, but I could not say that. I could not ask him, as a man and a warrior, to put away his honour because his death would cut me to the heart, and leave me hollow with grief. I could not say that without him, our daughters would be lonely too. How could I tell him that he must not go because his death would destroy all three of us with grief? I tried as best I could, but it was weak and lame, and I knew it would not be enough. "It's not what either of us want, but if we refuse him that means war. Isn't it better for them if we just give him what he wants?"

Gorlois strode back over towards me, and took hold of me by the arms, lifting me a little towards him. But it was both gentle and desperate rather than rough, and if I had thought he would let me, I would have taken his face in my hands and kissed him.

"It is precisely for our daughters' sake that I will not. What happens once we give him what he wants? If I give you up to him, and he has you, he will have learned that another man's wife is easy to take, and that he can do whatever he pleases with anyone he pleases. What then would stop him taking another man's wife, and another? What reason would he have to be kind to you, if he knows he has bought you from me? And what next? What about when he turns his attention to someone else? What if he decides he wants one of our daughters next? Morgawse?" Gorlois sighed, and it was a strange sigh, a sigh of distress. "And to think it was that which I was more afraid of. Him thinking she was fourteen years old, his hints about marriage. No. If we want our daughters to be safe, we must refuse him. I don't want my daughters to grow up in a world where men give their wives away because they are afraid. I would be no good father to them if I did not do everything in my power to defend you all from men like Uther."

"What good will all this be to us once you are dead?" I asked in a voice barely more than a whisper. Gorlois let go of me and stepped away. I had given all I had; that was all I had to persuade him. Was he too proud to understand? I needed him alive more than I needed his honour, or to have him as my husband. Perhaps I was selfish. Perhaps he thought it would destroy him to see me as another man's wife.

Gorlois pressed the heel of his hand into his forehead. "Igraine," he sighed once more, heavily, and I felt as though I was going to cry, but I held it back. "When I married you, I made a promise to you that I would protect you. And our daughters. You made a promise to me, too, that you would keep faith with me. I'm asking you to trust me. This is the only thing I can do."

I lifted his hand away gently and took his face in my hands, staring hard into his eyes. I had to make him understand, and yet as I looked at him, at the face of the man I loved, my protector, the father of my children, I felt an awful desperation sink into me.

"Gorlois," I said, throwing the last of my strength into a final plea. "He will kill you. Cornwall's armies can't possibly keep him out. Surrender. Live. Keep the girls with you. Besides, with you dead he won't have to marry me. He can just take what he wants and throw me aside for someone else. Please. We can make this look like an agreement. I have given you only daughters. No man would blame you for setting me aside. Send me to Uther, marry someone else who can make sure Morgawse and Morgan will be safe. This can be done with the appearance of honour."

"The appearance of honour is not the same as honour," Gorlois said gruffly. I closed my eyes tight. I had lost. I could not make him understand. Why did he have to be so proud, so sure of right and wrong? Why did he understand it all so differently from how I did?

"Igraine," he sighed again, and his tone grew soft. He lay one of his big, gentle hands on my hair, and I pressed my head into it, longing for a little comfort. He stroked my hair, and I choked back my tears. "There is no other way. Listen." With his other hand, he tilted my face up towards his, and I opened my eyes once more. "I will ride out tonight, with those knights that are here, and we will take him by surprise. That's the only chance we have. We'll make our camp at the border-castle in secret, and attack once it gets dark. If all is well, I will return to you tonight. It will be over quickly, either way."

"Promise you'll come back alive," I whispered, remembering the promise that I had asked him to make long ago, that he had not made but that he had kept. Gorlois said nothing, but drew me into a kiss that was as tender, as deep, as loving and as desperate as our hopes, and I said nothing more, for I knew that I had lost.

* * *

I sat in the window seat and watched as Gorlois strapped on his armour in the fading light. As the sun dipped low, it shone orange-red on the iron greaves on his arms, and on his breastplate; it looked like blood spilling down him, and it made me feel sick. He did not speak, but stared hard at each piece of armour as he did it, as though if he concentrated hard enough, everything else would pass away. It would not be so.

After I had failed to persuade him, I had tried to draw him from our kiss to one last moment of marital lovemaking, but he suspected me of being afraid, and he refused to take me into his arms out of desperation. I think he was too proud. He did not want to believe that he could be killed by Uther Pendragon, and he drew away from my kisses, promising me that he would love me as a husband as soon as he came back alive. I was upset. It would have made me feel less lonely, less desperate. He had left, and come back with his armour hours later, when I had given up on him saying goodbye to sit in the window reading. We did not speak, but I watched him strap each piece of platemail on, and prayed on every piece that it would keep him safe.

When he was finished I slipped from the seat and ran into his arms, and he let me run my fingers into his hair, and kiss him. He wrapped his arms around me, but they were hard and cold in their armour, and I felt awfully fragile and hopeless in his iron embrace.

* * *

He said goodnight to Morgan and Morgawse as though he were only going out to the courtyard for a little while. Morgan did not seem to be suspicious, but I noticed Morgawse's wary look, her sulky pout as he tried to leave. Perhaps she was more alert and sensitive than I thought. She certainly seemed to have noticed something.

Chapter eighteen

Uther was no longer far from Tintagel. Still, I feared that it would be longer than a single night before I heard anything. I hated the waiting. I hated trying not to imagine Gorlois, and Ulfius and Brastias, slaughtered among the scrubby grass and dark rocks of our home. I hated trying not to imagine what it would be like to tell Morgawse. She was old enough to understand that there was something that I might have done to prevent it, though I had tried with all my strength.

I sat in the window seat, watching the stars come out, one by one. When the moon, full and round, rose to the apex of the sky, I was still awake. I knew that I would not sleep. I played over everything in my head. My marriage to Gorlois; the night afterwards, when he had lifted the little wreath of flowers from my hair, when he had been gentle and tender, and I had felt safe in his arms. I remembered him returning from war, and the look on his face when he had seen Morgawse. I remembered our coming together out under the stars the night Morgan had been conceived. Gorlois was my life, my home, my safety. Worse than asking me to give myself up for his sake, he had asked me to risk giving *him* up.

I thought then about Uther, about the two different men he seemed to be. He made me uneasy, and he made me afraid, but there was something about him that I could not forget. But that was not love. Love was steady, and gentle, and it filled you to the core, and became a part of your bones. That was the love I had with Gorlois, and I prayed to all the gods I knew that he would return.

* * *

Then, like a gift from the White Goddess herself, in the soft white light of her moon, I was sure I saw three knights riding towards Tintagel castle. That could not have been an invading force. I jumped to my feet, my heart hammering in my chest. *He is alive*, I thought. But coming back through the depths of the night, like this? No, I should not get ahead of myself with hope.

And yet I was. Overcome with hope, and struck with a sudden memory of the potion Viviane had given me. I rushed to the shelf where I had hidden it among my dresses, and with a rush of uncharacteristic impulsiveness, I swallowed everything left in the bottle. It tasted worse even than I remembered it. More acrid, more thick with iron. I wondered if in the four years since I had drunk it last, it had curdled or gone bad, but it was done now. If Gorlois returned, we might hope for a child, and if that child were a son, I could be just a little surer about Tintagel's safety, about the future of my home.

But as soon as it was done, I regretted it. I went back over to the window, and the men I was so sure I had seen riding towards the castle were no longer in sight. Had I imagined it? What if Gorlois did return, later, and I had used the last of Viviane's magical drink? I was not sure that I could have a child without it, and I did not feel as though I had time anymore – not with men pressing at our borders – to wait on the chance of nature.

But, as my hope was subsiding into panic, I heard the sounds of men in armour moving outside the bedroom. I rushed to the door and threw it open. A dizzying wave of relief came over me to see that it was Ulfius, Brastias, and, standing between them, Gorlois. Or at least, I knew the three of them from their armour, for all three were fully armed, with helms on their heads.

Brastias was the first to pull off his helm, and give me a quiet nod. He seemed more serious, more sensible than he had when we had spoken that morning, though I supposed he was fresh back from the fighting. There was blood on his armour.

They were all quiet, and it made me wary again, but as Ulfius nodded to me, Gorlois stepped past them, and into the room with me, closing the door and drawing the bolt behind him. I felt the unease begin to melt away from me, replaced with heady relief. He was still wearing his helm, as though he had jumped from his horse and run right up here, to me.

I stepped towards him, and he pulled off his gauntlets. I reached up, my hands shaking a little, to lift the helm from his head. I was afraid that he kept it on because he was wounded in the face, but when I lifted it off and let it drop to the ground with a clatter, it was the same handsome, familiar face – broad, freckled, gentle and honest – that I knew and loved so well. I gasped with joy, and I could not keep from smiling, though I knew that they must have come from the most awful fighting, for Gorlois' armour too was smeared with blood.

I took his face in my hands.

"Gorlois," I breathed, my voice thick with relief. "You're alive–"

I was going to ask how, going to ask if it was all over, but he put his fingers against my lips, and I sighed against them and fell silent, closing my eyes with relief. *It is over*, I thought, *and we are all safe.* He turned me roughly around in his arms, holding me against him, and I felt his hands run into my hair, and the cold harness of his armour against my back, and then his lips against my neck, and I weakened deliciously under it. He had already loosened the laces of my dress, and was pushing it down off my shoulders, letting his lips trail after it, down to my shoulder. I leant back against him, and his hand brushed softly down my throat, down to the laces of the underdress, drawing them open, sliding inside. The feel of his hand, so large, so strong, so familiar against my breast sent the wave of relief through me again, and with it desire, and I leaned back over my shoulder to meet his mouth with mine in a kiss that was deep and passionate. He pushed the underdress down off my shoulders and I stepped out of it. I was aware that he was in his armour still, and I could feel the cold steel of it against my skin. I turned around in his arms and pulled open the buckles of it, helping him lift the breastplate over his head. We fumbled with the buckles and the ungainly sheets of metal, both rushing. The woollen breeches and shirt underneath were dirty with rust and sweat, but I did not care as he pulled me against him again. I felt his huge hand curl around the back of my neck. He was rougher than he usually was, wild with his victory, the relief for his life. I sank into it. I wanted it.

I drew him with me towards the bed, pulling his shirt over his head. I wanted to touch his body, to feel him, strong and alive. I ran my hand over his chest, the hard muscle, its huge broadness, its lovely strength. He was so solid, so real. I could smell the familiar smell of his skin, and the smells of battle: steel, and horses and sweat. He threw me down on the bed, and I thought he would leap on top of me immediately, but he did not, he stood at the foot of the bed for a moment, his eyes running over me. My hair had fallen loose, and I was utterly naked before him; I was not sure why he hesitated. I reached a hand out towards him, and he pulled off his breeches and climbed onto the bed on top of me. After his initial wildness, he was slow. He trailed his kisses up my body to my mouth, where his kiss was suddenly tender. He paused there, his hand against my cheek.

"Tell me you want me, Igraine," he whispered.

"I want you," I said.

"Tell me you love me," he said. I could already feel him pressing against me, hard, and ready to push inside, and my body arched towards his, filled with desire.

"I love you," I told him. And he went inside me, and I moaned softly with the delight of it. His strong hands held me tight against him, and he pressed his lips against my neck. I held tight to him. I had been so afraid, so afraid that he was lost from me forever. His hand ran up my thigh, under my back to pull me harder against him, and I sighed more deeply, feeling the sweetness of our love gather within me. His lips brushed against my nipples, soft first, then harder as I pressed myself against him for more. He was hard, and rough, and right then it was exactly what I wanted. I felt myself brighten inside with it, until I felt it shake through me. And I moaned deep with it as he did. And he wrapped me in his arms when he rolled off me, and I fell asleep on his chest, swimming with pleasure, and relief, and happiness.

But when I was asleep, I did not dream sweet dreams. I dreamt that I was not with my husband, but with Uther Pendragon, and his grip on me was hard and forceful rather than rough with passion as my husband had been, and his hands tangling in my hair were rough not with heady desire, but with jealous punishment. And when I awoke I was alone and cold, and naked and afraid.

* * *

I had slept only a few hours, and woke before it was full light. I dressed slowly, carefully. My body felt fragile and small, and I could not understand what had happened. There was no trace of Gorlois in the room, no discarded piece of armour, nothing but the feeling deep within me that he had been with me. It had not been a dream, I was sure of that. But the castle was quiet, and Gorlois was gone.

I tied up my hair, and dressed carefully, and placed the white gold circlet on my head, but none of it made me feel any better.

Morgawse rushed in late in the morning. Although she had obviously only just woken, it appeared as though there was something that she was expecting to see in our bedroom. I thought that she was looking for her father, for when she saw only me, she went suddenly still and quiet, and her brow wrinkled in confusion. It made me feel a little better that someone else had expected to see him in the morning.

"What is it, Morgawse?" I asked her gently.

She shook her head thoughtfully, and looked up at me. Her bright blue eyes, so like Gorlois', sent a pang of desperate longing through me that I had not imagined that he had survived.

"I thought I saw my father and Ulfius and Brastias riding into the castle last night," she said, and I wrapped my arms around her, and kissed her on the top of her head.

"Perhaps they did, my love," I said, gently. "Shall we go down to the courtyard and see if we can find them?"

She nodded, and slipped her hand into mine. Morgan had come to the doorway as well, to see what was going on. She was so little and delicate that I could lift her easily with my other hand, and she wrapped her little arms around my neck, and rested her head on my shoulder as I held both my daughters tight to me. And we walked down to the courtyard to see what had happened. I was so distracted that I did not even realise that Morgawse was still in her nightdress.

* * *

Out in the courtyard it was quiet. The garrison of men Gorlois had led out did not seem to be here anymore. That boded ill, but I kept quiet and calm. It was helping me, having Morgawse and Morgan with me. I had to be strong for them, to be sure.

Then, suddenly, I heard a horn sound from the guard tower, and I could see knights down at the end of the narrow walkway that linked us to the mainland by a thin bridge of rock. Morgawse jumped a little in excitement beside me. Had Gorlois returned, only having gone out very early in the morning to ensure the safety of his guard posts? That did not seem like him, but in that moment I deeply, deeply wanted to believe it.

Then, suddenly, Morgawse slipped her hand from mine, and with a bright cry of *Father*, began to run barefoot down the path. I worried about her little feet catching on the stones, and she stumbled a little in her excitement, because it was steep. The gates were opening, and the men were coming inside, but I could see already that these were not Gorlois' men. Across one of the horses at the head of the party was a cloth of white, marked in blue-green with the figure of a dragon, its mouth open in a roar, and its back twisted into an ugly coil. And it was too late to call Morgawse back.

The man at the head of the party jumped from his horse, and pulled off his helm. It was Uther Pendragon. He bent to one knee as Morgawse, carried by the steepness of the slope, ran into his hands, and he caught her roughly. I knew what he was saying to her, although the wind carried it away, because I knew what the news must be if Uther rode through my castle gates unhindered. Gorlois was dead.

Chapter nineteen

I could not feel the ground beneath my feet any more. I was not aware of the cold wind, or really of Morgan, her arms around my neck and her head resting against my shoulder. I was aware only of Uther Pendragon, striding up the steep slope towards Tintagel. I could see the sea breeze lifting the sandy-gold strands of his hair. I could see his sharp green eyes – I was sure, even from where I stood – piercing through me. A knight still visored but wearing Brastias' armour had taken Morgawse by the hand, and led her behind, but I suddenly found myself unable to trust the visored face. If Uther was here now, and Gorlois was not, it was not Gorlois who I had lain with last night, whom I had told that I loved. It had not been a dream. I was sure enough of that. I wished that I had been less sure. That would have made it easier.

As Uther stopped before me, pulling off his leather gauntlets in the easy, arrogant way he always seemed to when he had something to say, the world rushed back to me, and I was painfully aware of everything. The cold air against my skin, my loose hair blowing against my face where it escaped from the clasp. Morgan in my arms, shivering.

"My lord Uther," I managed to say, my voice tight with the effort of keeping it under control. He barely acknowledged that I had spoken. I noticed that Brastias, who stood behind him, to his right hand side, had taken off his helm and was staring down at his boots. *Is it possible that Gorlois lives, and is his prisoner?* I hardly dared to hope. It did not seem likely, not likely at all.

"Shall we go inside, lady Igraine?" Uther said, his steady gaze meeting mine. I felt it shoot through me, and the shock run through my body. He was so calm. Would he come, fresh from murdering my husband, to demand I treat him as a guest – or more than a guest?

He held out his hand to me. I did not have a choice. I was a woman alone, standing before a group of armoured men, with my little daughter in my arms. I put Morgan gently down, and she ran over to Morgawse, to take her free hand. Morgan did not seem afraid, merely curious, staring up at the unfamiliar faces around her. She was young enough not to understand. Not to be in pain. Morgawse was white, her lips pale, and trembling slightly. She looked as though she was about to cry. *Don't cry*, I begged her, silently. *Don't draw attention to yourself.* I was already running through my mind if there were a way to sneak them out of Tintagel, to safety. If I had time to write to Viviane...

Uther took a step towards me, and I was jerked from my thoughts to take his hand. No. No privacy or space for those anymore. His hand was steady as it held mine, and dry, and calm. I could feel the pulse in the base of my thumb racing where he held my hand tight in his, and I was sure that he felt it too.

* * *

I was distanced from myself, stunned. I felt myself going through the motions of being a good hostess as we entered the castle. Calling for the hearth-fire to be lit, and ale and food to be brought to the men. I caught myself before I called for men to fetch the lord of the castle. He would not come, whatever had befallen him.

Uther sat at Gorlois' place on the top trestle table. I was sure it was on purpose, and I bristled against it. He began unbuckling his armour, and pulling it off. I was reminded painfully of watching Gorlois buckle himself into his armour and kissing him goodbye. I had *warned* him. I had told him not to go. He had not listened. When Uther was stripped to the dirty, sweaty clothes he wore beneath the armour – the woollen leggings, the sweat-stained shirt of rough cloth – I sat beside him, tense and careful. I did not know what would happen next. I had not decided yet how much I was prepared to fight – how much I *dared* to fight. I was not sure how much danger my daughters were in, how much I could rely on Uther's assertions of love to keep them from his violence. I was not sure I could rely on them at all.

"My lady Igraine," Uther said, staring down the hall at his men as they fell like hungry animals on the bread and cheese and cured meats my servants had brought for them, "I do not know if your husband informed you of the nature of our conflict."

Had he forgotten that I was there when he demanded me as a possession? Was he testing me? Or was this a public show, for the men around us, for Morgan and Morgawse – who I noticed had crept up to sit behind me, hiding from Uther, Morgan on her sister's lap.

I nodded. "He did, my lord."

"Then you understand what this means for you," Uther said flatly. No, I did not understand what this meant for me. I did not understand what it meant for anything other than my own person, my body and my safety. Those hardly mattered in comparison with the safety of Morgan and Morgawse, and my castle, and those whom I had taken into my protection. What if Uther's men raped the servant girls I had promised my protection to here? Those were the violent acts of war that awaited the people who lived in the castle. Uther's knights would steal their food and horses, rape the women, kill those who opposed them. I – *Gorlois* and I – had owed something to these people, and allowing Uther to come through our gates was a violation of all of that. No, I did not *understand* what this meant for me.

"I think so, my lord."

I had not realised that I was staring down at my hands until I felt Uther's hand under my chin, turning my face to his. His expression was unreadable, impassive. I could not tell if he was a cold, heartless man, or if this was his way of being sincere.

"I will not hurt you, Igraine," he said, very softly. I felt my breath catch a little within me, and something in his look reminded me of when he had kissed me in the corridor, and reminded me, with a pang of guilt, of my having half-wanted it. He brushed his fingers softly against my cheek, in something like a gesture of comfort. I was not sure if I should trust it.

But then he stood, and held his hand out to me again, and I realised with a flash of panic what he meant. Then Gorlois was dead for sure. And was he so cold that he could expect me to take his hand and follow him up to the bedroom where I had slept for twelve years beside my husband the day after Uther had killed him? What position was I in to refuse? Could I hope that if I went willingly, Brastias would have the initiative to take Morgan and Morgawse from the castle, and off to Avalon, to safety?

"Now my lord?" I asked. I wanted to be calm, but my voice sounded weak and breathy with panic.

"If you might be so kind, I should like you to show me the castle. Where my men and I might stay. When we are rested, I will take you back to Camelot. It will be as my wife, Igraine. I do not mean you harm, or dishonour."

Uther left his hand out for me to take. He was careful, formal in public, but I was not sure that he would be the same when we were alone. I stood slowly, forcing myself to be steady, not to tremble, and slipped my hand back into his.

* * *

Uther was quiet as I led him around the castle, showing him the places where his men could sleep. I offered him the room that Enid had slept in last time she was there. It was rich and well-appointed enough, and he seemed satisfied. He did not ask if he could sleep in my bedroom with me, and I was glad. I did not think I could bear, after the night before, to lie with any man at all, especially Uther Pendragon. He did not ask about Morgan and Morgawse, and I was glad.

It was only when I excused myself to go to my own chamber, and turned to leave, that Uther caught me by the wrist, and drew me back to him, and spoke.

"Be assured, Igraine," he said, "that no harm will come to you and your people from me and my men. We will gather ourselves here, and before the end of the week we will ride to Camelot, where you and I will be married. I am a kind man, Igraine, though I know you do not think me so. I will give you time to grieve. You can burn your husband's body. But then we must leave."

I nodded, and I felt it hit me. Gorlois truly was dead. And he thought a week – only a week, after years of marriage – was a kindness to me. But then I supposed he did not have to. I was only a woman, and I had no power over him.

* * *

When I got back to my room, I found that Brastias was waiting for me, still in his armour, with his helm in his hand, sitting in the window seat. As I came through the door, he stepped from it, and dropped to his knee, bending his head.

"Igraine," he said, his voice thick with emotion, "I am here to beg your forgiveness."

I sighed, rubbing my face with my hands. I just wanted to be alone. I could feel the tears gathering behind my eyes, and I did not want to cry. I could not bear the thought of letting it all go. It would wash over me, overwhelm me, and leave me hollow.

"Brastias –"

I protested, but I think he thought it was an invitation for him to continue his supplication, for he, still kneeling, took both my hands.

"My lady, I fought as much as I could, and I want you to know that I did not swear myself to Uther except in the final moments."

"Oh Brastias," I sighed, "I hardly care about that now."

Men had done worse things to save themselves. It was not me that Brastias had to reconcile himself with; it was his God, and Gorlois' ghost.

I walked over to the window seat, and sunk down into it. I did not realise that I had been shaking until then. I drew in a deep breath and then another. I began to feel a little more steady. Just a little.

"What happened, Brastias?" I asked softly. I wanted to know. I wanted to know if he and Ulfius truly had come last night with Gorlois, or if I had been abused by some devil in my husband's shape. I knew Merlin's strength, his power, and long ago I had half-heard a similar tale from Viviane, and I feared the same trick had been played on me.

"My lady, I am not sure –"

"Brastias," I interrupted, "I want to know."

Brastias nodded, shifting on his feet, uneasy. He was really little more than a boy. A boy in a man's shape, in a man's armour. He drew in a deep breath. I only realised then that he was shaking too.

"We came to Uther's camp as dusk was beginning to fall. It was at the edge of a forest, hidden in the hollow of a little valley. The campfires were smoking, half of them out, and we thought that the men would be climbing back into their tents and falling asleep. We thought that Uther would not be expecting us.

"At first, it went well. We were a small, lightly-armed force, and Uther's men were used to fighting in heavy armour with broadswords, and they couldn't get their armour on or their weapons in their hands in time. But what we hadn't realised was that there were twice as many of them as we thought. Half of the camp was hidden within the woods themselves, and we did not see the tents until the men began rushing from the woods. We were outnumbered ten to one, but Gorlois would not retreat or surrender. Not even when the men began to run because they saw, among Uther's men, the witch Merlin, in his black cowl and hood. Some of them said he touched men with his bare hands, and their bones twisted and broke and blood poured from their eyes, and their tongues swelled until they choked. I did not see these things, but it was enough for our men to panic, and for those who were young, or cowardly, to run.

"In all this time, we had not seen Uther Pendragon himself. I was with Gorlois and Ulfius, and we were cutting through to the centre of the camp, where we could see Uther's tent. I thought we might make it, kill him before he was ready, and then Tintagel would be safe. It was smoky from the fires, and some of the tents were burning, but we were almost there.

"Then, out of nowhere, there were four men upon us, and one of them was Merlin the witch. Ulfius stepped out in front of Gorlois, and one of the men sliced right through him. Merlin did not seem to be doing anything, and yet I felt my limbs grow slow, and I felt heavy and weak. Gorlois, who would have easily thrown off six or seven men the size of those who took hold of him, seemed unable to throw the two that held him aside, and two others took hold of me.

"It was only then that Uther Pendragon stepped from his tent, as though he had been disturbed from his sleep. He was dressed only in his breeches, his chest and feet were bare, but he had his sword drawn and gripped in his hand.

"The men holding Gorlois forced him to his knees, and –"

Brastias stopped, his gaze on me hesitant, wary.

"Brastias, please," I said. "Continue."

Brastias drew in another deep breath, and crossed his arms over his chest, as though he was trying to contain something awful.

"Uther stepped forward, his sword raised. He told Gorlois that he would spare his life, and allow him to take his daughters to Wales. And he could live there in peace, if he would only –" Brastias drew in another sharp breath, as though he was in pain to remember it. "If he would only hand you over to Uther, to be Uther's wife. Gorlois refused. Uther raised his sword –"

I put up a hand for Brastias to stop, and he fell silent. In the end, I was not brave enough to hear what had happened to Gorlois. He was dead. That was all I needed to know.

"He died bravely, my lady. He did not beg for his life."

Bravely? No. Proudly. He should have begged. What would have been brave would have been to put away his honour, and to take Morgawse and Morgan away to somewhere they could be safe. To have not cared what men said about him, but only to have cared that his daughters were safe. To have lived on and made sure that those who relied on him were taken care of. Why did all men think that death was the bravest choice?

"After that, I pledged myself into Uther's service, on the condition that he would allow us to wrap Gorlois' body in linen cloths and bring it back to Tintagel castle."

112

"You did right in this, Brastias," I said softly, and he sighed as though he had been afraid that I would blame him, and be unkind. But he had done right. He had stayed alive. I supposed that there were those who would blame him for it, but I would not be among them. I, too, had made choices in order to live.

Brastias seemed to be satisfied with my thanking him; he nodded gently, and left. As he did, I asked him to bring Morgan and Morgawse to me. That night, I slept with them either side of me in the bed. Normally Morgawse would have been excited, but without her father there, falling asleep in the big bed wasn't a treat. There was no reading, no singing, and she was pale and silent as her little sister, who curled up beside me and fell asleep with all the sudden innocence of a child who has understood nothing. Morgawse and I lay side by side in silence through the night, staring up at the darkness over us, eyes wide open, neither of us knowing what to say to one another, neither one knowing quite who we were, without Gorlois there.

Chapter twenty

The next day, I lay half-awake for a long time, trying to remember why it was that I felt so awful, so paralysed and empty. Still fogged with dreams, it was a long time before the realisation sank through that it was because Gorlois was dead, and someone had come to me in his shape after he had died, and I had given them the last moments of love and togetherness I ought to have owed to him. I had betrayed him, against my own will, and now I and my daughters were the property of Uther Pendragon.

Uther did not seek me out, and I was glad to be alone. I stood with Morgawse beside me, and Morgan in my arms, and we watched Gorlois' body burn in Tintagel's courtyard. Morgawse was still and tense and silent. Quieter than she had ever been in her life. Morgan watched it all, her grey eyes wide, but without understanding. As we turned our backs on the pile of ash and walked up towards the castle, she asked me when her father was coming home.

When I overheard Morgawse telling the story of those days as an adult, she told it all as though it were a matter of days we were at Tintagel, waiting for Uther to give the command for us to ride back to Camelot, when really it was more than a week. She must have been in shock. But so was I; disorientated and afraid, unable to put into words what I needed to for her, because I was grieving for her father as well. But worse, worse, beneath it all was the knowledge that some unknown man had come in his place. I had heard too much of Merlin's shape-shifting magic not to fear the worst, and the thought of it made me sick.

* * *

It was almost as though Uther had forgotten, now that he had Tintagel castle, that what he had longed for was me as his wife. I had hoped that he would not find my father's gold, but he did. I saw his men dragging it up from the vaults in its heavy mahogany trunks. It would all be wasted. I knew what men were like. Some of the soldiers would give it to their women, or spend it on mead and ale and wine, dissipating it through the alehouses – and whorehouses – of every town between here and Camelot. What would Uther do with his share? Equip an army? I knew that he still resented the Bretons for failing to support his claim to the throne. He would have loved to have humbled them, as he had humbled Lot. He, like Gorlois, was a proud man. Such proud men. I hated them all.

It was almost a week later that Uther came to me alone at last. He was no different from how he ever was. He strode into the room without announcing himself, leaving the door hanging open, and seized hold of me, kissing me as though no time at all had passed between when he had kissed me in the hallway, in the light of the crescent moon, and now. I was hardly aware of him, and it was strange. I was aware of the red light of the setting sun pouring like blood through the window, and I was aware of my own body, small and tired and frail, his hands closing around my arms. But I was not aware of how I felt. I was empty, and numb. I wished that he would leave me alone.

I stepped back away from him, and he took a step towards me, backing me against the wall. I pushed him more firmly off and he looked a little surprised. Perhaps he thought that I, like he, was only waiting for Gorlois to be gone before our desires could be one.

"What have you come here for, Uther?" I asked. I was sure I knew the answer, but I wanted him to know that I was not his slave, although I was in his power.

He spread out his hands against my stomach, pressing me back more firmly against the wall. I could feel my heart in my throat, racing, and it felt strangely distant to me. He took a step closer.

"Long ago, I told you that you would one day be my wife, although then it was only because of Merlin's words to me." He leaned down towards me, his hands sliding up the bodice of my dress, towards my breasts. I wrapped my hands around his wrists, holding

114

him back, but he barely seemed to feel it. "But when I saw you again, when I watched you dancing, I remembered all of it, all of how you were: proud and stubborn and beautiful. I love you, Igraine. Be sure of that. You need fear no dishonour from me. I love you, and I shall make you my wife when I bring you back to Camelot."

He leaned in, as though to kiss me again, and I turned my face aside. He slid his hands around my waist, seeming not to feel at all my grip on his wrists, and pulled me up against him, pressing his body against mine.

"Igraine," he whispered at my ear. "Believe me, I mean you no harm. You have my promise that I will make you my wife."

I turned my face up to meet his eye. "Not before you have made me your whore, it seems, my lord."

His hands slid up my back, and one of them into my hair, drawing my mouth closer to his. He did not seem to be listening to what I had to say. He did not seem to understand or care that only a short time ago I had woken in the morning thinking myself a wife, only to find I was a widow. I was tired, and heavy with grief, and confused.

"Please." I turned my face away from his again. "Let me go."

He stepped away, his look strange; angry, but cold and steady. "You have nothing to fear from me, Igraine," he said again, as though he could not understand how I had not taken it in.

"Do my daughters have anything to fear from you?" I asked, carefully.

Uther shrugged. I felt the panic flash through me again.

"Promise me that they do not," I insisted. But I could hear the fear in my own voice, and I was sure that he did, too.

"All I can promise you is my love, Igraine. Those girls are my enemy's daughters. For your sake, I will be as merciful as is reasonable. But not more."

I opened my mouth to speak, and Uther took hold of my face, his fingers curling up around my jaw, turning my eyes up to his. I could feel the pulse in my neck fluttering against his hand, and I was aware that the touch, for what it could have been, was careful and light.

"You would have been in a stronger position to bargain for them if you had not refused me until it became necessary for me to kill their father."

Before I could speak, he left, and I sank into the window seat, too numb, too cold to even feel afraid. I wished that Viviane was there. She could have told me the truth about what had happened to me. She could have taken the girls away.

I woke next morning feeling awful and sick. I was not sure if it was because Merlin had come to Tintagel castle, and the thought of him repulsed me, or because the potion that Viviane had given me had worked, and the night a man had come to me in Gorlois' shape, I had conceived a child. The feeling was familiar, the weakness in my limbs, the sickness in the pit of my stomach. It filled me, also, with dread, for it would make me weak when I needed to be strong, and it would make me vulnerable when I needed to be like a stone.

* * *

It was after that, after Uther's men had dragged more gold from my father's vaults, and after they had eaten all they could from Tintagel's stores and wasted the rest, a man in armour came early in the morning to tell us that it was time to leave for Camelot. I would have to say goodbye to my home at last. The home I had married Gorlois to keep. My place of safety. I had fought my whole life to stay in this place that was mine, and now it was finally lost to me. I felt hollow, and empty, and heavy and sick. My whole body was sore, and I was sure now, sure with the kind of certainty that I had never felt before – never this soon – that I was pregnant with some stranger's child.

Morgawse came in with Morgan while I was sitting at the little dressing table, my hands shaking, trying to plait my hair. I was dressing myself slowly, carefully in all of the finest things I owned, desperate for a little protection. I wanted to leave my home looking like its queen, not like a prisoner. I was trying to weave a cloth of silver ribbon through the plait, but my fingers did not seem to want to grip properly, nor to be steady and sure as I needed them to be, and it was all I could do not to cry.

Morgawse sat down on the bed, heavy and sulky as an overgrown child, and I could not fight away the violent stab of irritation I felt towards her. Morgan beside her was still and calm, staring at the patterns on the bedpost. I did not think that she understood at all. In a small way, I was glad. I did not want to have two angry, grieving daughters on my hands.

"I don't know why you have to marry him," Morgawse complained, drawing her knees up to her chin and pouting. I could see in the mirror what a picture of petulance she was. I could not help thinking that it was something of Gorlois' fault that Morgawse thought that she ought to have whatever she wanted. She was old enough to be strong, old enough to help. I fought back the urge to stride across the room and slap some sense into her.

"I just do, Morgawse," I replied, terse and tense, trying to keep my eyes fixed on myself in the hammered surface on the mirror. My image was puckered, distorted, as though I were looking at myself from the bottom of a rippling pond. I did not know what I wanted. I did not want Gorlois to be dead, but now that he was, perhaps I *did* want to marry Uther. I could not continue alone, and who else was there? I was not going to put myself into the protection of another man who was vassal to Uther, and I could hardly run to France, seeking the protection of the sister who seemed to have forgotten me. Avalon would not harbour *me* from Uther, even if it did take my daughters, because Uther was Avalon's king. Once, I might have loved Uther. I did not know what I felt now. Hollowness. Emptiness. Cold.

"We could run away." Morgawse's childish insistent voice cut through my thoughts, and I felt myself tense with hostility against it. "Buy a ship and sail to Ireland. Or France."

It was as though she had stepped into my thoughts, and was accusing me of being too cowardly, too prudent by nature to run from Uther. I picked up my circlet and set it on my head, holding it on tight, as though I were steadying myself.

"No, Morgawse," I replied.

Morgawse jumped from the bed to her feet, and I could see her cheeks were flushed with upset, and I knew that she was angry with me. But there was nothing I could do, nothing I had done. We were here because of Uther, and because of her father.

"We could do it. Brastias would help us. Or we could go to Avalon. They would hide us there," she cried.

"No, Morgawse," I said again.

Morgan, still staring at the bedpost in front of her, her little fingers against the delicate carvings, made a little noise as though she were going to speak, but did not. She looked at me, and I could see in her lovely, big grey eyes that she did not understand why her sister was afraid, or why we were arguing. She thought it was all the same as it had always been, and she was – as always – lost in some faraway thought. She still expected to see her father walk through the door and scoop her up in his arms.

"Why don't you want to run away? King Uther is a monster. I hate him. I want to run away," Morgawse complained again. It was awful. She sounded as though she was going to cry. I ought to have been patient, to have explained to her that we could not run, and that we had nowhere to go, and that besides I was pregnant, and sick, and tired, and both flooded with emotion and empty of feeling all at once. And I could not be strong for her. And she was almost a woman, and could not rely on me like a child.

"Morgawse, just be quiet," I snapped, slamming down the bottle of perfume in my hand that I had been holding, not quite sure if I could bear its smell without retching in my newfound nausea. "I have to marry him. That is the end of it. I don't want to hear you saying these things ever again, do you understand? Especially not in front of Morgan."

Morgan had a chance for a different kind of life. She was young enough for this to be a distant memory soon. She didn't have to live with Morgawse's bitterness and anger. I knew Morgawse well enough to know that she would never forgive Uther for this, even if she had to.

Morgawse shrank back, hurt. I wished that she could try to be more sensible, try to understand that we had to make choices we did not want to make to survive. I felt a sudden stab of anger that Enid had just left me, had run back to France while I was in Camelot all those years ago at Christmas time. Morgawse could have gone to her aunt, if I had had any idea where she was. And it would have done Morgawse some good to see that my own sister was just like she was. She was getting old enough to realise that she and I were not alike, and I supposed that now her father was dead he was going to become a kind of idol in her memory. Her perfect father, who had let her run about the castle like a boy, spilling honey everywhere and scraping her knees, while her stern mother scolded her and forced her to accept a stepfather she hated. Even now, I could see the way it was going to go. But Morgawse's resentment was just something else I would have to bear in order for us to survive. I would have to. I did not come this far to buckle under the sulking of an eleven-year-old child. If she had to hate me to survive, then I would endure that as well. I would weather this. We all would.

* * *

Uther came before long, and as though he did not see my daughters in the room, he put his hand against the back of my neck, sliding into the hair at the base of my plait. I felt his fingers against my scalp and closed my eyes. There was something tender about the touch, though it was with the usual confident firmness that he had. As though I were his already.

"You are ready to leave?" he asked, gently. "You have everything that you need?"

I nodded as I felt his fingers brush up deeper into my hair, and then down lightly across my jaw, turning my face towards his as he leant down towards me, his other hand braced against the little dressing table. His eyes flickered over my face, thoughtful.

"Are you quite well, Igraine?" he asked, as though he knew that I was not.

I nodded briskly. I was afraid to speak.

Uther offered me his hand, and I took it, allowing him to help me to stand. Truly, I did not know at all how I felt about him. He had killed Gorlois, he had *demanded* me, but with his hand in mine I felt steadier. I felt a little comfort. I remembered long ago in Aurelianus' courtyard the way that he had kissed me, and I could not pretend that I had felt how I did with him with any other man. But he had proved himself not to be trusted.

When I turned to leave with him, all of the momentary comfort I had felt drained out of me. Merlin stood in the doorway in his dirty black cowled robe, his skullish teeth grinning at me and his eyes black as beetles in the shadow of his hood. I felt a new wave of nausea rush over me. I saw his hands folded together, stained and blackened with something that might have been ink, but might also have been some awful poisonous herb from the Otherworld. I tried not to imagine that it had been him in Gorlois' shape. It could not have been. It could *not*. The man who had come to me in my husband's shape had been passionate, had been tender. Merlin was not capable of that. I told myself this, but it did me little comfort. I was sure, too, just for a second, that I saw a line of ugly little black ants weaving between the fingers of Merlin's folded hands. But I blinked, and they were gone.

PART II
MERLIN'S CURSE

Then Queen Igraine grew daily greater and greater, so it befell within half a year, as King Uther lay by his queen, he asked her, by the faith she owed to him, who was the father; then she was sore abashed to give her answer. Dismay you not, said the king, but tell me the truth, and I shall love you the better, by the faith of my body. Sir, said she, I shall tell you the truth. The same night that my lord was dead, the hour of his death, as his knights record, there came into my castle of Tintagel a man like my lord in speech and in countenance, and two knights with him in likeness of his two knights, and so I went to bed with him as I ought to do with my lord, and the same night, as I shall answer before God, this child was begotten upon me. That is truth, said the king, as you say; for it was I myself that came in the likeness, and therefore dismay you not, for I am father of the child; and there he told her how it had come about, and that it was by Merlin's counsel. Then the queen made great joy when she knew who was the father of her child.

Sir Thomas Malory, *Le Morte d'Arthur*

Chapter twenty-one

As we rode away from Tintagel, I looked over my shoulder, watching as it disappeared behind me. It was a long time before its tall, spiked towers and the wild black rocks they were set among disappeared from view. I felt as though I had lost something as they did.

I rode at the head of the party with Uther. He wanted me beside him, in case I tried to escape. I did not blame him. I had considered it, but I was not sure that I would make it alive with my daughters all the way to Avalon. Certainly not with the child inside me, who might be the last piece of Gorlois in this world. Brastias rode behind us with Morgan and Morgawse. I was glad that he had survived. I knew that men would blame him. Call him a coward. Accuse him of being selfish. But it was a different kind of bravery, his courage to live with the shame, rather than to leave me and my daughters without a protector.

The journey was long, and I felt sick, but I dared not show it. I knew I was only safe until Uther realised that there was another man's child inside me. I wanted to turn back all the time to see that Morgan and Morgawse were safe, but I did not. If I turned around and looked at them, that would bring them to Uther's attention, and that I was sure I did *not* want.

We stopped at the shores of Avalon, and Uther slid from his horse, throwing off his helm and gloves, unbuckling his breastplate and throwing it off, and even stripping down to his bare chest to kneel before Viviane, who stood at the shore of the lake to greet him. Her gaze on him was impassive, and I somewhat suspected that she did not support Merlin's choice for king as wholeheartedly as she had before he had proven himself a man willing to kill for jealousy and desire. Still, as she stood knee-deep in the lake, the fabric of her long blue robe darkening upwards as it soaked up the water, she still placed her hand on his head in blessing, spoke the old words, and lifted the water of the enchanted lake to wash his head.

Merlin, on his horse beside me, leaned over. "Uther Pendragon is no shy Christian man like Gorlois was. He observes the ancient ways, and the gods of the land and the sky, of the earth and the moon have rewarded him."

"That hardly bothers me," I said flatly. "I was not raised a Christian."

It had come to us late, and we had taken it because it was

important to the French kings in the south, and my father wanted their trade. For my father, religion had always been a matter indistinguishable from politics. I had had to forget the White Goddess and the Hanged God, and the Drowned God and the Mother, and learn God and Christ at ten years old. I, like my father, was a pragmatist, and I would learn the ways I had to learn in order to survive.

Uther stood once more; Viviane kissed him on each cheek, and placed her hands on his head in blessing. I somewhat wished that Avalon would deny him a little of its magic. I wanted it all for myself, all of its protection. Although I was about to be his wife, Uther and I were enemies in many ways. Certainly, we were enemies when it came to the fate of my daughters.

I wanted to slip down from the horse and run to Viviane myself, to whisper in her ear, to beg her to take me and my daughters away, or at least little Morgan. She could at least take Morgan. But Merlin closed his fist around the reins of my horse, and led it with his as Uther pulled his armour back on, and the column of men and women and children turned away towards Camelot.

* * *

On the road, I slept with Morgan and Morgawse beside me. I was neither surprised nor jealous to see other women go into Uther's tent, since I had declined a place there. I would not be shamed. It made me wonder again about all the time Gorlois had been at war in the north. What if there were women caring for half-brothers or sisters of Morgan and Morgawse, who might be persuaded, for the sake of an old love, to take my daughters into their protection? No, more likely they would come to harm there, as well. People would be circling like vultures over everything Gorlois' death had left behind: Tintagel castle, the gold, everything that Uther had already snatched, but that he might be persuaded to distribute once more if the price was right. Or if the threat was great enough.

I thought, too, of the other women with Uther. He swore he loved me, and yet he had no shame in that. No thought for jealousy *I* might feel. He was strange. Stony, yet passionate. Quiet, but commanding. I could not tell if it was simply that he cared little for the act between a man and a woman. He had cared enough when he thought of me with Gorlois.

I wondered where Imogen was. No news had come to us that she was dead. Would he keep her once he was married to me? She was twice my age. Surely, the time when she would have been desirable was waning. Yet she still had some power, as the only one of

Aurelianus' blood who survived him.

It always starts with a king's death, I thought. Every war, every strife. A king's death without a son. This would all have been different if Morgawse could have held Tintagel. Those used to be the old ways, though I supposed it would only have meant that Uther would have tried to take it from her.

* * *

I barely slept, and when the morning light came in cold through the thin fabric of the tent, it drew me from the half-slumber I had fallen into, and I felt cold and achy and sick.

I slipped from the tent, hoping no men would be awake and out of their tents to see me, and ran bare-foot through the cold, dewy autumn grass to the forest, where I ran in among the trees. When I was sure I was far enough away not to be heard, I allowed myself to bend over double and retch, giving in to the nausea that was making my head swim and my limbs tremble. But I had not eaten, not properly, not for days, and all I could throw up was bile that burned in my throat. Across my foot, I was suddenly aware of a line of black ants trailing across the flesh, white with the morning chill, and I felt my heart race with panic.

"Lady Igraine."

I heard an unfamiliar voice behind me, and I wheeled around, wiping my mouth with the sleeve of my nightdress. It was a knight of Uther's, and on his face he wore a strange, unpleasant smile. I wondered if he understood what he had seen.

"Are you well, lady?"

I nodded, quiet.

He took another step towards me, and I flinched. I knew that I had lost any advantage I might have had then, for I had shown fear. I could feel my heart fluttering in my chest, and I cursed the weakness of my woman's body. If I had been wearing my shoes, I might have run, for I would have been faster than the knight in his heavy armour, and I was sure I still remembered how to climb trees as easily as I had done when I was a child.

We stared at one another for a moment, both braced, both unsure of whether the other was thinking what they feared. I moved before he did, turning to run deep into the woods, but he grabbed me about the wrist, pulling me back towards him. I slammed into the hard metal of his breastplate, and I felt my teeth grate together. Before I could gather myself, he had turned me around in his arms. I had been afraid that he was going to drag me back to Uther, and complain that I had been trying to escape, or that he was going to tell everyone that I was with child – the father of whom I could not know – but this was worse.

Before I could force myself free, we were on the ground. I could feel the cold, wet earth seeping through my thin nightdress, clammy and unpleasant against my skin. I opened my mouth to scream, but he shoved his hand half-inside before the noise could escape from my lungs. I bit down on his palm, which tasted of the earth, and of old meat, and the sweat of horses, but he did not pull his hand away. I could feel him struggling to pull open the buckles of his armour, and I pushed against him harder. I bit harder and harder into his hand, until my mouth began to fill with his blood. I could taste it, iron and acrid. Growling with rage and pain, he pulled his hand out to strike me across the face.

"Best for you to be quiet, Lady Igraine," he hissed at my ear. "It's only the whores who scream."

"Uther will have you killed," I spat.

He hit me across the face again, hard.

"You will not tell him, and he will not know. You come to him no virgin, after all, and with child – whether it be by that half-peasant Gorlois or some stable boy. Another man will make little difference."

I felt his hand suddenly against my thigh, pushing my nightdress up. I opened my mouth to scream, but before the sound came out, the man fell suddenly still, his eyes blinking slowly. His mouth fell open, closed, then slowly opened again, like a fish pulled from the water. His face went red, then purple, and his mouth continued to open and close. His eyes showed white all the way around and he looked down at me in blank panic, but I would not have helped him even if I could. His hand went to his throat as though feeling for some imaginary hand that had closed around it, but there was none. He fell limp against me eventually. It was only when I pushed his heavy form off me and sat up that I saw, standing right over us, Merlin the witch, his face hidden in the shadow of his cowl but his white hands, veined blue with patterns of woad, stretched out towards me.

I did not know what to say. I had thought that Merlin was my enemy.

Slowly, I pushed myself up to my elbows, and then got to my feet. He did not offer me a hand to help me stand. I was not sure if I would have taken it. I was wary of him still.

Neither of us spoke. I knew I should have thanked him for killing the knight, and I knew that he should have asked me if I was alright. There was mud all over my nightdress, smeared across it from the hem all the way up the back. I did not know how I would explain walking from the woods with Merlin, my dress covered with mud.

It was only then that Merlin reached out his hand towards me in a gesture of encouragement, and only then that I gently put my hand into his. As I did, I instantly regretted it. The world pitched and spun around me, and I felt yet another wave of nausea rush through me – worse, far worse, than what the child was giving me. But when I opened my eyes, I was back in my tent, where little Morgan and Morgawse were sleeping as though nothing had happened. Merlin was not there anymore either.

I slipped out of the nightdress, pulled on a clean underdress and climbed back onto the little sleeping-mat between my children. Only then could I feel myself beginning to shake. I needed to get Uther to take me as his wife as soon as possible. Until then I was a woman in-between. Neither virgin nor wife, neither captured princess nor native queen. As long as I did not belong to any man, I was not under any man's protection. I loathed the thought of belonging, but I was beginning to fear that the only thing worse was to be no man's possession at all. What the knight had said was true. I was no virgin; Uther would not be expecting a virgin on the night he took me as his wife. If another man seized hold of me, there was nothing but that man's word against mine.

* * *

Determined to know my own fate, as soon as it was full light I dressed myself and went to Uther's tent. I had left Morgawse still sleeping, wrapped in the blankets and furs, and Morgan sitting up, her bright grey eyes looking attentively around her – still, and quiet and calm. I would have sent Brastias in to watch them, but Morgawse was now too old for that to be seemly. I did not want to encourage her to treat Brastias half like a brother, half like a sweetheart. It would only do her harm in years to come.

When I got to Uther's tent, there was a knight at the entrance who tried to deny me, but when he heard my voice, Uther called me in. I felt myself tense as he said my name, and I was not sure if it was with apprehension, or with something only yet half-recognised in me.

As I stepped in, I understood why the knight had been trying to stop me from entering. Uther sat naked in a tin bathtub, rubbing the steaming water on his arms, washing away dirt. I had only sat in a bath that smelled of lavender and rose oils before, so it was strange to see the steam rising and smell nothing but the clean smell of hot water. It reminded me of the kitchens, and the smell of boiling water there, and it seemed odd, as though Uther were cooking himself.

I did not see what the harm was in looking at him. He had invited me in, after all, and did not seem to be shy about himself. *I* was clothed. I let my eyes trail over the shape of his bare shoulders, tensing and moving as he wrung out the cloth. His chest was broad and lightly covered with dark gold hair. I knew that he was large, for I had heard men say so, but after Gorlois, who had been like a giant, Uther seemed small. He looked harder, though, sturdier than Gorlois, who had been huge and muscular, but always had something strangely gentle about his ways.

"What is it, Igraine?" Uther asked directly, without looking at me.

I crossed my arms over my chest. He was going to be rude to me, then, now that he had killed my husband and captured me as his prize. I had been going to ask him how long the ride to Camelot would be, but I felt myself harden, and a strange desire to hurt him for his brusqueness sank over me.

"Your witch killed a knight of yours who tried to lay hands on me only this morning," I said coldly. "Is this how you treat the woman you swear you will have as your wife? With carelessness? You have offered me hardly any protection."

Uther looked up at me, and when our eyes met at last, I felt it go through me like a shard of light.

"I offered you the protection of my bed. You disdained it."

"So," I replied, forcing my voice lower than a shout, "because you cannot have me like a whore, you are happy to let any other man do so?"

Uther sighed in annoyance, as though I were a child, irritating him; as though I were weak of understanding. I felt myself tense against it even more.

"Do not be ridiculous, Igraine. That is not what I am saying." He braced his hands against the bathtub and pushed himself up. "I am simply saying that you are unharmed, are you not? I have set my witch to protecting you, I have offered you the protection that I can, and you have refused out of pride."

I looked away as he stood and wrapped himself in a linen sheet, still dripping with water. I tried not to imagine how it would feel to have those wet hands clasp my body, to feel the warmth of his bare skin against my own. I was a new widow. I should not even imagine.

I was so lost in my thoughts – in *hiding from* my thoughts – that I did not realise that he had come to stand beside me until he said, softly, "Look at me, Igraine."

I turned back over my shoulder, and I was surprised by how

close he was. I thought I could feel the heat of his skin, still warm from the steaming water of the bath. I could certainly feel my own heart racing. I did not know if it was fear that I felt, or desire. I half-wondered if the two were one. After all, part of the reason Gorlois had made me feel so safe was that I was not afraid that a passion for him would overwhelm me, and wipe me out. As our eyes met, I felt my breath catch, and I tried not to show it. I did not want Uther to think he had any power over me that extended beyond the fact that he had me in his possession. And yet I would have liked it; I would have liked to know once more what it felt like to be kissed by him. I remembered how his mouth felt against mine. I remembered what *passion* felt like, though I had indulged it only a moment. And yet, also, I felt Gorlois' ghost between us in the tent, and I held back, drew further back into myself. I could not shake the feeling that in some small way, in the reality of my desire, I had betrayed Gorlois to his death. Would he have been so proud if he did not believe that Uther had won some part of me from him? But he had not. Not enough that I would have thrown away all my safety for it. I wished he would have listened.

"Igraine," Uther said once more, in his rough, throaty voice, and I felt his thumb brush across my jaw and then slowly, tentatively, across my lips. If it had been at another moment, just a few weeks ago, before he had killed Gorlois, or even if he had touched me like this in Tintagel courtyard in the moments before I first met Gorlois, I would have closed my eyes and sighed, and let my lips part at the soft touch, but I did not. "Do you truly believe that I do not care if you are harmed?"

I did not answer, but I leaned a little towards him, and he towards me. I felt the wet strands of his hair brush against my forehead, and then his nose brush softly against mine, and I gave a little gasp of anticipation – I was not quite sure what of – but I resisted.

"Promise me that we will be married as soon as we reach Camelot," I whispered. Uther opened his mouth, and I was sure that he was going to give me what I needed – an assurance of my safety – when I heard from the door of the tent the unpleasant rasping voice of Merlin.

"Do not promise, Uther," he said. "Remember those promises that you made to me a long time ago? You are to make no vow, not even to this woman, without my permission, and I do not give it."

"I see no reason why you should refuse me, old man," Uther replied, but his tone was peevish rather than authoritative, and he turned away from me to reach for a clean shirt and pull it over his head. He behaved with Merlin something like a son with his father, so I could see why people believed the rumours about Uther's birth. But I could not believe it, not now I knew what an unnatural creature Merlin was.

"The time must be right, Uther," Merlin replied, but his nasty black eyes were fixed on me, and drifted towards my stomach. I was not surprised that Merlin had guessed that I carried a child inside me, but I could not see why he would not want people to think that this child was Uther's, since it was his wish that I become Uther's wife.

"What ambition of yours does this serve, Merlin?" I demanded, bolder perhaps than I should have been, hot from a sudden confusing closeness that I had wanted to give in to.

Merlin ignored me.

"Uther," he said evenly — every part of his harsh voice was unpleasant, and laden half with threat and half with a kind of low, wheedling persuasion – "you have made your promises to me, that you will obey me in all things, and make no pacts without me. I have changed you from one man into another." Uther flinched at this, tensed. I saw it in the muscles of his jaw. Of course he was not pleased to be reminded that his blood was lowly and his place as King was entirely at the conjuring of Merlin. "I have given you power. All the while, have I not cautioned you in patience? Be patient now, and I will make sure that you have all that you have desired."

"What difference does it make – a few days, a few weeks, a month – to you, Merlin?" I asked.

Merlin grinned. "In a hurry, my lady?"

"We have waited long enough," Uther replied, brusquely.

"You must make proper arrangements, my lord," Merlin insisted. "The proper ceremony. You would not want people to believe that you – or your wife – had anything to hide."

Chapter twenty-two

When I came back to the tent, Brastias was there, and Morgawse was putting her cloak around her shoulders. I wondered if he had helped her to dress, as he might have done when she was a child. She was too old for it, and I felt wary, and irritated with him for pandering to her need for his attention. Even now she was batting her eyelids at him, and swishing the cloak around herself. I drew her into my embrace and kissed the top of her hair, as though she were a child.

She wriggled away, angry, upset, still blaming me for us leaving Tintagel.

She sulked on the journey. I was glad, in that moment, for Morgan's strange, obtuse nature, the way she did not seem to notice the world around her. Perhaps if she had a little more she would have been angry with me as well, and I was glad that this was something I did not have to be wary of. I hugged her before me on the horse, and she snuggled back against me, quiet and watchful as always.

It was only when she said, as Camelot appeared over the horizon, "Will father be there, to meet us?" that I realised that she had understood just enough of what had happened to be awfully confused by it.

I kissed the top of her head, and said, "He is gone, love. He will not be there."

And she nodded, as though I were explaining what kind of bird it was she saw in the sky, or why the plants grow, and said nothing.

* * *

Our greeting at Camelot was muted and tense. Imogen was still there, dressed in the kind of robes a queen might wear: rich, dark red samite, jewels in her hair and about her throat, and over her shoulders a thick pelt of pale grey fur fastened with a golden clasp. I felt shabby and dirty beside her, dressed in my riding clothes. Her clouded eyes moved over us, and I knew that she was seeing that I was there, and Uther was there, and that her place in Camelot had changed. I did not know if she would be an enemy or an ally here. I knew that, if I were her, I would not be pleased to see a rival. The knights waiting for Uther greeted him warmly enough, and his steward Owain; they had the easy friendship between them of brothers at arms. I was pleased, too, to see that Viviane had somehow come ahead of us, and stood beside Imogen. She smiled at Merlin politely and kissed him on the cheek when he came forward to greet her, but I knew enough to know that it was false, and illusory, and that made me feel more tense. When Viviane came forward to kiss me, she whispered at my ear:

"Have courage, Igraine. It will get easier."

She smiled down at Morgan standing before me, with my fingertips resting on her shoulders, gazing up with her grey eyes wide with curiosity.

"Good morning, Lady Morgan," Viviane said. Morgan just blinked up back at her, as though she were simple, but Viviane did not seem to mind.

Morgawse beside her crossed her arms over her chest, doubly affronted to be brought here, and then be ignored in favour of her little sister. Still, she became suddenly shy when Viviane turned to her. Viviane leaned down a little to talk to Morgawse, although she was almost grown.

"You are the Princess Morgawse," Viviane said kindly – and though I could see that Morgawse was afraid of the woad, she drew herself up, trying to be brave, responding to the kindness in Viviane's voice.

"I am, Lady," she said, for once quiet and careful.

Viviane touched her cheek fondly, and Morgawse gave her a wary, shy smile that I was utterly unused to on her bold, sulking face.

"You do not know me, little Morgawse, but I brought you into this world. You were a beautiful baby girl, and now I see you are almost a beautiful woman."

Morgawse smiled more broadly at this. I found, guiltily, that I was disappointed at how easily flattered my daughter was.

Uther gestured for us to follow him inside. I felt the panic flash within me, and I was pleased – and surprised – when, on an impulse, I took Viviane's hand and she did not slip it out of my grip.

* * *

I was relieved that we were provided with our own rooms, and no one tried to separate Brastias from us. I felt better having a knight of my own that I knew well by my side. There was a room for Morgan and Morgawse to share, with a big adult's bed that they could sleep in side by side, and one in my own room too. I had also brought Margaret the old nun from Tintagel, to help look after the girls, and she could sleep in the room with me if I needed someone else. I wondered where Brastias thought he would sleep. When we settled into the room, Morgawse went to sit on his lap and have him wrap his arms around her, but I tutted and shooed her away from him. He should have done that himself.

In the end, I slept with Morgan beside me in the bed, and Morgawse beside Margaret in the room next door. Morgawse was so angry with me that she would not be kissed or comforted by me, and instead screwed up her face and threatened to scream. I wished that I could have screamed with her, and we could both have screamed and screamed until the whole horror of it was undone. But I was a grown woman, and a widow, and she a girl almost of age. We had to be careful, and calm.

By the time I woke in the morning, Morgan had gone back to her sister next door with the precocious independence that I knew so well. And I woke up cold and alone in an unfamiliar bed, with no idea what would become of me.

I was nauseous and pale. Even in the hammered, poorly-polished mirror – not so fine as the one I had left behind at Tintagel – I could see that my skin was white and my eyes were puffy. I was conscious that, though Imogen was blind, men could still see *her*, and though she was twenty years older than I, she was beautiful still. I did not know why I should care for Uther's sake; it was ridiculous of me to think so sentimentally of the man who was my captor.

In the morning, Morgawse shuffled in, wearing her nightdress with her hair loose and breadcrumbs down her front as though she had eaten in bed. There was, too, I noticed, a little honey stuck in her hair. She had always loved sweet things – little fruits, honey, and cakes. Always greedy for everything pleasant. Always looking for the next pleasure, rather than planning for the future. I put out a hand to fondly stroke her hair, and she let me, still a little sulky, but sadder now the morning had come and her sulks had not got her taken home from Camelot. I held her close to me, and kissed the top of her head, remembering how she used to potter about as a little girl, grabbing at things with her fingers sticky with honey, and giggling when Gorlois picked her up in his arms, kicking her little feet with delight when he sang to her. All of a sudden, I wanted to cry. But I did not. I just held Morgawse tight and kissed the top of her head over and over again, and she turned in my arms and nuzzled her head into my chest as she had done when she was small.

"When will this be over?" she asked. Her voice was muffled, but I could hear the tears in it.

I sighed, smoothing down her hair. "I don't know, my love," I replied, though I knew the truth was that it would never be over. It could not be undone.

Morgan, who had come in silently behind her, and who was perfectly neat although she must have eaten the same breakfast, burrowed in between us. We stood there in a quiet embrace for a while, and I felt that if the rest of the world had fallen away, all might have been well; we might have been happy in a perfect world where it was just me and my girls.

I dressed them carefully, brushing their hair, and even found a coral necklace that had belonged to my mother and tied it around Morgawse's neck. Just months ago she would have been wild with excitement; today, she just smiled gently and at last let me kiss her on the cheek. Morgan fidgeted when I brushed her hair, but was quiet, and curled into my arms as I sat in the window seat and opened Gorlois' old book of Pwyll and began to read to her.

Morgawse was happy enough to sit beside us with her head resting against my leg. It was blissful, suddenly, to be with them like this, even though the rest of the world had changed.

It was all the more jarring and painful, and too soon, when a woman came to tell me to make ready to dine with Uther.

I took care to make myself as beautiful as I could. Not because I cared whether Uther looked on me with desire, but because I wanted to keep myself as safe and protected as possible. Looking like a proud queen was the best way to do that. I hoped that Uther would declare in public his intention to marry me, but I feared it was too much to hope for.

But he did, and it was worse than anything I could have feared. The place they set for me was far from Morgan and Morgawse, who were with the old nun Margaret, whom Morgan sat obediently beside but next to whom Morgawse wrinkled her nose in annoyance, while looking up at Brastias every few moments to see if he was watching her. I sat instead between Uther and Imogen. I was not sure if it was a place of honour, or of disgrace. Uther was seating me beside his whore, as though to remind me that there was another woman ready to take my place if I were too resistant. I did not turn to look at Imogen because, coward that I was, I was afraid to look into her blank, cloudy eyes. They were like the eyes of a fairy-person, and I was afraid they would put some spell over me. Imogen had not been raised a Christian, and I had heard it whispered that she had learned things in Avalon that had caused her to be cast out. I wondered if she used them on Uther to make him keep at his court a woman who was old, and blind, and barren. As I was wondering this, and watching her hands – still young and smooth-looking from years indoors, and decked in thick, ugly gold rings set with bright stones that she could not have possibly appreciated the look of herself – grip her cutlery and cut the food on her plate expertly into little pieces, Uther stood, his cup in his hand, and silence fell throughout the hall.

"There will be many men here," he began, his voice low, but carrying through the hall, "who wonder why it is that I have brought the Lady Igraine back to Camelot, and seated her at my side." He glanced at me then, and I felt my insides clench, though I was not sure if it was through fear, or a strange, perverse excitement. "The lady is late the widow of Duke Gorlois, and it is my intention to take her as my wife. I would have all men stand, to raise their cups and their voices in celebration of their new High Queen."

There was a raucous shouting, and a clanging of goblets. Uther's hall was a soldiers' barracks more than a court. He preferred to associate with his men, for he knew their pain and their struggles. He found politics hard, and I could see he would have preferred to be down there with the common soldiery, drinking and carousing and shouting. I thought of Ector, and his calm, suave, courtly ways, and of Gorlois, who had always complained of low birth, but who had been raised like a prince along with his foster-brothers in Rheged castle. It was only then that I caught the eye of a man sitting on the other side of the table, just a little way from the places of honour, as though deliberately left in the shade. Our eyes met, and I felt a jolt of familiarity pass through me that was not entirely pleasant. I knew his wolfish features, his sly, intelligent stare; I knew, too, the arrogant curl of his lip as he raised his gold cup to it. And yet I could not place him. He was *still* staring at me. I wished that Viviane were sat beside me, not Imogen, but Uther had her at his other side, and I was sure that, that night, he would take counsel of her and Merlin together.

"Who are you staring at, Igraine?" Imogen asked, making me jump. Her voice was attractive, low and rich and lovely, yet it made me tense right through.

"No one," I said sharply, entirely unsure how a blind woman would know I was staring.

Imogen raised a hand to her auburn hair, threaded lightly with grey at the temples, deftly tucking a stray lock back into place. Truly, she was graceful and beautiful despite everything. I felt an ugly spasm of jealousy deep in my stomach.

"Is it not King Lot of Lothian that you stare at?" she asked. I realised that she was right, though I did not know how she could have known that he was here, or that that was where I was looking. But the man *was*, unmistakably, Lot. He had grown what I was sure he fancied as a somewhat rakish beard – one that he was currently preening rather vainly with his fingertips – but apart from that he was hardly changed. I glanced back at him, unable to help myself. As though sensing the touch of my eyes, he turned and his eyes met mine, and he gave me a slight smile that I could not read. I smiled back, warily. The only memory I had of him was of a proud, bold youth in Aurelianus' courtyard, throwing off his rich surcoat to wrestle with Uther. I could not imagine what manner of man he was now, now he had surrendered himself and his armies to the man he had thrown into the dirt as a boy.

"It is no use to be telling me lies, Igraine," Imogen said, carefully. "You see, everyone is so sure that I see nothing with my eyes that they never bother to hide anything from me."

"No, I am sure it is not," I said, hostile, unwilling to get into a conversation with her. Uther had sat once more and was talking to Viviane beside him. He seemed careless, relaxed, unaware that beside me his lover was accusing me of lying, of *staring* at Lot of Lothian.

I felt Imogen lean closer beside me, but still I did not turn to look at her. I would not weaken, I would not show her that she had any effect on me. I would be Uther's wife; I had nothing to fear from a barren, ageing princess. Still, her breath brushed against my skin as she whispered in my ear, and it made my skin crawl.

"I would counsel you, sweet, pretty young Igraine," she hissed – making sure I knew that she could tell I was young and sweet and pretty – reaching out and stroking the smooth, fine strands of my hair, "not to imagine that every woman who has been in Uther Pendragon's bed is an enemy of yours. If it were so, you would be swiftly out of friends at court. Why, even Viviane, your bosom friend, coupled with Uther when he was made king by the old rites, after the crusty old bishop crowned him in the chapel."

I was sure she was lying.

* * *

That night I went to Uther, to his chamber, bold with my anger, and defiant. He was not surprised to see me when he opened the door. He had seen Imogen talking to me as we dined, and I could see the angry resignation on his face.

"Send Imogen from court," I demanded.

Uther gestured me into the room, and I came, so blinded by the emotion within me, my desperation not to be shamed, that I forgot all the danger of coming alone to Uther's bedchamber. Suddenly, instead of remembering what I ought to have done, I remembered how it had felt to have his arms around me, hot from the bath, in his tent, which I ought not to have been thinking about.

Uther shut the door behind me, rubbing his face with one hand.

"I cannot, Igraine."

"Why not?" I crossed my arms over my chest.

He sighed deeply. "She is Aurelianus' daughter. If I send her from here, some ambitious man will marry her and use it as an excuse to challenge me in everything that I do. I have to keep her here. It needs to be clear to everyone that no man can claim her –"

"So you have made her your *concubine*?" I said, derisively.

Uther shrugged. "Is this so different from how you behaved with Gorlois? I do what I must to keep myself safe. To stake my claim to my home."

Uther reached out to take my arm, and I took a step back, feeling the anger burn in my veins. It was *not* the same. He sighed again; this time the irritation was a little more throaty, a little more forceful.

"Don't play the innocent little maiden with me, Igraine. I never came to you wooing with promises that I would never take another woman to my bed. I promised you love, which I have never promised any other woman, and marriage, which I have also promised to no one else. I do not think that you can say the same."

I felt my cheeks burn. Perhaps he was right, but it wasn't fair, it wasn't fair of her to flaunt it in front of my face.

"Send her away, Uther. I don't want her there when we are married."

Uther gave a rough laugh. "Do you think she will push you aside at the altar and try to steal your place? It is as much an act of survival for her as it is for me, Igraine. This is not some silly love-story."

"Do you expect me to believe that? When you have lived with her almost as man and wife in Camelot for *years*, since you were crowned?"

Uther shrugged again. "A man likes to have a woman warm his bed. That is the natural way of it, Igraine. Do you think Gorlois lay every night in chastity, thinking of his lady wife all the time he was at war at my side? I do not ask you, either, if you gave in to nature's longing while he was away. I have seen you bend your head in the chapel, and wish away all of the gifts and delights that nature brings us. Or perhaps it is that you pray so eagerly for the sake of that handsome young knight of yours, Brastias, who pledged to me to live another day for the chance of seeing his lady again –"

"You are full of crude talk, Uther," I snapped, stepping forward, feeling my fists clench. "But I think you are trying to distract me from your own long list of sins. I can yet refuse to become your wife."

Uther grabbed my arm, hard, and pulled me up against him. I could feel his chest rising and falling with rough breaths against mine, and – or so I thought – his heart racing.

"You will not refuse. Do not toy with me, Igraine," he growled, close. His eyes moved over my face, taking it in, trying to read me, to see if I would really dare. He pulled me just a little closer, and I tilted my face up towards his, defiant. But as I did so, it also brought us closer, and I could not keep my eyes from his lips.

Suddenly he was kissing me once more, and I was kissing him in return, and his hands on me became passionate rather than forceful, one sliding into my hair, pulling my mouth deeper against his. I forgot for a moment, in the bliss of his touch, why I had been angry; forgot that I had wanted anything in coming to his chamber other than this heady passion. But, as his arm slid tight around my waist and drew me against him, I remembered, and I pushed him back. He did not move back – no, not very much at all – and he kept his forehead pressed against mine so that our breaths mingled between us, hot and quick, and I could not slip away and deny that I had felt what he had felt when we had come together in that kiss.

"If you are jealous, Igraine," he whispered, "stay here tonight. Lie with me in my bed, in this great king's bed in which I have had no other women, and I will turn all others away, for the rest of my life."

I shook my head. "Not until we are married."

He had his arms tight around me, and I was small and weak in comparison with him, so my protest would hardly have meant anything if he intended to have me in his bed anyway, but I was still a noble lady, and if I screamed there might be someone who would hear me. But instead, Uther brushed his hand down my cheek, and gently down my neck, and across the soft skin of my chest above the neckline of my dress, and said, "If you are satisfied with waiting, when you can have all you desire this very night, and I will let no shame fall on you…"

I looked him deep in the eyes and said, with all the cold detachment I could muster, "If you think you are *all* I desire, you are mistaken, my lord."

"And yet, Igraine," he whispered, his lips brushing against my ear, his teeth grazing it gently as I felt myself soften in his grip, and the flush of desire rise on my neck, "I think beneath the duty, and the piety and the prayers there is a woman of flesh and blood, and –"

Uther did not finish, for I had turned my face to his and, sliding my hands into his hair, pulled his mouth against mine in a passionate kiss. I was not sure. I was not sure if I was behaving wisely, if it was safe for me to give in to what I wanted, and yet in that moment I did not care. I had always been so sensible, so careful, and yet I had not felt a desire, a longing, as strong as I felt through my body in that moment. Uther's hands were already unwinding my hair, tugging at it a little, making me gasp, and he took my lip softly between his teeth, a little rough, a little teasing, and I felt with a delight that I had never dared to think I would feel that I was out of control of myself. I was lost in the rush of sensation, and a pleasant hunger that filled my limbs with warmth and made my head grow dizzy and light. Uther was murmuring my name and pulling at the laces of my dress, and I was sighing for him in return. It was just as I felt he was about to throw me down on the bed, and we would both be lost in a passionate wildness that I had always longed for yet never dared to know, that there was a knocking at the door that shattered through all of it.

It was only Uther's seneschal, a grizzled old warrior named Drusus with an ugly limp, bringing Uther some water for washing, but it broke the spell, and made me aware of myself once more. I hid behind the bed curtains, ashamed and afraid, and my daring did not hold. Uther thought I was some fool concerned with God and his angry saints, but I did not care for all that. I cared for my safety, and the lives of my daughters. I was aware of how precarious my position was.

When Drusus had gone, shuffling away on his maimed foot, and Uther came back to take me into his arms, I shied away from him, plaiting my hair back into place, hurrying towards the door. He caught me by the wrist and pulled me back towards him, but I was no longer so overtaken with desire that I would cast myself, and my reputation, into his hands.

Chapter twenty-three

I lay awake a long time wondering if I had made the right choice. It was easy to think that I had, with Morgan curled up tight beside me, sleeping peacefully as a cat, because it meant that I could be sure my daughters were safe, but then when I fell asleep, I dreamed that I had stayed in Uther's bed, and in the dream we twined together in all the blissful abandon I had shied away from. I felt my body grow hot with it, and I was sure I felt his lips against me in my dreams where I had never known them before: brushing over my nipples, and my stomach, and, softly, in the secret parts that longed for him.

The touch of his lips filled me with eagerness. I pulled him to me, and at our coming together I felt the beginnings of such a wild ecstasy that it woke me from my sleep, gasping and filmed with sweat, and ashamed. I was afraid, too, that I might have woken my little daughter with my shameful dream.

* * *

The next morning, I watched as Morgawse begged Brastias to comb her hair for her, and I saw the careful way he did it, wary of touching her too fondly; he must have been aware that we were alone, and Morgawse was approaching the age where she could be married. Tintagel would fall to her, and her heirs, and there must have been men at Uther's court who remembered that I had a daughter, and that she had a rich fortune. I had to make sure that Uther did not throw her to some solider of his as a final act of malice against Gorlois. I felt my heart quicken in fear. I would have to act fast, and perhaps Uther would be angry.

I set out looking for Viviane. I did not see why she would refuse me. Morgawse had no magic art in her, and yet I thought Viviane would take her and foster her in Avalon if I asked. She had always been kind to me, almost like the mother I had never known. I wondered if that was because she felt guilty for having been unable to save my mother from the childbed death from which she had saved me. I would not think of that now.

* * *

But I did not make it to Viviane, not that day. I did not make it because, as I rushed through the corridors, I was halted by the sight of Imogen emerging from her room, tucking a few strands of dark auburn hair back into her plait. Right behind her followed Uther. He was dressed, though in the casual way he always was, with his rich surcoat hanging open as though he could not bear to be neat as all the other men were, and yet the way he stepped out behind her, closing the door carefully, I knew that he had spent the night sleeping by her side. I shrank back, watching them walk their separate ways, as though they had done nothing of note at all.

I felt hot and breathless with my anger, and yet I was not sure that I had any right to it. Uther had been clear about his intentions, and he had not acted other than he had said. And yet I hated it. It felt like disrespect to me, and to everything he had promised me.

"It surprises me also, Lady Igraine, that Uther would prefer to take an old, blind woman to his bed, rather than one so lovely as you."

I jumped around at the deep voice behind me, and saw that Lot was standing there, leaning casually against the wall. I had not seen Lot for well over ten years, yet he had just spoken to me as though we were halfway through an intimate conversation. He, too, did not treat me with respect. I opened my mouth to protest, but he continued, leaning a little towards me conspiratorially.

"Yet, I have heard men say of Imogen that to take a blind woman as a lover is a delight. Women love to look at men, and if all a woman has to look with are her hands, then she will explore a man as thoroughly as a woman might with her eyes, and for the man there will be all the more pleasure."

I felt myself blush, and resented it. I was not some shy milkmaid. I had been wed. I knew what it was to feel the delight of another's touch. How was it that the men could talk about it so, and we could not? The secrets I knew about what women wanted might have shocked even one so smug as Lot. For he was still smug. Still handsome and strong-limbed, still sly and calculating – all dark eyes and thick, black hair, and a voice so persuasive that it could only be telling lies. I felt myself tighten against his presence. I could see that he had grown from a bold young man into a practised seducer of women. I could tell by the way he leant a little towards me that he thought himself attractive, and I met it with bold defiance.

"Have you then, sir, enjoyed the caresses of the Lady Imogen?"

He laughed again. "Long ago, perhaps. I would not like to say." He leaned a little closer to whisper, "Though I would not wish to deny you the pleasure of your sight if you would –"

"You forget yourself, Lot," I said sharply, crossing my arms over my chest, squaring up to him. "Has the north grown so barbarous that all men speak to all women this way?"

Lot gave a strange, thoughtful smile, and said, "Has the south grown so pious and dull that it is now considered an offence to tell a lady she is beautiful?"

He was gone before I could protest, and I resented it. He had caught me off-guard.

* * *

I did not find Viviane. Viviane came to me as I sat in the evening with Brastias and my little girls. I wondered if Uther knew that Brastias still attended me. It was only right. He was my husband's faithful knight, and I knew it would cause him pain to be separated from us. But I could only imagine Uther's face tightening with anger to know that it was Brastias, and not he, who spent the evenings by my side. Oh, Uther would have me dine beside him, but then he would go as I grew tired and the evening grew late. It was not his will. Merlin would take him by the hand and lead him off, to whisper in his ear. And I saw that I was not the only one to be displeased. The men whispered among one another to see it, and even blind old Imogen followed them with her unseeing gaze as they left, and folded her hands in unhappy contemplation in her lap.

As the door opened and Viviane stepped in, I got to my feet. I rushed over to greet her, and she kissed me on each cheek.

"Igraine, my dear, you look tired," she said; her tone was gentle and kind. I nodded, feeling – as I always did around Viviane – like a girl of fifteen once more.

"Brastias," I said, half-turning over my shoulder towards him, "will you take the girls to their room?"

Morgawse grumbled and pouted, and would not put her face up

to be kissed goodnight on the cheek, but Morgan took her kiss meekly as she always did, as though it were nothing more than a passing breeze, and said 'Goodnight, Mother' in her quiet voice, following her sister and Brastias out.

"Morgawse grows beautiful," Viviane said; her tone was thoughtful and anxious.

"She is still a child yet," I said.

Viviane shook her head. "Not by the old measure of childhood and womanhood, Igraine."

I knew she was right. But I had been married years after I began to bleed, and I had other hopes for Morgawse. Now was the time I had to be brave. I drew in a deep breath, taking Viviane by each hand and fixing her with the steadiest stare I had within me.

"I want you to take Morgawse away, as soon as you can, and foster her in Avalon."

Viviane sighed, and I thought for a moment that she would agree, but then her face creased into an awful look of sorrow and resignation. "Igraine, I cannot."

"Why not?" I pleaded, holding her hands tighter as she tried to step back from me. I knew that she could feel my desperation, but I had no room in my heart for shame. "*Please*, Viviane. I will pledge you anything you wish in return. *Please*. Uther is not happy to have her here, and she is young and heir to Cornwall. There are many who would –"

"Igraine," Viviane interrupted, and I fell silent. "It is not for lack of my own wishing that I do not take Morgawse to Avalon. If I could –"

"Why can you not?" I begged.

"Igraine." Her voice was low, and I could see in her eyes that she was truly sorry, but I felt my heart sink. "She would not survive it. She would for a while, but she does not have the blood of our people in her. She would grow sick, after a time –"

"But could you not keep her there long enough –"

Viviane shook her head. "I could not, in good conscience. I can only suggest that you find her a husband who can take care of her."

"That is not much better!" I protested, feeling my cheeks flush. "How safe will her young life be when some man gets her with child? Better she should take her chances in Avalon –"

"Igraine, be *reasonable* –"

"At least take Morgan now, for you will have her in the end."

Viviane sighed heavily once more. "But I am not in Avalon now, and I must stay at court a little while. I hesitate to entrust Morgan's education to another. She is strong; she does not know it, you would not sense it, but there is powerful magic in her blood. She can heal with her touch. I have seen her pick up an injured mouse, and after the moment she holds it, it runs from her hands, full of life. With the wrong teacher –"

I nodded. So that was the excuse. I was ignorant. I had no magic. Viviane would not take my child. I had no blood guarantee from Avalon that they would help me.

"It must be to the nuns at Amesbury, then, for Morgan?" I said.

Viviane nodded. "They will teach her well and she will become wise, and that is no bad thing. But why not the nuns for Morgawse?"

I gave a harsh laugh. "You know Avalon, Viviane, but I know my daughters. Morgawse will prefer marriage and childbearing to a home with the nuns."

Viviane nodded in silent thoughtfulness, kissed me on the cheek, and left. It was only after she had gone that I remembered what Imogen had said about Viviane and Uther, and I lay awake all night, trying not to picture it in my mind.

Chapter twenty-four

The solution struck me, quite by accident, the next time I was compelled to sit at a public dinner at Uther's side, less his wife than Imogen at my own side, in whose bed he slept at night. I was staring into space, trying to remember what Tintagel's great hall had looked like, when Imogen leaned down beside me. I did not hear what she said because I was remembering what she had said to me the last time she had done this. *Is it not King Lot of Lothian that you stare at?* There he was, sat right there before me, his head held low over his plate of food – for all his fine clothes and neat beard, eating like a savage, for he had long been among only men in his halls. I remembered a story, long ago, that he had married among the Pictish tribes, but lost his wife to the childbed along with their first child. Despite what he had said about Picts and mixed blood, he had mixed his own *noble ancient blood* with one of them. Never the man of principle. Never the man of his word. And yet he had married for love. That was what they had said. And he had loved her so dearly that he had not married again in the long years since her death. He had been a young man then, and more than ten years had passed. He looked in need of a woman's care, a woman's civilizing presence. Morgawse would not bring him that, but he need not know it until he had accepted her as his wife.

Morgawse grows beautiful, I heard Viviane say once again, and as though she had heard her own voice echoing in my head, she turned to look at me, her eyes hesitant and wary. I looked away. It was what must be done.

Imogen beside me continued, "And you, always staring like the rustic you are –"

"Better to be always staring, Imogen," I interrupted, "than always talking."

She was quiet for a moment, bereft of a reply.

* * *

I sent Brastias for Lot that night, with my message. I could feel my heart thudding. I was glad that Morgan, who slept always like a little cat, sudden and deep, could be left in her room and trusted not to wake, with the old nun Margaret sleeping in a chair by the door like a guardian statue. Morgawse was quiet for once, nervous. She half-understood what I had told her about the man coming to see her, about what this meant for her.

Viviane had called her beautiful, but she still looked like a child to me, and beautiful was too much the word for a grown woman. She looked, also, so much like Gorlois. His bright blue eyes were even more lovely on her face. They suited her feminine features far more than his rough, soldierly looks, and his red-gold hair grown long in her girls' style showed its full beauty – and yet she was still a girl. It was the promise of loveliness, nothing more. What was I doing? She was so young. Was this really the only way?

"Are you sure about this, Igraine?" Brastias' voice – low, intrusive, judgemental – cut through my thoughts. I tensed against it, and all my doubts fell away in obstinate resistance to his questioning. "He is almost as old as her father."

I would not scold Brastias like the boy he was in front of Morgawse, but he ought not to have dared to question me.

"Then he will be a good protector for her," I answered sharply. I turned my back on Brastias deliberately, turning to Morgawse. She looked up at me; so small, and soft, and young. I put my hand against her cheek. It was still a child's cheek, soft as velvet, warm, a little damp. Either she had got it sticky with sweets and been freshly scrubbed by the nurse, or she had been crying. I shied away from that possibility. I gave her the bravest smile I could. She had to think that I was pleased, that this was good. This *was* ordinary. Because I had avoided an arranged marriage did not mean that there were not hundreds of brides in Britain who had gone to their marriage beds as she would: to a much older man, young and afraid.

"He is one of the most powerful kings in Britain. It is an honour for you, Morgawse," I told her, and she nodded, mustering all the seriousness she could. She was not even twelve years old.

"He is one of the *richest* kings," Brastias said behind me, pointedly, and I bristled against it. Why did he think he had a right to act as though he were Morgawse's protector and I was not? He was neither mother, nor father, nor brother to her. I ignored him, and kissed Morgawse tenderly on the forehead.

"When he comes, Morgawse, be good and quiet."

For once, she did not object.

* * *

Lot came dressed in his finest clothes. I was sure he wanted to impress upon me that he was strong, and I was vulnerable, and that if he took my daughter as his wife, then I would be obliged to him for the years to come. I would *not* give Morgawse into his hands on those terms. In the low firelight the gold thread in his midnight-blue surcoat glinted, and I could see that he had combed and oiled his black hair to a glossy, lacquer-like sheen.

"My lady, Queen Igraine." Lot greeted me with a polite bow, as though he had not, after over a decade, crept up behind me to ask me crude questions about Uther and Imogen. Was he putting on this act for Brastias' benefit? For Morgawse's? Or just to play with me? I got the sense he liked a game.

"Is this the girl?" he said, baldly, as though he were inspecting a horse. He looked at Morgawse. I saw her tense under his gaze, hold back a flinch. He must have looked so old to her. I felt a knot of pain tighten inside me. She was being brave. She must have understood on some level that it must be done. Brave like her father. No, I would not think of him. Lot turned back to me, his brow knitted in displeasure. "My Lady Igraine… she is a child."

He turned to her before I could protest, and asked her, "How old are you, Morgawse?"

I answered for her. "She is twelve years old. If the marriage takes place the day we have agreed for it, she will be a month away from turning thirteen. She is of age."

There were girls married before their time, but I did not want Lot to have any excuse to treat her as less than a royal princess, of equal station with him.

Lot made a doubtful noise in his throat.

"She is a woman," I added, softly. "She has bled."

He turned back to her. "Is that true?" he asked her, and she nodded, blushing so dark against her pale skin that her freckles seemed to disappear among the red. He *was* measuring her like a horse. Was she fertile? Was she strong? Then came the question I had expected.

"So, what is the dowry? Tintagel castle, of course, and Cornwall. What else has she inherited? Will King Uther add anything?"

I could feel Brastias' eyes on me, his burning desire to say, *King Uther does not know.* He held his tongue.

"My lord Uther wishes to keep Tintagel castle in his possession, and Gorlois' gold, until Morgawse bears a son," I said. In truth, I did not know what Uther would do, only that he would not be pleased, and that he would not part willingly with Gorlois' gold. Still, this would buy Morgawse time. Once she had a son, Lot would not rid himself of her – not if he had any sense.

I saw Lot's gaze darken, his jaw tense. I knew that would displease him. I drew myself up to my full height.

"So there is nothing?" he demanded. I shook my head, ready to protest, but he carried on. I could see the whites of his eyes, and the angry flush on his cheeks. "There are adult princesses in Britain with coffers full of gold and rich lands whom I could marry. Not just in Britain; in Brittany and France. In Scandinavia. Why would I want to marry a child with nothing to offer but herself?"

"Which princesses, Lot?" I demanded in return, my own anger rising to meet his. I *knew* I was right. There were women in their thirties, and infant princesses in Ireland, and Brittany, and in the southern French lands, but no one of his station Morgawse's age. None who would want to ally themselves to a vassal king. No one who would want to go to the awful, savage north. "I know what goes on in my own lands, and there is no one of Morgawse's lineage and status who is of age. Is gold what you want, Lot? You have plenty of gold. Morgawse is the King of Britain's daughter by marriage. Her father was a great warrior; she will bear strong sons, and marriage with her will give you honour."

Lot nodded, and I was surprised that he seemed to be yielding to my persuasion so easily. Perhaps he had not thought of it. Men had said that he loved the wife he had lost, and that no man had been able to persuade him to marry since. Perhaps he was, beneath it all, a sensitive man, and he would take good care of Morgawse.

He looked back up at me, and the look in his eye caught my breath. It was awful: sadness, mixed with pity and loss. "My lady," he said, "I knew Gorlois. He was a brave man."

I suddenly felt as though Lot and I were alone, and for a moment he was not an arrogant, greedy young man, but an old and intimate friend, and I felt the colour rise in my cheeks as I became aware of my vulnerability, the closeness of the wound of Gorlois' loss to the surface of my skin. "The news of his death saddened me."

I turned away, suddenly afraid that for the first time I would cry in public for Gorlois' loss. Brastias put his arm around my shoulders, and I did not turn him away. I was aware, obliquely, of the scent of his skin, like straw, like horses, and awfully that reminded me even more of Gorlois.

I heard Lot say, thoughtfully, "She has his look."

I turned back, composing myself, running a comforting hand over my hair, and realised that he was looking at Morgawse, his fingers lightly under her chin, turning her face up towards the firelight.

"So then," I said, in the steadiest voice I could manage, "we have an agreement?"

He let his hand drop, and fixed me with the same harsh, beady look I knew – all the intimacy and sympathy dissolved away, replaced with the gold he saw reflected in Morgawse's red-gold locks and Celtic looks.

"I will consider it," he said impassively.

* * *

Brastias took Morgawse to bed; I expected him to leave, but he did not. He came back and silently put his arms around me. I closed my eyes, leant my head into his broad chest, and wept without a sound. I felt his breath on the top of my head, and the warmth of his body wrapped around mine; with my eyes closed, he could have been Gorlois. It had been like a knife thrust into me to hear his name again. I had closed that off, I had pushed it to the depths of my mind.

After a long time – too long, too long for a lady to stand embracing her lost husband's knight – I pushed him away. Brastias placed a soft kiss against my cheek, over the tears that had fallen there, and left.

* * *

I could not sleep, so I walked out into the corridor when all were sleeping. It was a clear winter night, and the moon was out – big as a dragon's eye, hanging fat in the sky. I stood in the narrow corridor, staring at it, and the sight of it made me feel a little better, though it made me think also of the White Goddess, of love and death. I could not think of her without feeling horribly guilty for Gorlois' death. I was not sure, really, why I should think it was my fault.

I heard my name softly behind me, and turned to see that Lot was there, hanging back, hesitating, as though there were something that he wanted to say but did not quite have the courage for. It was strange. I had never thought of him as a hesitant man, but I supposed that I didn't really know him. No, I didn't know him at all, but I was going to entrust my daughter to his care anyway.

"Lot," I said, turning my back on the window, on the empty sky I had been staring out into. "You aren't sleeping either."

He shook his head.

"Igraine." He came closer and leaned against the wall the other side of the narrow little corridor we stood in, his arms crossed over his chest, looking at me, thoughtful. "Is this really what you want?"

"What do you mean?" I asked. I didn't want to volunteer anything myself, but also I did not really want to talk to him about it. I was afraid it would all spill out of me. I felt emotional, vulnerable, as though every feeling was close to the surface; my skin was dangerously fragile for holding all of it in.

He shrugged. "All of this, I suppose. Are you sure you want me to marry Morgawse, take her all the way back north with me? You will not see much of her."

"Lot," I sighed, pressing the heel of my hand into my forehead, "do you think I have that much of a choice?"

I did not know why I was being so honest with him. Perhaps it was the late night, or the way he had spoken about Gorlois, but I felt that my guard was suddenly down around him.

"What do you mean?" He was pushing me, and I was not sure why. I was not sure if he was going to offer me his sympathy, or if he was just self-interested. He took another step closer. "Has Uther threatened her?"

I shook my head, "No, Lot –"

"He has, hasn't he?"

"No, and you shouldn't say that," I snapped. I was conscious that we were alone, late at night, huddled together talking in half-whispers in some nook of the castle, and the worst thing for both of my children would be if I was thought to be speaking against Uther, especially to one of his vassals. "But she's another man's child. That's enough. He hasn't said anything, but I don't think it's wise to keep her here. You've seen her. No one will be mistaking who her father is."

Lot planted one of his hands on the wall I was leaning against, and leant closer. I remembered, with a sudden flash, the first time I had seen him, when he had been nothing more than a bold young prince with an eye on Aurelianus' empty throne. I realised that that was what I had been seeing before me. But now he had been king of his own kingdom long, and he had tasted defeat and subjugation at Uther's hands. He was hardened, and fully a man, a sovereign and a warrior, and I had been underestimating him. He wore the years on him worse than I did. He was scarred on his hands, and on his face. I could see a thin line, white and puckered, just at the edge of his dark beard.

"This is not your only choice, Igraine," he said quietly.

"I think it is," I whispered back.

He leaned a little closer, and I felt myself tense. "Come with me, and be Queen of Lothian."

He moved as though to kiss me, and I turned my face away from his, moving to slip under his arm and run away, but he caught me with his other hand by the shoulder, and pinned me back against the wall.

"*Consider it*, Igraine," he insisted. Still pressing my shoulder into the wall, with his other hand he brushed his fingers lightly against my throat. I felt my heart thud against his touch in fear, though it was gentle, as it trailed up my throat. Curling a finger under my chin, he turned my face to his. "Do you think that I have forgotten, all those years ago, that Uther and I fought over you in Aurelianus' great courtyard? Oh, it was a boy's game, but I remember who won it."

"I remember, too," I said, "who won the wars in the north, and who swore vassalage to whom."

Lot leaned the weight of his body further in towards me, and we were almost pressed together. I could not tell if he was trying to intimidate me, or if he thought he was being seductive.

"If you feel so sure there is nothing between us," he continued, changing the subject as though he did not want to speak of his past failures, but also – strangely – with the assumption that we had some kind of history, "then why should I accept Morgawse as my wife, when you are offering me *so little* in return?"

"I am offering you *everything I have*." It was hard to keep my voice below a shout, and to keep my desperation from it. "Tintagel castle, my home, Gorlois' gold, my father's gold. *Everything I have to give*, Lot. It will all be yours, when it belongs to your sons with Morgawse. Sons who will be brave, strong men like Gorlois was. That is all I have to give, and I am offering you all of it."

I felt Lot's arm slide down from my shoulder and around my back to pull me up against him. "Not all, Igraine."

I slapped him, hard, across the face. I wished that someone would come, although I would be in as much trouble as he was. I wanted to get away. I felt as though I was on the verge of crying once more, and I would *not* cry in front of Lot.

He pressed his fingers tentatively to his cheek where my hand had caught him, and looked at them, but there was no blood. I had not hit him as hard as I could have done. But I was prepared to, the second time. He looked from his fingers to me. The look was cold, and I was acutely aware in that moment that he was a man with a veneer of public charm; underneath there was an endless well of cruelty.

"Do you think Uther Pendragon lies chaste in his bed, while you refuse to fuck him until he makes you his wife? It seems clear to me that you are pregnant with his child."

I should have denied that I was pregnant, but he had caught me too much by surprise and my hand had already gone to my stomach, though it showed nothing.

"If I *am* with child, it is *my husband*'s child," I hissed.

Lot grabbed my arm again, pulling me up towards him. "Which husband, Igraine? Your dead husband? Your future husband? Do you think Uther Pendragon and his witch do not know that you have a child growing inside you?"

"What makes *you* so sure I have?" I demanded, though I knew I had given myself away. I wanted to know if people were talking. Who I could trust.

"Your breasts are swollen," he said with an unpleasant smile, and made a move as though he would try to press his hand against them. I slapped him again, harder this time, and made sure my ring caught against his lip. It seemed appropriate; it was Gorlois who had given it to me. I wished, painfully, that he was alive. Men had respected him for his goodness, in a way that they never would with Uther, though they feared his strength, and not one of them would have spoken to me like this while he lived.

"How dare you treat me this way," I said, my voice low with anger.

Lot shook me, hard, his hands tight around my arms. A thin trail of blood ran down from his lip, where my ring had caught it.

"I am trying to make you understand what kind of a man I am, Igraine. Aside from the fact that she has no lands, no wealth and barely a name, you are giving me a twelve-year-old girl as a bed mate and expecting me to be *satisfied*. I would prefer a woman my own age."

"I don't expect you to be *satisfied*," I cried. "I am asking you to take her into your protection. And don't pretend that she has nothing. Don't pretend that you don't want Tintagel. That you don't want *sons*.

You are old to be beginning a family, Lot. Many men have three or four sons already by now."

"Not Uther. Not Gorlois," he said, deliberately cruel.

"Morgawse is young. She is strong, she is brave. She will give you sons like her father. I will give you none."

"I think, Igraine…" He pulled me closer once more, and I wished that I had the strength to throw him off me, "you underestimate what a woman like you, who has been given proper instruction by a husband already, has to offer a man like me." He pulled me closer still, pressing his mouth against my ear. I felt his breath, warm and unpleasantly intimate against my neck. "Once, Igraine. Come to bed with me just once, tonight, and I will accept your daughter as my wife."

I pushed him back, as far as I could, and I shook my head.

"You will take her anyway, Lot, because you are vain and greedy and you want the gold. You won't have me as well. There are other men in Britain that would be glad to wed my daughter."

"Then *be aware*, Igraine," he said, his hand tightening on my arm one last time as I tried to slip away, "that I have no intention of waiting until your daughter is grown, or until she grows old enough and curious enough to ask me for it. I am not going to accept your offer only to have someone else come and claim her. I will make sure no one else can. And I will have these sons you promise me as soon as I can get them."

I felt sick. Morgawse *was* still a child, and Lot was not just a man grown, but a brutal and ruthless king.

"Don't hurt her," I said, though my voice was more pleading than commanding. Lot let go of me, and I stumbled back a step. I did not realise until then that I had been holding my breath. He shrugged.

"I can make no promises on that account. It is beyond *my* control."

"*Stop*," I hissed, but he had already turned to go, bored and disappointed since he had not got what he wanted. I waited until I could no longer hear his footsteps, and then threw myself into the nearest empty room to vomit. There was nothing in my stomach but bile, but it kept coming, as though my body was desperate to rid itself of his touch, his words. When at last it abated I drew myself back up to standing. I drew in my breath, and smoothed down my dress and wiped the tears from my cheeks. I tucked the stray strands of hair back into their little clasp, and then I was ready to go back to my room, to Morgan and Morgawse and Brastias as though nothing had happened. As though I were not afraid for them, or for myself. Or for the child who was still inside me, barely yet alive, not yet even quickening in my womb, but a still, silent promise of a memory of Gorlois. I tried not to think about what Uther would do when the child was born. I would face that when it came to it.

Chapter twenty-five

When I got back to my room, Morgan was asleep, curled up like a cat on the corner of the bed, but Morgawse was sitting with Brastias in the window-seat, as though neither of them could sleep either. I was annoyed that they were all in my bedroom, that I could not have a little privacy; that Brastias who I had set to putting the girls to sleep had let Morgawse stay up and wriggle coquettishly in his lap when I had been trying to secure her a husband. He was reading to her, or trying to, and she was leaning over the book, pointing at the words, leaning towards him, her bright mischievous eyes on his face, rather than the words on the page. After everything I had just endured for her sake, I felt a flash of anger in me that I knew I did not have a right to feel. But it was bright and painful and intense all the same.

"Morgawse, why are you still awake? Go to bed. And why did you let your sister fall asleep here? You were supposed to be taking care of her. Honestly, Morgawse. You're a woman now, but I wouldn't know it from the way you behave."

I was harsher with her than I should have been, but she had to understand. She couldn't flirt with Brastias, as had always been her game before she had even known what it was, or run through the castle, or spend her days in reckless freedom. She was about to become someone's wife. She had to understand that.

Morgawse made a face, sliding down sulkily from the window seat. She poked Morgan's arm with one finger, and Morgan, quiet and unfazed as she always was, blinked slowly awake.

"Time to go to bed, Morgan," Morgawse said, her voice still the voice of a sulking child. It was as though she had forgotten that, just hours before, she had endured Lot's measuring looks, and had not understood it at all.

Morgan nodded, rubbing her eyes, and slipped from the bed to take her sister's hand. I stopped as they went past me to scoop Morgan up into a tight embrace and kiss her cheek. She wrapped her little arms around my neck, and rested her head on my shoulder. Morgawse scowled up at me. She was angry that she was in trouble and her sister was not, but Morgan was quiet and well-behaved, and

Morgawse refused to even try to understand the rules, let alone abide by them.

"Goodnight, Morgawse," I said, mustering all the kindness I had the patience for. She glowered at me as I set Morgan back down beside her, and she led her little sister out of the room. I watched them go with a small sigh. I wished I could make them understand how difficult a position we were in. Wards of their father's enemy, prisoners – just three vulnerable, disenfranchised women. They had taken my castle, they had killed Gorlois' men. It was just us three women and Brastias, who was Uther's knight now, really. Although his heart was with us, he would not – could not – act against his lord.

"Lady Igraine," Brastias began hesitantly from the window-seat, but I turned to him and cut him off before he could speak.

"Brastias, you need to be careful how you behave around Morgawse. She's young and… imaginative. And she's bound to be someone else's wife. I don't want her getting upset, or you getting into trouble –"

"It's settled, then?" Brastias said, and I could hear the disapproval in his voice. He had no right to disapprove. He was neither Morgawse's father nor her guardian.

"Yes," I said tersely, "it is settled."

He paused, as though there was something he dared not say, but I knew what it was.

"Are you sure that this is for the best, Igraine?" he said.

I put my hand against my forehead, shaking my head. "No, Brastias, it is not *for the best*, but it is the only thing to be done."

I felt him take hold of a little of the sleeve of my dress, just below the shoulder, and give it a tug. I turned and looked. The shoulder seam of my dress was ripped open, where Lot's rough grip had torn the fabric, and on the other side there was a little tear at the neck, near the top of the shoulder. It was a fine dress, delicate silk. It had torn easily.

"*How* did you settle it?" Brastias asked, very quiet.

I shook my head.

"That's a bruise," he said softly, and began to pull back the dress fabric at my shoulder to look further. I stepped back, defensive, angry, upset.

"Brastias, what are you doing?" I snapped, "get your hands off me. I suppose you think because you share little teenage confidences with my daughter that we are more than just a lady and her knight, but don't confuse *vassalage* with anything else, and do not touch me, or my clothes without my express permission again. You overstep the bounds of your place, Brastias."

Brastias stepped back; I could see the hurt pass across his face, but I was afraid. I felt like an animal, my heart racing, afraid of another's touch, afraid of showing any vulnerability.

"Leave, Brastias. Please," I said, turning my face away from him, choking on the words. I was not going to cry again. I wanted to be on my own.

"My Lady Igraine," he said with a bow. When he reached the door, he stopped, and turned back, and said very softly, "I will not stop caring for you, or your daughters, my lady, just because it is beyond my place."

* * *

I spent the day alone. No one wanted to see me. They were all angry with me for something or other. Morgawse because I had scolded her; Brastias because I had scolded him; Lot and Uther because I would not go to bed with them. Only Morgan was not angry, but Morgawse must have been keeping her to herself because she did not climb in through the bed curtains in the morning asking to be read to. And she did not come in the afternoon as I read by myself the same old book of stories Gorlois had given me when he had asked me to be his wife. I loved those stories. I loved how they never changed. Every time I read them, the same people were there. No one died who was not expected to die, no mystery was new. I knew it all. Every page. Every lovely word. But I had never learned to read it in his own language, or to speak the words he knew, and eventually the thought made me sad. I closed it and instead watched the men out of the window, training in the courtyard below.

* * *

It was only in the evening, when I sat by the light of the candle brushing out my hair, staring through the window at the stars in the crisp winter night, that someone came. Two people. Uther and Brastias, right through the door, without knocking.

I stood as Uther strode in. His face was dark with anger, and when I caught Brastias' eye, I saw guilt and regret, and I knew what he had done.

"Igraine," Uther began, his voice tense with anger. "Brastias tells me that Lot has harmed you. Tell me what happened."

I shook my head. "Brastias is mistaken. We argued. That is all."

"About your daughter's marriage?" Uther asked. I nodded, feeling my stomach drop away from inside me. *Brastias has told him, even about that. Brastias has betrayed me.* I felt sick, vulnerable, and alone.

"Take off your dress," he ordered.

I crossed my arms over my chest, looking between him and Brastias. Brastias turned to leave, but Uther put out a hand against his chest, stopping him.

"No, Brastias, you will stay and the truth of what you said will be proved or disproved. Besides…" There was a cruel flicker in Uther's eye, as he stared straight at me. "I am sure you have already pictured in your mind the sight of your mistress slipping out of her dress, and perhaps her underdress as well. I doubt there was a man in her service that did not imagine himself pressing his lips against the white skin of her throat, her breasts –"

"My lord Uther," Brastias pleaded. I could see that he was blushing, and he looked down at his boots, one hand shielding his eyes from me, as though from the painful brightness of the sun. I was about to protest when Uther spoke again.

"Take off your dress, Igraine."

I could feel my heart racing inside me, my blood rushing with nowhere to go. I supposed he expected me to refuse, to be shy and demure. I wasn't afraid of him, though. If he wanted to look at what he had driven me to, so be it. Slowly, I reached behind me to pull the laces of my dress open, and slid it down off my shoulders and let it fall to the ground. The truth of what Brastias had said was painfully obvious. In my underdress, the dark purpling marks of Lot's fingers showed around both of my arms, and some marks, too, against my collarbone and shoulder on one side.

"Look at her, Brastias," Uther said, quietly.

Slowly, Brastias looked up at me. He avoided my eye, and I did not blame him.

"You lied to me, Igraine," Uther said. "Where else has he touched you?"

I didn't answer. I was staring at Brastias. I could not quite understand why he had done this. Did he think he was helping me? Or did he think it would make Uther stop the marriage? I knew he was against it. Of course he was. He wasn't thinking about his responsibilities. He was thinking about Morgawse, and giving her what she wanted, just like her father had always done. This was all about *her*, about his thinking he had some special role protecting her. It left me in the position where I always had to be the one saying no to her. It wasn't fair.

"No, Uther, listen. We argued, and he took hold of me – he was angry, it was –"

"Why was he angry?" Uther demanded.

I opened my mouth to speak but I did not know what I wanted

to say. I did not know what the right answer was. Uther strode across the room and took my hands in his. Holding them out, his eyes glossed over the bruises on my arms and lighted on the one at my shoulder. His fingers went to the laces at the front of my underdress and my body tensed with apprehension. I closed my hand around his.

"My lord Uther, no, I –"

But he swatted my hand away from his, and loosened the laces, sliding the underdress down off my shoulder and tracing his fingers along the bruise. The touch was gentle, and his gaze was soft now that he was looking at me this close. I realised it had been a long time, an awfully long time since I had felt the friendly touch of someone else. Despite everything, despite his barging in here and demanding that I take off my dress, despite the war, despite his roughness, and his unkindness, I felt myself weaken. I remembered the moment before his seneschal had knocked at his door, when I had almost given in. I wanted to close my eyes against it, but Brastias was there, and besides we were not yet married.

Uther slid the dress down a little further, and out of the corner of my eye, I could see Brastias look down at his feet once more. Uther's fingers left the bruise, tracing down across the curve of the top of my breasts. My chest rose and fell against his touch with the breaths that were coming to me harder and faster now. After Lot's roughness, and my deep loneliness, I ached for more. My head was swimming.

Though Brastias was there, Uther slid his other arm around my waist, and pulled me against him, into a kiss. It was deep and sensual, protective, and I was lonely. I was fragile, and afraid. I was half-naked and bruised, and the comfort of a man's kiss seemed to bring warmth back to my body. If Brastias had not been there, I would have sighed aloud with it.

"Brastias," Uther said, drawing away from the kiss, but not turning over his shoulder to face Brastias, "you may leave now."

Brastias caught my eye over Uther's shoulder. He was stuck. He could not disobey his lord but he did not want to leave me alone with him. I gave him the slightest nod I could to tell him I understood. With a bow, he left and closed the door. Uther slid the other sleeve of the underdress over my shoulder, and it fell down to my waist. His fingers brushed the sides of my breasts, and the skin there grew warm and bright with it, but I resisted. He would not bring me here to shame me and throw me away. Whatever he said, whatever Merlin said, I was not so foolish that I did not believe that was possible. He let his forehead rest against mine. I felt his breath against my lips, his nose brush against mine, his lips against my lips. And my mouth opened in just a small sigh of anticipation for him as he took my breasts fully in his hands and I felt the warmth of his touch against my bare skin. Gorlois had never been like this, never confident and commanding, never assertive, never daring. But he had always been careful, and gentle, and tender. His desire had been a natural part of his love, whereas with Uther I was sure that desire was by far the leader of his emotions. He brushed his thumbs over my nipples, first soft and light, then more firmly, and I felt myself flush with desire and pleasure at his touch. *I should not want this*, I thought. Bruised from Gorlois' loss, from Lot's violence, I ought to have been repulsed by the touch of any man, and yet there was a peculiar comfort in Uther's touch. *I should not*, I thought, distantly. Only a few weeks widowed. I should not.

But at the touch of his tongue against mine, and his hands against my skin, I pushed aside my guilt, and I leaned into the little comfort I was being offered. Uther began pushing back the skirts of the underdress as he walked us back into the alcove of the window seat. I felt his hands slide up my thighs, and then his fingers brushing, just teasing, dangerously tempting. I put my hands on his.

"It is only a few days until we will be married," I said.

Uther drew away and I found that I was disappointed. I felt hot and tense, and though I knew this was what I ought to have done, I wished deeply that I had not. Uther braced one of his hands against the window frame, and leaned down over me, giving me a long, steady look.

"I have waited twelve years to have you as my wife, Igraine. I can wait a few days more."

I reached out and took his free hand, guiding it up beneath my skirts. He closed his eyes, and I saw his jaw tense.

"Igraine –"

I seized hold of him by the front of his shirt and pulled his mouth down onto mine. His fingers went inside me, hard at first, making me gasp, but then softer, teasing, pressing and drawing away. His other arm slid around my waist, lifting me against him. I was already lost in it, in the tightening frustrations of coming delight. His teeth grazed my neck, my breast, and I shivered against his touch. I was still swimming in it, still heavy and foggy with fading pleasure when he leaned down and whispered in my ear.

"If Lot touches you again – if he comes near you – you can tell him that I will treat his wife with the same disrespect as he has treated mine."

He left before I could protest and, still reeling from his touch, from Brastias' betrayal, from all of it, I was struck with the horror of his words.

The warmth on my skin evaporated as fast as it had come, and when I climbed into bed I felt small, and terribly alone again. When I slept, I dreamed that there was a man sleeping beside me. I was sure it was Gorlois and I reached out to wind my arms around him; he rolled onto me and took me in his arms. It was only when our mouths met and I felt the brush of a rough beard against my lips, that I knew that the man I was dreaming of was not Gorlois, but Lot. I struggled against him in the dream until I woke myself, tangled in my sheets and gasping for my breath.

Chapter twenty-six

The next day when Brastias came, I was cold and aloof with him. He had Morgan in his arms, and when he put her down, she ran over to me and climbed into my lap. I wrapped her tightly in my embrace, and kissed the top of her head. She turned around to face me, her grey eyes wide with incomprehension.

"Mother," she said in her quiet, careful voice, "when Morgawse is married, can we go home?"

I felt like crying, but I did not. I brushed the loose strands of hair back from her face, and tucked them into her plait. It was messy, and uneven. Morgawse must have done it.

"Camelot is our home now, Morgan," I said gently.

Morgan shook her head in a strangely adult gesture, as though I did not understand and she had to explain it to me.

"Home. Tintagel home. Morgawse and I don't belong here."

I did not know how to answer her. It was as though she understood that *I* belonged here now, but she did not. How was I to explain to a child who seemed to understand so much, but who was still yet a child? She wasn't safe here either.

I would lose her and Morgawse in one fatal swoop, for I could not keep Morgan here with her suffering. It would be the nuns for her, and a dull life in an abbey until she was a woman and Viviane could take her to Avalon. I smoothed her hair down and kissed her on the forehead. Of course, Uther did not pay her any mind now, with Morgawse carrying Gorlois' looks and approaching womanhood, but when she was gone, his eyes would turn to the last remnant of Gorlois' life, and he would seek to destroy it. I wanted Morgan long gone, and safe, before it came to that.

Morgan slipped off my lap, and settled into the window-seat to watch the men moving about below. Brastias came up behind me, uneasy. He ought to have been. I was furious with him.

"Lady Igraine," he whispered. I ignored him, running the comb through my hair. I wondered if there had been any truth in Uther's teasing of him. I was ten years older than he was, and he had been my husband's knight, but it was not so uncommon for young knights to foolishly desire their ladies. I knew by now that I was beautiful.

"My lady," he persisted, "you must forgive me for telling the King. I did not know what else to do. I was afraid."

"We are all afraid, Brastias," I hissed, not wanting to distract Morgan from what was giving her peace and distraction. "That was why we ought to have been *loyal* to one another. You are so besotted with Morgawse that you would do *anything* to keep her from marrying Lot –"

"I am *not* besotted with Morgawse, I –" Brastias protested.

"Be careful, Brastias," I warned, fixing him with a steady gaze. I had felt his lips against my cheek as I cried against his chest, I had seen the shy look in his eye as I slipped out of my dress. Better that neither of us gave it voice, better that he agreed that he was too close with my daughter. Anything else was death to us both.

"A man is careful, or a man is brave," Brastias said bitterly. "And already men say that I am not brave, because I did not die alongside my lord. So perhaps all that is left to me is your *careful*."

Before I could reprimand him, he got up and left, and I felt the hot anger of frustration cloy in my veins. I was trapped, and everyone blamed me for whatever I did.

* * *

I found Uther in his council chamber, alone, staring hard at a map spread out and weighted with stones. I knew that he heard me come in, because I saw his eyes flicker towards the door, but he was ignoring me. Even after last night, he was still angry with me.

"Uther," I said, quietly. I should have begun with *my lord*, but I dared to play on his affection for me. I would need everything I had to convince him to let me marry Morgawse to Lot.

"How long were you going to keep me ignorant about your intention to marry Morgawse?"

I tensed, drew myself back.

"I am not yet your wife, Uther, and she is not yet your stepdaughter. I do not see how this concerns you."

He turned to me then, and I could see that I had already

overstepped the place of a prisoner queen, a widowed wife of a defeated vassal. I did not think I cared.

"Is that what this is, Igraine? So that I will wed you quicker?"

I crossed my arms over my chest and I drew myself up to my full height. I let him wait a moment for my answer.

"Is that not also what you desire, my lord Uther? I know well enough that the only thing holding you back is Merlin's prohibition–"

Uther stepped forward towards me with such suddenness that it startled me. His voice was low and threatening. "Do not presume to know what has passed between Merlin and me."

So, this was the way that it was.

"So, you can give me nothing that I want," I said. I meant to sound cold, steady and calm, but my voice cracked a little. Uther opened his mouth to speak, but I did not wait. I knew that if I waited, then I would weep before him, and that would be worse than anything else. "My lord Uther, if I am neither your wife nor your prisoner, then let me go. Let me take my daughters and go back to Tintagel until Merlin gives you his permission –"

"*No*, Igraine." He stepped towards me. I moved away as he reached out to take my hand, but he was quicker than I was, and caught me about the wrist, drawing me back towards him. I could not read him; his tone was a mix of pleading and commanding, and a small part of me was sorry that Merlin had such a hold on him. But that had been *his* choice, his decision. I did not see why *I* should have to suffer for it.

"*Yes*, Uther," I replied, and I was almost shouting now, struggling not to let my voice rise to a scream. "Or will you force me to stay? I miss my home. I fear for my daughters. Oh, and you can come and collect me again once you are ready, as I am sure you will. I am a woman and have not the strength to stop you. Just let me go *home*."

Uther dropped my wrist, and turned back to his map. Dispassionately he said, "You should make Camelot your home, and so should your daughter Morgawse, for she will not go to Lothian any more than you will go back to Tintagel."

* * *

When I got back to my room Morgawse was there, sitting in my chair, patting drops of my perfume on to her throat with her chubby hands.

"Morgawse," I scolded sharply, "what are you doing?"

She blushed, knowing she had been caught at something. Brastias was there, sitting in the window seat, staring out, and Morgan sat on the bed with a book open that she could not possibly have understood. Brastias had not stopped Morgawse playing at being a little woman. I grabbed her hard around the wrist and pulled her up from the chair.

"Mother, I'm sorry –" she complained.

"You're young for this, Morgawse," I said, "and that perfume is expensive."

In that instant her contrition melted, and she screwed her little face up in anger. "Not too young for marriage, though, am I, Mother?"

I slapped her hard across the face. I was sorry for it as soon as I did it, but I did not have the patience for her, not then, not when I was fighting everyone to keep her safe and she could not be safe and sensible herself.

"Go to your room, Morgawse," I said.

She pulled her hand away from mine, cradling her cheek in it where I had slapped it. I felt guilty, and Brastias gave me a dark, judgemental look as he gathered Morgan up into his arms and carried her out, following Morgawse. I did not want to fight with him, did not want to speak with him, so I let him take her, though I had hoped I could have sat a while with Morgan.

When I was alone, I pulled the circlet from my head, the bracelets from my wrists, and the jewels from around my throat, and threw them down onto my dressing table. I supposed I could have sold them, or used them to bribe a knight to smuggle me out of the city. I could have left, disappeared. I could have gone to Tintagel, though Uther would have dragged me back. I could have gone to Lothian, if I were willing to submit myself to Lot's protection. I could have gone to Rheged castle in Gore, and begged for sanctuary from Gorlois' relatives. Perhaps I should have done that then, but I could only have escaped by leaving my daughters behind, and that I would never do.

I was lonely, and the child inside me was making me feel vulnerable. I already felt ashamed that I had slapped Morgawse, and I wished that I could have explained to her, to all of them, why I was so anxious to be married, why I was so afraid for all of our futures. I just wanted to run back to Tintagel, and hide there until my child was born and I could send him to be safely fostered somewhere. Perhaps Viviane would take the child, if it were a child like Morgan. And it made me think about Gorlois, about our last moments together, those I could be sure of, when he had been jealous, and possessive, and without affection. When he had believed that I had led Uther to think that I wanted to betray him. *He* had betrayed *me*. He had failed to trust me, and he had thrown himself into the path of Uther's destruction. Why had he preferred death to dishonour? If he had given in, then Morgawse and Morgan would have been safely with him. He would have found a stepmother to take care of them. I would not be here, in fear of my life, and their lives, and the fate of our home. I was struck with the thought that Gorlois had, in the end, been selfish.

* * *

I wanted to be alone, and I knew where I could go that Uther would not find me.

I didn't like dealing with Imogen, but at least she was easy to find, sitting in the public room of the queen's tower holding court as if this were her palace. At least Uther had moved her out of the bedroom.

"Imogen."

She looked up from the lute she was fiddling idly with. I had heard her play before. She was very musical. "Are there any services in the chapel today?"

Two of the women beside Imogen whispered to one another. I could imagine what they were saying.

Imogen, from where she was sprawled decadently in a pile of silk cushions, shrugged.

"We only have services there at the great festivals. Do you need someone to hear your confession, Igraine? There's no priest or bishop there; we haven't had need of one."

I coloured, and I was glad she could not see it.

"No, I only wish to have a quiet moment to pray."

Imogen shrugged haughtily. The other women had stopped their spinning and sewing to look at me incredulously. Prayer was obviously deeply unfashionable in Camelot.

"I don't see why you should not, Igraine, if that's what you truly desire to do. Though you would be welcome to sit here with us and take some entertainment, instead."

"You don't pray?" I asked, challenging. "I thought it was your father who had that great chapel built."

Imogen swept the auburn hair off her shoulder, and turned back to her lute.

"He did. For foreign dignitaries. And, besides, I was raised by my mother. I would have thought a good girl of pure British blood like you might cleave more to the traditions of her people than continental fashions."

Your father was a filthy Roman, I thought. I did not say it.

"Lady Imogen," I said, as politely as I could manage, "I look to the future. Your ways are those of the past."

I left before she could say anything else belittling. I didn't like fighting with her; it felt petty. If I was going to be Uther's queen, then she was beneath my concern.

* * *

The chapel was empty and smelled dusty. What must have been new fifty years ago was already old and tarnished. The rich red and gold silk hangings hadn't been beaten, and the dark wooden pews were greying with dust. The altar was set as though the priest had only just stepped out, but the gold cup was dull with disuse and empty. The chapel was quiet the way that nowhere else in Camelot was quiet. The castle was filled with the noise of servants moving around, of animals, of life busying around. The chapel was completely silent, and rather dark and cold. I stood beneath the figure of Christ on the cross. The missionary who had come to us at Cornwall had spoken again and again of Christ's power to forgive and to redeem. I would rather have stood before the figure of the Holy Mother Mary. She had borne a child to one man and married another. She had surrendered herself into the hands of fate, the hands of God. I wished I could muster that kind of acceptance, but no angel had given me my child, and I was not worthy of that kind of endless mercy.

I knelt at the wooden rail before the altar, folded my hands together, and rested my forehead down on them. I did not want any of the things I had been taught to pray for, like patience, mercy, forgiveness. I wanted strength. I wanted knowledge. Imogen and that gaggle of stupid women were probably tittering at me right now. Silly Igraine, in the chapel all alone. Silly Igraine, too young and foolish to see that God does not really care.

"Igraine?"

I jumped. I looked up to see Uther standing beside me. So, Imogen had told him.

"What are you doing?"

He had an infuriating little smile playing about his lips. I turned back to my clasped hands.

"I am praying for my husband's soul," I said, closing my eyes.

Uther laughed softly.

"I have heard men say that I do not have one. That I have sold it to Merlin."

"I didn't mean you."

There was a long silence in which I continued to pretend to

163

pray. I heard no sound from Uther, but I was sure that he was not praying as well.

"Go back to your castle if that is what you need, Igraine," Uther said at last, and the gentleness of his voice surprised me. I opened my eyes and looked up at him beside me. He was staring up at the figure of Christ hanging above him. Those five gory wounds. I was sure Uther had seen worse. Men cut open on the battlefield like sheep at the butcher's block.

He looked down at me. "That's what you want, isn't it?"

I did not know what I wanted.

"Where is the priest?" I asked.

"I sent him to Winchester. He kept trying to meddle in state affairs."

I almost said, *Was it because Merlin did not like that?* but I thought better of it.

"Do you need a priest?" he asked me seriously.

I opened my mouth to say something sharp in response, as I might have done to Imogen, but I could not. Men like Uther were dismissive enough of faith, but God had watched over me the way that the White Goddess and the Hanged God had done my whole life, and I would not forswear any of them. And we had done wrong, Uther and I. I knew well enough I had sins to confess.

"Uther," I sighed, "do you not? I was a married woman, and I… and you *killed* Gorlois. You killed him. And he has not even been dead a month and we have already… *I* have –"

Uther pulled me to my feet roughly, his hand around my arm, into the path of his piercing stare.

"How old were you, Igraine, when the priests taught this to you?"

"I suppose I was about ten years old."

"So, since then you have believed that what is written in a book is more important than the heat of your own blood? Than the turning of the seasons, and the natural desire of a man and a woman to become one?"

I felt the same weakness pass through me that I had felt all those years ago in Tintagel courtyard when he had whispered to me of the same.

"These are old ways, Igraine. Old virtues. Gorlois chose death. He could have lived, but he loved these new virtues. I care for nothing, Igraine, but the blood and the bones of my body, the old powers that run through me, and that always bring me back to you."

He leaned in and brushed his lips very lightly against my cheek.

He knew I wanted him. He knew that I had burned for his touch before, and he knew I remembered the pleasure I had felt under his hands. He knew that I was weak. Slowly, his lips brushed down the curve of my cheek, and I opened my lips for him. But we were not married, and I could not be sure of him, could not be sure that he would not dispose of me, or keep me as a concubine like Imogen, until I had that promise from him.

I pushed him back and he pulled me against him again, his fingers working my hair loose, tangling there, filling me with heat I wanted to resist. I pushed him away, harder this time, and fell to my knees. My hair was falling around my face where his hands had loosened it.

"Is this what you want?" I said. "Is this how you want me? Begging for you to treat me honourably? Begging for you to protect me?"

Uther took hold of me hard and pulled me back up to my feet.

"Of course that's not what I want," he said thickly. "You know that isn't what I want."

"What do you want?"

"I want to be free of… of all of this. We can. You and I, Igraine, we are all the world that matters."

"We are not," I said, turning away from him, striding down the aisle. He lunged for me, pulling me back into his arms. We stumbled together, the weight of his body hard against me, the heat of his mouth against my temple, my cheek. My mouth found his, and I remembered his hands slipping my underdress from my shoulders. His touch against my skin. I itched beneath my clothes.

"You and I were meant for one another," he said against my mouth. "I am tired of fighting."

His lips moved down, across my jawbone to my neck, and I softened in his grip. I half-opened my eyes, and met the disapproving gaze of the figure of Christ.

"Not here," I hissed. "Not here."

Uther's eyes were wild, his chest rising and falling hard with desire. He glanced over his shoulder at the altar and back at me. We would not make it across the great courtyard and up to either of our rooms without being noticed.

"Wherever my lady wishes," he said gruffly, taking my ear gently between his teeth. "Just let it be close by."

I gripped his coat, dragged him back with me through a narrow stone doorway off the transept. We tumbled through, he braces his hand against the wall to stop us both from falling, me wound against him, already tearing the coat off his shoulders. Something clattered to the floor, and something else. Uther pushed me up onto something, some low table – it was dark in the little room, and smelled of dust and vellum – but I would not have noticed my surroundings anyway. I was aware only of his mouth, his tongue, his hands working my clothing loose. Lips against my collarbone, me tangling in my underdress in fevered desperation to feel them against my breasts. His skin beneath my hands, the hard contours of muscle, the softness of his lips, the coarse hair that grew thicker as my fingers travelled down. Just when I was sighing every breath, drunk on the sweetness of bare skin against bare skin, Uther seized me hard by the thighs.

"Tell me you want me, Igraine," he growled. "I want to hear you say it."

I was beyond words. I grabbed him by the hips and pulled him against me. He thrust inside me with a low animal groan, and I arched against him. He covered my mouth with his to hide my cry of relief. It was rough, but on my part as much as his. I wound my fingers into his hair, and pulled. He took the tender skin at the base of my neck between his teeth, and knew how to hurt me just the right amount. It was all the wilder for how long I had waited; perhaps I had truly wanted this since that first moment, almost fourteen years ago.

After the ecstasy of release, Uther was unexpectedly tender, and brushed soft kisses against my brow, my closed eyelids, my lips, which were still burning from his mouth. I ached all over – a pleasant ache that went right to my core. Slowly, reluctantly, we drew apart, and I pulled my clothes back into place. Uther pushed open the door that had slammed shut behind us as we tumbled in, and the dim light that filled the chapel spilled in. At my feet, knocked from the table as Uther had pushed me up onto it, was the gold thurible, now dented and with the block of incense half-spilled out. I leant down and picked it up, tidying it as best I could, setting it back on the table. I looked up to see Uther, fully dressed and silhouetted in the dim light of the doorway, turned over his shoulder and watching me. We didn't speak. I glanced behind me at the scattered books and fallen gold candlesticks – the candles broken to pieces – but I left them. We walked side by side out of the chapel in silence, and I did everything I could to avoid meeting the eye of the dying figure of Christ.

Only later did everything else creep back around me. I dreamed of Gorlois wrapping his arms around me, and pressing his lips against mine, and saying, *Tell me you love me, Igraine*, and *tell me you want me*. And when I woke I felt strange, and hollow, and unsettled, as though something had been done to me, some trick had been played on me once more, but I did not quite know what.

Chapter twenty-seven

The next day I felt wary and ashamed around my daughters. As Morgan sat in my lap listening to me reading to her in a soft, distant voice, I remembered the feel of Uther's hands against my thighs, hard and rough. I blushed and I pushed the thought away. I wished that Brastias was not there, for I imagined that he was watching me, and trying to guess what I was thinking. Morgawse was still sulking, but I was no longer in any state of mind to scold her for it. If she knew what I had done, what I had said, what I had felt in the arms of the man who had killed her father then I was sure that she would never look me in the eye again.

I was sitting there with Morgan, stroking her hair gently and pointing to the words when Viviane came in. I felt a rush of gladness, for she had been away at some business of Avalon's and I had missed her. I jumped from my seat and ran over to her, overtaken by a sudden affectionate impulse quite unlike myself, and I only just held myself back from throwing my arms around her in joy when I remembered that she was the Lady of Avalon, and that was beneath her dignity.

"Viviane," I breathed, "I am pleased to see you."

She smiled gently, and took my hand in hers. "And I you, Igraine. I am glad you are well. I have been worried about you."

I felt myself smile like a child to be told that someone had worried about me, that someone was taking care of me. It was foolish, but now that Viviane was here again I felt as though she had come to keep me safe, and I wanted to commit myself into someone else's care, and be saved.

"I am well enough, I –"

But Viviane had stopped listening to me. She walked past me to half-kneel before Morgan. Morgan looked at her with her big, quiet, thoughtful eyes.

"Do you remember me, Morgan?" she said. Morgan nodded. I saw Morgawse bristle with annoyance that she had been ignored again in preference for her sister, and for once I felt the same thing as my eldest daughter, and I realised that I had a habit of thinking of them as though Morgan were like myself, and Morgawse like Gorlois, when Morgawse was just as much my child as Morgan was, and it was Gorlois' blood that had destined Morgan for Avalon.

Viviane put a gentle hand on Morgan's shoulder, and stood again, turning back to me.

"Igraine, I wish I had the leisure time to speak with you, to hear more about how you and the girls are, but I must take you to Uther and Merlin right away."

I slipped my hand into the hand she offered and followed her. What was going to happen? I felt an awful panic settle on me, and I felt sure that it was because I had given in to the desire I should not have felt, and done so before I was fully married to Uther. What would they do? Send me away? I had given up the only power I had. I felt sick, and fragile, and shaky.

As we arrived outside Uther's chamber door, Viviane kissed me gently on the forehead. She said, "I have come to make Merlin end his games. Do as I say, Igraine, and all will be well."

I nodded, but suddenly I remembered what Imogen had said. *Uther has lain with your friend Viviane.* But I pushed the thought aside. I could not imagine Viviane with a man, not in the way that normal men and women were, hot with desire. Imogen must have been lying.

Viviane opened the door without knocking. I wondered why we were meeting in Uther's bedchamber, and then I realised that Viviane meant to surprise them. Uther was in his shirt and breeches, and there was an old, old man with him, whom I had not expected to see. The old man was thin, and bent over, with a long, white beard that grew down as far as his belly, and white-blue eyes that made him look as though he would be blind as Imogen. But he was not, for the eyes flickered over us as we stepped in. Uther, too, looked up, and when our eyes met I felt a jolt of heat go through me that was half shame, half delicious remembering. I closed my eyes for a moment, and I was sure I could feel once more his mouth against mine, his hands in my hair. I suppressed a shiver.

"Merlin," Viviane said coldly to the old man, who was *not* Merlin, not as I knew him, "news has reached Avalon that King Uther is yet to wed Igraine."

The old man nodded. "That is so, my sweet Viviane," he said. His voice rasped like old parchment, and he turned a mean, sarcastic smile on her.

Viviane regarded him coldly, and I kept my eyes on the old man, for I could feel Uther's eyes on me, and I felt the flush rise up my throat, on to my cheeks. I wished that we were not there with others to witness it.

"Merlin, I have not obstructed you, because we want the same things. We want peace in this kingdom, we want to protect the heir of the Pendragon –"

"And so, Viviane, you are coming here to demand that I beseech my King to take his wife to the chapel and wed her in the eyes of the god of the Christians?" Merlin sneered, as though it meant nothing. "Such things can wait. What is important has already come to pass. He has lain with her already."

I opened my mouth to protest, feeling myself flush dark with embarrassment, with horror that Uther had told Merlin. He was looking away from me then, down at his feet. I did not know why he could be so harsh and unyielding with everyone else, but so utterly obedient to Merlin.

Merlin saw my face, and a cruel smile spread across it.

"All the more reason, Merlin," Viviane continued, seeming not to have noticed my distress beside her. "The Emperor in Rome and the kings in France and Ireland are now Christians. We can hardly wait until after Igraine's child is born."

So it was spoken aloud, in public. I glanced at Uther, and he was staring back at me. I could not tell what he was thinking. Was he angry because he knew it could not be his? Would he force himself to believe that it was? A spasm of fear went through me at the thought that Gorlois' infant child would be in danger when it was born. A child born after the father's death, an unwanted stepchild. What would I do?

Merlin shrugged as though he hardly cared at all.

"Let it be done, then," he said.

I got the sense that he had only been playing for power with Viviane, and Uther and I had been dragged into this. I knew that they were enemies, and yet half the time she was kind to him, and half the time harsh. I felt awfully as though I had been thrown around between them, too, and bruised by it, and I was not sure if I should be angry with Viviane.

"Uther," Viviane said sharply, "let arrangements be made for your marriage as soon as possible. It has been unkind of you to leave Igraine unsure of her position, whatever Merlin's instructions."

Uther looked as though he did not know how to answer her. I hoped that she and Merlin would leave, and Uther and I could be alone, for I had never felt more unsure of my position with him until this moment. I opened my mouth to speak; I could feel his eyes on me, and could see that he wanted to say something to me as well, but neither of us had the chance with Viviane and Merlin fighting over us. I remembered running my hands into his hair, and feeling his breath against my neck, and I wished that I could have lingered, to see what he had felt, and what he thought, but Viviane had her hand around my arm and was pulling me from the room.

* * *

Viviane was angry so I sent Brastias and my daughters away when we came back to my room.

"Igraine," she said, her voice tense with concern and harsh, although the harshness not directed towards me, "I am sorry that Uther seems to be so ruled by Merlin. I am glad that your knight Brastias thought to send me word of his concerns. I do not know what game Merlin is playing –"

Brastias. Brastias had written to Viviane to tell her that I was in trouble. I was not sure how I felt about that. I had been unkind to him, and cold, and I had thought he was too involved, dealt too personally with me and my daughters. I had told him to be careful, and he had still written to Viviane. *I* should have thought of it. I had been too caught up in trying to get her to take my daughters away to think of myself.

Viviane sighed heavily. "I think Merlin wants to be sure that your child will be born at such a time that it will be impossible to believe that it was conceived within your marriage."

"Why would he want that?" I asked quietly.

"I don't know," Viviane replied, darkly. "I don't know."

* * *

Late that evening, when Morgawse and Morgan had gone to bed, I put a hand against Brastias' arm to stop him leaving. He stopped where he stood, and looked down at me with gentle resignation. He knew that I knew now what he had done for me. I opened my mouth to thank him, but he put his hand gently over mine.

"It was no more than my duty, Lady Igraine," he said. There was both affection and coldness in his voice.

* * *

I did not know if I was safe or not. It seemed to be known by everyone now that I had a child growing inside me. I did not know what Uther thought, or what Merlin wanted, or, for that matter, what interest Viviane might have in all of this. I wanted to feel sure.

When I slept, I dreamed a strange, vivid dream. I dreamed of Uther, covered with blood from head to foot, dressed in light leather armour, his arms bare and smeared with blood and dirt. It was also spattered across his face, and he was climbing a tall hill, up to a circle of stones. There was low mist, as though it were very late at night or very early in the morning, and there were torches up in the circle,

170

casting light and long shadows. In the centre of the circle stood Viviane, naked, her body painted all over with the patterns of blue woad, her hair loose around her. Like that, I realised that she could not have been more than five or six years older than I was. I had thought her much older because of her woad patterns and the robes of the Lady of Avalon, but she was a young woman, and beautiful; her long golden hair was like the fresh corn of the harvest, and she was lovely. Far lovelier than I was. Uther stopped when he saw her, and threw down the short spear in his hand. He stood at the edge of the circle of stones, staring at her, his chest rising and falling as though he had just run there, hard, from some kind of hunt, until she beckoned him forward. And he came, and pulled her hard into his arms, smearing her white skin with blood. Then they lay down together on the ground, and the dream faded away. I wished I had not seen it.

I felt sick when I woke up. Confused, guilty, somehow betrayed. I did not know who to trust, or what to believe, only that everyone had been playing with me, and I could not rely on anyone.

Chapter twenty-eight

They came to tell me that I would wed Uther soon after that, and I went blankly through the preparations as though I was sleepwalking. Viviane was by my side, and was kind in her usual detached, auntish way. Morgan stared, Morgawse moped, Brastias fussed, and I avoided Uther and Merlin as much as I could.

The day came, and I felt sick, exhausted and unsteady. I remembered that wild moment with Uther – the rough passion, the delight, the desire – but I also remembered him submitting my entire fate to Merlin, and that he had been with Viviane and refused to give up Imogen.

Imogen came to help me weave the ribbons into my hair for my wedding. She would be among my attendants for it, as was her right as the daughter of the previous king. I hated having her there. It was like a curse. Morgawse, too, sulked under the touch of her hands, and seemed to be afraid of her blank, white eyes. I put on my jewels; they felt heavy. I looked at myself in the mirror: I looked pale, tired and drawn. Viviane kissed me on the forehead. I felt empty and alone. I had wanted this. Now all I wanted was to close my eyes and sleep until it had passed.

* * *

In the chapel, I said the words that I was bid, and everyone clapped and cheered as Uther put his arms around me and kissed me. I closed my eyes into it, and for a moment I felt a little better. As Uther drew away from me, he whispered close, "I am glad this day has finally come."

I gave him an unsteady smile in return.

* * *

I worried for Morgan and Morgawse during the feast, and could not relax. I could not stop myself from looking over at them every few minutes, and I knew that Uther was watching me do it. I was glad that Merlin was not at the feast and Viviane was, though I resented having Imogen at the high table. I barely tasted the food, and I barely drank the wine; I was just tense and waiting for it all to be over. I thought I would feel better once Uther and I were alone. But then came the awful, tedious ceremony where Uther and I sat side by side on the thrones of Logrys in the great hall, and one by one the lesser kings came and bowed to their new queen. I was exhausted, and sick, and it was only Uther's hand in mine that saw me through it.

Halfway through the ceremony, I saw Brastias standing at the front of the line with Morgan and Morgawse, and I felt my stomach clench with fear. I saw Morgawse's face. She would not do it. I knew that as soon as I saw her. There was a murmur in the room, for those who had known Gorlois and fought by his side recognised Morgawse as his daughter. She was wearing the circlet that had belonged to his mother, a lovely red-gold Celtic-made piece of jewellery that publicly declared that she was his child, and his heir. She must have picked it out from among my things after I had left.

I tensed myself, prepared for the fight that I knew was about to come. *Why do they all have to be against me?* I thought. Merlin, Morgawse, Imogen; perhaps Viviane as well.

Morgawse looked up at me from the centre of the aisle set out before the thrones, and I saw a cold flash of defiance in her blue eyes.

"Come and greet your new stepfather," I said gently, as loudly as I dared. Morgawse heard, and shuffled forward reluctantly.

"*Please.*" She let me beg. There, in front of Uther, and in front of all the gathered nobles of my new kingdom, my daughter made me beg, and stood glowering until I came down from my seat, down the dais, to take her hand and lead her with me. Her hand was hot, but dry. She wasn't panicking; she knew what she was doing. Perhaps this was not the petulance of a child. She was old enough that she ought to have understood the danger she was in.

Stood in the aisle beside her, I suddenly saw Uther as she must have seen him, sat in the throne with the heavy crown of Logrys on his head, rich white furs across his shoulders, his fingers covered in gold rings, gold around his neck, and beneath all that, the red and gold surcoat embroidered with the gold dragon. He made a fearsome-looking king. I had forgotten that this was what my daughter saw, when I saw only Uther as I had first met him, more soldier than ruler. I caught my breath a little to look on him. I had forgotten what a powerful man he was, for I had last seen him struck dumb before Viviane and Merlin. But their power was something beyond the power of the world, of kings and queens. Theirs was the power of the earth and the sea and the sky, and no human man could rule over that. Uther was wise to fear them.

When we reached the foot of the dais, I gave Morgawse an encouraging kiss on the cheek and squeezed her hand. I knew she was angry with me. I knew she resented it all, and I had not had the patience to be kind to her, but I wanted her to be good. I slipped back into my seat beside Uther, and he rested his hand on mine. It was heavy, and comforting, and warm and real – far removed from the secret threats and games of Viviane and Merlin. Perhaps we would be better like this, joined together, and they would think of us less as their playthings, their pawns.

"Come and greet your stepfather, Morgawse," I said again, trying to be encouraging. There was a distinct murmuring in the crowd now. She stood there, still, glowering. I felt myself tense inside, and it sent a pain through me, sharp and unbearable. She was punishing me for marrying again. I closed my eyes as I felt a wave of nausea pass over me, and I was not sure if it was the child inside me making me ill, or the fear running through me – my dread for Morgawse, and for myself.

"Come and kiss me, Morgawse," Uther said beside me, and his tone was low and dangerous with threat.

I opened my eyes to see Morgawse look back over her shoulder at her little sister. Why was she looking at Morgan? When she looked back, it was not at me, it was at Uther, and I saw her flush with anger. She was not going to come forwards, not going to be obedient. Why did she always have to throw herself recklessly into danger? She crossed her arms over her chest, and her face screwed tight into an angry pout.

"I won't come and kiss you. You're a monster." Her voice was quiet, but it carried through the hall as far as Uther. The men around her were murmuring that Uther's stepdaughter dared to defy him in public. It seemed that this strengthened her resolve to provoke Uther, though, for I saw her draw herself up to launch herself into more. "I hate you. Everyone here knows you murdered my father because you wanted my mother for yourself. I won't do it. I won't. You're a monster and a brute and I hate you." Morgawse's voice had risen to a shrill scream that filled the hall, and Uther beside me had got to his feet. I wanted to stand, to hold him back, but the room was spinning around me and I could feel my heart thudding in my chest. Then Morgawse turned her eyes on me, bright blue, shining with tears, and harsh with accusation. "How could you do it? He killed my father. He killed my father! How could you marry him? See? He's a monster!"

As she spoke, Uther reached her across the dais, and grasped hold of her by a handful of her hair. She screamed, he shook her, and she screamed louder. He shook her harder. I saw him bring his hand back, to strike her.

"Uther, *no!*" I shouted, and he froze. But he did not let go of her hair. His pride was hurt; he had been insulted in his own hall. Morgawse would not be humbled before anyone, her father's spoiling had made sure of that, so it was left to me that I should humble myself once more, and beg.

"My lord Uther, please. She is only a child. She does not understand what she is saying. Please."

Slowly, Uther released his grip on her hair; she went to run away, but he put a hand around her throat. Not tight, not yet, but he turned her face up to his.

"In future, Morgawse," he said, soft and threatening, "you will show me respect in public."

I felt it strike through me, cold and awful. Why could she not have just shown him respect? Why did he have to react with such violence? When Uther stood up straight once more, turning his back to her, she ran away and into the arms of her nurse and the old nun Margaret. I hoped that they would scold her, so that I did not have to. I did not want to have to always be telling Morgawse to be different, for her own safety.

When Morgan stepped forward afterwards, I was relieved that she was silent. I had not expected her to shout like Morgawse, but she might have said something in that thoughtful voice of hers that would have been just as disrespectful. I asked her to come forward and greet Uther, too, but she just blinked at me slowly, as though she did not understand. I knew that she did, and this was her own way of being defiant. In part I blamed Morgawse. She talked to Morgan all day long of how she hated Uther, of how their father had been a perfect, wonderful man and Uther was a brute. What chance did Morgan have of any kind of happiness with her stepfather, if her sister was so set against him?

I glanced at Uther beside me as Morgan slipped away to join her sister. His jaw was clenched tight, and I felt myself shrink back a little from him. They were just children, and the loss of their father was still fresh to them, still raw. He did not have to have been so rough with Morgawse.

He did not put his hand over mine again as the rest of the lords came to pledge, and the atmosphere had changed from one of celebration to one of angry wariness.

* * *

When the rituals of pledging faith were over, Uther stood, and took me by the hand. It was strange; we had already come together as lovers, yet I was nervous now that I knew he would take me up to his chamber as his wife. This time it would not just be the blank release of years of frustrated desire. I was not sure if I intended to refuse him, or not; not sure how much I blamed him, and how much I blamed Morgawse for the moment of violence between them. She was old enough to know better, but she was my own daughter, and he could have been kind.

By the time Uther closed the door behind us, I knew that I was wary because I was angry, and so was he. He pulled off the cloak of furs about his shoulders and threw it to the ground.

"Who has been responsible for disciplining your girl, Igraine?" he demanded.

I crossed my arms over my chest, stepping back from him. "She is only a child. You did not have to be so rough –"

He turned back to me and I jumped back at the power of his rage.

"How long will peace in Britain last if a child can challenge me in my own hall, on the day of my own wedding?"

"How long will men respect you if you behave as though you must show force against a child to protect your *pride*?"

Uther's hand closed hard around my arm, and he pulled me up against him. I could see that he was flushed with fury, shaking with it, but I was angry, too. He was pushing me and Morgawse apart, and so was she. They were both tearing at me, forcing me to choose one way or the other and I did not want that, could not bear that.

"You will not speak to me that way, Igraine," he said, low.

"You will not treat my daughter that way, sir, if you want my love."

"You will teach her respect, if you want her to be safe."

We were still, eyes locked together. I could feel my heart thudding. In part, I knew that he was right. That he could not be seen to be tolerating Morgawse's open defiance of him. Yet he did not have to be so rough, and so cruel. He would have won her better with kindness, but he was so jealous of Gorlois that he did not have it in him.

"Gorlois is gone, Uther, and she is just a girl." Very softly, I added, "Men will think that you are afraid of her."

"*She* ought to be afraid of *me*. I will make her afraid, if that is what it takes."

I slapped him hard across the face.

Uther stepped back from me, holding his hand against his cheek. I could see his chest rising and falling hard. He looked up at me, slowly, and there as a strange flash in his eyes. It was anger, mixed with something else, something stranger and darker and more ambiguous. He leaned very close, and he whispered, "I would be within my rights to make the girl my slave."

I hit him again, and Uther took hold of me about the waist. I pulled away from him and he pulled me back roughly. I slapped him hard again. As I did he made a noise low in his throat, of *enjoyment*. That stopped me still where I was. As I hesitated, he wrapped his arms around me and pressed his mouth against mine. I was still angry, and I pushed him back once more, and slapped him again. He grasped my wrist, twisting my arm behind me, crushing me against him, pressing his forehead against mine. He *was* excited. I felt a strange jolt of excitement go through me as well; a strange jolt of power.

"You are a pervert, Uther Pendragon," I said thickly as he kissed me again, and I felt myself weaken into his grip.

"So are you, Igraine," he said softly at my ear. And I felt his teeth graze against it, and a delicious weakness run down my spine. "You wanted me to fight for you, to bring you here by force, to kill Gorlois –"

I pushed him away and raised my free hand to hit him again. He grasped hold of it, and held that behind me as well. His kiss this time was more forceful, but I found that I wanted it. I could taste the wine on his lips and I knew that he was drunk, but I didn't mind. I had been hot with anger, and it had changed fast to desire. One of his hands slid down and pulled up the skirts of my dress, and grasped hold of the underdress beneath and tore. I heard the fabric shred to pieces in his grip and shivered, half in revulsion, half in excitement. With his lips still close by my ear, he whispered, "You love the chase,

Igraine."

"I do not."

I felt his hand brush up my throat, and rest where I could feel my heart beating hard against his fingertips. "You do, Igraine," he whispered. "I can feel your heart racing."

I pushed him away again, but now only because I knew that it was what he wanted, what *I* wanted, and he grabbed me harder. And the hand still gripping the underdress tore it further, and his other hand slid into my hair, pulling my mouth against his. And I let it overwhelm me, and I was lost in it. Before I was aware what had happened, we were on the bed and I was pulling at the buttons of his surcoat, pushing it off his shoulders, and he was kicking off his boots, and pushing me over underneath him to pull open the lacing of the heavy brocade overdress. When he pulled it away, I saw that my underclothes beneath were ripped to the waist, the skirt of the underdress in pieces. Uther did not pause, did not seem to notice. His lips found my breasts, and he pulled the lacing of the underdress open and drew it down. I was wild with it, intoxicated, lost to everything apart from the sensation of his skin against my skin, of his lips, his tongue, my hands as they felt the shape of his muscular shoulders, and his chest, coarse and rough with dark gold hair, scarred from battle. By the time he pulled his breeches away and we came together I was lost in the same rapturous, gasping ecstasy that I had known with him before. And I sighed his name and clasped him tight against me, and the delight I had longed to know with him before came fast on me, and sudden, and we sank down together, both sighing with blissful relief. And in that haze, tangled together, I fell asleep before the candles had even guttered out.

Chapter twenty-nine

When I woke in the morning, I was once again no longer sure if I knew, or if I had ever known, truly, what kind of a man Uther Pendragon was. I had thought he was a proud man, yet he had wanted to be fought, and slapped, by his wife. I had thought he was a cruel man, but when we were alone, though his touch was rough, he could also be caring, and he was as keen for my pleasure as for his own. It was not Gorlois' dutiful, husbandly lovemaking either; it was wild, and it was passion rather than politeness that made Uther's touch so pleasant, his love so overwhelming.

It was the depths of winter still, so it was half-dark. When I pushed myself up on my elbows to look at him sleeping beside me, he looked so different from how I had seen him when I was a young girl, and then later from afar. I had seen him so often angry, so often fighting for men to respect his role as their king, and I had had, really, almost no time alone with him. In his sleep, I was surprised to see that his look was gentle, his brow not creased by anger or concern. He looked younger, too, without that. He was older than I was, older than Gorlois had been. Of an age, I supposed, with Lot, though Uther looked older. He was harsher, stockier, more tanned from the battlefield, more scarred from it, better at impressing men with his terrifying power. In his sleep I saw none of that. His dark gold hair, though cut short in a soldierly style, was tousled from lying against the pillow, and looked inviting to touch. His rough face, relaxed, looked young, slightly boyish even, though I would never have thought that about him before. Men never said that Uther was handsome – they said that about Lot, but they said that Uther was brave, and ruthless, and strong. But, I thought, how he was now, as I had him all alone and without all of his striving to be considered King, he was the finest man I had ever seen. Would I have run away with him against my father's wishes all those years ago if I could have guessed at this? Perhaps. But I would not wish for it. I would not wish away my daughters.

I remembered how he had been, all those years ago, dressed in his soldier's clothes while Lot and the other young princes of Britain had swaggered around in rich surcoats, when all he had had was the blessing of Avalon, and the tricks of Merlin to make him King. He had not held his court in London, or at Winchester at Aurelianus' great palace. I wondered, distantly, if he was afraid that men would compare him to King Aurelianus, and find him less. He had taken the gold and the jewels and the tapestries and silks from the palace, but Camelot was a fortress, and they looked different here. Why had he wanted it so badly? Why had *Merlin* wanted it so badly? Why had my father disliked the choice so much? A trace of Roman blood, I supposed, but it was too late for that in Logrys. Perhaps in the border kingdoms, in Lothian and Orkney, in Cornwall and Gore and Ireland, there it would be always Celtic kings, but the world had changed. My father had accepted Christ with ease, but somehow still resented mixing blood with the Romans. I didn't care. Uther was Avalon's man more than any other race, or allegiance or people. Or perhaps he was Merlin's. That thought unsettled me. He had promised Merlin his son, so I would one day be left with either bearing him no heir, or giving away a child.

But I didn't want to think about that now. Alone, with him, in the half-light of dawn with the bed curtains closed, I could pretend that everything else did not exist. Perhaps it was childish of me, but I wanted to believe it for a moment.

I leaned over and brushed my lips lightly against his closed eyelids; they flickered, and in his sleep he smiled, reaching out for me, and drawing me onto his chest.

"Igraine," he murmured, his mouth finding mine, his arms wrapping around my back. This was different again – gentle, tender, and utterly absorbing in its own way. Both warm and sleepy still, we were lazy with each other, and I felt the pleasure of his touch fill me with a warm, gentle heat. In the rising light of the morning, with the secret, gentle Uther that I had not really known before, it was as powerful and as lovely as it had been with the rough man who had torn my underclothes to pieces the night before.

We lay in bed still as I listened to the bells ringing for prime, he with his arm gently around my waist, and a hand idly tangled in my hair. I closed my eyes as he kissed me softly on the bridge of my nose, and then on the lips, and I sighed again. I felt his hand slide down and rest against my stomach, which was yet to show the first signs of the life inside. I felt myself clench with fear that this would shatter everything that was warm and safe and lovely about the morning.

Uther's lips found mine again, gently, for a moment, before he asked me, "Whose child, Igraine, is this?"

I screwed my eyes shut for a second, pushing back the fear, and the dread, and the awful heavy unknowing. I did not know. I did not know what had been done to me. But all I could tell him was the truth. I shook my head.

"I don't know," I said, turning my face away from him, upset and ashamed. Gently he put his hand to my cheek and turned my face back to his.

"What do you mean?" he asked, and I could see concern in his eyes, and kindness. I was afraid that would all pass away.

I drew in a deep breath.

I shrank closer to him, into the protective circle of his arms, and I laid a hand gently against his chest. Slowly, I began. "It was all so strange, I… I don't know. Gorlois and I had been long apart. That night, at the pass, when his men invaded the camp near Tintagel, it was midwinter night. I remember that, for it seemed special. Gorlois said he would come back as soon as it was done. I waited, and I watched for a rider though the gates. One did not come. It was only very late when a man came. I thought – I was *sure* – it was Gorlois.

Ulfius and Brastias were with him. The man wore his armour, bore his sword, and underneath that – it was *him*. I don't know how – it was Gorlois. I was sure it was, and he was my husband, and I did not turn him away, for I was so sure that it was he. But the next morning, you were at the gates of Tintagel, and I was told that Gorlois had died the day before, before the sun had even set, I…" I shook my head, fighting back tears of upset, of confusion, remembering how that night had been – tender and loving. And the man had spoken with Gorlois' words, and I had given myself to him in relief, and love, and hope. "I don't know who he was."

Uther hushed me gently, and stroked my hair. I thought he would be angry; I thought he would demand that the child of a stranger should be cast out, but he did not. He kissed me softly on the forehead, and turned my face gently up to kiss me again, and I felt the panic subside from me a little.

"Hush. Don't be sorry, sweet Igraine," he said, his fingers running through my hair, his other hand sliding up my back in a gesture halfway between comfort and desire. "It was I, Igraine," he said.

I looked up at him, spreading a hand out against his chest to still him, my brow wrinkling in confusion. "What do you mean?"

He smiled, and brushed his fingers fondly down my cheek. "I could not wait. The time called for it to be done, and I could not wait to have you. I had the witch Merlin change my shape, and the shapes of two of my knights so that they would seem to you like Ulfius and Brastias. And it was I who came to you in the form of your husband. Be glad, Igraine, for the child is mine."

I was not glad. I felt sick. I heard, once again, Gorlois' voice: *Tell me you love me, Igraine. Tell me you want me.* And then Uther's: *Tell me you want me. I need to hear you say it.* I could hear my blood rushing in my veins, I could feel my skin grow cold, and clammy, and crawl. When Uther reached towards me to draw me into his embrace once more, I pushed him roughly away, sitting up, pulling the sheets of the bed around me, aware though I was what an inadequate protection against him this was. I could feel the tears gathering in my eyes, and I bit them back.

"It was *you*?" I demanded.

Uther sat up beside me, and I could see that he was angry. How could he have been so stupid as to think I would be pleased?

"Igraine," he said, sharply, "you will come to see in time that it was for the best."

"*For the best?*" I cried. I jumped back out of the bed as he leaned forward to try and take my hand.

"Igraine, you are being hysterical," he said. And what was worse than anything else was the irritation in his voice, as though some awful horror had not been committed against me. As though *I* were the one at fault for not understanding. "Igraine," he continued, "come back to bed. Be reasonable. Igraine, where are you going? You can't go out like that."

I had pulled the underdress over my head. It was in pieces, the skirt torn, one of the sleeves ripped. I didn't care. I did not have any other clothes here yet, so I would go out like that if I had to. My fingers trembled on the laces, and it was hard to tie them. I was angry, and disgusted, and desperate to be away from him. How could he have told me he loved me, and been passionate and loving and tender as though he were honest? Why had he even bothered trying to persuade me, if he had had me already by trickery? It was all the more awful that I had let myself be won round by one who had already had what he wanted by deceit. It made it all a lie, and I hated it.

"I will go out like this, and if anyone asks me, I will tell them why."

"Igraine, just consider, *for a moment*."

I pulled the dress of grey and silver thread over my head. It was my finest dress, and it was crumpled from spending the night in a heap on the floor.

"Igraine." His voice had changed from annoyance to pleading, and it was the tone I would have used on one of my daughters if they were making a fuss about something unimportant. And it was the worst thing he could have done to convince me to stay. "Where are you going? Come back to bed. Wait until you are calm. Don't distress yourself. Think of the child –"

"Do *not* talk to me about my child –"

"*Igraine* –" he shouted, and his voice was so loud that I felt it shake through me, and the room, and I stepped back from him again. We stopped for a moment there, he still in the bed, the covers crumpled around him, and I dressed but with my hair loose, my dress unlaced at the back, my underclothes torn. For a moment we were both still, like two animals bracing for a fight. Then I turned and I ran, before he could stop me, out of the door, down, barefoot, until I threw myself against the door of the room that Viviane slept in, if she stayed. And I prayed to all the gods I knew that she would open the door.

And she did. I gasped with relief and threw myself into her arms. She led me into the room with her, and closed the door, and took my face in her hands with a look of motherly concern.

"Oh, the brute," she sighed. "He told you, didn't he?"

I jumped back from her. "You *knew*?"

"I knew, Igraine, and I am no more pleased than you are."

It struck me suddenly that Viviane was selfish and cold. *I am no more pleased than you are.* She had no idea how I felt. To imagine it was the same for her – Uther and Merlin going against her wishes – as it was for me. I could not believe that she thought it was the same.

Viviane shook her head, as though in annoyance at a pair of disobedient boys. I did not know what I had expected from her, but I had not expected this.

"Merlin had seen it, Igraine, long ago, that you would bear a child. A son, a great king. Merlin says the greatest king that Britain will ever know. He said also that it would be to Uther, and conceived midwinter night, in this year. And all these things were said to me, by Merlin, in Uther's presence. What man would ignore such a prophecy, of greatness for his own son? But there were other ways for this to be done. Uther thought it would be easy to persuade Gorlois, but it was not. He delayed too long, waiting for Gorlois to yield, and he became desperate. The measures he took under Merlin's guidance were extreme. Console yourself, Igraine, that fate had a hand in this, as well as your husband."

I did not feel better. I felt worse.

A son.

"Merlin will take my child," I said, wrapping my hands over my stomach. "Uther has promised him his first-born son."

"You will have others, Igraine," Viviane said gently. "You are young yet. If there is trouble again, you have the drink I gave you."

I shook my head. "I do not."

"Why?" I could see anger pinch a little at Viviane's kindly look. She thought I had been careless.

"I drank it all." I felt the tears gathering in my eyes once more.

"Igraine, *why*?" Viviane said sharply.

I shook my head, unable to explain the moment of desperation when I saw what I had thought was Gorlois riding through the gates.

"Can you not give me more?"

Viviane shook her head, and she suddenly looked cold, and closed-off and stern.

"There is no more, Igraine. The world is not endlessly full of magic. Such a potion takes years to prepare. By the time another is ready, you will be past your childbearing years."

"Can you not stop Merlin taking my child?" I begged her.

She took my hands in hers, and I could see that she was as comforting as her station allowed, but it did not help me much in feeling better. I had the awful sense that she only cared for me up to a point. She and Merlin, the whole lot of them in Avalon, cared only for themselves, for the futures they had seen. I was less to her than the dreams she had dreamed.

"I will do all I can, Igraine," she said, and I nodded. I was not sure what she could do. I was not sure that she would truly do *anything* if it did not suit her own wishes, or further her own ends.

Chapter thirty

When I came back to the room where I had been staying, Morgawse was sitting in the window seat, her arms wrapped around her legs, her forehead resting on her drawn-up knees. When I opened the door, she looked up. Her eyes were red, as though she had been crying all night. She didn't seem to notice that my hair was loose, my dress ill-laced and that I too was red-eyed and exhausted. She glowered at me, and put her forehead back down on her knees. There were servants rushing around us, packing up my things. I supposed they were taking them to the queen's apartments in Camelot.

I thought of all that Uther had been prepared to do to me, and his threats about Lot and Morgawse, and I knew that it had to be done. I had to get her to safety.

I called one of the servant girls to me, and instructed her to brush out and plait my hair, and bring me fresh clothes. I chose another of my finest dresses, blue like the summer sky, and set a string of wild ocean pearls around my neck. They had been my own mother's, and my father had said they came from the warm seas far in the south. They were lovely. I wanted to look lovely. I wanted men to think me so lovely that I would not have the sense in me to do anything but stand there to be looked at. I placed my old circlet on my head, wary, still, of the crown of Logrys. It was far away, besides, in Uther's chamber where I had left it, and I did not want to see him.

Carefully dressed and clean, neat and composed, I went to inspect my new rooms. They were in a tower of their own, and I had a chamber to hold audience in, and a council room, and my own bedchamber. Things were a little dusty everywhere but the audience chamber, for Camelot had lacked a queen. I was glad that Imogen had not been occupying the queen's bedroom. I ordered for things to be cleaned, for fresh candles, and more silk covers and furs for the bed as it was cold still, and deep into winter. I wanted it all to be how a queen's rooms should be. I was Uther's queen now, and I would face him as such. If it was his son I carried inside me, he would have to give me what I wanted. He would have to show me some respect. I could be fairly sure that he would not rid himself of me. Not even if I took every measure possible to remove Morgawse from danger.

As the servants were finishing, I called Brastias to me.

"Send for King Lot, Brastias," I said.

He opened his mouth as though he were going to protest, but he did not. I was glad, for I did not want to scold Brastias.

"And," I added as he turned to leave, "afterwards, go to my daughters and make sure they have all they need."

There were no rooms for my little daughters in this tower, and I felt the ache of my separation from them, even though they were only a few minutes' walk away. I wanted them by my side. I wanted little Morgan wriggling into bed beside me in the morning, and asking to be read to. I wanted to see Morgawse's sulky face, and stroke her red-gold hair.

* * *

I had asked for Lot to meet me in my council chamber, and he came in his fine surcoat, which was dark blue and sewn with the bronze two-headed gryphon of his house. It was getting towards evening then, and the days were short, so I had lit the candles on the table, and in their flickering light, the bronze thread glinted bright. Lot had obviously preened himself for the meeting as carefully as I had. I had stood before the hammered mirror before I came, and peered at myself, and reminded myself that I was beautiful, and that that might be something else I could use to fight against this place I now found myself in.

"Lady Igraine," he said, with a bow. "Being queen suits you well."

I nodded in acceptance of his compliment.

"It is still my wish, Lot, that you and my daughter be married."

The corners of Lot's mouth twitched up into a slight smile. He had been there when Uther had shaken Morgawse by her hair. He did not know what else there was behind all that that made me feel sick and afraid.

Lot took a step forward towards me, his fingers trailing across the surface of the table.

"My previous offer still stands, Lady Igraine."

"And which was that?" I replied, my voice a half-whisper. I had been half-sure that he had been playing with me, trying to shock me, before. I felt my heart thud, hard, for a second as our eyes locked together. I prayed that he had been only testing me.

"Tonight." Lot reached out, and took the end of my plaited hair between his fingers, rubbing the silky-fine strands of it, a look of bored approval passing across his face. I slapped his hand away, and he turned his sharp eyes up to mine. "If you come to me, and accept the offer I made you before, I will pledge all in my power to keep your daughter safe, to treat her with kindness, and the honour deserving of her station, of the greatness of her father, and the power of her mother."

"Do you swear it, on the name of God?"

Lot bristled a little. I had not held him for a pious man, but one did not have to be pious to be afraid. He knew the exchange he was asking of me was ungodly, but he swore anyway.

* * *

I was still not sure if I would go. If I would commit myself to that in order to have Morgawse as far as possible from her stepfather. If Uther had come, if he had begged my forgiveness, if he had promised to be kind to my daughters, and to protect my unborn son from Merlin, then I might have put it from my mind, and put my trust in him. But he did not come to apologise. He thought that I ought to have *been reasonable*, seen the sense of it.

I thought, across the courtyard, that I saw lights in Imogen's bedchamber.

* * *

When darkness had truly fallen, and the moon had risen in the sky, and I had no sign that my new husband was coming to try to win me around, I resolved that Lot was my only choice. Uther was with Imogen, pouring his anger into lust. I was disgusted at the thought, but more disgusted still by the thought that he had come to me in Gorlois' shape, and not cared that I had said *I love you* to someone else, to the man whose face he wore. He had not cared. If he could do that to me, I dared not think what he might do to my daughter, whom he resented. *I could take her as my slave*, he had said. He would not.

I felt sick and nervous and disgusted with myself already, but I would do what was required. I could not close my eyes and picture once more Uther's hand tangled in Morgawse's hair, her screaming, the look of raw anger in his eyes. I could not keep her here with the kind of man who could deceive a woman as Uther had deceived me.

Lot was standing at the window of his room in his shirt and breeches when I came in alone, quietly, closing the door behind me. I could feel myself shaking, but I held it back. I was *not* weak. I would do this.

"Igraine –" he breathed, and I rushed across the room, and pressed my fingers against his lips to silence him. If he questioned me, I would break and I would not be able to.

"One night," I whispered, my voice quavering. "And you must promise me that you will be kind, and protect her, and take care of her –"

Lot gently lifted my hand from his lips, and away, and, sliding his other arm around my waist, pulled me against him and into a tender kiss. His beard was a little rough, but his lips were soft and sensual. And yet all I could feel was disgust. He was going to be my daughter's husband, and I did not love him. He was handsome, and young and strong, but I did not desire him. I only hated him.

"You have my word," he murmured through his kisses, pushing us back towards his bed. I felt his hands running over my body, and I felt my skin crawl with repulsion in response. I could hear him, his voice low at my ear, sighing with delight as he held me to him.

When he lay me down beneath him, and I felt his body pressed against mine, and his hand pushing back my skirts and pushing my legs apart, I could not bear it any more. I could not bear to do this to myself, or to Morgawse, but most of all to the child inside me who would suffer this indignity with me. At the thought of that child, and the last moments I had had – I had *thought* I had – with Gorlois, I began to cry.

At first, Lot did not notice. He had unbuckled his belt and begun to open his breeches by the time he realised. When he did, he jumped back from me.

"In the name of God, Igraine," he demanded, his face an ugly mix of anger and disgust, "why are you crying?"

I looked up at him in disbelief, my dress crumpled around my legs, my hair coming loose. "Why do you think?" I asked bitterly.

He shook his head, running his hands through his hair. "I thought this was what you *wanted*, Igraine. I thought this was just another one of your games, like when you married Gorlois just to get Uther to chase you for fourteen years –"

"That is *not* –" I snarled, but Lot cut me off.

"What kind of woman *are* you?" he demanded.

"I am a mother, *my lord*," I hissed at him, "and I would do anything to keep my child safe."

"Get out of my chamber," Lot said, coldly.

I pushed myself up from the bed, still shaking, glaring at him.

186

He was behaving as though I had done some shameful wrong, but it was *he* who ought to have been ashamed. As I went to go past him, he grabbed me hard by the arm, and pulled me back to him.

"I will not be played by you, *Queen* Igraine," he said, his voice low with threat, and then he pushed me roughly towards the door. By the time I returned to my own chamber, the disgust of it all had overtaken me, and I bent double and retched into my little copper basin until I could barely breathe.

I pushed open the window and leaned out, breathing in the clear, late-night air. I could not hold in my mind all the things that had happened to me in the last day. I felt an awful dizzying vertigo when I tried to think of it all. All I could do was push it back, and face my situation cold, and hard, and calm. I had woken in the morning suddenly happy, suddenly hopeful, and in that time I had found that my child was conceived under a deception, and I had offered myself as a whore to save my daughter's life, and been too much of a coward to see it through. I was trembling, but with the cold night air against my face, I felt suddenly clear. *This is the worst it can get*, I thought, and it gave me a strange kind of comfort.

"Lady Igraine?" I heard Brastias' voice behind me, thick with concern, and I turned around. He saw my loosened hair, my crumpled dress, and he knew that I had spoken with Lot. I opened my mouth, ready to lie, ready to protest, but no words came out. He had Morgan in his arms. "Forgive me, lady. Morgan could not sleep. I thought I would bring her to you. Though... I thought King Uther might be here."

I shook my head, walking over to take Morgan into my arms. She had been bright-eyed, but when I held her, she closed her eyes and rested her head on my shoulder, wrapping her arms around my neck. I kissed her cheek. She was cool and soft, and it was a comfort to me to hold her in my arms.

"Brastias," I said, evenly, "tell me again what happened, the night Gorlois died."

He looked uncomfortable, staring down at his boots. What a boy he still was.

"Brastias, please. Just tell me what you did."

He drew himself up, and I could see that he was trying to be brave. "Yes, my lady. I... I pledged myself to Uther, and then they took me away, with the rest of the prisoners, and they gave us food, and wine, and Uther went into his tent with the witch Merlin. There were not many of us. Most of the men decided that they would rather die. Sometimes I wish that I had been that brave."

I stroked Morgan's hair absently. It was an excuse to look at her, not at Brastias. With all the casualness I could muster, I asked, "So, you did not return to Tintagel that night?"

"No, my lady," he replied, and I knew the confusion in his voice was genuine.

"Someone did, Brastias, wearing your armour, and bearing your face." I continued petting Morgan's dark silky hair, and pressed a kiss against her temple. She moved a little in her sleep. "And a man who seemed to be Ulfius, and a man who seemed to be Gorlois. I let that man into my bedchamber, and I let him take me to bed, as is only right for a wife to do with her husband. But now I learn that it was not Gorlois after all, but Uther Pendragon. I am pregnant with his child, and I do not know what in the world to do, Brastias. I do not know what to do."

I looked up at him then, and his face was slack and pale with shock.

Very quietly, I said, "If I asked you to pack a few essential things, and saddle a horse, and take me and the girls back to Tintagel, would you do it, Brastias? Would you do it and not tell a soul?"

Brastias bowed his head. "I would do anything you asked of me, Lady Igraine."

Chapter thirty-one

I felt an awful calm settle over me then. I did not have to give Morgawse to a brute like Lot, or submit myself to Uther, who had deceived and abused me. I could hide myself and my child from Merlin, and I could return to my home and be free. Nothing else mattered. Perhaps they would come for me. Perhaps they would throw themselves against the walls of Tintagel castle, but it would not matter because I would not be any man's slave. *I can make your daughter my slave.* He had wanted to make *me* his slave. And as soon as I had defied him, he had lost interest in me. I was sure he was spending his nights with Imogen.

I fussed at Morgan and Morgawse, dressing them carefully in their travelling clothes, kissing them on the cheek over and over again. Morgawse was still moping because she did not understand, and I could not tell her where we were going, and Morgan was quiet and compliant as always. Brastias hovered always with us, ready, but wary.

"Is everything packed?" I asked him, quietly, and he nodded. I kissed them both once more.

"Take them to the back of the castle," I told Brastias softly, as I slipped away to collect my small parcel of things before I left. I had wanted to make sure that at least they would have a chance to escape, if I were caught, and I would not leave behind the book that Gorlois had given me. To abandon that would have felt like betraying him all over again.

* * *

I was full of the rushing thrill of escape. I was not a prisoner. I was the Queen. No one would try to stop me, and as soon as we were out of sight of Camelot, we could ride hard – it would be weeks before they could reach us. I had allies elsewhere. Perhaps even my sister's husband in Ireland would send troops if I begged, and Erec in France, and perhaps the Bretons. They had been against Uther, once. I felt my freedom close around me as I rushed up to my room. I had tucked the small bag under my bed, and I was sure that Uther was occupied in council with Merlin. Now was the time for me to make my escape.

But when I opened the door to my room, I saw that Viviane was standing before the window, and beside her was Merlin, and beside him Uther. I felt my heart race, and my stomach sink.

"Come in, Igraine," Viviane said gently, as I stood in the doorway. Uther stood in his shirt and breeches; he had come in a hurry. His arms were crossed over his chest, his face was an unreadable mask. He did not look at me, but stared hard at the floor before him. I was surprised, as I always was, by how different he was around Merlin. Every other man, he would have shown the full force of his aggression, but the witch ruled him too much, and that made me afraid.

I stepped through, closing the door, feeling my heart grow heavy in my chest. I had thought that Viviane was on my side.

Viviane glanced at Uther, and back to me. "I understand that you are upset, Igraine –"

"*Upset* –" I cried, but Viviane continued.

"But that will pass. We cannot allow you to leave for Tintagel." I opened my mouth to deny it, but Viviane raised an authoritative hand for silence. "The time is early, and you may yet lose the child. I have seen what will come to pass if your son is not born, and if Britain is left without the king that he will become. Do not think, Igraine, because the future has been seen one way, that this cannot be changed. Merlin, who sees all things, thinks the boy will live, but no man's life is certain. A flight to Tintagel castle, a siege – how many children, just a few weeks old in their mother's womb, would survive this? This is larger than you, Igraine."

"Consider, also, Igraine," Merlin said, his nasty face twisting into a skull-like grin, back in his usual form, the bald-headed hollow-eyed ageless man, "that Uther was acting under my instructions. It is easy, I know, for women to grow affronted with their lovers, but if I can urge you to understand that it was I who impressed upon Uther the importance of conceiving his son at the appointed time –"

Somehow that made it *worse* – that Uther had deceived me for Merlin's sake.

"Do you have *nothing* to say, Uther?" I demanded. He said nothing. I turned to Viviane. "So I have no choice in the matter? I cannot even leave Camelot?"

"I would not advise it, Igraine." Viviane replied gently, but I did not have the patience for her.

"I *will not stay*. Am I a prisoner, then? A prisoner of all three of you?"

"Igraine, *please*," Viviane said. "We do not want to force you to do anything you do not want to do. We only want to make you understand how important your child is, to all of us. To Britain."

I opened my mouth, but I did not know what to say. It did not seem that I had a choice.

"If I go to Tintagel," I persisted, stubbornly, "you will fetch me back, then?"

"We will, Igraine," Merlin said, his black eyes boring into me. I felt sick, and naked under his gaze. No, worse: hollow, as though he saw right through my body and to the child in my womb. "If you must blame someone, blame me, and not Uther, for he did only as I bid him."

Viviane walked over, as though she were going to leave, and she kissed me on the cheek in the same auntish way she had always done. But I no longer felt the warm affection that I had, for she had given me into their hands without mercy. I was not sure I could forgive her. *And I have promised her Morgan*, I thought. It was all in tatters, everything, and I had thought I could not suffer more.

After Viviane had gone, Merlin whispered something to Uther, who nodded, and slipped past me and left.

"You have *nothing* to say to me, Uther?" I demanded again. I had hoped for more from him now we were alone.

He rounded on me then, and I had not expected him to be angry. He had been so passive with Merlin there, so silent, and I had expected him to be *sorry*.

"You do not even *try* to understand Igraine. Do not forget that I remember how you were that night, when you thought I was your husband. And now you and I are bound together, and I must remember how you were with him, and how you told him you loved him. And I must know always that I had to force you to come to me, but you went willingly as his wife."

I felt myself flush dark with anger. "How *dare* you –"

"I have never loved *anyone* but you, Igraine. I did as I had to. Merlin told me that it had to be done, if I wanted a son to follow me –"

"If you loved me you would never have deceived me. You cannot love me, if you treat me this way. You cannot. You *cannot*. And I hate you, Uther. I *hate* you, I –"

I felt a nauseating wave of dizziness pass over me, and Uther jumped forward to catch me as I fell forwards. I felt a sickening, hot trickle down my leg, and when I pulled up my skirts there was a thin, awful, bright red seam of blood. *No*, I thought. *No, not after everything.* My vision was closing in, and I could hear a ringing in my ears. The only solid thing around me was Uther's arm around my waist, and outside of that there was only darkness and the pounding of my heart, and the iron smell of blood.

"Fetch Viviane," I managed to gasp before the darkness swallowed me up entirely.

* * *

It felt as though a long time had passed, and I had spent it in darkness, where there was nothing apart from the smell of blood. *This must be what it is like to die on the battlefield*, I thought. *Alone with the darkness, and blood.* What had happened? I was not sure. I had been about to run to Tintagel. Oh, and then they had found me, and stopped me. And the child. I felt the darkness close a little closer around me at the thought. Through the darkness, I could hear voices. Voices I recognised. A woman's voice, rich and low, and slightly motherly in tone. *Viviane.* I felt her hand press against my forehead, dry, and cool, and soothing.

"She will be well enough, but she must rest. Arrangements must be made for the girls, too. Brastias, you must see to that. I believe Igraine had made arrangements for Morgawse to marry Lot of Lothian. Make sure that that is seen to as soon as possible. If needs be, remind the King of Lothian that it is I, now, who gives the order for it."

Very quietly, and more sadly than I could have imagined, I heard Uther speak. "This is my doing, is it not?"

"No, Uther," Viviane said briskly, and I wished I had the strength to wake and tell Uther that this *was* all his fault. Worst of all, he had made me a prisoner of my own body, for I knew now that I did not have the strength to run. I wondered if I had lost the child. If I had, it would all have been for nothing. "It has been the fault of all three of us. I should have prepared her better. You should have not told her so soon. Merlin should never have allowed you to –" Viviane choked on her words a little, and I realised that she had been harsher with me than she meant, for she was so set on the child, on the king that would bring Britain together. She knew what Uther and Merlin had done to me for the brutality that it was. "Igraine would not have refused you, if you had come offering her love. She loved you, though perhaps she did not know it."

I felt Viviane stroke the hair back from my brow, and in my delirious, half-conscious state, I murmured against her touch.

"I have been a fool," Uther said, darkly, "and my crimes cannot be undone."

"They cannot, Uther," Viviane agreed, her voice blank of compassion. "But your wife lives, and your son lives, so all may yet be worth what we have sacrificed to the future that Merlin and I have seen."

Your son lives. My child was alive within me. That was the thought I held onto tightly as I slipped out of consciousness once more. *Your son lives.*

Chapter thirty-two

It felt slow, the time it took for me to be able to stand, and walk about the room without my body aching and my head spinning, but Viviane told me it was only a few days, not even a week. She told me that she had used all the magic she knew to save my son, and that I had to stay calm, and be gentle with myself. *I will not be able to save him a second time*, she had said. She told me, too, that she had made all of the arrangements for Morgawse to marry Lot. I supposed that was for the best. He would keep her safe, for the sake of Tintagel castle, and my father's gold.

Uther came, and we shouted about it, and he said that Tintagel castle was his, by a conqueror's right, and I said that Tintagel belonged to my daughter, to Morgawse. He pleaded with me, in rough terms, while Viviane stood by and listened to it all with quiet detachment.

"You know as well as I do, Igraine," he said, sharply, "that your father, the man everyone called the *poor King of Cornwall,* was *not* poor, but sat on his gold like a dragon. And the vaults of Tintagel castle are so full of it that with all my men and wagons I could not bring it back to Camelot. That gold will buy *peace.*"

"It is Morgawse's dowry –" I protested, but there was no point, and quickly Viviane shushed me, and told me that I should not shout, and Uther that he should leave. He went, but he had won, and my daughter would have nothing. Lot would take her anyway.

I was bored, and unwell, and lonely. Viviane and Brastias could not sit with me always, and sometimes Imogen was sent by I did not know whom to sit beside me, and tell me stories that she had memorised when she could see. But I turned my face away from her and was resentful.

* * *

It was when I was just strong enough once more to stand that the day of Morgawse's wedding came. I went to her in the morning. For once, Morgawse was quiet and still. I think at last she was understanding the gravity of the situation, and to see her subdued – her bright eyes cast downwards, hidden by her long, thick lashes, her voice soft, and her movements slow and wary – I realised how painfully I missed her usual energetic brightness. I wrapped my arms around her, and kissed her on the forehead, and she leant against me and closed her eyes as I sat beside her on the bed.

I took her hand in mine, drew in a deep breath, and began. "Now, Morgawse, tonight you will begin your duties as a wife. Don't be afraid. Your husband will know what he is expected to do. Just be gentle, and obedient. It is not pleasant, at first, but you will grow to like it. I hope you will be happy with your marriage, Morgawse."

She nodded, but I knew that she was afraid. I stood, and gently led her over to the mirror. We did not talk much as I brushed out her red-gold hair and wound it into plaits, weaving a cloth-of-gold ribbon through it. We were both thinking of her father. Perhaps she was thinking of running through Tintagel castle barefoot, and stumbling down its steps to be swept up into his arms and thrown into the air. Or she was thinking of all the stories he used to tell, of giants, and dragons, and impossible tasks undertaken for the sake of the love of a beautiful young girl. She loved the story of Culwuch and Olwen, but I loved best the story of Pwyll, and its message: be sensible, be careful, be safe. Keep your promises. I was thinking of Gorlois too, but it made me feel heavy and sad. All of my memories of him had become tangled in my memory of the last night I had spent with him – that I *thought* I had spent with him – and somehow I could barely remember any other time I had been in his arms. I had held so tight to that memory in the days just after his death, and it had turned out to be hollow and false, and I had let the others slip out of my grip, just a little bit. If I had been alone, if I had not been in Camelot, perhaps I could have closed my eyes and remembered the night I had come back from Avalon with the little flask of potion clasped in my hand, and we had lain under the stars. I was sure that that was the night that had made Morgan, for she was special, such a child as one might expect the stars to make.

But Morgawse was special too. I felt that, more strongly than ever before, as I stood there with her, twisting the lovely, thick strands of her hair, which were like gold, between my fingers. So like her father. She was all that was left of him in the world: his gentleness, his goodness. She would be strong, too, as he had been, and she would have sons that would be like her father. I hoped that she would. I hoped that they would not be like Lot.

"Tell me about your wedding to my father," Morgawse asked softly, as though she were afraid I would be angry. I carried on running the comb through her hair for a few more moments.

I sighed, but it was in fond remembrance. "Ah, I was an old bride, Morgawse," I began, letting my hands fall from her hair to rest on her shoulders. She turned round to face me. She was smiling, but I could see that she was holding back tears.

"I was almost sixteen years old – or was I already sixteen? I do not remember. But I loved your father. He had been the greatest knight at the tournament my father held while he was looking for a man to be my husband. Mostly it was to distract the young men from fighting each other, but as it turned out, for once it was also the winner of the games who won himself a wife as well."

She wrapped her arms around my waist and rested her head on my shoulder. If it had been any other day, I would have told her not to be so childish, but today was not a day for it, and I wanted her to hug me close as though she were a little girl.

"What happened next, Mother?"

"Well, my father gave his permission, and all the knights and lords gathered." They had been long gone, I remembered that, and it had been quick, and small, but I had liked it that way. Still, I knew that Morgawse would want it to be like a story in romance, and for that it would have to have all of the pageantry. "It was a sunny day, late in summer, or was it early in autumn? But your father was the tallest, finest, bravest man that I had ever seen, and I remember seeing him come into the chapel, and feeling sure that I would always be safe with him by my side. I loved him." I was not sure that I had then, but remembering now all I could feel was that I had.

"I was a foolish girl." I could hear myself becoming harsh, but as I relived it, I remembered the completeness of my happiness in those years. Gorlois had sacrificed all of that to his pride. Why could he not just have let me go? Morgawse's face had crumpled when hearing me regret my happiness, but she had to understand the truth of the world. I took her firmly by the shoulders. "It is best, Morgawse, to marry a man who can protect you. I have chosen a man who has the power to keep you safe, Morgawse. *Forever.*"

She shifted in my grip, and turned away. I was not sure if she was crying.

"Morgawse –" I began, aware that it had not been the right time to talk that way with her. She turned back to me, her eyes shining, but her cheeks dry.

"Why do you always talk like you regret it, Mother?" she said, and I took her face in my hands and I kissed her on the forehead.

"I do not, Morgawse, my love. Of course I do not. I have you, and Morgan. I have nothing to regret."

She nodded, but she did not seem entirely satisfied. She wanted to hear me say that I longed for her father, that I suffered his loss every day. I would not say those words. If I did, I was sure it would kill me.

I clipped her hair into place with a little gold clasp that had been my own, and I helped her into a dress of thick orange-red brocade sewn with gold thread. It was a woman's dress, and most of the time she wore the plainer dresses that children wore. When I had it on her, and pulled it tight, I realised that my little daughter was looking more and more like a woman, had the beginnings of a woman's shape, and she was almost beautiful. She looked so much like Gorlois, I had never expected it. She was not yet fully a beautiful woman, but she would be. Her eyes were large, and gorgeously blue, like the wild cornflowers that grew in the countryside around Tintagel, and her features were gentle and soft and feminine. I put, last of all, a thread of amber beads that had once been mine around her neck. They suited her far better than they would ever have suited me. I would not have known, standing beside her, looking with her into the mirror, that she was not quite twelve years old. It occurred to me that staring into that mirror I was staring into the future. Morgan looked so much like I did. One day she would stand beside her sister, and they would look just like this, and I would be old, and faded and gone, but they would have each other.

I kissed Morgawse on the cheek once more.

"You look like a woman, Morgawse," I said, and Morgawse closed her eyes.

* * *

I was still unwell, and grew tired in the evenings, but that evening I was a little glad of it, for it took the edge off my sorrow. I sat with Morgan in my lap as Uther led Morgawse by the hand up the aisle of Camelot's great chapel – both were tense and angry and resistant. He did not want her married, did not want Lot getting ideas about following him onto the throne of Logrys, or taking Tintagel castle for himself, and she did not want to be married. Of course she did not. She was just a child.

Morgan fidgeted in my lap, but her face was impassive as always, her big, grey eyes following her sister's movements as though she saw nothing else.

I barely ate the food at the feast. Morgan had to be left with Margaret the nun and Emer the old nurse, and I had to sit beside Uther. I was not yet willing to speak with him, and I was exhausted. As soon as the plates of meat were cleared away, I left before the sweet cakes came and picked Morgan up in my arms, carrying her off to bed with me.

I lay down in the dark in the cold in my clothes, under the covers and with the bedcurtains drawn with Morgan nestled beside me, and she snuggled close, and reached out and put her arms around my neck.

"Can we go home now, Mother?" she asked quietly, but I did not answer; I stroked her hair and said nothing.

I was afraid that when I fell asleep I would dream of Lot with Morgawse, for he had glared at me throughout the wedding feast and I had felt sick of the thought of him with her. It was all the worse having had a little knowledge of it myself, for it meant that I could picture with awful vividness him lying on top of her, pushing his hands up under her skirts, and I could not bear it. But I did not dream of him. I dreamt of Gorlois, of him taking me by the hand, and leading me up to our old bedroom in Tintagel. He drew me into his arms in the window seat, and I sat against him, and he read to me in the Welsh Gaelic that I did not understand, but that sounded gorgeous like the singing of the mermaids. And I wanted to cry, but it was a dream, so I could not. And I felt his hands against my arms – strong, and safe and comforting – and his chest against my back. And I felt a longing as deep as the rocks beneath the castle burn through me. I did not know how I could bear it, to live like this, though I knew I would have to, for the sake of my son.

* * *

When I woke in the morning, the dream seemed silly and distant compared to the real concerns of the world outside. Morgawse crept into my room, and into the bed, wriggling between me and Morgan. It was late in the morning, and usually I would be up, and usually I would scold Morgawse for climbing into the bed like a child. But I did not. I did not dare ask her how her husband had been with her last night, not with Morgan there with us, not when I knew that the truth might go through me like a knife. So I said nothing, but put my arms around her as well, and the three of us lay still in a mutual sorrow, and a mutual comfort. I glanced over Morgawse for signs of harm, but I saw none. Only that she was quiet and still, and did not meet me with her eyes.

Chapter thirty-three

I was not surprised when before too long Viviane came and told me that it was time that Morgan went to the abbey. In a way, I was glad of it. I thought that she would be lonely when her sister left for Lothian, and I thought that it would be easier for me to do it all at once.

I was bitterly sorry that I was too sick to travel with her, but I was glad that Lot was not so enamoured of his new wife that he did not try to stop Morgawse accompanying her sister to say goodbye. I kissed Morgan and promised that I would visit her when I could, but I was not sure when that would be. I was glad that I was ill, and shaken through with everything that had happened, for it meant that I barely registered the loss of my little daughter through the painful fog of everything else.

After that, Morgawse left with Lot. Before they departed, he came to my rooms. I had not expected to see him. I thought he would be embarrassed, or ashamed, or angry, or an awful combination of the three, but he was not.

"Lady Igraine," he said gently from the doorway, and I turned from staring out of the window to look back at him over my shoulder. "We are going to return to Lothian."

I nodded. He took another wary step into the room, closing the door behind himself. I felt myself tense a little, but if he came over and tried to touch me, I only had to scream and someone would come. I wished that I had a man's strength, and a man's place in the world, that I did not have to be afraid of him, or shamed.

"I will come and say goodbye to Morgawse," I said flatly. I tested the place that realised that both my daughters would be gone, and it was numb, and awful.

"Igraine," Lot said, and his voice was so sincere that it shocked me, "please, listen to me. It is my intention to keep my part in our agreement, though you did not keep yours. I will protect Morgawse. I will be kind. I will not use her claim to Tintagel to make war with you and Uther." He took another few steps into the middle of the room, and I turned fully to face him, still unsure. He stopped before me, and sighed. "She is a brave girl, Igraine. Braver than you. She is so much like her father."

I nodded, gazing down at the wooden floorboards between us, feeling distant and disconnected as though I were in the middle of some awful dream that I would wake from. But I knew I would not.

"So like Gorlois," I echoed, and at last I looked up and met his eye. He was staring at me hard, his sharp gaze gentle for once. "So like him indeed. So, if you find her brave then you have already –"

I could not finish, and he saved me the trouble by nodding curtly. The thought made me feel sick, but she was his wife, and in the eyes of the law, a girl of her age was ready to be so. My sister Elaine had been the same age when she had married, but her husband had been young as well, and I think it had been a long while before they had been together fully as man and wife.

"One of the serving women thinks that she is with child already," he said.

I pressed my palm against my forehead, fighting back the splitting headache that I could feel beginning to spread through from the front of my brow to the centre of my head. It was an awful thought. She was too young. If she were sick, it would be because she was so nervous about her new life. She was just a girl, just a girl.

I did not realise that I had been standing with my eyes closed and my head spinning until I heard Lot say my name, and felt a hand close around my arm. When I opened my eyes it was onto spinning and darkness; I could hear people shouting, and arms lifting me into the bed, but I did not know whose. I thought I heard Uther and Viviane, and Lot, and Merlin, but I called out for Morgawse. I was going to miss her leaving.

* * *

When I woke, late into the night, there was someone sitting up in the bed beside me. I propped myself up onto my elbows, peering into the darkness. In faint outline, against the white light of the moon that peeped through the bedcurtains, I made out Brastias' profile, and I was surprised.

"Brastias," I whispered. "Should you be in here?"

He turned to me, as though he had not realised that I was awake, and the moonlight picked out his features. He looked concerned, and tired, and much older. I realised that I thought of him as a boy, and he had been fifteen when Gorlois had taken him on as a young knight, but he must have been twenty years old now. I thought of him as a boy, but he was a man. I had been brusque and dismissive with him, but he had travelled through all of this with me.

He opened his mouth as though he was going to say something, but he did not. Slowly, he leaned down towards me and pressed his lips softly against mine. In the strange, midnight world, between the bedcurtains, sealed off from everyone else, I yielded for a moment, and my lips parted under his, and I sighed. His kiss was soft, and pleasant. I thought of Gorlois, and how in the end his pride had been more of a concern than his daughters' safety, and Uther, and how he would have done anything to be made King. But that was not all of it, and we were not all the world.

Gently, I pushed him back and turned over, pulling the covers more tightly around me, and went back to sleep.

* * *

When I woke in the morning, I wondered if it was a dream. I put it from my mind. Brastias was gone, called to some duty riding out with Uther to check the borders, or to deal with some petty complaint, or train those knights who were younger than he was. It hit me once more than Morgan and Morgawse were gone. But I felt better about it, because it meant that they were safe.

I had saved two of my children. All that was left now was to save my unborn son from Merlin.

* * *

The days passed slowly, and I was bored, and lonely. Viviane and Brastias came by to see me, to tell me how things were, from time to time. Viviane brought me drinks of medicine that she said would strengthen my blood. I had been afraid that I was in danger of losing my child again when I had fainted talking to Lot, but Viviane said it was just the blood that I had lost, and I was slow to heal. Brastias did not try to kiss me again, and I wondered if I had imagined it.

Imogen came by once or twice, half concerned and kind, half preening. She delighted in dressing to be looked at, with little gold ornaments in her thick auburn hair – though it was streaked now with white – and rings on her fingers, and gorgeous dresses of samite the colour of exotic jewels, sewn with gold thread and pearls. They must have been her mother's, Aurelianus' queen's, for Britain had not been that rich since his reign. She wanted me to see that I was not the only queen at Uther's court. I hated her.

Uther came a few times, but he was formal, for Viviane was there, and he felt her cold blue-green eyes narrow on him. And I was glad, for I knew that though Viviane would say nothing of it to me, she blamed him, and she knew that he had done me a great wrong.

* * *

I thought it had been months, of loneliness, and tiredness, and hostility, but when Viviane put her hand against my stomach and said that the child was strong, despite everything, for three moons of life, I realised that it was the middle of the third month of the year, and it had all passed unbearably slowly. Morgawse must have been married just a few days after I married Uther, and that was within the same month that we came from Tintagel. I was exhausted from my sorrow and my anger, and I wanted it to be over, but I did not want to go back to Uther unless he begged me and said he was sorry and that he had been wrong.

* * *

At last he came, one bright morning at the end of winter. I stood at the window, looking down at the pretty little walled garden beneath, when I heard the door, and I knew from the sound of the footsteps that it was him.

I looked up, back over my shoulder, but I did not speak.

"Igraine," he said, gruffly. "We must end this. We are man and wife. We must –"

I put out a hand for him to stop, and to my surprise he fell quiet. "I will not do anything you say I 'must'. There is no need for 'must', for I know, Uther, if I refuse, you will make certain that I comply anyway, by force or trickery."

I expected him to tense, to become angry at my defiance, but he hung his head and sighed.

"I did only as I was advised, Igraine."

"Then," I said, drawing in a breath that shook through me, fighting back the tears, "you are not sorry?"

There was a long silence, where we stood staring at one another. I by the window, he halfway across the room. I was glad I was dressed in one of my fine dresses, with the white-gold circlet of Cornwall on my head, not the crown of queenship I had left, purposely, in his chamber. I felt strong like this, and able to be harsh with him. He had come in his shirt and breeches, without his fine gold surcoat and his crown. It was only an illusion that I was powerful and he was not, but it helped me, just a little.

Then at last, very quietly, his voice strained, Uther began. "I regret, Igraine, the pledges that I cannot unpledge. I regret the things that I have done to you. I regret the men that I have killed in anger on the battlefield when I could have spared their lives. I regret believing that Merlin's price would be a simple one to pay, but I was a young man, and I did not think of the future. Most of all, Igraine," his voice dropped, and cracked with emotion, but I still held back, "I regret that I am a man of deeds, and not a man of words. I regret that I cannot find the words to tell you, to explain to you, that I never meant harm, or violence, or cruelty by you. I have only ever loved you. I thought you were mine, because I loved you, and I thought you loved me too. I am not a man of words, like Gorlois must have been. No, Igraine – let me finish. I know that he must have been, because I *know* that you loved me, all those years ago. I know it. Even after you married him, at Christmas when you told me you did not, I know you loved me then. He must have been a man of great words to talk you out of that. I felt it, you felt it. It was the world, to me."

I opened my mouth to speak, but my eyes, and my throat, were filling with tears. I was sure, long ago, that I had been strong.

Uther stepped forward, and when he put his arms around me I did not push him away. He drew me to him, and buried his face in my hair. I could feel the heat of it against the cool skin of the back of my neck. By my ear, he murmured,

"I am only a solider, Igraine. I know only the ways of a man of war. I will not change. I will love you, always." He grasped me tighter, his hands gripping the fabric at the back of my dress, and I felt the heat of his body against mine. And I felt a distant memory stir within me, a memory of love, and brief, brief happiness when I had woken in the morning as his wife. Uther turned back to me, pressing his forehead against mine. I should have thrown him off, I should have slapped him and told him he would never win me round, but there was some truth, some moving truth in what he said, and I could feel my body weakening into his touch, feel myself yearning, feel the desire to slip away melting.

I took his face in my hands, and I whispered, "Promise me you will not let Merlin take our child."

To my surprise, without hesitation, he nodded, and his mouth found mine, and we came together in a rough kiss, wild with relief, and sudden passion. Through his kisses he said, thickly, "Yes, Igraine, I promise. I promise." His mouth was hot against mine, his hands pulling my hair loose, and running into it. I let out a sigh I had meant to hide. "I will do everything in my power."

Just before I was lost in the heady swirl of forgotten desire, I thought, *That will not be enough.* But then beyond that was the knowledge that for Uther's sake, it was enough that he would pledge to give all he could for our child. It was more than Gorlois had ever promised.

Chapter thirty-four

So, Uther and I reconciled. It was tentative, and wary, and after that first moment of passion I was hesitant, and guarded. I knew I would have to tolerate Imogen, and make my peace with only rarely seeing Morgawse. But this was life as I had it. As I grew stronger, less sick, I found it easier to return to the way I had been, to find again the sensible, cold way to see the world around me. I had suffered, yes. But I could count my advantages now. I was Queen. I would bear an heir. Uther had harmed me, but he had pledged a promise to me. I desired him; I had perhaps, as he said, loved him once. There were many women in the world who could not say such things about their husbands.

I learned, too, that Uther had no head for politics. He did not like it. He would say, as he had said to me, *I am a soldier*, whenever he was faced with a complex political problem, and part of me suspected that what kept Imogen by his side was the careful way she gave advice, both authoritative and deferential at once. I knew I could be that to him. I knew I was clever, and wise. I would wait my time, I would gain his trust, and I would grow powerful. That would be. But the more pressing concern for me was to keep Merlin from taking my child. He had left court, and that made it all the worse, for I did not know where he was.

* * *

The opportunity for me to prove myself came sooner than I thought, and unexpectedly. It was fully spring, and I was standing out in the little walled garden beneath the queen's tower instructing the servants on which bushes to prune and which to leave when Brastias came.

"Igraine?"

I didn't correct him. I turned and strode the few steps over to him. The bright sun caught in his dark hair, and on his armour, though it was dull and dented, and made me squint against it.

"What is it, Brastias?"

"There's a missionary here, Lady Igraine. He wants to speak with you."

* * *

Up in my public room – a room where I had last been exchanging unfriendly conversation with Imogen about the chapel – sat an old man in Roman clothes, his hands neatly folded in his lap. When he saw me, he rose to his feet and gave me a broad smile.

"My Lady Queen Ygerna – look at you! I would recognise you anywhere – though of course you are a beautiful woman now."

He saw my brow crease, my hesitancy.

"Oh – you don't remember me. You were just a child."

I did not remember the face of the young missionary who had come to Tintagel when I was just a girl and taught my father the ways of God and Christ, but I did remember his name.

"Father Ninian? What are you doing here?"

He took my hands in his. His hands were very soft – the hands of a man who had aged with them pressed together in prayer. But I supposed I was used to warriors.

"I was so happy when I learned that King Uther had married at last, and even happier when I learned the wife was you."

I could not meet his kind old eyes. I nodded, staring down at our clasped hands. Mine, set now with gold rings and gems, pale and slender and young. His, unadorned, the nails short but clean, the skin slack and mottled with age. He had seen me last twenty years ago. I was not the woman he thought I was.

I shook my head. "I do not know, Father, that my husband would welcome you."

"This, my dear Ygerna, is why I came. Sanctificatus est enim vir infidelis per mulierem fidelem."

I knew that verse well enough. Through the believing wife, the heathen man is sanctified. There would be no sanctifying Uther. I sighed.

"I have been in the Highlands. The King of the Picts is a Christian now."

I fought the urge to smile. "I hope you did not call him that when you were in Lothian."

Father Ninian gave a reserved smile in return. "Lady Ygerna, I am a diplomat as well as a churchman."

I motioned to the chair where he had sat before, and I pulled one up to the little table beside him. Down in the yard, Uther was equipping himself for a hunt. We had not spoken alone the past few days. It was difficult. Whenever we wanted to negotiate with one another, we could not be alone. Too easy, then, to slip into the lures of closeness, of flesh and desire.

"You would like me to help you to convert Uther."

"I would like you, Lady, to intercede with your husband on behalf of the Church. As queens have done before you. Think of Esther, and of Saint Helena. Think of the Virgin Mother, Queen of Heaven, who intercedes for all of us." I was unsure, and he could tell. Another argument with Uther, leading nowhere.

"There is talk in Rome of a Holy War. A war of conversion. Some eyes in Ireland are turned towards Logrys and ask why Uther is the only King in Britain who keeps the old ways, and heeds no authority beyond himself."

"Uther is no challenge to Rome," I said quietly.

Ninian nodded. "I know, but Britain is rich, and Rome remembers a time when you were one of its provinces. Only give this court every appearance of being a Christian one, and that will be enough. I will, of course, speak for you."

He did not say *if you manage to convince Uther*, but I understood it anyway.

* * *

At the next council, I waited for a quiet moment after Uther had grumbled about taxes in the north and Imogen had once more asked for gold from the crown to sustain the household she kept in my castle, to speak.

"My Lord Uther, I have something I wish to say."

Viviane was watching me carefully. I wondered if she would consider this a betrayal. That was not my concern.

"Father Ninian," I gestured to him, sitting quietly in the corner in his strange Roman clothes, "has come as a missionary to this court. It would be well for us to put aside pagan ways and live according to the law of Christ."

Imogen was already speaking even before I had finished, lounging in her chair, gold and jewels from around her neck trailing on the table as she leaned forward towards me.

"Saint Igraine preaches the gospel once again. We would be just as well having your nun in here, wouldn't we?"

Imogen knew that I had sent Margaret north with Morgawse. She laughed when she felt my indignation.

"Save your prayers. You think you're a regular Saint Helena, don't you? Go to the chapel, sit down and pray. Let those of us with a head for it talk politics."

"Saint Helena was a warrior as well, Imogen," I said coldly. "She led an army. She supervised the torture of those who denied the true faith."

Imogen bristled, but Uther was already out of patience.

"What has this to do with me? This is simply a matter of household arrangement –"

"It has everything to do with you," I said forcefully. "If we do not make every show of being a good Christian realm then Rome may aid the Christian kings of Britain in taking Logrys from you. And I can think of at least one man with Christ at his side and an army under his command who would delight in doing so."

"Lot." Uther's voice was dark. I nodded.

"What of Avalon?" Viviane asked.

I glanced around the table. They were all looking at me; not just Uther and Imogen, but all of the knights and the lords. I took a deep breath.

"Nothing need change in our relations with Avalon. But Uther and I will set a Christian example. This is what must be done."

Uther nodded, and the talk around us turned to something else. I felt an overwhelming rush of strength. I was wise. I was careful. Uther needed me. After that, I attended every council, and more and more I spoke out. Although at first Uther was annoyed, as was Imogen – both being used to talking as they pleased – when Uther saw that Viviane listened to what I had to say, and the lords often agreed with me, he began to listen as well. Imogen did not warm to it as much, or perhaps I imagined it. I was not quite sure with her whether she hated me or not. I kept Ninian as long as I could, but he had a calling, and he followed it back to Rome. Sometimes, Uther came to my chamber at night, and often we would argue – either about Tintagel, or some tedious affair of state in Logrys – and then we would hurl ourselves together. It was easier that way: to blur the white-hot anger with the heat of passion. It meant that neither of us had to face what we had done to one another. We did not have to be tender. We did not have to be honest. Part of me liked it too. I felt as though I were in control of him, though I was sure that I was not.

Brastias was always by my side, but he did not try to kiss me again, and it faded away in my consciousness, like a dream.

* * *

We did not talk about Merlin, we did not talk about my daughters, and we did not talk about Gorlois. Uther talked often about his son, though now that Merlin had gone, and the prophesying had died down, I wondered that everyone was sure, after just a few months of life, that the child in my womb would be a boy. I had never shown any indication that I would bear anything but daughters. I wondered, besides, whether since the child had been conceived to a man in Gorlois' shape, it would look like him. That seemed to me the more obvious outcome than what Uther seemed to assume, that he would, like God, make progeny in his own image.

* * *

The days grew longer, and I grew steadier, but my illness had been enough of an obvious disturbance in the household and people began to whisper that the queen was with child so soon. Uther was not pleased that it was being rumoured everywhere like that. Knowing his promise to Merlin, and not wanting the common folk to hear of it, he tried to order me to stay in my rooms. I refused, but he was there more and more, staying with me so that I had to stay inside. Partly, too, he liked to have me and the growing child to himself. He liked to run his hands over my swelling belly, and kiss it, and I would lie beneath him, angry and resistant for a while, but always overtaken by it in the end. It reminded me of the tender Uther that I had known in glimpses, the man who was half-lost being the soldier-King, afraid that any man would question him. In the end, I gave in to the dream that I had of who Uther Pendragon was, in those moments, and I offered him my mouth to be kissed, I twined my limbs with his, and I allowed myself to believe in the man I had imagined. It was that, and the angry passion of our fights, that held us together. I did not see him often in the daytime, but sat reading, or spinning, or sewing with Imogen and Viviane and the other ladies of court. Viviane, of course, did not sew or spin, but she read, or sat and watched, and I found her presence a comfort, though I was not sure I trusted her. Still, she was the closest thing I had to an ally, and I was glad of her. I was sorry, too, when she left, because troubles on the Isle called her back to Avalon. I missed her, and I disliked sitting beside Imogen in silence, so I took to going to the chapel to pray. It was a moment of peace, alone. A moment with the Virgin Mary, who too had borne a son for a man whose true shape she could not see, and had given him to a destiny she had no say in. She was not the goddess of my childhood, but I looked at her and I saw myself, however prideful that might have been.

* * *

One morning, late in spring, stirring, half-awake, I became aware of someone moving about in the room. Groggily, I murmured in

206

protest at being woken, but I did not really mind. It was light outside already, I could see that through the bed-curtains, and there were things that must be attended to, things I had to do before my swelling stomach made it harder for me to get around. There were matters of politics to attend to. Tributes unpaid, oaths unsworn, matters of the coin and the equipment for men, the taking of harvest; all those things that Uther did not have the patience for. I would have to have the patience for them, while there was still time for me to organise it.

Slowly, I pushed myself up to sitting among the cushions, and rubbed my eyes. I didn't feel nauseous anymore, which was a mercy, and the small swell of my stomach was only just visible underneath my loose nightdress. Once I was dressed no one would guess at it unless they were sitting right beside me. It was the maids, who knew that I had been sick in the morning, who looked out for it, but as of yet it was still gossip and rumour.

I pushed back the bed curtains to see that the person I had heard moving around was a young woman, pretty, with thick, glossy brown curls falling down her back, pulled back simply from her temples, the way I had dressed my own hair as a young girl. Her skin was slightly dark – not from the sun or work in the field, but as though she had been born in some gorgeous southern place – and she was delicate-boned and graceful in the way she moved. I paused for a minute, watching her as she sat with her head bent over one of my dresses, sewing a little tear on the hem carefully. It was so nice to watch her. She was young, and lovely, and her careful concentration was as attractive as her neat, pretty features. I wondered with a jolt if she were some favourite of Uther's, but I put the thought from my mind. Imogen was worth my jealousy – she had been a princess – but I need not be jealous of a servant.

As though she had heard my petty little thoughts about her, she looked up, with big, sweet brown eyes, bright as chestnuts, and smiled.

"Good morning, Lady Igraine," she said. Her voice was low, and soft and musical, and I wondered where such an enchanting creature had come from, if she were a fairy, wandered in from the woodlands. I was about to ask her who she was when she spoke once more. "My name is Melusine, and I have been set by Lord Uther to be your maidservant, and to take care of you in all things."

I laughed brightly. "Melusine, like the lady of the waters?"

Elaine had used to tell me the tale while she sat spinning, before she was married. She had disliked spinning, but she had liked me sitting at her feet to listen to her stories, and Melusine the shape-changer had been one of my favourites.

The girl smiled. "Yes, like her."

She pulled out the chair I put before my dressing table, and gestured for me to sit in it. And I came, and sat, and she began to brush through my hair. I closed my eyes against the pleasant feeling, the gentle, familiar feeling of having my hair brushed, and I was surprised how it made me feel as though I might cry. It was a long time since I had felt the tender, friendly touch of another woman. Not since Elaine had brushed my hair as a girl. I felt her loss within me – a dull, heavy pain. It had happened far away, in the midst of other things, and I had never properly grieved for my oldest sister. If only she were alive still, she would not have abandoned me like the selfish, capricious Enid. There was so much lost. I had parted my daughters from one another.

"Your hair is so soft, my lady," Melusine said, cutting through my thoughts, her nimble fingers weaving the strands into a plait. "Like strands of fine silk."

I laughed softly, and I realised that already, with Melusine, I had laughed more than I had done in a long time. I supposed I missed the company of women.

"You are too kind, Melusine. Where are you from? I can't place your accent."

"Oh," she said breezily, "I was raised near Avalon, but my parents are from the south countries near the Mediterranean Sea."

"Near Avalon," I said thoughtfully, as Melusine picked up a blue ribbon, and began weaving that through my hair, a style more elegant, more elaborate than anything I could have managed myself. I realised that I had been negligent in not providing myself with a servant before this. There had been serving women around in Tintagel, but I had asked the help of whoever had come by. And I had missed out. I knew women whose maidservants were their confidantes, their intimates, their friends. Already, I liked Melusine, but I was not sure that I was ready for a confidante. Not quite yet. "It is beautiful there, I hear."

"Oh, it is," Melusine sighed, picking a silver torque from the dressing table for around my neck without even asking me what I would like to wear. I did not mind. I found it tedious, choosing, and I was glad that she did not interrupt the conversation with asking. She had a soft, almost seductive voice, and I realised that already I was trying to induce her to speak more about herself, just to listen to it. "There are groves of trees so thick that it is always darkness within, and the fairy-folk live there, they say. And there are springs of clear water hidden in the woods that hide the groves at the centre. And the land is ancient, and the trees whisper to one another…" She laughed to herself a little then. "Though the men say those are women's tales, as though they do not believe them. Perhaps it is better for them not to."

"It is better, certainly, not to repeat such tales," I found myself saying, more sharply than I meant to, and I felt myself blush, as though I were ashamed, even though she was only a servant. I ought not to have been embarrassed at all in front of her, and yet I was. I was because I believed all that she believed, about the land of fairies, beyond our own land, and the strength of the Otherworld. It had given me Morgan, and the child within me. Yet, I knew too well the jealous god of the Christians, and I knew that not all of his priests would be pragmatic, compassionate men like Ninian, and I was afraid more and more – afraid the way Uther never would be – that the world was changing, and that those who did not change with it would be silenced. These were not the old Romans, who had come and gone, and adopted our old gods with their own. Rome, which had once been strong in war, was now strong in religious might, and I thought it wisest, thought it best, if we all bowed our heads to Rome's god. And deep, deep below that, I still remembered Gorlois taking the garland from my hair, and kissing me, and calling me the White Goddess, and the acute awareness I had at that moment that he was from a passing time, an age that was dissolving away. I wanted to stride into the new world, and if that meant turning my eyes away from the secrets of the woodlands, then so be it. The woodland had no armies. I had to live – to survive – in the world of men.

"But my lady," she said, a little more meekly, "they are only tales."

I put out my hand, and placed it gently on top of hers, and smiled.

"I know you meant no harm, Melusine," I said, and she smiled in return.

* * *

Uther came in as Melusine was helping me pin a cloak about my shoulders, and he crinkled his brow at the sight of her and turned to me.

"Who is this girl?" he asked.

She turned to him and curtseyed, "I am Melusine, my lord. The Lady of Avalon sent me to care for Igraine, for her health, and all her requirements."

He did not look at her. He was looking at me, still. "She looks familiar to me."

I waved a dismissive hand at him. "It is hardly worth embarrassing yourself, Uther, over trying to remember the faces of all the servant-girls whom you have –"

Uther cut me off, seizing hold of me, hard, about the wrist, and we stared at each other.

"Forgive me, my lord Uther, but we have not met." Melusine spoke softly, and Uther released his grip on my wrist a little. "I shall return, Lady," she said to me, and slipped away tactfully as Uther stepped forward, and took my face in his hands, and kissed me roughly.

"You are a shrew, Igraine," he murmured through his kisses. And I felt his arms come around me, and I let myself sink into it.

Chapter thirty-five

The days were slow, and without event. The child inside me grew, and so did the faith of the men of the council in my good judgement. Uther wanted always to fight those who did not respect him into submission because it was all he knew, but I understood the complexities of tribute, the customs of each of the peoples of Britain, and even he began to ask me what I thought. I was pleased about this, though he was always the same to me in private, half demanding, half tender, and we did not talk.

One day, as spring was drawing to an end, and the air was bright but still fresh, I sat in the walled garden, reading, and listening to Melusine play the harp, which she did wonderfully. I found that, when a cry went up as the knights came back from the hunt with Uther, most of the women scurried away to greet husbands, and paramours, and I was left alone with Melusine and Imogen.

I went to stand, to leave, and Imogen put a hand over mine. Her hand was wrinkled a little at the knuckles and, I saw in the harsh daylight, tanned in patches with age, her skin a little slack to the touch. I supposed that she was more than forty years old, perhaps even fifty, but her hair was still so bright and thick, and her presence so powerful and beautiful, that I always forgot how old she was. Her white, sightless eyes blinked at nothing, though Melusine, young and lovely, plucked the strings of the harp before her.

Very low, she said to me, "I know that you hate me, Igraine."

I said nothing. I was not going to fight with her over Uther. What they were involved in was far beyond what I ought to have been concerned with. She tightened her grip on my hand, and I felt her rings bite into my skin.

"You will not be young forever, Igraine," she said. "And I know you have a head for politics, for I have heard all those clever things you have to say for yourself when the council meets." Her tone was wry, slightly mocking, and I did not like it. "So before you are fully resolved to hate me, just understand that what I have done was an act of necessary politics for me and Uther both. He keeps me so that no other man will try to use me as a standard to rally around, and I allow him to keep me, because I do not want some young, upstart soldier to carry me away, and use me in ways I will not like. I *like* Uther. We are used to one another. We know what we are to one another. It is not love, or the reckless passion that drove him to you, but it has its own domestic virtue. I do not deserve your hate for wanting to be safe, or to enjoy the embraces of a man even though I am old and barren and blind."

I did not say anything, but I did understand. I knew my hate of her was childish.

"Why are you telling me this now?" I asked after a long time. I could see that Melusine's fingers had fallen still on the harp and that she was listening.

"I am dying, Igraine. I have seen a physician who says there are short months left of my life. It is a sickness in my lifeless womb, and I will not live long. I wanted you to understand, before I died, that I never meant you harm, and for you to see that you have misunderstood me in this. You are wise with everyone else's wishes and desires, but not with your own."

"That is *not true*," I hissed, and I was angry that she had gone on to lecture me when I had just been melting to her, feeling weak and sympathetic.

She put her hand on mine in a gesture which I was sure was meant to be comforting. "I am only trying to give you my advice, as a faded princess to a young queen."

I nodded, and I allowed her to lean over and kiss me on the forehead. But I was not sure how I felt about her.

* * *

Late that night, as I sat in a tub of steaming bathwater and Melusine combed through my hair, I was still thinking about Imogen. I ran my hands over my body under the water, over the new, round shape of my stomach, over my little breasts, grown larger and heavier in anticipation of a child to nurse, and then over my long, thin arms, rubbing away the dirt and the tiredness. When she had finished combing through my hair, Melusine pressed her fingertips against my temples, and rubbed them against my scalp until I sighed with pleasure, and then across my shoulders, which were hot and wet from the bathwater, until I groaned low, feeling my muscles relax. I had not realised how tense I had been until I felt the strong, competent touch of Melusine's nimble fingers. She was a skilled and useful woman to have in my service. She did my hair so nicely, and played the harp so prettily, and sang in a low, sweet voice. Already, I was fond of her, and now as I felt her fingers press into the knots of tension in my shoulders, and down my back, I was sure that I would not part with her unless I had to.

After a long while, still kneading at my back with her fingers, she said, softly, "I heard what the Lady Imogen said."

"Hmmmm," I replied, closing my eyes and sinking down further into the bathwater.

She was quiet again for a long time, and then she said, "If the Lady Imogen is sick and dying anyway, I could give her a drink – it would be painless, and that would be kinder than a long sickness –"

I sat up sharply in the bath, and some of the water spilled onto the floorboards.

"Melusine, *no*," I said sharply.

"If I were you," Melusine said, archly but quiet, "I would want her gone."

"Well," I replied, relaxing back into the water, "perhaps that is so, but murder is not the answer."

"It would be an act of mercy," Melusine persisted, but when I insisted, she was quiet.

* * *

Still, only a few days after that, Imogen died in the night, as peacefully as if a drink of magic herbs *had* put her to sleep. I surprised myself with my own grief. Imogen had been a presence in my life for more than ten years, and we had not been friends. But I had recognised something of myself in her, something of my own determination, my own careful persistence, and I only blamed her for her life as concubine to Uther because that was easier than blaming him. He stared at me in disbelief as I wept watching them burn her body, but I could not help feeling that I had lost my double, my shadow at Uther's side, and someone worse might come to fill her empty space.

Uther came that night, blank with grief, and I did not ask questions, or berate him for mourning the woman who had been his lover. Imogen had been at his side when I had married another man, and she had been the guidance that I now had to give on my own to stop a hot-headed soldier throwing himself into war after war just because he had a crown on his head. He only waited a moment for Melusine to slip out of the room before he pulled me from my prayers and caught me up in his arms and threw us both down on the bed, whispering my name over and over, his hands gripping me, hard, as though he wanted to be sure that I was there, real and solid, beneath him. When we sank apart, I was still trembling with it, with the power of the pleasure of my own body, and it was only then that I realised that we were still half-dressed, he with his shirt pulled open, but not removed, and his breeches only half-kicked away, and I with my dress loosened and pulled open, but the skirts crumpled beneath me. We fell asleep like that, exhausted, empty of feeling, and when I woke in the morning, Uther was gone.

I did not ask Melusine if she had had a hand in Imogen's peaceful death, because I did not want to know. I knew that if I knew that she had, I would feel responsible.

* * *

Mostly it was tedious, domestic affairs that occupied my days. Drusus, Uther's seneschal, was old and lazy, and I suspected him of being a philanderer. Though he limped badly when Uther set him about some task or other, I had seen him try to pull Melusine into his lap as lithely as any young man. It was only because she was so young and nimble and quick that she had managed to slip away from him. I didn't like him, although he did respect me, and listen to my instructions; I noticed that he passed many of the tasks off to the younger men, and complained besides of aching bones from dragging his heavy, maimed foot, so more and more often I left the tasks to Brastias, who was always by my side. He sat with me, often, in the council chamber below my bedchamber, and we would, until the stars were out and the candles low, comb through the accounts of the castle, the treatises Uther held with the local lords and the lesser kings of Britain. And we made sure that there was peace and order in Britain. I did not think that Uther, riding out to hunt, checking his coat of mail, harrying his smiths for more swords and armour and demanding every few days that another man ride out in search of Merlin, realised that it was Brastias and I who held his kingdom together.

In the letters that came and went, I learned that the captain of the garrison at Tintagel was living in it like a lord, and I pressed Uther to send men to stop him. Because he cared about the gold in the vaults, he did, but I was not sure it would be long until someone else decided that they wanted the castle for themselves. I longed to return. I hoped that when my child was born, Uther would let me go back to my home. I missed the sea, and the dark rocks, and the smell of the wide waters. I missed the cry of the gulls, though it was harsh and horrid. I missed it all. In comparison, Camelot was neat and tame, and I could not honestly say I preferred it to my cold, wild home.

There was a letter, too, one day, from Lot. It was addressed to me, but Brastias tore it open anyway, giving me a wary look that I did not like. It was not his place to be protective of me. But it was not from him. It bore his seal because it came from his castle, but it was written in neat little letters from Margaret, the nun I had sent with Morgawse when she married, who had been her teacher as a girl, saying that Morgawse was well, and there was every sign that she had a strong and healthy child growing inside her. I knew that it was supposed to be good news, but Morgawse was so young, barely more than a child herself, and I was afraid for her. I prayed for her as well, though this was to the Mother I had prayed to as a child. I hoped that her husband was being kind. I dared not think of it. From what I knew of him, he was hardly a kind man. Though he had had his moments. He had not wanted me when I had cried.

* * *

One night, late, Brastias came to me to say he had a letter from Viviane for me, saying that she was returning to Camelot to check that I was well. I remembered how I had felt when I had found out about the child: betrayed, cold, angry with her. I did not feel those things now. I felt as though a beloved aunt was returning to me, and I longed to see her, to have her kiss me on the forehead like a child, and call me 'Little Igraine' – though I was taller than she was – to tell me that my child was safe, and that in my illness I had done him no harm. I needed to ask her, as well, what assurances she could give me that Merlin would not take my child. Oh, I had made Uther promise that, but he hardly had the power to deny Merlin anything.

I noticed that Brastias sat strangely in his chair, stiffly, and leaning to one side. As he read from the letter, I came to stand behind him, and pressed my hand gently against his shoulder. He drew in his breath sharply, though his teeth, as though he were in pain.

"Brastias," I asked quietly, "are you hurt?"

"No, Lady Igraine, I –"

"Stand up," I said briskly, "and take off that jacket. Let me see."

"No, I –"

"Just do it, Brastias," I said, and reluctantly he stood and shrugged off the leather jerkin the knights all wore for training. His shirt underneath was dark with blood at the shoulder, and it was turning a rusty brown as though he had left it to bleed and no one had seen to it. I felt a flutter of fear deep in my stomach. If they had only been training at arms, then why was Brastias so badly hurt, and why was he trying to hide it?

"Take off your shirt, Brastias," I said, very softly, my voice tense with fear. Slowly, he pulled it over his head. Beneath, in the candlelight, I saw the muscular shape of his chest, the skin tanned a little from the early spring sun, the fine, dark hairs of his chest, and I felt myself blush just a little. I was glad of the half-darkness that hid it. Beneath his shirt, I saw the wound of his shoulder was deep, and dark with dried blood. I gasped, pressing my fingers lightly against the edge of the wound as he sat down once more, so that I could look down at it.

"Brastias," I breathed, "what happened to you?"

He shrugged away from me a little, and I put my hand against his other shoulder, drawing him back a little. His bare skin was warm, and smooth, and soft, and I tried to pay it no attention. He was almost ten years younger than I was, and I was a married woman – more, a woman married to a jealous man. And yet, he had been beside me all this time, and been steadfast, and reliable, and faithful.

"Tell me how this happened." I interrupted my own thoughts, forcing myself to concentrate on the wound, on the problem before us.

"There was an accident, training. The man I was paired with, I think he slipped, and the blow was harder than he meant it."

I did not believe him.

"Who was it, Brastias?" I asked, and I let my hand trail up to his cheek and turned his face to mine. I had not noticed before how dark his eyes were, and I wondered once more where Gorlois had found him, when he had brought him back to be one of our knights. I had often wondered if he were some bastard child of Gorlois', to whom he had felt a responsibility, but he did not have his look. If he were, his mother must have been some dark-eyed fairy maiden, like the one with whom Prince Ector had disappeared in the middle of the night.

"Igraine, please," he begged, his voice cracking with desperation, looking away from me, trying to rise. But I put out my hand to stop him once more, and he fell still.

"It was Uther, wasn't it?" I asked very softly, and Brastias nodded. Uther was never finished punishing Brastias for having once been Gorlois' knight, and for still being more mine than his.

"Stay here," I ordered gently, "and I will get something to clean this."

So, Brastias was either too proud to ask for help after being injured in a fight with his King, or Uther had forbidden it. As I put the water to heat on the fire, I wondered what I thought of it. I did not know how I felt. I was confused, I was weary, and the child inside me was making me feel unsteady, likely to pitch one way or another with wild emotion. I did not remember being this way with either of my daughters, though Gorlois had been by my side the whole time Morgan had been in my womb. And Morgawse – I had had the thought of war in the north to occupy me, then.

I tore up some herbs to put them in the hot water, and tore some strips of linen to bind the wound. It was not so bad, and it would heal cleanly, if I could treat it properly. When I came back down, Brastias was sat in the chair, looking as if he had not moved at all.

He was quiet when I pressed the strips of linen into the wound, though I knew it must have hurt him, and I felt him tense with the pain under my hands. When the wound was clean, and bound, I pressed my hand on top of it, like a blessing, as I had seen the women of Avalon do. There was no healing in my touch, but I liked to do it anyway. I had done it to Morgan and Morgawse whenever they had hurt themselves, and needed comforting.

I closed my eyes, and leant my head, just a little, against his. Slowly, I felt his hands come to hold me about the hips, and I opened my eyes and looked down at him. I could feel my heart thudding, hard. It was half dark with the candles beginning gutter out, and late, and the room smelled pleasantly of steam and the herbs I had put in the basin of hot water. I opened my mouth to protest, or to say something mundane and business-like, to pretend that we were not stood here, alone, staring at each other like teenaged idiots, when Brastias pulled me closer, and I leaned down to let my lips brush against those he offered up to me. And he stood, and lifted me gently on to the table, his hands running softly up my thighs, my back, into my hair. And I let my hands run over his bare chest, his muscular arms, and it was a blissful moment of forgetting, of sensation. The warm air, the young man under my hands, the lips against mine, soft but firm, and gentle, and sensual. And I was lying down beneath him as he climbed onto the table on top of me, and I was sighing as I felt his hands push back the skirts of my dress, and his bare skin against the skin of my thigh.

But then, as he slid his arm under my waist to pull me closer against him, his arm knocked the little copper basin from the table, and it clattered and rang against the stone floor. And it was like waking from a dream. He jumped back, and I stood up, both of us flushed, and suddenly aware of the cold chill of reality, that we had been shocked back from the brink of a dangerous mistake.

He opened his mouth as if to speak, but I had already slipped down from the table, pushing my skirts down and smoothing them, and picked up the little copper basin. I turned to him then, as though nothing had happened between my bandaging his wound and now, and I said, "Make sure you rest, Brastias."

He nodded and said, "Of course, Lady Igraine."

I rushed out to my own room where Melusine was waiting to help me pull off my gown, and my underdress, and to comb out my hair, and fetch me a drink of hot honey water before I got into bed. Yet all the time, whenever I closed my eyes, I could feel his mouth against mine, and I was aware that if I could not forget this, it would cost Brastias his life.

Chapter thirty-six

The next day, I confronted Uther when he came to me in the evening and tried to wrap me in his arms.

"Why did you injure Brastias on purpose, and not allow him to go to one of the medicine-women?" I demanded, stepping back from him as he reached for me. An unpleasant smile spread across his face, and I felt myself tense against him.

"That's what Brastias told you, is it?" he said, his voice low, and thick with threat.

I drew myself up to my full height.

"It is," I said.

"Well," Uther said, unbuttoning his surcoat and shrugging it off, tossing it casually onto a chair, though I knew it was the most expensive piece of clothing he had ever owned, "I had to teach him a lesson, had to instil some discipline among the men. Did he tell you what he said, that made me believe that was necessary?"

I felt my blood run cold. I shook my head.

Uther gave a rough, cruel laugh before he spoke, fixing me with his grey-green eyes. "I did not think that he would have done. Oh, little boys love to run to their mother when their father scolds them, but I suspect it is more than this with our young Brastias. You are not quite a mother to him, are you? Too close in age. Too comely. Too easily drawn into sympathy, and perhaps even affection. No, Igraine. I shall tell you, and you shall hear." His hand closed around my wrist as I tried to step away. "Brastias and some of the other knights were amusing themselves making fun of King Lot, and his wife." I felt my stomach twist within me, and I put a hand to it, afraid. The memory of my fragility was still too immediate, too raw, for me to not fear my own raging emotions. "Some of the jokes were crude. There was some degree of… miming."

Uther didn't leave it to me to imagine what gestures were made. I'd seen them before, made behind my sister Enid's back after she had dragged herself home, not half as shame-faced as she should have been with a new husband in tow. But to know that men were making them about my twelve-year-old daughter was obscene. I ran to the window as I felt the bile rise up my throat, and I retched. Uther stood still, watching me dispassionately as I leaned out of the window, gasping for my breath. I hated the thought of Lot with my daughter badly enough when I was not forced to picture it, and to hear that the men were joking about it made it almost unbearable. They were also joking about me, and what kind of mother would give her daughter up to that kind of rough treatment by a much older man.

"Now," Uther continued, his voice cold, and awfully calm, "you know I do not have much affection for my stepdaughter, but nonetheless, she is the child of my wife, and I will not suffer men to speak so of my kin. I know that Brastias had a lot of licence with Gorlois, and he was close with the girl. I do not ask those things that other men have asked: if there was a hurry to marry her to Lot, because Brastias had her with child already; whether Brastias is some illegitimate child of Gorlois, to have earned such… undue favour from his master. I do not know these things, and I suspect that you do not know them, either, Igraine, for if you did, you would not shower him with your favour and affection so freely."

If I were not still sick, not still shaking, not fighting to keep down what was left in my stomach, I would have stood, and shouted at him, and beat him with my fists. It burned me, somewhere deep inside, that he thought the same things that I had thought about Brastias. That he *was* too close with Morgawse, that he was Gorlois' own son, rescued from some farm, or brothel, or – worse – from some half-noble lady who, with her in his arms, might have been a threat to me and our daughters. *It cannot be true*, I told myself, but I was not sure I believed it.

* * *

Brastias came the next morning, after I had lain all night cold and still as a stone in Uther's embrace. He did not question my silence, he did not really seek to comfort me. I think he enjoyed my suffering, because it made him believe that what he had done was right.

When Brastias came in, Uther was long gone, and I waved Melusine away. I saw the colour rise in his cheeks and I knew what he thought.

"Igraine," he began, his voice thick with some dangerous emotion. And as he stepped towards me, I stepped back, and I saw painful confusion flicker across his face. He had been ready to take me into his arms and kiss me. He had been thinking about it, since it had happened, wishing that he had not left, that he had called me back and made me stay. I was glad I had not, knowing what a man he was.

I crossed my arms over my chest. "*Lady* Igraine, Brastias. And I called you here because I have learned from my lord Uther exactly what it was that he punished you for."

I saw Brastias tense. He was not going to deny it. An awful mix of anger, betrayal and disgust coursed through my veins. I had wanted it not to be true.

"Igraine, please, you do not understand –"

"*Lady* Igraine, Brastias. Do not speak to me as if you are anything more than a sworn servant of my husband. Do you need me to repeat what my lord King Uther tells me you said about my daughter?"

I was fighting back the tears. Whatever else he had been, however brazenly she had behaved, he had been her *friend*, and that he would say those things made me sick with him, and furious at the whole world of men. I had thought Brastias was different.

"Igraine," he said, ignoring my instruction once more, staring down at his boots. I could see that he was sorry, but he was not sorry that he had said it, only that he had been caught at it. "It is just men's talk. There is not a knight in Camelot who does not make some crude jest or other on the field. Besides…" He looked up at me slowly, and I could see that he struggled to give me the truth, though I knew what it would be. "I cannot be seen among the men to… have a special affection for Morgawse. I must… say the things that they say. Make the jokes that they do. I cannot be seen to have more regard for her than other women. She is a twelve-year-old girl, and she is someone else's wife."

"*Do you?*" I asked, very low, forcing myself back from slapping him, from attacking him with every strength in my weak little body.

"No." Brastias rubbed the heel of his hand into his forehead.

"No, that is not what I mean to say – but men talk, Igraine. A man is only so good as his reputation. I... forgive me –"

I crossed my arms slowly.

"What do they say about me, Brastias? What do the men on the field say? What do *you* say, when you are among them?"

"Lady Igraine, *please*." Now that he wanted me to spare him, to let him go, he had returned to his formal way of talking. Perhaps he was every bit the coward he feared he was.

"Tell me, what do you say about *me*, Brastias?" I insisted.

He cowered back from me a little as I stared at him, hard and cold and unmoving. He would not have sympathy from me for his suffering. He drew in a long, unsteady breath. He knew he would have to tell me the truth.

"Men say that you and Uther were lovers while Gorlois still lived, that you had been for years. That your child was conceived before you and Uther were married. They say a bastard king will sit on the throne of Logrys, and they laugh. They say, also, that Viviane has taught you the arts of seduction known among the witches of Avalon, and that you used them to lure Uther to your side."

"What do *you* say, Brastias?" I pushed a little more.

He hung his head.

"*Brastias*."

"I said nothing, lady, but I did laugh with them, for there was nothing else I could have done."

"Leave me, Brastias."

"Igraine, *please*."

"*Go*."

And he went, because he was neither brave enough to stand up to the other men, nor to stand his ground with me.

* * *

When Melusine came back, she fussed at me a little. She knew I was sad, and worried, and she undid my hair, and brushed it out, and twisted it up again. I liked that, for it felt like being petted like an innocent little creature, and I leant into the comfort.

"You are tired, Lady Igraine," she said gently, her hands brushing softly down my shoulders, and I nodded, and sighed. I felt her fingers drawing open the lacing at the back of my dress.

"A lady with child as you are should rest. Go back to bed. Come, I will help you." I nodded, suddenly feeling very sleepy under the soft, soothing touch of her hand. I wondered if she, too, was one of the fairy people, to have such a gentle, comforting touch. A touch that could heal, or put someone to sleep. I thought of the young girl,

Viviane, with her hands tight on the front of Ector's surcoat, which glinted with gold in the moonlight, like her hair, and the way he closed his eyes and leant his forehead against hers, as though slipping under a spell. I was slipping further away from the world around me. I was aware of Melusine's little hand in mine, and then the softness of the bed, the light covers, just changed for the warmth of the summer, and somewhere in the half-sleep I was fallen deep into, I was aware of a lovely dream gathering around me, of tender lips pressed softly against my own. And I was sure that I lay on the grass outside; the fresh, slightly scrubby grass outside Tintagel.

Chapter thirty-seven

I slept deeply, and woke only when I heard the hunting horns sound in the courtyard. Some king was coming, or queen, so I ought to make ready. I pushed myself up, and saw that beside me on the bed Melusine had also fallen asleep, in all her clothes. I blushed to remember the dream I had had, as though somehow it would have crept out of my thoughts into hers, and she would have seen my desires – to be out in the wild, and back in the arms of a man long dead. I pushed the memory away, and shook her gently awake. She blinked slowly, and rubbed her eyes.

"I did not mean to sleep," she said, groggily.

I put my hand to my hair. It was all fallen out of place. The horns sounded again and Melusine started up.

"My lady, we must make you ready. That will be Viviane."

Viviane. How did Melusine know that it was Viviane? *I was raised near Avalon.* What if she were one of the women of the Isle, as Morgan would be? But no, if she were so she would be painted with the woad of the druids. Perhaps she had been sent away in disgrace. I thought of Imogen, dying in her sleep, and I wondered.

* * *

When Viviane came, Melusine was already gone. I wanted to ask her to play the harp, but she disappeared before I could, to some task or other. Viviane kissed me on the cheek as well as she could, for she had a small boy with her, no more than two years old. I forgot all of my fears and mistrust when I saw her, and I kissed her on the cheek, and asked how well things were in Avalon. I led her to sit beside me on my window-seat, I asked her about the child, and what had brought her to Camelot.

Viviane handed the little boy to me. He was the most beautiful child I had ever seen, and I could not suppress a gasp of delight. He was perfect, with bright black hair and blue eyes as clear as the sky above. His little fingers closed around my thumb, and he kicked his little feet in delight where he sat between us to have captured it, but was quiet and content. He reminded me a little of how Morgan had been when she was smaller. Always wide-eyed and quiet. But he was more energetic, wriggling between us as though excited for something, without yet knowing what.

"He is a beautiful child," I said, turning to Viviane with a smile. When she smiled in return, I noticed that the skin around her eyes wrinkled more than it had seemed to before, and that she looked a little weary. "How did he come to be in your care?"

She reached over, and offered her hand to the little boy, and he grabbed at it, his face brightening into a smile.

"He is an orphan. I've been caring for him since he was born, poor lost thing. His mother was one with the gifts of the Otherworld, and trained in Avalon. A very promising girl. But King Ban of southern France came to seek my council, and that of Merlin, and of course he saw her. She was very beautiful. Wonderful blue eyes, like the sea, and hair white-gold and fine as silk. Truly, I do not know what happened between them, but I do not see how a fourteen-year-old girl could not fear to refuse a great king – though I know he is a great seducer of women. She always swore that it was love. Well, after I heard of it, he agreed to marry her at my suggestion, but she was so young, and weak. When it was time for her to birth the child he had given her, I brought her back to Avalon. By then she had her little baby sister Nimue as her charge as well, for their mother had died. I knew that she was young for it, and small, but I had hoped… Well, it was not to be. Some the White Goddess has already claimed, and she knew it. I did not allow Ban on to my island, and he was furious, but there were none to whom he could turn for revenge. He is dying now, of course. Some say of lovesickness for the wife he loved the most. I say it is the White Goddess drawing the life from him that he has ill-deserved. Either that or his god punishing him for lust. But when the mother died, I kept the son in my possession. I have not raised a child of my own, and he is a sweet boy. But I fear that I must raise him as a Christian. It was long ago that Merlin came into this world as a witch. I do not think they would accept another one now. And besides, this boy, whose mother named him Galahad, has little of the Otherworld blood in him. He will become a good knight of your own son one day, I am sure. Now his father is gone, I will take him often to the court in France, so that he can learn their ways, so that he can be a leader of his own men. But Avalon will be his home until he is grown. There is no place for him in Avalon as a grown man. No, better that I give him what he needs to be strong and great in the world of men."

Viviane nodded carefully, and I realised that we were two women of the same mould. Fierce, pragmatic.

I looked up at her, suddenly struck with a thought. If this boy and my son were meant to be companions, then why could they not begin now? I could feel my heart beginning to race. It was a great danger to defy Merlin, but I was brave enough for it. He was long gone, and my fear of him was receding, my awareness of his power. Surely if he were so great, he would not have disappeared, and left me with this chance? I could do it. I had been brave enough for worse.

"Take my son, too," I said, quietly. Viviane pretended that she hadn't heard. I knew that she was pretending, because she heard everything, and though I was quiet, I had been right beside her. She was giving me the chance to change my mind. To back out. I was not going to.

"When he is born, Viviane, I want you to take my son to Avalon. That is the only way that Merlin will not take him."

Viviane shook her head, sadly.

"I can take him, Igraine, but not to Avalon. I can take him and hide him so that Merlin will never find him. If I take him to Avalon, Merlin will come for him, and I do not have the power to stop him without damaging the magical defences of Avalon itself. I can hide him away. But... you will not see him until he is a man grown. If he were with Merlin –"

I shook my head. Already I loved the child inside me with all the pure love of a mother, and I knew that I had it in me to suffer the loss of him, if it kept him safe.

"Do it, Viviane."

"Once it is done," she said, "it cannot be undone."

"I know," I said, and she leaned down and kissed me on the cheek, as though I were still a child.

* * *

I hoped that Viviane would remain a long time, but her stay was only brief. She was occupied with her little fosterling, and had only come to check on my health, and to give her counsel to Uther. As I sat there, one hand on my stomach, imagining how it would feel to give my child to a stranger, Viviane and Uther talked. Through the mist of my thoughts, I realised that they were talking about something that Uther had deliberately kept from me. I had not heard him talk of this at other councils. They were talking about the Bretons, the King

223

of Carhais and his queen who had spoken for Lot and against Uther at the council after Aurelianus' death. They were refusing tribute. They were acting as an independent realm. I did not see why they shouldn't, and yet it made Uther furious.

I wished that he did not care so much for his pride.

That night he was angry and rough with me, but I was so with him. I was still angry with both him and Brastias, and I was glad of the chance to slap Uther, hard, about the face. I didn't care that he enjoyed it; I didn't begrudge him that, for I enjoyed doing it to him, imagining my tiny little body could make any difference. Uther pushed me up against the wall, closing his huge fists around my wrists and pinning me there until I sighed in defeat, and his hands slid up my skirt, and he grasped me hard and pulled me against him, and we struggled together, halfway between anger and delight.

* * *

After that, all the news was of conflict with the Bretons. Brastias crept back to my side, and I did not have the energy to be hostile, though I was no longer kind. I had lost my belief in him as someone unlike other men. They were all the same.

I began to feel my child move inside me, little kicks, little wriggles. I felt that I loved him already. But I would have to give him away, if he were a son. Viviane and Merlin had promised Uther it was an heir in my womb, but there was no real way to be sure.

The first time I felt him move, it was during council, and I took Uther's hand, under the table, and put it against my stomach, so that he could feel the little foot of his child kick. He fell silent, and all the men stared at him, but that night he held me with a new tenderness, as though at last he realised what a wondrous thing this new life was. I wanted to write to Morgawse, but he said no one could know, that this was the only way to keep the child safe, and I nodded, for I knew he was right. Though they all *did* know, the knights, and the men, and the servants. Camelot was like the house of rumour, and everyone talked. They talked of how Imogen had been a great lover of her day, and how this knight and this servant-woman spent their nights together, and how the queen wore many clothes for the summer, and ate a most uncommon amount of this or that, and that she had quarrelled with her knight Brastias over her daughter, who was even now carrying some secret child inside her, up in Lothian. Half lies, half truth, it was meaningless noise to me.

* * *

Summer drew on, and I grew heavier, and more uncomfortable in the heat. Camelot was stifling, and even when I sat with Melusine

224

and the other ladies in the little walled garden beneath my tower, I felt as if I could barely breathe. There was nothing of the cool breezes of the ocean that we felt at Tintagel. I lay in as much of the shade as I could find beneath the ornamental rose trees, and I prayed for the heat to break, as it sometimes did at the beginning of summer, and turn to thunderstorms. But it did not. It only grew hotter. Even the chapel was stifling, though the sun at least did not reach there. But air was thick and close, and the smell of incense stuck in my throat.

It was at the end of a long, hot day that Uther came back from the hunt; he was angry from the heat, as I was, but there was something more than that. I turned as I heard him come into my chamber, the summer evening sun slanting in orange and still hot behind me.

"The Bretons are coming to court," Uther said tersely, pulling off his gauntlets. I said nothing, drawing the folds of my cloak more firmly around me. More hiding, then, more secrecy. More small talk with strangers. More fighting. I resented it all, resented his devil's pact with Merlin, resented being a prisoner in my own body, resented Uther's inability to put away thoughts of taking the fortress city of Carhais for the sake of his pride. It was only one small kingdom. It hardly mattered. I didn't even look up at him.

"Igraine," he said more sharply, "did you hear what I said?"

I nodded.

"Do you speak Breton, Igraine?" he asked. His tone was brusque, business-like, impatient. He did not ask me how I was. He did not ask me if I had forgiven him yet for coming to me in disguise, and binding me into his black blood-pact with the witch I hated. He never asked. He did not care. Or perhaps he thought the matter was solved, and that I ought to be happy. I was *not* happy.

"I do not, my lord."

Uther sighed in annoyance, lifting the rough leather hauberk off over his head and throwing it down beside me. It smelled of old leather, and his sweat, and blood. The blood of men I had known, who had fought him to protect me. The thought stung me, from the anger of the past, and I cursed again the weakness of my woman's body. I wished again, suddenly, very strongly, that I could have run away, taken the child and disappeared. But there was nowhere on the earth that I could hide from Merlin. God would not give me sanctuary from him, for he could not keep out the sun and the sky and the beasts and the birds and the winds, so he could not keep out Merlin. It was all a mess now; I could not even trust Brastias, with whom I had tried to flee to Tintagel, and I was not sure I trusted

Uther, though he and the pleasure and pain that were all tangled up with him were all that I had. That, and my child.

"That is a pity, Igraine, for Leodegrance's wife does not speak a word of English. Do you speak French?"

"A little," I said, quiet and resistant.

"That will have to do." He shrugged. He was annoyed that I was not looking at him, but he preferred to pretend that he had not noticed, that I was not angry. I hated him the worse for it.

* * *

Uther did not warn me – chose not to, because he was still angry – that it was the next day that they were coming. I was tired from the child, and too hot in the layers of fabric I had wrapped myself in in an attempt to hide what could no longer be hidden. I wished it could be talked of openly, that I had a child inside me. I thought it would make it harder for Merlin to steal him away.

As it was, when Uther called the Breton king and queen into his throne-room, old King Leodegrance – whom I recognised from all those years ago at Aurelianus's council – gave a warm broad smile, and took my hand and said, "Ah, my lord Uther, I see the gods have blessed your marriage with a child already." He kissed my hand and said, "You, lady queen, are glowing with life."

I thanked him, quiet and polite, and he added, "It is a wonder, though, that you like to be so wrapped up. Melita, when she bore our last, complained constantly that she was too hot, though most of that time was the middle of winter." He turned and smiled at his wife, who did not understand what he was saying, but looked up at us with a hard, steady gaze not so unlike Uther's, while a little girl with the same wild red hair as the mother shifted in her arms like a cat.

Though Leodegrance wore a rich robe of brocade, I noticed that the Queen, Melita, was dressed like a savage in leather armour, her hair braided and held in place with leather ties which were studded with brass. She looked like one of the old tribal queens that the Romans both praised and mocked in their histories. Like Boadicea, like Cleopatra, like the Irish warrior queen Maev. But I had heard that these were Breton ways, and when Leodegrance, as though he were her servant announcing her, bowed before Uther and stood aside to let her pass, she handed him the little girl, who fell quiet in her father's arms, and bowed to Uther like a man.

She said something in Breton which sounded like a greeting, and I recognised Uther's name. To my surprise she turned then to me, and bowed to me, and greeted me. I had thought her older than I was, because her face was tanned and wrinkled from the sun, her skin a little scarred, her look tough and brave, but when she came close I saw that she was about my age. The boys standing behind her – men, almost, two of them – who must have been her sons, must have been born when she was only a little older than Morgawse was now. A young bride to an old king. But she did not seem unhappy with him; he seemed kind to her, even a little deferential. I wanted to believe that Morgawse's marriage would be the same.

Then the sons came forward, and introduced themselves: Rioch, Felix, Conan. *Felix*, a Roman name, and the mother's name *Melita* – was that not Roman as well? Were the Bretons trading with Rome more than we realised? Using Roman names when abroad? I did not believe that that woman's real name could be something as sweet and simple as *Melita*. It would not go well for Uther, if the Emperor in Rome found that he could call on the Bretons against Logrys and the vassal-lands of Britain. It made me feel wary and afraid, though it all seemed peaceful enough. Still, the two eldest sons, barely a year apart by the looks of it, were tall and looked strong – both handsome with youth, both bright of smile, with their mother's pretty bright blue eyes. One fair as gold, the other dark like the father. The youngest brother, Conan, had his mother's bright red hair, like the little girl, and he must, too, have been almost of age. The family of the Breton king and queen was almost a small garrison, and if the girl would be trained to fight like a boy as well, then I did not know where that left us.

Chapter thirty-eight

I prepared myself carefully for the feast that evening, as Uther paced the room behind me. I closed my eyes against it, and into the feeling of Melusine's light, deft fingers running through my hair. They were firm, but pleasant, and quick, and I wanted to shut everything else out.

Uther made sure that I was dressed in my finest gown, thick brocade though it was summer and sewn with gold thread, and that I had jewels about my throat, at my ears, around my wrists, on my fingers. Aurelianus' old riches. Things that Imogen had used to wear.

We came down late so that the Bretons would be already there, already waiting, so that Uther and I could enter with ceremony. I let my hand rest on his, but I did not turn to look at him. I was not sure how angry I was, because I was not sure how stubborn he planned to be with them. And beyond that, there was a part of me that knew that they were not my people, and my ways were not their ways, and though I would not let Uther plunge us into war for the sake of pride, I also knew that I did not *want* them to best us. A part of *me* was proud, a part of me wanted to win. A part of me wanted them to think that I was a great queen, not just some prize that Uther had won at his war-games.

At first the conversation was friendly. Rioch, the oldest of the Breton princes, who was perhaps seventeen years old, was confident and charismatic. He was the one who had his father's dark looks: the flashing smile, the swarthy skin, the wry flick of his eyebrow. He would be very handsome in a few years' time. He led the conversation easily, though I noticed that he, too, was deferential to his mother, and every so often appeared to lean towards her and summarize what everyone else had been saying for her, in Breton. She would nod as though she were taking it all in but carefully reserving her judgement. I noticed that the little girl was no longer with them, but was in the arms of a nurse – a pretty young woman with dark black hair and pale skin like milk who sat in the corner. I also noticed how Rioch's eyes flickered across in that direction more than any other, and I thought it was not just out of concern for his sister.

The talk was pleasant, and got more pleasant with wine. Leodegrance was a good storyteller, and he had a few wildly exaggerated tales to tell of the days of his youth, and the battles he had fought at Aurelianus' side. They were well-told, even though they were lies. The second son, Felix, grew bold with wine as well, and laughed and joked with his brothers, and Brastias and some of the other knights. Beside me, Uther was deathly quiet as though he were listening out for something or waiting for his chance to speak. I did not know what he would say. I was sure he had deliberately decided not to consult me. It was only late in the evening, when the little cakes had been cleared away and people were pouring the last of the wine into their cups that Uther cleared his throat, and shifted in his seat, and began. I noticed that Melusine, standing beside me, and leaning past to pick up my empty plate, froze where she was. I should have shooed her away, but I did not.

"Shall we at last discuss, Leodegrance, what you came here for? I know that you do not think of me as you ought, as a sovereign king, not since you opposed me at Aurelianus' last council."

"I did not *oppose* you, Uther," Leodegrance said tersely, and I saw his eldest son beside him tense. "I merely supported a different candidate."

Uther did not react, his face stony and cold in response to the older man's visible annoyance. But I remembered all those years ago the council at Aurelianus' great court in London, and I did not remember Leodegrance being particularly set against Uther. I remembered him appearing to think the whole council beneath him, entirely, and his support for Lot being born of a complacent nonchalance. Uther must have remembered it differently. Uther and Leodegrance – and the Breton queen, though it made no difference since she did not speak English – seemed to be the only ones apart from me who were still sober, and that made it all the more dangerous. I was afraid that one of the princes would say something, or one of Uther's knights, and it would erupt into a fight, right there.

"I have not received any tribute from the Bretons," Uther said evenly. "Not since I came to the throne." I saw Leodegrance's face darken, and I knew that this was not just political conversation; something was about to be decided between these two men.

Leodegrance gave a wry smile, still giving the impression of casual interest rather than anger, but his wife was silent and looking at him, and even the red-haired little girl in the arms of her nurse at the end of the table had fallen still and fixed her bright, round eyes on her father, as though she understood what was about happen, though of course, she could not have done.

"Ah, Uther, well…" He folded his hands together before him on the table, fixing Uther with a steady stare to match that which Uther was giving to him. He had a strange tone to his voice: soft, low, persuasive. I could see what people meant when they said that he was one of the old blood of the fairy people. And I had heard men say things about him, about his family, about the powerful bloodlines that met in King Leodegrance of the Bretons. I had not believed it until I saw him now. "This is because Brittany is no vassal kingdom of yours. We are allies – yes – friends, also. But the sea lies between us, so we do not fear your violence, though I know you rained that down on Lot of Lothian, and let him be torn between you and the highland tribes until he submitted. But we will not submit. You may march your army into Brittany, and you will not find a soul that you can lay your hands on. You are a man of the sword, Uther Pendragon, and I have respect for you as a warrior. You have ruled Logrys, and Britain, with strength, but you are a man who understands nothing of the mysteries of the world. If you bring your armoured men into my lands, our forests will swallow you. Our lakes will draw you in until you drown. Our fruits will choke in your throats. Take my friendship, Uther, for I offer it freely. Do not ask me for *money*."

The table fell silent, and Leodegrance's eldest two sons looked at each other. They were not calm and steady like their father, and their fear and unease showed on their faces. I wondered if it would have done on their mother's face as well, if she had understood what had been said, if she had not been occupied, in that moment, with taking her little daughter from the arms of the nurse, whom she was quick to dismiss now that the conversation had turned dangerous. I wondered why she would want to keep her little girl there, but I supposed it would be comforting to hold a little creature. The girl was such a pretty child, and I, so weary and emotional from the child within me, wanted to hold her myself. I missed Morgan, and her quiet, sincere affection, and I thought that it would have given me huge comfort to hold a little girl about her age. But I dared not ask, and besides the little girl was winding her arms around her mother's neck and closing her eyes and resting her head on her mother's shoulder to sleep, oblivious that her people might be thrown into war. It was not the time for me to ask.

"You cannot threaten me with magic, Leodegrance," Uther said softly, "when I have Merlin the witch on my side."

Leodegrance nodded thoughtfully. He seemed a calm, sensible man, and I wished that he and Uther could put away their pride and be accorded. "I think it is better, Uther, if we do not threaten each other at all. We will not pay you tribute as your vassals, for we are not, but I am sure we can reach some kind of mutual agreement where we can both be satisfied."

Uther took a bite from the chicken leg left on his plate, which he had refused to let the servants clear, and the juices smeared across his face. The sister of Leodegrance's queen, sat beside her, wrinkled up her nose in distaste. She was a young girl, looked only just of the age to be married, perhaps as much as ten years younger than her sister, and had not yet learned to hide her feelings in public, it seemed. She had not been with the party who greeted us, and I only knew who she was from the striking resemblance she bore to the queen – though where the queen's hair was bright red, the sister's hair was dark brown, and glossy as ebony. She seemed to be there to translate for her sister as well, for I had noticed that she had begun, now that the talk was serious and Rioch was no longer whispering to his mother, to lean down and whisper in the queen's ear.

"Have arrangements been made for the girl?" Uther gestured towards the sleeping child in the Breton queen's arms. "My wife will bear me a son, and he will be king after me, and must have a wife. We might make a suitable alliance that way."

The two eldest sons looked at each other once more, wary, and I knew what was coming. Uther knew it as well. He had not meant to compromise or be reasonable. He was only trying to appear so.

"Forgive me, Uther," Leodegrance said carefully. "But it is not Breton custom to give our daughters away to foreign kings as brides. If your wife bears a daughter, that girl may choose any of my sons –"

"Not your custom?" Uther insisted.

"No, Uther –"

"Yet I have heard of other Breton girls given away to foreign kings. I think you begrudge me your only daughter for my son because you were hoping to join with that old lecher Ban of Benwick castle and strengthen yourselves against me. What is so special about this girl that makes her too great for the throne of Logrys?"

Leodegrance shook his head. "She is betrothed already, to one of her own people. This is our custom, these are our ways."

Uther tensed in his seat. "This is because she has witches' blood in her, is it not?"

There was a silence, and I knew that it was true. So, Leodegrance was loath to give away the child who had inherited his ancient fairy-blood, the blood of the Otherworld. I had heard things said about him. Someone had told me once that although he could be wounded, he never spilled a drop of blood. Someone else that he was over a hundred years old. Someone else that he could bring a spring forth from the dry ground. More besides about the warrior-days of his youth, a charmed life, the gifts of the Otherworld: weapons, magic, secrets that I longed to know. Lies, perhaps, but that didn't matter. The magic was real. It was in his blood. The blood, some said, of Maev of Cruachan. He wanted that power to stay in Carhais. I did not blame him for it. I thought of Morgan, and the blood she had in her, magic and powerful and great, and I knew – with a stab of guilt – that it was not just circumstance that would make me more careful of whom I married her to than I had been with Morgawse. Once I had admitted that to myself, I felt mean and low and cruel, and I was surprised that Leodegrance and his wife spoke so in front of their sons.

Uther took a large gulp of the wine in his cup, and said, brusquely, "You have three fine sons, Leodegrance. Surely one among them must be fit to be King in Carhais?"

"My lord Uther," Felix, the second brother, said, his voice steady, calm, still slightly lighter than a man's, though deep. I would have guessed that he was fifteen years old. "My brothers and I are warriors, not rulers."

Uther shrugged. "You are young, you will learn. I was just a soldier, once."

The boy continued, "The Breton people like to keep their queen in Carhais, and for her consort to be a great warrior, so the people might be safe both with the protection of a father, and a mother to care for them. The mother must be one of the land, so we cannot give our sister away, even for so great a prince as the son your queen might bear."

Leodegrance put a hand, in gentle, fatherly comfort, on his son's arm.

"My son has put it better than I ever could, Uther. Guinevere will not leave Carhais."

Guinevere. The girl was named for the White Goddess. Hearing her name, the girl woke and slowly blinked her eyes. She tried to wriggle away from her mother to reach her father, and when her mother held her tight she pouted and screwed up her face as though she wanted to cry, but she did not.

* * *

That night, Uther was mad with rage, and I could not convince him to put it aside. He paced wildly, deaf to everything I said. I could see the corded muscles standing out on his arms as he clenched his fists, and at the side of his neck where his jaw was painfully tensed.

"Uther –" I began, warily, but he was talking to himself, staring hard in front of him.

"The Bretons think that they can do whatever they please. They will not give up their heathen gods and yield the practices of their religion to Rome, as the rest of us have had to do. They do not *control their women.*" He turned to me, then, his eyes wild. "Did you see the queen? How brazen. And that little girl. Too good for our son, Igraine, they say."

I wrapped my arms around my swelling stomach. I wished that Uther would stop saying that it was a son inside me. He would be angry and disappointed if it were a girl. I wished for a girl; a girl that Merlin could not take away from me.

"Are you listening to me, Igraine?" Uther said sharply, and I nodded, looking up at him.

"Uther," I said, as gently as I could manage. "It is well for a king to be proud, but it is the duty of a queen to remind him to temper that with pragmatism. This is not worth making war over."

Uther growled with rage. "*Igraine*, now is not the time for your talk of kings and queens and duty. Do you have any blood in your veins, or is it only wise words and holy water?"

I stood, slow, awkward, tired from the child inside me, and

heavy with it, crossing my arms over my chest.

"Please yourself, Uther. I do not know why I imagined that you had it in you to be prudent and listen to what I had to say –"

"You will speak to me with respect, Igraine –"

"I will, Uther, when you have deserved it of me."

We stood for a moment, staring hard at each other. What cruel force of destiny had brought us together, both too stubborn to back down, he wild with his anger, and I careful, sensible and intractable. I had the thought once more than we did not belong together. I could see Uther's chest rising and falling hard with his anger, but he was unsure what to say to me, what response he could give to what I had said.

He lunged towards me, and I stepped back, but I was weary and he was faster. He caught me hard about the arms and slammed me against the wall. I suppressed a cry.

"If you were any other woman," he growled, "I would beat you until you learned respect."

"But I am not *any other woman*," I hissed. "Did you beat Imogen? Is that what you did? I don't believe that. I bet that you begged her, too, to slap you. To treat you like the savage dog you are."

He shoved me harder against the wall, and I felt my heart race. If I had not been worried about my child, I would have grasped hold of his shirt, and torn. I would have run my fingers into his hair, and pulled him to me. His eyes searched my face for some sign, but I gave none. I could feel my skin burning, my muscles tensing. My back arched towards him, and I felt how thin the few layers of fabric between us were. He leant down towards me, his lips parting. I could feel him trembling with desire.

"Let go of me, my lord," I breathed. It was only after he dropped me, and turned his back to stride from the room and slam the door behind him, that I realised I had been holding my breath. I threw open the shutters and gulped in the cold night air. Down in the garden below it was silent, and I stared into the empty night stretching out above me, my blood pounding and my head fogged with Uther, with his touch, with my anger and my hate. And I fought against him. We were in danger if he could not yield a little. I did not know how to stop him. I did not know what to do.

Chapter thirty-nine

Uther did not return. I could see the light burning in his bedchamber across the courtyard. Perhaps someone else was in there. It was not beyond what he was capable of. I knew him well enough. Overtaken with anger, fired with desire. I felt the same, but one of us had to be wise. One of us had to be careful. I could not sleep either, though I forced myself to return to my room and lie down in my bed. Late into the night, when sleep had not come, I climbed out of the bed, and wrapped my cloak around the nightdress, and slipped out of my room. Long ago, in Tintagel, I had done this, and I had wandered into Uther, and we had kissed in the moonlight. How distant that seemed now, how childish, when I felt our child heavy inside me, and I knew all that Uther had been willing to do to me to have it there – his son, his heir, the child of destiny.

I stood in the corridor, arms crossed protectively over myself, and leant against the wall, staring out of the narrow window at the moon. It was a crescent, growing. If I counted through the moons, I supposed that I was perhaps as few as two away from my time, and then the child inside me would be out in the world, and everyone would tear at him, for he was closest to the throne.

"Lady Igraine." A soft voice behind me spoke, and I turned to see Leodegrance was there. "Forgive me, I did not mean to startle you. I, too, am not yet tired." He came to stand beside me, but he did not look at me. He gazed out at the moon. I looked at him. He was not a tall man, not quite so tall as I was, but he was strong-built. He had the look about him of a man who had once been a great warrior, but was no longer, gone slightly to seed. He was soft about the belly, and there were flecks of grey in his dark beard, but he had quick, bright eyes of dark, dark green, and a smile that flickered suddenly across his face, and he seemed full of life as a young man.

"It is a beautiful night," he added, after a moment. I realised I liked the sound of his voice, the soft, thick accent of the Bretons, the calm way he spoke. He seemed like such a reasonable man. Why could he not be reasonable and play at politics with Uther like he ought?

I sighed in annoyance. "I suppose." I was irritable; I could feel the child moving about inside me, and I was heavy and uncomfortable, and far too hot. "Though all I can think about is how foolish men are with their pride, and how peace is the greatest of all virtues."

Leodegrance nodded slowly beside me. "You lost your first husband, did you not, to war with Uther?"

I nodded.

"Because he would not play at politics with him, then?"

I nodded again. I felt myself stiffen inside. I did not think that anyone would dare to speak of Gorlois in Uther's castle, nor did I want to hear his name.

"Perhaps it is so," Leodegrance said, evenly. "Perhaps men are proud and foolish, and we crash against each other in war for no good reason. Perhaps you do not realise that as a woman you have the gift of being allowed to be gentle. A man cannot be gentle; if he is weak, then he is lost. Even I, and I come from a people, and a land, of sovereign queens and consort kings. You can show softness, and kindness. There are days that I wish that men could do the same. Perhaps your husband Uther thinks so, too."

I almost gave a rough laugh of derision at the thought of Uther longing to be gentle, but I held it back. Uther was a soldier, and that was all he knew, but he had learned it from having been raised a boy.

"You will not consider, then, pledging the girl as wife to any son we might have?"

Beside me, Leodegrance shook his head. "To the Bretons, their queen is their land. Just as you would not consider sending your son to be married in a foreign place, we would not send our daughter."

I thought of the Breton princes, and with a sudden flash of regret I realised that I should have thought to marry Morgawse to one of them. One close to her own age, one that would put the sea between her and her stepfather. As it was, her marriage had delivered her into the hands of an ambitious man.

"Besides," Leodegrance continued, more softly, and I was surprised at his honesty, "she is the only child who has inherited the Otherworld blood I have carried in my veins, that has been a part of my family for generations. It was a mistake – her mother – it was for the sake of love, and I do not regret, but she does not have it in her. The boys, my sons, I love them, but they do not have it. Guinevere – more perhaps even than myself; she was born among the stone giants at Carnac."

"The stone giants?" I asked, turning to him, and he nodded, but he did not explain. I supposed he thought I knew what he meant.

"We were riding through that land, and it was as though in her mother's womb she sensed that it was a special place, where the Otherworld touched the surface, and longed to come then, for she did. And after she was born, she was always the same. Stubborn. She is no wife for a king of Logrys, my lady, where you make your women curtsey and wear fine silk dresses. She is a Breton girl, and she was born to rule in Carhais."

I nodded thoughtfully. I wondered if all his wild idealism would lead him to the future he hoped for, where his daughter took his wife's place as sovereign queen. There were men who hoped so for their sons, and got it, but the Bretons could not stay pagan forever, and either Christ would reach them, or the armies of the Holy Roman Empire, and they would have to live by God's word that said that woman was servant to man, and there would be no more Breton queens. The thought made me feel horribly sad, though I could not have said why.

"My sister," I offered. "She lived in Ireland. She was married to one of the princes. Máel. Is he one of your blood?"

Leodegrance smiled and shook his head. "No. I know Máel, but he is not of my kin. Those who rule in Emain Macha are the Ulstermen now. My grandmother Maev of Cruachan was not one of them. Oh, we are not so different, I suppose, but they are not my blood, and I am not theirs. Emain Macha and the Ulaid have not seen the queens of my blood since my grandmother Maev fought the great hero Cu Chulainn on the plains. But those are days long past, and enemies long forgotten. I should like to see Emain Macha once more. I was fostered there, as a boy, for a little time. Tell me, does your sister like it well?"

I looked away, down, at my hands folded before me. "She died in childbed, long ago."

Leodegrance nodded quietly beside me. After a long pause he said, "That happens more and more, now that the ancient magic has been replaced with prayers, and charms, and the superstition of the Virgin Mother. What could a virgin mother possibly know about childbirth? The White Goddess –"

I hushed him, more forcefully than I ought to have done.

"You must not say such things here," I said.

He made a noise of annoyance deep within his throat. "So, your Christ not only excludes me from his heaven, but he bans my voice from the world, because I am faithful enough not to forget those gods who have cared for me since I was a child?"

I looked up at him once more, and met his angry stare with my own gaze, cold and impassive.

"Honour whatever god you please, sir. I only speak to remind you that all things are politics here, and to be wise. We are wise, sir, or we perish. These are the gods of Camelot: gossip and rumour. And Christ is their seneschal, listening out for both."

There was a long, slightly hostile silence between us. I supposed that we were both stubborn. I waited a long time, until I felt daring enough to give one more little push towards what I wanted. "So," I said softly, "there is no chance that you will make a peaceful end of this with my husband?"

He shook his head. "Not if the only way to see that done is to give him my daughter."

I turned to him fully then, and I almost reached out and took his hand, but I did not. He was a serious but kindly man, but he was also a king, and I dared not be too familiar, too emotional with him.

"What harm would it do, for her to live here? You could see her, she would not be lost to you. I would promise to let her children come back to Carhais, if it still lacked a ruler of your magic blood."

He shook his head, and I saw that there would be no argument. "I cannot, Igraine. It is not our way. And it is not just a question of bloodlines. I have seen how men treat women in Logrys – forgive me, lady Igraine – but, I have seen how King Uther treats even his lady wife. He holds you on his lap to be petted, like a house dog, and when he is tired, he waves you away, and there is another, and perhaps another, that he toys with. But though you are wise, good lady, he does not listen, and though you are gentle, and I know you love him, he has not been taught to love, for in Logrys men hold their women as chattel, not as companions and friends. If I give you my daughter, she will suffocate here. You have little daughters, do you not, lady Igraine?"

I nodded. I did not want to speak to him. He was wrong about Uther, and about me, and he was insulting about our people and our culture.

"But they are not at court?"

I shook my head.

"Morgawse is married, and is Queen in Lothian, and Morgan, who is just a little child, is at school in an abbey, in the west."

"Forgive me once more, lady, but they are sent from here because in your land, the father is considered more important than the mother?"

I bristled against that, for it was true.

"I sent them to safety because Uther is a jealous man. I think in Carhais you do not know what a strong king is. Uther is strong – he is harsh, and jealous and cruel, but he is strong. Stronger than you. Stronger than your wife, and your Breton army of barbarians and savages. My husband Gorlois was a greater warrior than you will ever be, and Uther Pendragon tore him and his army to pieces, and left a trail of blood from the borders of Cornwall to Tintagel castle. It is *wise* to give heed to fear, and hide from harm. So, you look down on our ways, you do not like them. If you do not yield Uther the land that he wishes, or the tribute payment, or your Otherworld girl, then you will know what I have known, and there will be nothing left of what is precious to you, and you will look back on this moment, and you will curse yourself that you did not listen to me."

He gave me a long, even look that hid in it something awfully like pity, and nodded, and turned away to stare out of the window again.

"As I said, I envy the women of Britain, who can be gentle, and yield, and need not bear the shame."

It was only then that I realised what a foolish man he truly was.

Chapter forty

The next day there were more talks, but I did not go. I was bored and disgusted by the idea of Uther and the Breton king and queen tangling up in their pride.

I was left to entertain the Breton guests who were not called to the council. These were the Breton princess, the queen's sister, Aurelie, who was young and pretty and bright, and the youngest of the Breton princes, Conan, and the little girl. There were a few servants as well, Melusine among them, and they seemed to be all from Camelot, though I knew that the Bretons had servants just like everybody else. I did not see the pretty nurse I had glimpsed with the girl, and I wondered where she was.

I sat down heavily among the cushions scattered in the corner of my public room, and tried to think of what I ought to suggest to entertain them. I thought I might ask Melusine to sing and play, but she was suddenly quiet and shy, hanging back. I was sure Uther would be irritated that I had not organised something more lavish to show our might, but I did not really care.

To my surprise, with a bright, rich laugh, Aurelie picked up the lute from the corner of the room and ran her deft, slender fingers across the strings. She was, I would have guessed, not quite twenty. She was very beautiful; white skin, dark brown glossy thick hair, blue-green eyes, and the same little red mouth as her sister. Though the Breton queen's mouth was harsh with authority, Aurelie's was soft, slightly coquettish. In among the discussions, I had heard that she had a husband back in Carhais somewhere, and I was glad of it.

The little girl walked over to me with purposeful steps beyond her years. How old had her mother said she was? Not yet two? She was small, but confident and steady, and had already the same dark green eyes her father had – thoughtful and intense. Her hair was a mess of red curls that made me wonder if her mother fussed her and combed them as I had done with my little girls. I had the urge to pull the girl into my lap and go at the hair with a comb, but I resisted.

She said a word in Breton in a sweet, sulky voice, and I was painfully reminded of Morgawse as a child.

Conan stepped forward with a laugh, scooping up his little sister in his arms, and she laughed and kicked her little feet in delight. He, the Breton Prince, was not many years younger than his aunt. Perhaps thirteen, and growing handsome already, with his mother's pale skin, red hair, and striking features.

"She wants a story," he laughed, and in response she cried, "Story!" and clapped her little hands together. So the mother did not speak English, but all the children did.

"I can tell you one," Aurelie offered, her eyes flashing with sly promise. She folded herself lithely into a little wooden chair, and cradled the lute in her lap. She began to sing, a little *Lai* in Breton. I thought it was rude of her, to sing in a language that I did not understand, but I knew the story anyway, from the names of the characters. It was the tale of a jealous husband who kills his wife's beloved pet nightingale. I flushed with anger, sure that the song was directed at me, sure that Leodegrance had mocked me and gossiped about me with his sister-in-law and his sons.

I opened my mouth to protest, but before I could, Conan was clicking his tongue in good-natured disapproval. "Aunt, it is not friendly to sing a song that the lady Igraine cannot understand. Here, I will tell a story." He turned his little sister around so that she sat on top of his bent knees, her little feet resting on his stomach where he lazed in the window seat as though it were his own home, not an enemy's castle. She reached out and took his hands as he began to tell the story, and I saw her dark little eyes fix on him with excited intent though I was sure that she could not have understood all that he said.

"Long ago, little Guinevere, there was a beautiful queen named Maev, and she had a handsome husband, called Ailill. Maev was brave and Maev was strong, and Ailill was brave and Ailill was strong, and they were very happy together. One night, as they lay in their bed, as husbands and wives do, they talked. Ailill said, 'You are lucky to have a husband such as I, who is handsome and brave and strong, who has besides brought you many lands and riches.' And Maev said, 'No, husband, it is you who are lucky to have a wife who is beautiful and brave and strong, and who has besides brought *you* many riches.' And they could not agree who was the more powerful, and who had the most to give. And so they woke the servants, and they counted the gold, and they saw that it was both the same. And then they counted the furniture and the servants. And they saw that they had both the same. Then the servants went out into the fields to count the cattle. Maev had a great herd, and Ailill had a great herd, but that night the White Bull, a great bull gifted with strength from the Otherworld, not wanting to be led by a woman, had run away from Maev's herd, and joined Ailill.

"Maev was furious, and her anger shook the mountains, and made the seas draw back. But Ailill, because he loved her, said that he would bring her the Brown Bull of the Ulstermen for her herd, so that they should be equal. Maev sent her men to buy the bull, but Conchobor, King of the Ulstermen, sent them away. He was a cruel man, a selfish man, a man who had once long ago been Maev's husband – and she had given him sons, but he had been rough and rude, and now they hated each other. So Maev gathered her army, and Ailill called his Galeoin, who were the greatest fighting men in the world. And Maev led her army out beside the great knight Fergus, who was the strongest man in the world, and was her lover. But he betrayed her for, though he loved her, he loved Conchobor the more.

"Maev's army marched to Emain Macha, and by that time the hero they called the Hound of the Ulstermen had come to fight for Conchobor's army." At the mention of the hero, Guinevere laughed again and clapped her hands, and Conan laughed softly, ruffling his hand through her messy hair, "No, Guin," he said fondly, "we don't like him. He is the enemy." Her little face puckered in confusion or displeasure, I could not tell which. "And he fought many men to keep his King safe, men who Maev sent out to fight him with the promise of her love, and the love of her beautiful daughter Finnabair, who was the loveliest of all maidens, like your aunt Aurelie." The young boy flashed a daring smile at his aunt, who bit her lip and crossed her legs where she sat in response to his inappropriate interest. Were such things tolerated among the Bretons? "And out they went, one after the other, and he killed them all. But Conchobor could not hide in Emain Macha forever, and Maev called on the great raven of the White Goddess, the Morrigan, who came, and with her great cry like a scream began the battle. And the armies crashed against one another, and the blood that poured carved a chasm in the land. But it was not the blood of men. No, it was the blood of Queen Maev – her woman's blood. And when the hero Cu Chulainn saw it, he was afraid, and fled, and the Connachtmen – who were the men of your great-grandmother Maev, and your great-grandfather Ailill – took away the Brown Bull, and their victory was known throughout the land."

What an awful, crude story, I thought. Besides, I was sure when I had heard Máel tell the same tale to my father, long ago, it was the Ulstermen who had claimed the victory, and Maev of Cruachan and her Connaught consort had been little more than cattle rustlers throwing themselves at the gates of Conchobor's mighty fortress.

"Oh, Conan," Aurelie laughed, and I was surprised that her tone with the young man was flirtatious as she came to lift his little sister out of his arms. "Don't fill her head with that rubbish your father talks, about magical bulls and queens of the Otherworld."

Guinevere wriggled in her aunt's embrace. I wondered, then, at the gap between them. Conan was fully ten years older than his little sister. Leodegrance and his queen must have thought themselves to be barren together for a long time, and she a late surprise, a child blessed not only with being an ageing man's late child, but also having inherited what he had longed to pass on to his sons. His wife, too, was about my own age, and childbearing for her would be more difficult year on year, and that little girl would probably be their last. I understood why he did not want to let her go, but I had not wanted to let my daughters go, and I had done what I had to do for the sake of my safety, and that of my family. But he was a king, and kings could afford to be selfish.

* * *

Later, when Conan had taken his little sister away to sleep, Aurelie slipped down into the pile of cushions beside me and bit her lip at me the way she had done to her young nephew.

"You disapprove of me, don't you, Lady Igraine?" she said. Her voice was lovely, rich and soft. I was aware of how lithe and young she was, and how I, weighed down with my child and my slow and heavy anger, was very poor in comparison – although before I grew fat and heavy men had called me beautiful. She was dressed in the strange way the Breton women were, in leather vests and breeches like a young squire. At the side of her vest, I could see the beginning of the curve of her breast, soft and white, and full despite her muscular arms and legs, whose enticing shape I could see through her leather breeches. She shrugged when I did not reply.

"I think you would like it, Carhais. You might surprise yourself. Some things that seem strange at first are often just what we require."

Had she seen me watching her make eyes at her thirteen-year-old nephew and known I was judging her?

"Are you not married?" I asked, sharply. Aurelie laughed.

"I am, but I am not sure I see what that has to do with it. Marriage hardly helps a woman discover new things. Oh – one, I suppose." She was teasing me, trying to be playful, but I wasn't in the mood.

I pushed myself back up from the cushions, moving to leave. As I went Aurelie shouted after me. "This is why Breton women don't belong in Logrys – you are all prudes."

I hated her, though I was not exactly sure why. I think I hated her because she thought what everyone else thought about me – that I was prudish, and pious, and uptight. And I was not any of those things. I had taken a magic drink from Avalon and lain with my husband out under the open sky. I had kissed and refused the man I longed for as my lover when I was married, and I still prayed to the old gods of the land, to the Mother *and* the Virgin Mother. And I had not always lived a life of piety and goodness – no, not ever. But because I was careful, and clever, they all thought I was dull, and I hated it.

* * *

It was out in the corridor that I spied the nurse I had missed earlier, and I hung back, for I saw that she was talking to the oldest son, Rioch. I could just about hear their low voices, though they were talking in Breton. Still, I did not need to understand their language to see what was happening.

Rioch was leaning down towards her, and she had a hand pressed flat against his chest, under his leather jerkin which hung open, so that some of her fingers brushed bare skin at the neck of the shirt. She was young, but I would have guessed that she was older than he was. He could not have been more than eighteen years old, and she looked to me five or more years older. But she *was* very beautiful; slender, tall, clear blue eyes and bright black hair. His hand brushed gently down her cheek, and she closed her eyes. Though she shook her head as though she might send him away, her lips parted just a little, and he leaned down and kissed her. She pushed him back, shaking her head, looking around. I heard her say the queen's name, and I knew what was happening. *No,* she was saying, *the queen will send me away if she catches us.* The young prince was half-laughing, shaking his head, and pressing his lips against her cheek, her brow, and then her mouth again as she turned her face up to his. Her hands closed around the front of his shirt, and she pulled him back with her into the chamber that must have been hers. As she did, I heard him murmur her name, *Christina,* and a chill went through me. *Unmistakably* a Christian name; a *Roman* name.

I rushed to Uther's chamber, and threw the door open without knocking. He stood at the window, his hands pressed down against the sill, leaning into it, bowed down under the weight of his anger. He turned around, surprised to see me, and opened his mouth, but breathless, I spoke first.

"The nurse," I said, but Uther spoke before I could finish, while I was still catching my breath.

He shook his head. "I have made enquiries, Igraine, for I know that it is often the job of a younger sister, or a close relative. But she is nothing more than a tradesman's daughter with a knowledge of medicine, and this is why they have her. She is a widow already, yes, but also we have no one her age. She would be getting to be past her years when our son is born. The sister, too, is married and too old."

I shook my head, drawing in deep breaths from my run up the stairs. Censoriously, Uther stepped forward, and slid his arm around my waist, steadying me.

"You should not run about the castle, Igraine. You will do yourself harm."

"The nurse," I said firmly, "is called *Christina*. Don't you think that's strange?"

"Hardly," Uther said, and I could hear the cold annoyance in his voice.

"And Felix, the son? Those are *Roman* names, Uther."

Uther shrugged. "Why should they not be?"

I sighed in annoyance. "The Bretons are not Christians, so they will not have got such names from their Latin Bible. The girl Christina must be Christian, and if the Christians are sending their daughters to Carhais, and the Bretons are taking Roman names then this means —"

At last Uther had caught on. He said, darkly, "The Bretons have been trading with the Romans. They're not saving the girl for one of their own — they want to make an alliance with the Emperor. The Bretons would rather join with Rome, than with me."

"I think so, Uther," I said. "I think so."

* * *

But nothing seemed to come of it. Uther stormed away, and only came back late to wake me roughly, where I had fallen asleep in his bed, and press his hot mouth against my temple, into my hair, with a frustrated passion that only seemed to tangle with everything else he was lost in. He was gone in the morning when I woke, and when Melusine came in with my clothes, and a hot bath of water, she told me that the Bretons had left as well, an uneasy half-truce struck between them and Uther. I was sure that it was not sincere.

Chapter forty-one

I was right. It was only a few days after the Bretons left that Uther gathered his knights and told them to assemble all the men they could, to sail across the sea to Brittany, to catch the Bretons before they reached their fortress city. He also swore that he would reward the man that brought him Merlin, for I knew that he was afraid to go into Leodegrance's land without him, after the threats of magical forests and deadly lakes. But Merlin was nowhere to be found, and I hardly thought that Uther would have any success in commanding him to come.

As it was, Uther managed to prevail upon Viviane to send some of the women of Avalon to accompany him on the campaign. It was hurried, careless, but I was glad that there would be women from Avalon there. I was not sure how much I had forgiven Uther for all of the horrors we had got tangled up in, but I knew that I did not want to lose another husband, and be thrown back and forth between the kings that remained and looked greedily to the throne of Logrys.

* * *

I did not want to stay in Camelot after Uther left, but I knew that I could not make the long journey to anywhere that I wanted to go. Tintagel was a week's ride away, in my heavy and uncomfortable state, and I would not go to Lothian. I did not think I would make it there with my own life and the child's, and I would have to lie to Morgawse.

I wrote to Viviane, asking her to come to Camelot, but she said that she could not. There were things to attend to in Avalon, and she had two little fosterlings to care for, the little boy Galahad, and the infant sister of his mother, and besides that the affairs of Avalon. I wrote to Morgan in the abbey, and she wrote to me in return, in her big, childish writing, but in Latin, saying that she was well. I wanted to go and see her, but then she would see the child, and she would remember, and she would ask. Perhaps if it had been Morgawse at that age, wild and scatty and forgetful, more interested in how fast she could run, and catch, and dance, then I would have risked it, but Morgan would remember, and she would ask.

Thinking of my daughters made me sad, and I spent the long nights alone reading with Melusine, or listening to her sing and play the harp or the lute. I let her sleep in the bed with me, because I did not like so much to be alone, and I was afraid that the child would be early, and I suspected that she knew more of the magic arts than she would like me to believe.

The summer drew on, hot and heavy, and even the little garden dried up, the grass turning yellow and the flowers dying on the honeysuckle vines. And there was nowhere that I, huge and pregnant, could go to get cool, so I sat in my room with the window open, and Melusine waving a fan for me, though that hardly helped. I wanted Uther to return, or the heat to break. It was getting close to autumn, and it was very unseasonably hot and I was sick of everything. Sick of waiting. Sick of being pregnant. Sick of missing my daughters. There were moments of relief. Melusine pressed her hands against my huge belly, and told me that she could feel the strong, true shape of the child. A foot, the head. She was sure, as Uther was, that it was a little boy. I worried again that it would look like Gorlois, but I dared not tell Melusine what had happened. I didn't want her to be sorry for me, because that would remind me what an awful thing it was.

* * *

It was, in truth, less than a month that Uther and his men were away, across the sea, but it felt like an age. It had been swift. They had not managed to get the vassalage they wanted, nor to get hold of the king and queen who had sealed themselves in the great fortress at Carhais, but Uther had torn their army into pieces and pillaged their towns, and that had satisfied his anger. No magic woods had swallowed them. No lakes had drowned them. They had picked the ripening apples off the trees and feasted on them, and no man had come to harm from it.

So Uther had not had the victory he had coveted, but he had, I saw with resentment, taken prisoners. The Breton princess Aurelie. I should have known that the men would not return without a pretty prize. She was bloodied and bruised, her hands bound behind her, but she walked among the other prisoners with her head held high and proud, and I noticed that many of the knights found it hard to take their eyes from her. I watched from the window of my council room, hiding from the eyes of the people of Camelot, though mine was a secret that everyone knew, and waiting for Uther.

* * *

He was pleased with himself when he came back, and I was too weary and irritated with him to give him the praise that he wanted for subduing the Bretons. He looked on my huge stomach, too, with concern, for it was less than a month, surely, until the child must be born. I think he had hoped that the time would come while he was away, and he would not have to deal with the blood and the mess; he would just come home to a son.

"What are you going to do with the prisoners?" I asked, as Uther pulled off his armour, throwing it to the floor piece by piece with a clatter, and shouted for a bath. He shrugged.

"We will take most of them as slaves. Then there is the princess. I am not sure what is to be done with her."

I knew what he, and the other men, were hoping was to be done with her.

"There is a chance to make peace, Uther. You can give her somewhere sensible, to be married. To another one of your vassals. There is Prince Uriens in Gore, or the brother of Lot of Lothian, the Duke of Orkney."

Uther shrugged. He wasn't listening. He glanced at me.

"You should be resting, Igraine."

"I am well enough," I replied sharply.

"Where is your woman?" he asked. Before I could reply, he said, "I will instruct her to make sure you stay in your bed."

"Do you not want me here with you tonight?" I demanded.

Uther shook his head.

"Not tonight, Igraine."

He had been away *a month*, and he had no interest in being with me tonight? I was his *wife*. Did he not even want to speak to me, to just lie beside me? Perhaps he was disgusted with me, now that I was so large.

When the bath came, I think he expected me to rub his aching muscles, and wash the dirt from his hair, but I left and went back to my own room. I was not in the mood to be kind to him. He had gone to war when I had told him not to, and he had come back only to ignore me. I could not help thinking of how Gorlois had been when back from a long war. He had longed to take me into his arms, and for us to remember together how our love had been.

Someone had put the Breton princess in one of *my* rooms, and Brastias and another knight were guarding the door. I supposed that it was only right that as a prisoner of royal blood she had the appropriate treatment, but I did not like her and did not want her close to me.

* * *

I did not sleep well with the child so near its time, and I wanted to go and walk in the moonlight until I could sleep again, but I was wary of what I would find. But then I felt resentful. It was *my* home, *my* castle. Uther was *my* husband. I did not see why I should hide away, as though I were ashamed. But still, I regretted it almost as soon as I was out of my chamber, and down a flight of stairs. I could hear low voices down the corridor, and I knew who it would be, what I would see if I peered around the corner. And I could not resist the temptation, though I knew it would cut me to the bone.

As I crept close, and leaned around, I saw the Breton girl, Aurelie, pressed up against Uther. I felt my stomach tighten with jealousy and hate, and I put a protective hand against my stomach, feeling the child stir in response inside. She was a prisoner, and yet she knew that at that moment she had him, just a little, in her power. I could see that. And they said that all Breton women were like this: beautiful, powerful, manipulative. Not like the wise, careful women of Britain, but all too much infected with wildness in their blood. I had thought it was a lie. I had thought it was ignorance and prejudice. I was not so sure any more.

Aurelie's hands were closed in fists around the fabric at the front of Uther's shirt, and she was pulling him towards her. He, too, held her fast, one hand tight in the thick, dark curls of her hair, pulling her face up towards his, the other so tight around her arm that the skin under his fingers was turning white, and then red.

"In Brittany," she was saying, her voice deep, her accent thick and gorgeous, far more alluring than anything I could have said in my neat, soft voice, "where women live by honour like men, for a man who can capture a woman with honour on the battlefield, it is considered right that she yields herself to him as a prize."

"Is that so?" Uther sounded bored, but he drew her tighter against him, and leaned a little in towards her, just slightly. I could see that he was about to close his eyes, about to lose himself. Perhaps she was hoping to escape, hoping he was the lust-mad fool he appeared to be, and that afterwards she could slip away.

"Besides," she said softly, her eyes fixed on his, "I have never fucked a king, and I should like to know if even a king, under his clothes is like a normal man after all."

Uther gave a low laugh, taking his hand from her arm to take hold of her around the jaw. His grip on her looked a little violent, and his thumb pressed hard into the soft flesh of her cheek. She showed no sign of pain or fear.

"Do you talk to your sister the queen with that dirty mouth?" Uther asked, but his tone was low and playful, and I could tell that it had excited him to hear her talk like that. He was imagining it already, what it would be like to entwine himself with such a woman. It would be exotic for him, daring. A pleasant change from his wife, who was angry and reserved, and careful now that she was heavy with child.

"My sister does not like to talk of such things. Oh, she is not shy, none of us in our country are, but my sister does not like to talk of men and women, for though she loves her ancient husband, she must make sure to lie perfectly still beneath him when they come together, for fear of shattering his aged bones." As Aurelie spoke, her voice thick, and slightly muffled by Uther's hand at her jaw, I saw her slide one of her hands down his chest, and stop over his breeches.

"You are not a young man anymore, Uther Pendragon," she whispered softly, and he leaned a little closer, and I saw her lips part in temptation, luring him towards her. "Yet I think you could survive a single night with me."

Uther groaned and closed his eyes as she slid her hand into his breeches, pulling her against him in a rough kiss.

I rushed away then, sick, angry, powerless. Even a woman that my husband had taken as his prisoner had more power over him than I had.

* * *

I had not cried for a long time, but when I got back to my chamber, I did. Hot tears of frustration that gave me no relief. Uther would always be able to make me suffer like this. I wished I could have not cared. I knew queens who lived their lives like that. Certainly, Elaine had spoken with casual nonchalance of Máel's bastard children, and I supposed that this was something that Morgawse would come to know as well. I wished that I did not love Uther so much. I wished that I did not *hate* Uther so much. It had all been so much easier with Gorlois, when I had been fond of him, and we had cared for each other.

Chapter forty-two

It was only late in the evening, a few days later, that Uther came at last to my chamber. I wondered if he felt guilty for not seeing how I was when I was so large with his child, but he did not seem sorry.

"Have you decided what you will do with the prisoner?" I asked him evenly, looking down at the sheet of parchment before me where I had been beginning a letter to Morgan, not yet meeting his eye.

When he did not answer, I glanced up. He was dressed in his red and gold surcoat, and he had gold chains around his neck, gold rings on his fingers. He had been making, to *someone*, a show of his kingly power. I felt a spasm of concern, for now I was so near my time, he would be taking care of the state affairs without my counsel.

"Come and greet me properly, Igraine," Uther said, and I could hear the annoyance in his voice, and I could feel my body tense for a fight.

I stood, slowly, but did I not come towards him. He took a step towards me.

"I only ask, Uther, if you have had any more thoughts, any more plans, regarding what you will do with the Breton princess."

"What do you mean, Igraine?" he asked, taking another step towards me. I did not move back. I did not want him to feel as though he could push me, either into stepping away, or into unsaying any of the things I wanted to say.

"I only mean to say, Uther, what will you do with her, now that you have fucked her?" Uther grasped hold of me, hard, about the arm, and pulled me up close to him, leaning down towards me so that his forehead pressed against mine, even as I shrank back.

"You are beginning to sound like a jealous old woman, Igraine," he said, and his voice was low, and cruel, and mean. I was glad, now, that any pretence was dropped between us.

"You are an animal," I hissed at him, "You can't even control yourself when you know she is playing with you –"

"Do you think I am simple, Igraine?" he asked, his other hand closing around the knot of my hair at the back of my head. His lips were so close to mine as he spoke that I could feel the heat of his breath. I tried to pull away, and he gripped me harder. I gave a little gasp of pain. "I have no intention of letting her go home. But you are jealous, sweet Igraine, are you not? You fear that another woman's soft caresses, another woman's kisses, will win me from your side." He slid his hand down from my hair, down around my throat, and slowly over the curve of my breasts. I closed my eyes, pushing away the rushing desire, anger, repulsion, longing, the powerful heady mix of it all.

"It is disrespect to me," I whispered, but his lips had already found mine, and swallowed it up, and his hands were pulling at my clothes, and running over my body, into my hair, his fingers rough and firm against my scalp, and tangling in my hair, pulling my head back to put his lips against my neck.

Softly, there, he murmured, "Tell me how you feel to think of me, like this, with the Breton girl."

I pushed him back away from me, but he pulled me into his embrace harder. "How do you feel to think of how I kissed her, and held her, and how underneath she was as white and lovely as the snow, and her nipples were pink and sweet and soft as the summer flowers. And I tasted them with my lips, and with my tongue, and when I was inside her she called out my name."

I slapped him, hard, though I knew he wanted it. His hand closed around the skirts of my underdress where he had pushed it up under the heavy brocade skirts of my dress, and he tore.

"I could call for them to bring her in here," he said, his lips brushing against my ear as he pressed us back against one of the hard posts of the bed, "and you could enjoy her as well. I have been with two women at once before now, and it was a delight not just to me, but to both of them."

I felt a hand slide the dress from my shoulder, and push it down until my breasts were bare and his hand closed over one of them, the touch of his fingers sending a dizzying wave of desire through me.

"She was young, Igraine, deliciously young. I have known too little the delights of young women. I thought I would have you, as an eager young virgin, just fifteen, and I *long* to know what you were like. Were you hesitant, and afraid? Or were you, like most young girls are, secretly eager."

The fingers of his hand, pushed up my skirts, suddenly found the place between my legs that made me gasp out again, and Uther pulled my head back once more, so that I had to look him in the eye. "Were you? Did you beg Gorlois for his cock?"

I slapped him again, and hissed, "You are disgusting."

"So are you, Igraine," he growled, and he pushed his fingers inside me, and I cried out with surprise. "You would have let me have you up against the wall in Tintagel courtyard, all those years ago, if we had not been interrupted. I felt the heat of your skin against mine. I felt you shiver. Did you dream of me, all those years with Gorlois? I dreamed of you – of what it would be like to lie you down beneath me, and put my lips against your skin, to hear you sigh my name."

He tightened his grip on my hair as his fingers went deeper inside me, and I was breathing hard already, half dizzy, half intoxicated, half repulsed by his touch, and his talk. I had wanted to be angry, to push him away, but I was weak, we were both weak with each other, and somehow we always came back to this. He drew his fingers out of me, slowly, and I closed my hands around the front of his shirt, pulling him against me, lost. I offered my mouth up to his, and he kissed me, roughly, for a moment. But he was not finished talking. I could feel myself burning with longing to have him by then. If I had been less lost with it, the strength of it, when I was angry and disgusted with him, it might have made me afraid.

"I used to dream, Igraine, of the feel of your body against mine, and know – I knew that you were dreaming the same." His hand closed over more of the underskirt, and he tore. He was wild with anger now, wild with desire, wild with saying to me all the things he longed to say, as he had been the night we married.

"And when I had my hands on your body at last, and you slipped out of your clothes as though it were nothing but habit, because you thought I was another man, I had to hold myself back from falling on you like a beast in the field. Gods, I remember that night so well. The moonlight." With his free hand, he traced along my jaw, down my throat. "Against your white skin, and the smell of your hair, like the salt of the sea, and the taste of your mouth, wine and honey. Every night is the same with you." Though his voice had dropped low, and was heavy with the lust that burned within him, his hands closed around more of the thin fabric of the underclothes. "The same rush to see your form, to smell your skin, to feel us become as one. I dream about it now, as vividly as if it never was. You are right beside me, and I still long for you." He suddenly stopped still, his eyes fixed on mine, and whispered, softly, "Now tell me, Igraine, that you have more to be jealous of than I do. I have my sport, as any man does, but you have my soul."

Before I could speak, Uther pulled me into a kiss once more, and I took his hand and thrust it back up my skirts. I did not know why he wanted to talk about Gorlois, or the past, or the night he had deceived me, but he did. I could hear his words, over and over in my head, that he had loved me all his life, that I possessed a part of him that no one else could, and I *wanted* to hear those things. I wanted to feel them, to feel sure, to feel his love could not be lessened by other women, or by the horrors of the past. And I could not pretend that I did not long for him, as he did for me. To hear those words, and to feel his hands on me, for that brief moment took everything else away.

* * *

It was almost a week later, when I sat with Melusine and Brastias in my council chamber, giving them their instructions for their day, that the child came. I felt the pain first, and the rush of water down my legs, and I closed my eyes as I felt the strangely familiar sensations close around me. I felt Melusine's hands wrap around my arm, and with a strength I thought she was too small for, she pulled me to my feet. I also felt Brastias' arm slide around my waist, and they carried me to my bed.

"Fetch Uther," I mumbled through the pain. "Fetch Viviane."

"Viviane will not have time to come," Melusine said gently, "but I will help you, lady. Drink this."

I did not realise until then that I was already lying in my bed, and I had in my hand the drink I had had before from the women of Avalon. I drank it in a huge gulp. Almost immediately, I felt its delicious sleepy numbness spread through me.

"Call for Uther," I tried to say again, but my lips felt heavy, and I thought the drink was stronger than it was before, because before it had sent me into a soft half-sleep where I had still been aware of what was around me, but now I was slipping into darkness, away from my body, and I thought I could hear Melusine telling Brastias to leave. Which he should have done, for she was pushing back the skirts of my dress. But suddenly I felt afraid, and as the blackness closed over me, I called out for Uther again, but I was sure that no one would hear.

Chapter forty-three

When I woke, I felt groggy, and sore. My breasts were swollen and aching with milk, but I could not hear the child. Had he died? Had he been born a girl, or bearing Gorlois' face. Had Uther had the child taken away? I felt panicked, and I could feel my heart race, but I felt still too drugged to move, still too exhausted. I tried to speak, but my throat was dry and my voice without strength, and I slipped into the darkness again.

When I woke again, I did not know if it was days later, or the same day, or weeks later. I knew that it was morning because the light was bright and clear, and I could smell bread baking far away. I was starving hungry, but I cared more about what had become of my child. Slowly, heavily, I pushed myself up onto my elbows. Uther sat in a chair at the foot of the bed, his head in his hands, but as though he sensed me waking, he looked up. His face was dark with some kind of unspeakable suffering, and I could not hear the child.

"Where is my child?" I asked, my voice weak, wavering, already filling with tears.

Uther shook his head. His eyes were red.

"Uther, where is he?"

He could not speak. I did not know if my child was alive or dead, if he was lost, or sickly and in another's care, or if he was gone forever.

"Where is Melusine?" She was not there, not there in the room. I had expected her to be there. She ought to have been there. What possible reason was there for her to leave just as my child was born? For her to leave me weak and sick? I felt an awful chill settle through my body.

No. Melusine, Melusine. Melusine, lady of the water. Melusine, *changer of shapes.* Melusine, Melusine, *Merlin.* He had taunted me with the truth, and I had been too distracted to see it. I pushed the covers back from me, and struggled forward towards Uther, reaching out to him, and he stood, and caught me in his arms. I heard Melusine's voice – *Viviane will not have time to come* – and thought of the drink that had put me to sleep for days, and Melusine sending Brastias away. Oh, and I had let her wash me in the bath, and sleep beside me, and all the while she had been *Merlin*, and that was why he was nowhere to be found in the whole kingdom all the while that she was here. She had been nervous before the Bretons, in case they sensed who she was, and she had disappeared whenever Viviane was here.

I grasped hold of Uther's shirt, pulling him down towards me.

"Melusine," I said, the words rasping from my dry throat. "Melusine is Merlin, and he has taken our child."

Uther looked back at me, his eyes blank and empty with loss. "I know, Igraine. I know."

* * *

We lay side by side in the bed, in silence, staring up at the canopy above us. It was all for nothing then. All that I had risked, all that I had begged for, it was all lost because I had not seen what was right before me.

I fell asleep again, swiftly, exhausted by sleep, by Merlin's drug still in my blood. When I slept, I felt myself sink deeply into a dream, and it was a dream that was almost as clear as the waking world, for I saw Viviane before me, beautiful and terrifying as she always was with her flaxen hair, and her woad, and her piercing blue-green eyes. She waved a hand before herself, and she dissolved into nothing, but I knew she was there, for I followed her. We came through a thick, dark forest, and to a clearing where a little fire burned. Hunched over the fire was a man in a dark cowled robe, and as I came closer, I peered beneath the cowl and I saw from the hollow, black eyes, and the woad, and the skullish grin that it was Merlin. In his arms he held, wrapped in a blanket, a little, wriggling creature. Viviane stood before him, but he could not see her. Only I knew she was there. He was hushing the little baby in his arms, but the baby cried and cried. At last, he settled the child on the soft grass, and turned his back for a moment to draw something from his pack – some drink, I thought, to soothe the child. And in that second Viviane leant down, and wrapped her cloak over the little baby, and both disappeared once more. Only this time, they melted into nothingness. My child was gone, but he was with Viviane, who would hide him somewhere that Merlin could not find, and he would be safe.

* * *

When I woke in the morning, I did not tell Uther. I did not trust him not to weaken and tell Merlin, and I did not want to earn him the witch's wrath. That was something I was willing to bear alone, so that my son – if he had been a little boy, for I had not even seen his face – could be safe.

* * *

I was weak, still, and exhausted from the birth of my child, so when the cry came that Merlin had returned and was demanding to speak with King Uther, I stayed in my rooms. I missed Melusine, though I knew she had been nothing but an illusion, for now I had no one to take care of me, to brush my hair and lace my dress. I supposed I ought to find someone else, but I did not know where to begin looking.

I wrapped myself in my cloak, and peered out of the window of my council chamber, down to the courtyard where Merlin and Uther met. I pushed open the window in time to hear Uther say, "Merlin, the debt is paid," and I was glad I had not told him, for he said it with such sorrow and conviction, even before his men, that I knew that Merlin would not doubt. He would know, then, that it was I who had somehow cheated him of his payment. I did not care.

* * *

I was prepared for Merlin when he came up to my room, as I knew he would. I knew that he would be angry, but it didn't matter anymore. I had already won. I felt my body tense right to the core as he shut the door behind him with a soft click of the latch, but I was ready to face him. He had done everything to me that he could.

I could not tell yet if he knew for sure that it was my doing, that Viviane had taken my son and hidden him away, or if he only suspected it. He fixed me with his awful, black, irisless eyes and I stared back, blank and cold as I had learned to be. I was grateful, then, for all the strength that I had learned since Gorlois' death. It had been worth it.

"What is it, Merlin?" I asked, flatly. I hoped that Uther would come back soon. He would not like Merlin being alone with me in my bedchamber, and though he was nothing more than a brute to Merlin,

I thought the strange witch was cowardly enough about the suffering of his body that he might scuttle off if Uther came.

Merlin folded his arms over his chest. With the hood of his ugly cowl pushed back, I could see the traces of blue-green on the deathly white skin of his scalp. His skull looked unpleasantly too large, as though it were straining at the semi-translucent skin. Once again I wondered how old he truly was, how long he had been alive, what kind of demon he had sold his soul to, in order to have so much of the dark Otherworld about him.

"Viviane has taken your boy," Merlin said, his blackened lips curling back from his nasty, peg-like teeth. "She has hidden him from me. Tell me where he is, Igraine."

Your boy. He was a son, and Uther's heir. I felt a rush of gladness for that. And he was safe.

I shook my head. Now was the time for me to be brave, and to be cold.

"I do not know where my child is, Merlin. If you have lost him, then you have only yourself to blame."

"Do not play games with me, Igraine," Merlin snarled, stepping towards me. I did not give any ground. I was not going to be backed into a corner. I was not frightened for my own safety, and I was sure that my children were safe. I did not feel any kind of desire to protect Uther, either, in that moment, from Merlin's vengeance. He had brought this man into our lives. He would bear the consequences, if the world was just. I only cared that he would not break, and tell Merlin my secret. "I know that it was you who told Viviane to hide the boy away. I will find him. And I will punish you for this."

I sighed heavily. It was hard, but I had to give the impression that Merlin did not frighten me. I could feel my heart racing, my palms sweating, but I knew that I appeared calm. I was practised at it now.

"What will you do, Merlin? You have lost. You will not turn my son into your slave, for you to rule through when he takes the throne. Uther is the last king you will have as your puppet. The priests and the bishops are chasing your old gods to the borders, and magic is draining out of the world. Go back to Avalon. Beg Viviane to forgive you. You have had your time."

Merlin's ugly mouth spread into an unpleasant grin, and I felt the panic flash though me, though I could not say why.

"Igraine, do you truly think that you have won? You think because you wear a crown on your head, and you are Queen of Britain that you rule me. But everything you rule is illusion. You cannot command me. You cannot *fight* me. You are a queen of men, but I am ruler of the earth and the sky, the fire and the oceans. You think that because you have won Uther away from me with your woman's tricks that I am crippled and I have no power, but you are wrong. I would have made your son great, the greatest king this land has ever known. I would have protected him from every evil. But you are selfish, and small-minded, and you do not see the whole grandness of time, just a woman's small, selfish view of family. You will regret defying me. I will tear your precious family to pieces. I will put your daughters to war against one another. I will go to Avalon, and I will make Morgan my pupil until all she knows is the blackest part of the Otherworld, and the dark magic consumes her. I will let your son walk the cursed way to the death the fates have set out for him, when I could have saved him if he had been mine, as Uther promised. And I will curse your womb so no matter what spell Viviane gives you, there will never be another child, and you will be alone."

"I am not going to bargain with you, Merlin," I said flatly.

"Indeed," he said, his black eyes still fixed on mine. "I did not mean to suggest that you could do anything to change this. I do not forget. I do not forgive."

"Neither do I, Merlin," I replied, and he melted away before me, into the air.

* * *

Viviane came, and told me I had to come with her to Lothian because Morgawse was about to have her child. Uther did not have the chance to stop me, because as soon as I put my hands into Viviane's as she offered them out to me, the room swayed sickeningly about me, and disappeared. And we were in an empty room in a different castle.

Before we went to find Morgawse and Lot, I begged Viviane to show me my son, to tell me where he was, but she shook her head, and only said, "I cannot, Igraine. He is somewhere safe, among good people who will care for him. He will have a father, and a mother, and an older brother, so he will learn first to be a squire, and will never as a child be the first into danger. He will be happy, and I will make sure that he will be safe, as I will make sure that Morgan is safe. But you cannot know where he is, or what his parents call him, because if you know, Merlin *will* find him. This is what you asked me for, Igraine," she added gently, and I nodded.

Lot was waiting outside the chamber, angry because he had counted up the months on his fingers, and realised that this birth was one month short of nine after he was married. I did not have time for him, and the same gossip and accusations that had hovered around Camelot like flies. I waved him away, and went in with Viviane.

Morgawse looked so small compared to the huge mound of her stomach, and she screamed and screamed, and blamed me, saying that I had killed her by giving her over to marriage so young. But she was not dying, she was making life, and I did not have the patience to be kind to her. And I was sharp and brusque because I was weak and exhausted, and because I was jealous that when her child was born she would hold it in her arms, and feed it, and love it, and it would not be taken from her.

And it was not just one child, but two; two little boys with her red hair, and with the look of their father about them, too. That would cease his complaining. After the first boy was born, Morgawse sobbed, and half slipped away into unconsciousness, and I knew that if Viviane had not been there, I would have wrapped the second little child up in a blanket and secreted him away with me. I wanted to cry when I saw their little hands and feet. They cried loud and strong, and Morgawse cried, too, with delight, and held them in her arms, with a new and rapturous wonder on her face. I kissed her on the side of her head, and I closed my eyes, for all I could think of was the loss of my own child, disappeared into the mists.

PART III
MOTHER OF THE KING

Then said the old man, Why are ye so sad? I may well be heavy, said Arthur, for many things. Also here was a child, and told me many things that meseemeth he should not know, for he was not of age to know my father. Yes, said the old man, the child told you truth, and more would he have told you an ye would have suffered him. But ye have done a thing late that God is displeased with you, for ye have lain by your sister, and on her ye have gotten a child that shall destroy you and all the knights of your realm.

Sir Thomas Malory, *Le Morte d'Arthur*

Chapter forty-four

When I returned to Camelot, it was to find Merlin firmly placed at Uther's side, whispering to him in councils and watching me with his empty black eyes. Uther, broken by the loss of his son, seemed to have submitted his will to Merlin's. Nor did I fight, because I knew now that Uther would be no king without Merlin, and without Merlin our son would have no future.

I dreamed about the boy all the time. In my dreams, he was small and perfect as Morgawse's little sons. Born before their time and tiny as kittens, they had been strong and lovely. So was my son. In my dreams I held him in my arms, and he was warm and heavy. He cried for me, and laughed when I kissed his cheek. His little hand closed around my finger. His eyes slowly grew from the empty blue of a newborn to grey and lovely like my own, and his hair was gold like Uther's. He was the most perfect creature that I had ever seen, and I did not even know if he was real. I did not talk about those dreams with Uther, and I hated to wake from them.

Uther and I were bound together now by our shared grief, as well as the desire and jealousy and anger that had tangled us together before; but he was different with me, and I with him. We were aware that we had lost, and some deeper world now existed between the two of us. He was tender and loving more of the time, less wild. He did not try to provoke me to hit him, or enjoy taunting me with the other women that he had from time to time. I did not mind them anymore. I knew that they could not come close to what existed between us. Understanding. Companionship. And, when the fires of disaster had burned everything else away, a love as deep as the rocks beneath the earth. I loved Uther, and I forgave him, for I saw that he had made the promise rashly as a young man, and that regret of it dogged him. I did not forgive, I would never forgive Merlin. He resented me. He resented my influence on Uther, and he was jealous of the secret hours of the night we spent together. Then, I could whisper to Uther without Merlin there to order his puppet king this way or that, to make this pact with this man, and this war with another. He knew that I had a part of Uther that he could never possess. I became more insistent in councils. I had knights of my own: Brastias, and the young men that he trained. They always stood with me, and the older men, too, often favoured my careful pragmatism over Uther's impulsive desire to dominate. Sometimes Merlin had his way, sometimes I mine. Rarely were they the same.

I learned, long after the fact, that Uther had married the Breton princess to Lot's younger brother, and I was glad that he had taken my advice. I was gladder still that she was across the border, and far, far north in the islands of Orkney where Uther would never see her again. More news came, too, that Morgawse had had another son. Uther had snorted with derision and, when he thought I could not hear him, said to his knights, "This will have Lot of Lothian thinking he is the finest stud-horse in Britain." I had cast him a narrow look which he ignored as the knights laughed into their hands, half ashamed, half amused – although a few of them were worried. They had noticed that although I had been pregnant, and none had been allowed to speak of it, no child had come forth, and in the years that followed I showed no sign of conceiving another. They counted the years. Though I was only just thirty years old, and Uther still years from forty, they said that we were too old – or at any rate too old to begin. My mother had been far older than that when I was born, and I knew it was foolish, but it hurt me all the same. I visited Morgan, sometimes, in the abbey. Whenever I was there, I looked out, carefully, for Merlin hiding in disguise as a nun, and I flicked through the books in her room, looking for black magic spells. I found none. Morgan always told me she was well, and that she liked the abbey. The abbess agreed that Morgan was a good student, and had learned her Greek and Latin letters well, but puckered her lips in disapproval and said that she was wilful. I was not sure that I would have described her so. But I had not raised my daughter to be pious, and perhaps she had resisted that.

* * *

The seasons came and went, and I dreamed less and less of my son, although, when I closed my eyes, if I wished it, I could picture him – a little boy, gold hair tousled, running everywhere with his little chubby hands in front of him, as though he knew that he would fall. But the pictures were dimmer, and the loss deeper, more empty, more hollow. I knew that it was only what I imagined, and perhaps my son was dark, like me, rather than fair like his father, or even red-haired like Morgawse. Whoever he was, I did not know him, and I would not until Uther was dead and he took the throne. I might be long dead by then.

I did not think that Uther remembered the day that we had lost him, until one morning, late into the fullness of summer, fully five years after it had happened, I woke as his arms wrapped around me, and his face nuzzled against my neck. He was a little rough with the stubble of a night's sleep, but I murmured with delight as I felt his weight on top of me, and his hands, gentle and loving, running over me, drawing me closer. His mouth found mine and, still warm with sleep, I sighed into him, pressing my body into his. That was when he paused and fixed me with his steady gaze.

"Today, he will be five years old." I closed my eyes tight and nodded, and I felt the tears gathering, close to the surface. "Oh Igraine," Uther said, his voice low, and soft with compassion. "I did not mean to make you sad."

He pressed his lips softly to my closed eyes, and pulled me closer, pushing back the nightdress, his mouth finding mine again. I felt him, hard against me, and I leaned into it, into the promise of forgetting, and I knew that he was offering me all the comfort that he could. I wished that I had a woman to share my pain with. I wished that my sisters had not abandoned me for death and exile. But, what I had, real and solid, was the oblivion of love that Uther offered me, and with a sigh of abandon I accepted it. I was glad to forget.

* * *

Our days were routine, without great event. Viviane came and went with news from Avalon, and sometimes with the fosterling boy, who was now tall and thin as a sapling and always quiet. I visited my daughters. Morgan told me that a knight from the nearby farm and his two sons sometimes visited her, for their mother was sick within the abbey. The abbess confirmed this, and promised me that it was no danger to my daughter. She clicked her tongue with disapproval, and said the mother was a pagan and refused to repent it, but only said, "All gods are one god, and all truth is one truth." She called the husband a handsome knight, and I did not think that a nun such as she ought to have been noticing that a man who might be about to lose his wife to illness was handsome, but I said nothing. She also said that the two sons were like brothers from a fairy-tale, one dark like the father, one fair like the mother, and it gladdened me to hear it, though I could not have said why. It was Morgawse who liked fairy stories, not Morgan, but I was glad nonetheless that there was something of that kind of innocence near her. Simple people with simple lives. Children her own age to play with. And she would be off to Avalon before she or the boys got any dangerous ideas.

* * *

People began to say things. Things they should not have said. They said that I was the power behind Uther's throne, and commanded his thoughts and deeds. I was not. Merlin was. But that was not so bad. What was bad was that they said that I had seduced Uther out of love for power when I was a married woman, and, witch that I was, had created a phantom child to induce him to marry me. But all the while I was barren as the northern wastes of ice. I had wished that I had the powers of a witch; I wished that the child had not been my flesh and blood that it had hurt me to lose. Uther did not care; he shrugged, and even laughed at the rumours. He told me that I ought to be pleased that people thought me as mysterious, as powerful, as dangerous as Viviane. I did not want people to listen to me because they were afraid. I did not want people to think I was a woman of no faith who had used and devoured one husband, and who now acted through another. True, Uther had no head for politics. It was by my word that those affairs were mostly conducted. But no more so than Merlin, silent as a spider, the shadow behind Uther's throne.

* * *

I did not realise how much time had passed until, one day, just as winter was creeping in, my sister found her way back to me. I supposed that I had let the time slip past me in a haze because I hated counting the days, the age of my lost son, the ages of my grandsons. Morgan's birthdays that slipped by until she was suddenly ten years old, and tall, almost, as I was; articulate, with a strangely adult manner of speaking, far beyond her years. That was the year that Enid came.

Uther and I sat in the great hall, in court, ready to receive supplicants for justice. Uther was there to dispense that justice, and I to dispense mercy. I was ready for that. I had arbitrated when I had to. This young man who had run away with this man's daughter must, if he wanted to keep his head, marry the girl and acknowledge the child. This man whose dog had killed this man's sheep must pay their price, and give up the dog. This knight who forced this girl must leave court, in exile, forever, but he need not face death. That was my place, that was my role, and I knew it well. I did not know what to do when, in the great throne room, which was usually quiet with reverence, I heard my name.

"Igraine, Igraine, I must see Queen Igraine."

When they brought her forward, I hardly recognised her. She was emaciated, thinned to the bone, and her thick gold hair that had been my envy as a girl was dirtied with mud and matted, and paling from the temples out. I supposed, since I was thirty-five years old, she must have been more than forty, and past her years of youth. She was still beautiful though. Thin, and dirty, and wild about the eyes, it was still obvious to me that I looked upon a beautiful woman. High cheekbones, the same lovely, clear grey eyes that our mother had possessed, and a slender, elegant frame. Her dress was rich – lovely fine samite in a periwinkle blue, the dye for which must have been costly indeed – but torn, as if by brambles, and her skin was a little bloodied, dark red, and rusty brown.

I ought to have felt sorry for her. I ought to have rushed down from the dais and thrown my arms around her. And yet she had slipped from Tintagel when I had needed her. She had run back to Erec, her love, and she had not cared about me, or my child, or if I would need her if the war had killed my husband; she had only cared for herself. And she had always been selfish. She had laughed off every duty she had ever had. Enid was a shallow person, a careless person, and she had not cared about me. If she had stayed by my side, I might not have been lured in by Melusine and the illusory promise of friendship. I might have given Morgawse and Morgan into her care, and kept them safe and close by. I stiffened in my seat, sitting as tall and straight as I could with the heavy crown of Logrys on my head. Uther was looking at me. I could feel the touch of his eyes on my face. He knew that this was someone to do with me, but he had never met Enid. He would not forget her after this.

Someone whispered something to Enid, and before I could speak, she dropped to her knees, and bent her head in deference. I should have rushed to her and pulled her to her feet. I did not.

"Stand, Enid," I said, coldly. Enid stood. She was trembling. If I had had the inclination to be compassionate and kind I would have called for someone to bring her food and wine. She looked as though she needed it. "What brings you to Camelot, sister?"

"Ygerna," Enid sighed, and I saw relief flood her face, and desperation. But I tensed against it, against her choice to call me by the name my mother had given me. No one had called me that since I was a very little girl. I knew what it was. It was an appeal to family, and it burned within me.

"Ygerna, little Igraine," she continued, "I have come to throw myself on your mercy."

I let her wait for a moment, let her stare at me expectantly before I spoke.

"Where is your husband, Enid?" I asked.

Her mouth opened as though she were about to speak, but her eyes filled with tears. I looked away from her. I did not want to see it. I would not be made to feel sorry for her. She had not felt sorry for me.

"That is why I came here, Igraine," she began, drawing in a deep breath. "Erec has gone mad." She waited for me to respond, but I did not. "Erec went – he went mad. At first, the knights started talking. They started saying that Erec did not do his duties anymore, that he was becoming like a woman, sitting with me while I sang, or read. Spending his days and nights with me. I heard them talking. They were laughing at him. I think he heard them too. But when I asked him if he would not prefer to sometimes be out riding with his men, he grew angry, he accused me of having a lover. That was when it began. He made me put on my riding clothes and saddle my horse, and he made me ride before him, out of the city. I did not know where I was going, but he forbade me from speaking. We rode into the forest. It was a dangerous place, full of bandits. When I saw them on the road, I cried out. He would have died if I had not, but when he had killed them, he beat me for disobeying him, and we carried on like this. We came to a lord's castle, and stayed, and the lord saw how cruel Erec was to me, and how sad I was, and he –" She choked on her words and I looked down, away from her face, where tears were now streaming clean tracks through the dirt. "I thought he was only being friendly, only comforting. He was so much older, I never thought – but I ran from him. I ran from him, and told Erec, and I begged him to take me away. And he beat me again, and set me to the road before him. Then again we came to another lord's castle. This lord was young, and handsome, and charming, but I did not like him. I loved Erec. I loved the man that Erec had been. This time, when the lord tried to seize hold of me, seeing how lonely I was, I slipped away, and saddled my horse, and I rode here. I rode all the way here, sister." She gave a rough laugh of relief, and I glanced up. She was smiling, desperately. She was so sure I was her saviour. "I rode all the way to you. To my sister. Igraine…"

She tailed off, and I could see her breaths racking her. I could see she was hungry, and weary and abused. I could see that Erec and his sudden cruelty had destroyed her, but I felt my heart within me grow cold.

"He is still your husband by law," I said. "And you must return to him. I cannot harbour you from your lawful husband, Enid."

"Igraine, Igraine, please," she begged. "I am your sister." I held up a hand for silence, and she fell quiet.

"You were my sister, Enid, almost twenty years ago. You were my sister when I was young and pregnant and alone in Tintagel Castle. But then, when I was called here to Camelot, you slipped away. You were not my sister then. You let me come home, sixteen years old, alone, afraid, with a husband at war, with my child near her time, to find an empty castle and the stores wasted by your carelessness. You did not come when your first niece was born, because you were too engrossed with Erec. You did not come when your second niece was born, because you were too engrossed with Erec. Do you even know their names? No. I did not think so. You did not come to mourn with me when Elaine died. You did not even write to me when my husband died." I was trembling too now, but with rage, with the anger that I had pushed down to the pit of my stomach, that I had suffered this all alone, because my sister was too self-centred to care. "You left me alone, Enid. You did not care if I lived or died. If my husband treated me well or badly. If I was lonely, if I was scared. You did not care, because you had Erec. I have lived more than half my life without you. You are a stranger to me. Less. Strangers have not betrayed me as you have. I have been alone. Alone while you indulged your passions, the forbidden love you thought was worth everything. I will not hide you here. Go back to your husband, and beg him to take you back. Long ago, you made the choice that he was all you needed. You must live by that choice now."

There was a murmur of discontent in the hall, and I could feel Uther and Merlin staring at me, and both were amazed that I could be so cold. I felt cold. I felt awful, and cruel, and yet – staring at the sister who had abandoned me – I could feel nothing else.

"Give her food, and drink, and fresh riding clothes, and send her on her way," I said.

Enid begged, and wept, and finally screamed as they led her from the hall. In the end they had to drag her. I closed my eyes, and leant my head back against the cold, dark, heavy wood of the throne that I sat in, and I tried to imagine that I was somewhere else, someone else; that the world was different.

That night Uther was wary with me, as though there was something he wanted to say. I ignored him as I sat in his bedchamber, rifling through the papers of the day's affairs, signing the last of them, checking the details, pressing them with Uther's seal. After a long time, when he had pulled off his boots, and shrugged off his surcoat, and taken off his crown and the gold chains he wore about his neck for state occasions, he said to me, "It is beyond me, Igraine, to know how things are between sisters, but –"

"Yes, Uther," I said, quiet but firm, "It is beyond you."

Chapter forty-five

Not long after that, more trouble came. I should have known that Lot would not sit quietly in his vassalage, not now that he had sons, and my daughter was grown. They had been a bad match. I had wed the two people in Britain who hated Uther the most. I should have seen that this was what it would become.

It seemed small. The piece of parchment I held in my hand was unassuming enough. But I was sure that it was a lie. I had seen the gold and jewels and fur that Lot draped over himself – and over Morgawse – all too frequently. There was no way that what he promised in taxes to Uther was enough.

"Look at this." I slid the sheet over to Uther. He grunted in assent and shrugged, without reading it. "Uther, read it."

The other side of him, Merlin began to peer. I should have waited until we were alone. At the edge of my vision, I could see Brastias and his latest squire watching me. Uther still did not seem to see what I was saying.

"Uther, that can't be right. He's not paying us what he owes."

Uther threw it down, and rubbed his chin. He did not look at me.

I pulled the document back towards me.

"It's Orkney – he's left out Orkney and his incomes there. He hoped we wouldn't notice," I said.

Uther would not have noticed. Perhaps this was not the first time.

"We should send letters, we should demand he pay –"

Because he knew I wanted peace, Merlin urged war. I still remembered his threat: I will set your daughters to war with one another. I will tear your precious family to pieces.

"Oh, no. It is more serious than that. You must go, and demonstrate to him who is lord. If Orkney is not paying you, then perhaps they now give tribute elsewhere. A show of strength must be made. If you do not go, my lord Uther," Merlin wheeled over the counsel table, "then what is to prevent the Lord of Orkney making an alliance with the King of the Ship-men across the sea? Or the Spear-Danes? You seem a very faraway threat to him. You should go with an army, and be prepared to subdue any insubordination with the sword."

I sighed, pulling the map a little closer towards Uther and myself. I avoided catching Brastias' eye, though I felt him looking at me.

"It's weeks and weeks of journeying, right to the far North. By the time we get there, it will be freezing winter. We'll be moving slowly, dragging an army behind us. There's no reason to believe that Orkney are planning to throw off your rule – Lot is just greedy with his gold, as he always has been."

"The Lord of Orkney is Lot of Lothian's brother, isn't he?" one of the lesser knights piped up, unhelpfully.

Merlin's black lips widened into a great, gloating smile. "Of course, we have no reason to believe that Lot of Lothian would allow any challenge to my lord Uther's rule."

Uther gave a rough grunt of wry assent. A small armed party of fifty men was ready to ride north within a week.

*　*　*

Because we wanted to move quickly, I rode at Uther's side astride a horse. I was happy not to be confined to a litter. Elaine had had one, and I had ridden in it once, and the swaying had made me sick. I was a good rider, and I didn't mind the cold, which got sharper and more bitter the further north we went. We should have sailed, of course. We should have taken a ship from the old Roman town at London and sailed, but Uther couldn't wait for spring, and it was too dangerous to sail now, with the storms of autumn heavy upon us.

It rained from when we joined the old Roman road to Northumbria, and the horses' hooves churned up mud that spattered all over my expensive furs, but I was glad not to be trudging knee-deep in it with the lesser soldiers. It was winter by the time we reached the Roman wall. I could see what Uther had once described – how Lot's army, twenty years ago, had begun ripping it down. I had never been so far north. It was freezing, and every day we woke to frost on the ground, but it was beautiful. I learned not to feel the throbbing from the cold in my hands through my gloves, and I learned to be grateful for water that did not have to have a skin of ice shattered before I washed in it.

The days were a bare few hours long when we boarded the ship that would take us the short trip across the freezing northern seas to Orkney. No expense had been spared by Lot to demonstrate to Uther that his brother, stuck out there in the sea on that icy rock, was a powerful man, so the ships were filled with rugs and silks, and somewhat alarming braziers filled with hot coals. I supposed if the ship pitched and sank, I would have greater concerns than the wood catching fire.

When we arrived in Orkney, I expected to meet again the gloating, preening Breton princess who had taunted me for being a prude years before. She was no longer there. Instead, a woman bearing her face greeted me formally, and kissed my cheek with icy lips. She wouldn't meet Uther's eye, and held the hood of her beautiful white-fur cloak so that it shaded her face from us both.

Inside, the reception was only slightly warmer. I had expected Lot's brother to be about the same age, and to be possessed of the same oily charm, but the Lord of Orkney was a nervous man in his mid-twenties with thinning hair.

When Uther demanded, "How many men do you keep here?" Orkney didn't seem to be able to give a definite answer. It only worsened.

"My Lord King Uther, my Lady, Queen Igraine, I'd like to present our daughter, Adaira."

The girl appeared seemingly from within her mother's cloak. She was very pretty: dark hair, blue eyes, clear white skin. She looked to me to be almost eight years old. So it was entirely possible that she was Uther's child.

Uther, pulling off the cloak of grey wolf fur that he had worn the whole ride and shoving it towards Brastias, grinned between them.

"What a pretty girl. I'm glad to see that my gift has pleased you these – eight, is it? nine? – these long years."

Uther let his eyes rove over Aurelie as she unpinned her own cloak and handed it to a servant. I hadn't noticed before, but underneath she was obviously pregnant. Another reminder of what I lacked.

"Your gift?" The young lord repeated, dumbly.

"Yes," Uther insisted. "I'm sure your brother made clear the circumstances in which I found your bride. We came upon her army when the Bretons tried to throw off my rule. The rest of her people just about escaped, but we caught a small band of them. The others were men, so we killed them. But we took Aurelie. I pulled her from the greedy hands of my men, and I protected her myself, so that I could give her to you."

Both Aurelie and Orkney coloured. The little girl Adaira shrank back behind her mother.

I heard them arguing about it later. Hissing at each other in their room. I had gone to look for more furs, but I had, too, also hoped to catch Uther sniffing around one of his old conquests.

"You've shamed us both, woman," I heard Orkney snarl through the door. I pressed my ear against it.

"I was a prisoner, Duncan. By the names of all the gods, I thought you knew, or at least would have had enough sense to piece it together."

In private, it seemed, she was the woman I remembered.

"And what about Adaira?"

"What about her, Duncan? She's your child. You know she's your child."

I slipped away. It was too painful. I had a child that age, lost somewhere in the world.

* * *

I was glad when it was time at last to leave for Lothian Castle. The journey was awful; it was almost midwinter by then, and the seas were rough. After a week in Orkney watching Uther swagger around Aurelie and bully Duncan, I was glad to leave. I found myself oddly wishing that Merlin had come with us, for I was sure Uther would not have been quite so undignified in front of him.

When we arrived, their Christmas celebrations were beginning. Everywhere was hung with bright cloth banners and wreaths of whatever rough, prickly plants grew in those northern heaths. I didn't feel like celebrating. I only wanted to see Morgawse and my grandsons. But it was not yet time.

Uther stood before me, fastening a heavy cloak of rich furs around his shoulders, watching his image move and ripple on the surface of the hammered mirror. It was all bright gold and dark fur, rich cloth and leather. If it had been another time, another place, I would have slipped my arms around his waist, let my hands burrow beneath the layers of expensive fabric until I found hot skin.

"What are you going to do?" I asked, quietly.

He turned over his shoulder back to me.

"What am I going to do?"

"Yes."

"You mean what are we going to do?"

I closed my eyes, leant my head against the bed post. I did not know that I could fight with Lot and Morgawse on this. I did not want any part of it, but without either Merlin or me beside him, how would Uther negotiate?

"I don't know," I said. I felt Uther kneel before me, one of his arms slide around my waist, pulling me against him, his mouth finding mine. I pushed him back. I would welcome the distraction later, not now.

* * *

"Where is Morgawse?"

Lot, dressed in more gold than I would ever have imagined possible, gave me his wolfish smile.

"She is out with the hunt, with our two eldest. She will be back before dark."

"They're just boys –"

Lot laughed. He still did not look at Uther, but was staring right at me.

"We start them early here. They will be safe in their mother's care, and among the knights. Please – sit down. I can call for anything you need."

Uneasily, I sat down. Lot made a point of striding around the table to sit beside me. Uther sat stiffly the other side. This was already going badly. Brastias settled himself the other side of Uther, but the rest of the table was taken up by lords from Lothian.

"What brings you all the way north, at this time of year?" Lot asked, leaning just a little towards me, his voice just a little too quiet, too intimate. He was playing some game with Uther, just as they had done when they were boys, and I did not like it. I turned fully to him.

"There was a mistake in the accounts. We haven't been being paid the tribute we are owed from your lands in Orkney, Lot."

Lot lounged back in his seat, that detestable smug smile playing around his lips.

"A careless error on my part," he shrugged. "My lord Uther is lucky to have a queen so wise and so beautiful as you, Lady Igraine."

He reached forward and brushed his fingers across the back of my hand. It would have been an innocent enough gesture from any other man, but I could feel Uther tense behind me. They were a pair of idiots; why could they not just deal honestly and honourably with one another?

"You will have to be more careful in the future."

Lot eyed me levelly. I could not tell what he was thinking behind that look of sly superiority.

* * *

Uther was furious as soon as we were alone. He paced before me, raged about war.

"I agree that something must be done to subdue him," I said, "but we do not need to make war with him. Just impress upon him his status as vassal. And do it without me there."

Uther rounded on me. "Without you there?"

I gave a rough sigh of irritation. "Don't you see what he's doing? He's trying to make you angry."

"Oh," Uther grinned savagely. "Yes, I do see. I see him looking at you, and touching you. Whenever you are not there, he is careful to remind me of all those years ago when you were just a child. Still thinks he won some right to you with a little wrestling. Perhaps he already claimed his prize –" Uther reached for me, and I jumped away – "in those years before I had you."

"Uther, stop."

"Do you like it? Do you like the way he looks at you?"

Uther caught me then, and I shoved him off me roughly.

"Of course I don't like it, Uther. But I like even less what a fool it makes you. He wants you to be angry. If I'm there, he'll do whatever he can to distract you. Go tonight. Make sure he knows that it is he who is vulnerable, not you. You can't let your vassals know that you are a jealous man. You can't let Lot play you like this, Uther." Uther made to grab me again, and I slapped him. He caught a breath, pressing his hand to his cheek, but he looked calmer. I felt the cold determination settle over me.

"Listen to me, Uther. If he had any strength to resist you, he would not resort to these kinds of games. Let it be known that you will deal with him as with any vassal, and he cannot hide this manner of thing from you again. It will be easier, without me there. He is beneath your concern, in such matters."

I took a step towards Uther, and seized him by the collar of his coat.

"He is jealous of you," I whispered. "Don't forget that."

"So he should be," he said, low, winding the length of my plait around his hand and tugging. I stepped back, pulling Uther with me, and we tumbled onto the bed.

* * *

The sun was already low when I saw Morgawse ride in with Gawain and Aggravain. The days were awfully short this far north in the winter.

I waited for her uneasily in her public audience room. I wondered how much she knew of the jostling for power between Lot and Uther. I wanted to keep her separate from it, but she was a grown woman now. She might have had her own ideas.

273

But when she flew through the door trailing fur, brocade, and several small boys, it was clear she did not have politics on her mind. She threw her arms around my neck and kissed my cheeks.

I took her face in my hands and smiled. She still had those plump cheeks and lips she had had as a girl, but something about her look now was a little tight, a little pinched and tense. I kissed her on the forehead.

"You look well, Morgawse," I said, warily.

She fussed a nurse who had followed her in, and took a burbling infant from the woman's arms. I felt the knot of jealousy in my stomach tighten.

"Another child?" I asked, hoping that I sounded pleased.

Morgawse turned to me, and her look was strange. She nodded tersely.

"This is Gareth. Would you like to hold him, Mother?"

I held out my arms for him. He had that heavy softness I did not realise I remembered so well. When I pressed my lips against his cheek he smelt clean and wonderful, the way all babies did. He looked a lot like Morgawse had done as an infant; red hair, wispy-fine and sticking straight up, and plump round cheeks.

"Another son," I sighed. "You have been blessed many times, Morgawse."

"Hmmm."

She turned away from me, apparently occupied with the second-youngest, a rather sulky-looking child with Lot's dark hair. She should have been grateful to have so many children. I would have given anything to be surrounded by my children. I would have given anything to give Uther another son.

"Grandmother." The boy standing before me caught my attention. He was holding a book in his hands. I thought it was Aggravain – he and Gawain were not so alike as they had seemed when they were born, but they still resembled each other enough for me to be a little unsure. "Grandmother, I can read now. May I show you?"

The book was romance – *The Earl of Tolouse*.

"Shouldn't you be reading to them from the Bible, Morgawse?" I asked. She ignored me, pretending to be busy with the little dark boy, Gaheris. It would be harder for them to play the political games they needed to in the south if Morgawse only filled their heads with nonsense. "Morgawse? Don't you even have any Caesar?"

She half-turned back towards me. "I don't read to them in Latin at all, Mother. I don't see the point."

No, she had not grown into politics.

It was a pleasant afternoon, and I found it grew more pleasant when Morgawse swept off to the feast Lot had planned and I was alone with the boys. I could hold little Gareth and pretend he was my own, and I could read with Aggravain, who was careful and precise as Morgan had been, while Gawain and Gaheris played some game they had invented together.

I was sorry when the nurse came to bring them one by one to their beds.

* * *

I was woken by Uther returning from the feast, trailing Brastias behind him. I knew he was drunk, because I did not think Brastias would otherwise have dared to argue with him.

"My lord," he was saying as they burst through the door, "you should not have –"

"Do not tell me what I should or should not –" Uther snarled, but he stopped when he saw me sitting up in the bed.

"What happened?" I demanded, deathly quiet.

Brastias looked between us.

"I attempted to impress upon Lot who was vassal to whom."

"How?"

There was a long quiet.

"He threatened Queen Morgawse," Brastias said, at last.

"Threatened with what?"

Uther glared at Brastias. Brastias said nothing. I felt bile burn the back of my throat. I thought of Aurelie, and how Uther had been in Orkney. I should have known that that was the only reasoning he would be capable of.

"She is my daughter."

"No," Uther bellowed. "She is our enemy's queen. Did you not counsel me to make it known that he was my servant? Did you not tell me that he was jealous of me, and I must play on that? You demand that I be strong, and you blame me for making use of another man's weakness. You sit there while he plays with you as though you enjoy it, and you advise me to play the same game!"

"I did not enjoy it, and I did not give you leave to threaten my daughter –"

"I do not need your leave, lady," Uther spat. "I only require your obedience."

I opened my mouth to shout, but he was already gone, and Brastias followed. I should never have left him to handle negotiations with Lot alone.

Chapter forty-six

I was still angry when we returned to Camelot, but the proper tribute came from the North the next time it was due, so Uther was unrepentant. We did not speak of it, but I refused to ride north again, for any reason.

I began once again to dream of my son, and I began to wonder if they were dreams that Viviane gave me, like little gifts, that were glimpses of his life. Even if they were not true, they were sweet. Two boys play-fighting together with wooden swords, one with Uther's golden hair and my fierce expression of concentration, the other tall and slender, with long, dark hair who, if he had not been holding a sword and dressed as a boy, I might have mistaken for a girl. I dreamed, too, of my son doing ordinary things. Carrying buckets of milk, or sacks of turnips, or squinting over his letters with a face dark with annoyance, that was wonderfully like Uther's own expression. They were sweet and lovely, those dreams, but they were without substance. Even if they were true and I knew him, he did not know me, and I doubted that if I ever saw him he would welcome the mother who had given him away.

Years later, too, I received a letter from Enid, saying that Erec had forgiven her whatever imagined offence she had committed, and taken her back, and was showering her with his love once more, and thanking me for my good advice. It rankled with me that no misfortune could ever seem to touch Enid, though I knew it was selfish of me, and cruel. After all, she still had no child, and though my son was lost, I had two daughters, and I was grateful for them.

News came and went of them, and I always longed to see my grandsons because the eldest were of an age with my son. I liked to imagine him at the age they were, doing the things they did. Playing at the same games.

* * *

Spring came, and news with it that Morgawse had come down from Lothian, and was waiting to see me. I hoped that she would bring her boys. Last time I had seen them, Gareth had been just a tiny baby, Gaheris had been small and sulky, but with a bright smile and his mother's pretty blue eyes, and the two older boys had been precocious and charming, both, in different ways. Aggravain like a serious little adult already, not so unlike Morgan as a child, with a clear, focussed gaze, and an oddly adult way of speaking. He had called me Lady Grandmother, though he was only six, and had wanted to show me that he could read from Morgawse's big tatty old book of romances. Gawain, on the other hand, had been loud and hearty, and had rushed about the place. He looked very much how I imagined Gorlois must have looked at his age – big, and very like the kind of son a king would hope for. Strong, and bold, and boisterous. They made a good pair of twins; one steady, one wild. Just as Morgan and Morgawse made a good pair of sisters – though I was sure that Morgawse benefitted more from Morgan's company than the other way around.

I had planned to ride out with the hunt, to enjoy a little leisure. I did not like hunting much, but I liked to ride outdoors, and to feel the breeze in my hair, and to be in the forest. But I would forgo that to see my daughter. It had been, truly, a long time indeed.

I rushed up the stairs when Brastias told me, jumping into his saddle, still eager for the hunt, that she was waiting for me in my council chamber. I was breathless by the time I got up there, and a little flushed. I threw the door open, ready to rush to my daughter's delighted embrace, when I froze, and I felt my blood go cold.

Morgawse was there, but she sat among a pile of half-scattered cushions, her hair falling loose, her arms wrapped around her knees which were drawn up to her chest, and an awful guilty blush on her cheeks. There was wine spilled across the floor. A few paces away, Uther stood, his surcoat hanging open in the lazy way he always wore it, and he was staring hard at her. Without looking away, he said, in a strange, flat voice, "Morgawse is not feeling well."

Morgawse peered up at me from under her thick eyelashes, from under the waves of red-gold hair that half fell, spilled, across her face, and I stared back at her, blank. I felt Uther's arm slide around my waist as if from far away, and his lips press against my cheek as if they were pressed against a stranger. Louder and more present than anything else, I could hear my heart beating, slow and heavy with dread, and I could hear the blood rushing in my ears.

"It is a long journey, and I think it has tired her. I will leave you two alone," Uther said softly, and he slipped away. Slipped away before I could scream. Before I could demand to know what I had almost seen. Oh, I had been grateful enough that Morgawse had grown to be so beautiful, but that was before I thought that it would come to do me harm. She rested her head down on her knees, as though she could not bear to look at me, but I took in all of her. The red and gold brocade dress, tight about the bodice where she was still small and dainty though she had borne four living sons. Plump where

I was skinny, about the breasts and hips. She was just growing to be unbearably lovely as I was growing to be old, my dark hair beginning to thread with grey, my skin wrinkling. But she was dressed, too, to be looked at. Gold ornaments in her hair, gold rings on her fingers, and bangles about her wrists. If she had had the courage to look me in the eye, I would have seen gold about her throat as well.

That night, I went to Uther's chamber, for I knew he would not come to me. He called me in when I knocked. He stood at his table, unlacing a leather gauntlet from his wrist. So, he had gone out hunting with a hawk afterwards. I suspected that he had wanted to for the sake of some pent-up emotion that I had interrupted him at, that could only then be expressed in the bloodlust of hunting, of watching the hawk tear something small and furry to pieces.

I crossed my arms over my chest, and waited. He was pretending that he did not see me.

"Are you going to make me ask exactly what it was I saw earlier?" I asked, my voice low with threat. Uther shrugged without looking at me. "What have you been doing? Things are settled with Lothian and Orkney – is this just more of your childish games with Lot? Besides that, Morgawse is my daughter," I snarled, "not any one of the other women you snatch up here and there about the castle –"

"How could I forget that she is your daughter?" Uther turned around, and I could see real rage on his face, not just the false annoyance of one rightly accused. I leaned into it, stepping towards him. I was ready for a fight. "Who else would have learned such tricks with men?"

"What are you suggesting?" I demanded.

Uther took a step towards me, and I did not give ground. He was still dirty from the hunt, still had mud on his arms, the marks of sweat on his brow. He leaned down towards me. "Morgawse has had the perfect example of how to play at puppets with men from the age of ten years old. I should have suspected that she would learn something of this kind from you."

I slapped him hard across the face, and he grabbed my wrist and pulled me up towards him. His hand was tight, and I feared for a moment, as he yanked me towards him, that my little bones would snap under his powerful grip.

"Don't be foolish, Igraine," he hissed. "What do you think I could want with a creature like Morgawse? Did you not consider that she might want something with me? Speak to her. Ask her how things fare between her and her husband. She has not come here just to see you. She wants nothing more than for me to dissolve her marriage and give her Tintagel Castle. I refused. She was determined to persuade me with the skills she learned from her mother."

I shook my head. "That is not possible. She hates you."

Uther laughed softly, his grip tightening until I gasped. "True. But she wants something that only I can give her: Cornwall. You must see, from her perspective, how she thought it would be persuasive. I had something she wanted, and she offered me what she thought I wanted. Her. A son."

He threw me hard across the room, and I landed sprawled out across the bed. He stood over me, his hands braced against the posts.

"You expect me to live differently from every other man in this land. Any other king, if his enemy's wife came to him, offering herself like that, would take her. And then that man would know who was his lord. So she is your child? She is a grown woman now. She is someone else's wife. I must be strong. I must take each advantage as I find it. You would not have me lose my position. This is how it was always done, Igraine. This is the position of a vassal queen. If you wanted Morgawse to be free of this, perhaps you should have sent her to the nuns as well."

I scrambled to my feet and threw myself against his chest. I got in one good blow across his jaw before he had hold of me.

"She is not just a player in your game, Uther," I hissed.

"Isn't she?" He pulled me against him, and I pushed, and we fell back onto the bed. "What do you think she dreams of during those long, cold winters in the North? The mother who sent her there. The stepfather she hates. Coming south. Going home to Tintagel Castle. Punishing the husband she hates, and the mother who gave her to him. Or – who knows? – perhaps this is part of Lot's plan. Perhaps he sent her here to drive us apart. She's a grown woman now. It's possible she's lying about wanting their marriage dissolved."

I pushed him over, trapping him beneath me, one hand over his throat, ready to press, the other flat against his chest. Of course, if I really did try to hurt him, he could throw me off, but for the moment he was still. I could feel his heart hammering against my hand.

"Think about it, Igraine," he said. "It was not so many years ago that we were playing the same games with them in Lothian. She's not your girl anymore; she's his wife. Who knows what they have plotted up there, together. They have, after all, an enemy in common."

I thought about it. Morgawse always complained about her marriage. And yet it was not so many years ago, before Gareth was born, that I had seen a change in Morgawse and Lot; they had been suddenly shy around one another in public, and I had seen him stroke her hair, and kiss her gently. She complained about childbirth, and about the North and the cold, and yet she always had more children. Perhaps he was right.

"They are our rivals for power in Britain, Igraine," Uther continued, and his hand slipped under my skirts and up my leg. I didn't loosen the hand around his throat. "You know they are both capable of such things. All either of us can be sure of is one another. You are mine. I am yours. We must be strong, together. We must make the future sure for our son."

I pressed my hand hard against his throat.

"Don't touch her again," I hissed. His fingers slid inside me and I shuddered.

"I have no interest," he whispered, "in anyone but you."

* * *

Late into the night I woke onto a memory that I thought I had forgotten. Of Morgawse, of a time long ago, when I had been weary with the loss of my son. Morgawse had come into my chamber in the morning. Though she had been a married woman, she had crawled into bed with me, and put her head on my shoulder, and said, softly, "Uther has tried to hurt me." And I had hushed her, and stroked her hair, though she was thirteen or fourteen years old, and I had said, "What do you mean, my love?" She had shaken her head, and refused to say anything more, except, "He is a monster, Mother, and he tries to hurt me."

Chapter forty-seven

I was glad that Morgawse left swiftly. I did not know how I could continue with her, now, as an enemy and rival. And Uther – things had changed between us as well. I still loved him, and I knew that he loved me, but it had all become tinged with pain, and secrecy, and mistrust. In the moment after he had denied it, I had believed it, but I had had his mouth against mine, and his hands holding me tight, and I was not sure I believed it when I was alone. Morgawse was beautiful, and Uther was a man who considered it his right as king to indulge his desires whenever and wherever it suited him. Brastias did not say anything, but I knew he glanced between Morgawse and Uther, looking for something. The threat of violence, perhaps, or something worse.

So I grew colder, and those I loved grew further from me. I saw Morgan in the abbey, and she was always pleased to have her mother there, to show me her books, to tell me what she had learned. I looked among them, always, for something wicked Merlin might have hidden there, but always it was the same. Virgil, Ovid, Homer, the Psalms, the Bible, the writings of Augustine and the histories of Livy. Safe, scholarly books. I held her tight, and kissed the top of her hair, but I could never stay long. Uther and I were allies in the council chamber and lovers in the bedchamber, but outside of that, we were almost strangers. He would not have tolerated me delaying with Morgan for long. Morgawse was lost to me through what she had done, or tried to do, and Brastias and I existed in the wary space of those who were once close. Viviane was ever busy in Avalon, and I was alone.

I dreamed more and more often of my son. In my dreams he was a tall, handsome boy with a bright, charming smile. I saw him play-fighting with wooden swords with the dark-haired boy, and sometimes other boys, and he was better, stronger than the others, even those who were older than he was, and taller. I was proud to see him, even if it was nothing more than an illusion. I saw, too, small domestic moments, which were the most painful to miss. I saw him lying awake in his bed, then shuffling over to the window to look out at the moon. I saw him picking blackberries and smearing the juice all over his face in his excitement to eat them, as Morgawse had done as a little girl.

Sometimes I regretted the choice I had made. Perhaps I had been wrong to mistrust Merlin. If I were honest with myself, I mistrusted him more than perhaps I should have done for the part he had taken in helping Uther to wrong me. I suspected him of using Uther as a puppet, but Uther needed wise counsel and guidance. He was rough and impulsive, inclined to sudden anger and a ruthless adherence to the letter of the law. He needed me, and he needed Merlin as well. But then I remembered what Merlin had said to me. The threats he had made. Those were not the threats of one who only wished to help a young man find his way safely to the throne. Merlin was dangerous.

Time went on, and people began to talk once more. They said that I was past my childbearing years, and it was true; I only bled irregularly, and I was no longer young, but there were women past my age who had another child or two. That was not what stopped me. It was Merlin's curse.

I wondered if things would have been different if Uther and I had had another child. Something to bind us together, something to distract us from the loss of our son. Something to distract him from other women. Something that would have made Merlin's price less awful.

I knew that people blamed me. Said that Uther should have married sooner, or younger. Said that a man could only expect to have no child if he first had as his mistress a barren woman, and then as his wife one who had used up her childbearing years with another man. It was all the more painful knowing that Uther's heir was hidden away, and that his father would never see him while he lived. Nor, perhaps, would I. If it was war that came to kill Uther, I doubted that I would survive it.

Perhaps it was all the price for my own sins. Maybe I too had made some kind of devil's pact without knowing it. I had coveted a husband who would let me stay in my home, who would be devoted to me, who would keep me safe. I had chosen for myself a man who had loved me, doted on me, adored me and obeyed me in every way, except to keep me safe. I had refused Uther time and again. I had refused my destiny, and it had come for me in the most brutal way imaginable.

My life began to feel bitter and small, and everything a tangle of politics around the secret that I had concealed. Uther was no longer a young man, and I was no longer a young woman. We had no child to be seen, and yet he would not acknowledge any bastard child, or name another king as successor. Máel in Ireland was furious, and Lot in the North, and one of my nephews, Mark, who was now of age and who had hoped to gain something from being the son of the sister of the Queen of Britain. Mark had been disinherited in Emain Macha as part of the bridal settlement with his father's second wife. The only king who did not pester Uther to be named was Leodegrance of Carhais, who sat smug as a cat in his fortress in Brittany as though he thought this was some visitation of revenge from his heathen gods onto Uther, for the dishonest way that he had attacked him. Certainly, if there were gods looking after kings, it would not be the God and Christ that Uther and I made a show of worshipping every sabbath day, for he was a God who disdained the world, and sought to tear it down and bring something more noble in its place. He would not help Uther; I could hardly hope that he would show mercy to a man who had made a deal with a sorcerer for his throne.

So it continued. For the moment, Uther was strong enough to silence any man who questioned him. To send away those who said that he should put me aside and take a fifteen-year-old bride to his bed while there was still time. I knew there were many among them who blamed me more than him. Who said that I had bewitched him. I was too ashamed to tell them the truth, that it was I who had been prey to his magical deceptions.

Chapter forty-eight

Christmas came once more, and with it Morgawse and Lot down from Lothian with their sons. Morgawse rode in beside Lot with a cloak of white furs about her shoulders, clasped with gold, and her red-gold hair all but loose, twisted back in the old Cornish fashion at the front, and shining in the cold winter sun. The pale gold freckles on her face were no longer those of a child, but were somehow gorgeous. They made her seem as though she was burnished with just a little gold all over.

Lot slipped from his horse first, and offered her his hand. I saw none of the open hostility I had feared between them, but Morgawse was tense as they bowed before us. I kissed her on the cheek, and she gave a slight smile as we greeted one another, but both of us now were wary. Something had shattered between us, and I knew that we had lost each other. In that moment, I wanted to hug her tight to me; in that moment, I was not sure if I had not blamed her for far more than she had done, but I was afraid that what I had suspected was true, and I could not bear that.

The Christmas feast was tense, and the festivities false. I felt brittle and unpleasant. Morgawse and Lot largely ignored each other, and their sons sat at the other end of the table, all boisterous and ill-behaved. I did not scold them. I did not have the energy. Besides, it was Christmas. The eldest two, the twins, were explaining the rules of one of the Christmas games to the younger two – the dark, skinny one who looked the very image of Lot, or would grow to, and the littlest one, Gareth, who was old enough to sit in his own chair and spill the gravy from the feast all over his face, and rub his sticky hands on his brothers as they complained and leaned away from him. I wanted to go and pick him up in my arms and wipe his face and kiss his soft red hair and pretend he was my own child, but I did not. His mother should have been watching him. Should have cared if he were dirty, or ill-behaved. She did not seem to notice.

When the food was cleared away and the music for the dancing began, I was surprised that Lot stood and offered me his hand, but I took it. I could not imagine what interest he could have in even being polite to an ageing queen when his wife had grown so beautiful. But, when we were alone among the dancers, our voices lost in the cheering and the singing and the music, I realised what he wanted. He waited until he had slipped his arm around my waist, and drawn me close enough to whisper in my ear. I was glad it was seedy politics rather than seedy desire that he wanted to discuss with me, at least.

"Who will follow Uther?" Lot hissed at my ear.

"I do not know," I said, blankly. I dared not close my eyes, for I would see the gold-haired boy, and it would spill out of me. His arm tightened around me.

"Yes you do, Igraine," he insisted, "or you can direct him. All of Britain knows who rules here, really. It is said that you yourself decided the corn tax laws, and set the price for importing saffron and pearls, and you sit in judgement beside Uther for the petty complaints, but he barely speaks. You can tell him who to name."

"All those things are true, Lot, except that I cannot tell my husband who to name as his heir."

I felt his lips brush my ear, he was so close when he whispered next.

"Name one of my sons, and it shall be done. He shall be left here when we depart for Lothian, and you can raise him, and train him in statecraft."

If I had had no son of my own, how I would have been relieved, been overjoyed by that offer, though it was only made in base, selfish ambition. But I could not. I could not raise one of my grandsons for disappointment, in the lie that they would be king after Uther. It would not be fair. I shook my head.

"Why not, Igraine?" he growled, and I felt his hand grip my arm hard enough to make me gasp. I wished that someone had noticed. I glanced around for Brastias. He was still sitting at the high table beside Morgawse. Morgawse and Uther sat side by side, staring out at the dancing and ignoring one another in such a way that I could not imagine that it was innocent, and I felt myself burn with anger.

"I am not Merlin the witch. Only he has Uther's ear in this matter."

Lot seemed to accept this, nodding to himself. He had never questioned me on the child he had known I had inside me before he married Morgawse. I supposed he assumed that I had lost it. Had I said so? I did not remember. But I knew that he had lost children before; the one that had taken his first wife, and a few with Morgawse. Someone who had suffered that was hardly likely to press for it.

* * *

I was glad when they left, but more and more those days I felt the danger gathering. Uther is old, men whispered, and he has not fathered a son that he can recognise as his heir. They said, too, it is all the spell of the witch Igraine, and of her friend Viviane, who seek to enslave him. That is why she refused him so long, so that he would be under her spell. Uther laughed at them, heartily, as though no one could possibly think I had any influence over him. Did he not listen to me in councils? I knew that he did, because without me, we would have lived in ruin. But he laughed with the other knights all the same. So did Brastias, though I had long ceased to believe that he was more loyal to me than to his brotherhood of fighting men. They would all laugh together at any woman, for fear that one day all we women would be laughing at them.

* * *

Late one summer, I wandered into Uther's chamber, coming with some charter documents I needed his seal on because it was almost harvest, and his last corn law – as I had said it would – had left people in Cornwall hungry and angry. I opened the door to see a girl who could not have been more than seventeen years old, who squealed in fear and embarrassment and, blushing deep red, clutched her underdress against her naked body.

With a sigh of annoyance, I turned my eyes to Uther, who sat at the end of his bed with his breeches pulled on, but not laced properly, and nothing else. The hair on the chest was almost all grey, and his muscular frame was going to seed, his skin slackening, his belly no longer hard and taught. With the young girl there, suddenly I saw him through her eyes. A lecherous, ageing king whom she dared not refuse. I wondered if someone had sent her to him, hoping that there was still time for him to conceive an heir. The dress that must have been hers, lying across the floor, was rich enough – fine silk, sewn with pearls and such – so she wasn't a prostitute or a servant.

I tossed the papers down on the little table by Uther's fireplace.

"These need your seal, Uther. See to it as soon as possible."

I turned to leave, and Uther called my name. I had hoped to get away before my anger and disgust clouded it all out. I didn't want to scream at him in front of the girl. That would hardly have been dignified.

"Igraine, don't feel the need to hurry away. Don't be childish. There's no need to be embarrassed."

"I'm not embarrassed," I hissed, wheeling around and slamming the door behind me. The poor girl was cowering back into the corner, unsure of whether she dared pull her underdress over her head. "It is you, Uther, who ought to be embarrassed. To have gone the way of all old men: always seeking young women to soothe your fading pride."

A slight, cruel smile spread across Uther's face. "It is the way of all men to seek young women when their wives go the way of all old women."

I opened my mouth to give him a sharp retort, when he jumped to his feet, and with a conciliatory laugh tried to come and take me in his arms. "Oh Igraine, don't be so serious. Don't look so angry. Hush. I am only making fun of you. You are as lovely as any maiden –"

I pushed him away from me.

"You think you can solve everything with flattery, do you? Oh, I hardly mind who you have in your bed. It's all the same to you. But it's hardly dignified for a man your age, is it?"

Uther half-turned over his shoulder to the girl, and said, his voice suddenly rough with authority, "Leave us."

She nodded, flustered, terrified, pulling her underdress over her head and rushing past us to collect her dress from the floor and hurriedly pull it on.

"Come, my love, don't be jealous." Uther's hands found my hair, and he slid his fingers in at the top of my neck, and despite myself, I closed my eyes, and sighed. "It was not in our bed, love. I swore I would never, and I hold by that. I did not have her in the bed. I must make some efforts to satisfy my men that there will be a king after me. I cannot very well tell them about –"

Uther rested his forehead against mine, but when he leant in to bring his mouth to mine, I leant away.

"It makes no difference. You are too old for it now."

He grasped me hard by the arm with his other hand, and pulled me up against him. I still felt it, the wave of delicious dizziness that ran through my body when he held me to him, but now it was muted, and it wasn't enough. And beyond that, I felt a cold, awful detachment, as though I were watching myself standing there with him.

"Lot is no older than I am, and still your pretty daughter's womb grows ripe with his seed year upon year. There are men who laugh at me, Igraine, and say that if Lot of Lothian's seed is so strong, perhaps he should be king. And then I wonder, perhaps it is time I took the most fertile woman in Britain to my bed, and gave her something a little better for her womb than that northern savage can offer."

I pulled away, and Uther crushed me against him, pressing his mouth against mine, but I was sickened by his talk, and sickened by him, and I pushed him, hard, back from me.

"We are too old for these games, Uther," I cried, and I heard my voice break, and felt the tears gathering in my eyes. How long were we going to carry on like this, as we grew old, half lovers, half enemies, tangling and choking on a love that was halfway between passion and hate? For he hated me as much as I hated him. For marrying Gorlois. For bearing him no other child but the one who had been taken.

"Igraine," he began. I saw his face soften, and grow sad. I saw the loss there, and the sensitivity that I glimpsed so rarely, but which always bound me to him and reminded me of what a man I loved: a man dark enough to draw me in, but gentle enough to hold me there. I opened my mouth to reply, to weaken, to pretend to forgive all that could never be forgiven, but then Uther began to cough, hard. When I went to put my hand on his shoulder, he shoved me roughly away. There was blood on his hand, and a little spattered across the floor. He had pushed me away because he had known that that would happen. How long had he been hiding it?

"Uther," I said, low with dread, "is that blood?"

"Leave, Igraine," he growled.

"Is that blood?" I shouted, and he pushed me roughly out of the door, and slammed it even as I threw all my little weight against it. I heard him draw the bolt.

I felt an awful, calm cold settle on me and seep into my core. Uther is dying, I thought, and my son is still only a boy.

Chapter forty-nine

I sent letters to Avalon, and to Rheged and to Emain Macha, to ask if there was anyone with knowledge of magic or medicine who could save Uther's life. I was not sure if I lay awake at night or if I dreamed, for I saw Uther sleeping beside me, and out of his mouth and down over his chest came the swarms and swarms of horrid little black ants that I had dreamed of when I was pregnant with Morgawse. I was too old now to fear it, only to accept it as the omen that it was. Uther's breath rattled in his sleep, and he became angry and suspicious of everyone. He wanted to be alone all of the time. He told himself that this way none of his knights would hear him coughing, would see the blood, would know that the King was dying.

Viviane came, and put her hand against his chest, and gave him a drink that eased his breathing, and for a while he stopped coughing. But it came again, and when I begged Viviane to do as she had done before, she shook her head.

"When it is time, it cannot be stopped. Better, Igraine, to let the White Goddess take him now."

I did not even think to scold her with Christ, but nodded my head, and said through my tears, "But my son is only twelve years old."

She put her hand on the top of my head and kissed my forehead, and said, "If it is time, it is time, and destiny shall claim him."

I thought that was the most frightening thing I had ever heard.

* * *

When Viviane had gone back to Avalon, Merlin came and locked himself in Uther's chamber for several days. The men grumbled, but they were used to me giving them their instructions, and they carried them out willingly enough. When the days were spent, Uther swaggered out from his room looking as though he had won back five years of his life, and for a whole week he did not cough, and he was back to the bold way he had been with me when we were younger. Whenever we were alone he pulled me into his arms and pressed his mouth to mine with all the wildness of his youthful passion, and he never looked at the young women of the castle. But it did not last. It had been a blissful reprise, and I had forgotten how much I missed him as he had been before he began to grow old and frightened and sick. But it was an illusion of Merlin's. I woke when only a week had passed to the sound of his hacking coughs, and the bedsheets spattered with blood.

A messenger came with a package from Emain Macha, but the herbs and poultices within made Uther woozy and delirious, and he shouted about our son and I had to send everyone away and tell them he was in an ill dream. When they were gone, I rested my head on his chest and he wrapped his arms around me. I wept, for the boy was still lost, and the breath was still wheezing in Uther's dying lungs. When I closed my eyes, when I dreamt, I no longer saw the boy. It was as though his father's death had pushed him back into the mist. Instead, I dreamed of following the little trail of black ants to a room full of them. When I opened my mouth to scream, the little blank ants rushed into it, choking out the sound.

* * *

Uther became more and more visibly sick, his skin greying and then cracking at his hands and around his mouth, his eyes bloodshot, and his fingernails bleeding. He wanted to prove to himself, and to everyone, that he was not dying, so he tried again and again to coax me to his bedchamber and have me lie with him. But I would not, because I saw his cracking skin, and the blood around his mouth, and his teeth where they met the gums, and I was disgusted and afraid.

* * *

"Uther is dying," I said softly to Brastias as we stood, with the sunset outside turning my council-room from orange to a dark, threatening red.

Brastias nodded beside me. "What of your son?"

I had forgotten that Brastias knew. It was such a secret, such a long-kept jealously-guarded secret that I had forgotten that anyone knew besides Uther, myself, and Viviane and Merlin.

I shrugged. "I do not know, Brastias. We can only hope that his fate calls him forth."

There was a long silence between us, and Brastias put his arm around my shoulder. After everything, he was still my friend, and I was grateful for him.

"In the end," Brastias said, gently, "I will be sorry to see him go from this world. He was my enemy, once, but he is a good king. A strong king. A brave king. He has held Britain together sometimes, I think, by the force of his own will. He has been a good king. Perhaps even a great one." There was a long pause once more, before Brastias added in little more than a whisper, "Sometimes I even think he is a good man."

I was not sure that that was true, but I nodded silently and we stood there still for a long time.

* * *

At last the time came when the vassal kings of Britain could not be prevented from knowing that Uther lay dying, cloistered with Merlin and clinging to life, but with his last few days seeping away from him. They all came, one by one, and I endured them all. First, Máel came, with his king, from Emain Macha. The king from Emain Macha was angry that there was nothing for him. He offered me a son to adopt. I shook my head. He left unsatisfied. Then old Ywain, with a son a little older than Morgawse, who was kind and careful but hopeful, too, that when he came with a man full-grown, unmarried and marked obviously with strength and royal Welsh blood, that he would be pledged as successor, and I was sure they grumbled on their horses as they rode away. Last to come were Lot and Morgawse, and

I only just endured them   Morgawse's seething petulance, even at that awful time, and Lot's greedy gold-counting and ugly, bright-eyed ambition. I wrote to the abbey and asked for Morgan, for I felt sure having my daughter at my side would comfort me, but they told me she was no longer there. Taken to Avalon. So, fate had claimed her as well.

I sat at night beside Uther, all that time, watching the breath come in and out, in and out of his rattling chest, and I thought, is this all that is left? Have we not had a love that carved Britain into pieces, and then seared it back together again? Will it end like this? I wept, sometimes, and laid my head on his chest, and he put his hand on top of my hair. I knew that he wished I would get into the bed beside him. I could not.

I could not stop myself running back through all our time together in my mind, as though he were already dead. I remembered the hot, dusty day at the end of summer in Aurelianus' courtyard, where he had lost his wrestling-match with Lot, and kissed me anyway. I had understood for the first time what had made my sister leave everything she had, risk angering my father and put herself into danger, to run away with Erec. But I had denied it. Someone or other had managed to impress upon me the importance of duty, and I had been afraid of the pact that Uther had made with Merlin and what it would cost me to go with him. If I had gone then, perhaps we would have had many children together, and it would have eased the pain. I remembered him riding into the courtyard in Tintagel, armed and mounted on his horse with his knights, demanding to have me as his bride. A painfully misjudged move against my proud father, who might have yielded if Uther had humbly requested it of him. And then the Christmas after I was married, when he demanded to know if I had done it just to spite him. I did not think at the time that I had, but now with the benefit of looking back over the years, I was not so sure. Not so sure that I had not resented the pact he had made with Merlin, and with Imogen. And, I supposed, with Viviane. That there would always be someone other than me that he was beholden to. And then, the wasteland of years where I lived simply in my marriage, which had been happy. We had been companions, and friends, and parents to our little girls. There had not been love. Not the kind of love that burns you to the bone and remakes you, but the kind that is steady, and comfortable. That had been enough, until I had seen Uther again. I remembered the moonlight, my fingers against the tattoos on his wrist, and a kiss that woke everything in me that had been sleeping. That had been the end for us, I think. The point at which neither of us could have turned back.

In those moments I forgot the lies, and the cruelty, and the struggle for power between us. That all seemed petty and small in the face of Uther's death. I took his hand in mine, and traced the blue-green line of the dragon curling at his wrist. It was faded now, and his skin was wrinkled and cracked. His illness had aged him years over just a few weeks. Our son would be raised by someone who did not know the ancient secrets of the kingmaking rituals, as Uther had done. We all called ourselves Christians now, and there would be no union with the land for him, no sacred meeting with the Sovereign Goddess of the Isles as there had been for Uther, and Aurelianus before him, and the kings before that. The thought made me afraid. What would anchor him here? There were still people who thought that way. The Bretons. Perhaps some in Emain Macha still believed it, for I knew that their ways were the same. Perhaps it could be done. Once Uther was gone, it would be I alone who would be able to keep our son safe. To set him on the right path, to be the King he was supposed to be.

"Uther," I sighed, brushing my fingers across the dragon at his wrist, and he murmured in response, his eyelids flickering. He was close to the end, without even the strength to speak. "Who would have thought that we would end this way?" I tried to give a weak smile, but there were tears in my eyes. Why was it that a man as strong, as obstinate as Uther, could be defeated by disease? I supposed that that was the way of the world, but it would all be a little less when he was no longer in it. I laid my head on his chest. His breath was so weak.

"I have loved you all my life, I think," I said softly. "Even that first moment, that first kiss, felt like something I had known before. Some people say we have all lived before. Perhaps long ago you and I, Uther, were simple people who lived their lives together in simple happiness, not kings, and queens. I did love you though. I do love you. That will always be a part of me. A part of both of us."

I realised that I had not said it before then. Uther had often told me that he loved me, but so much of our life together had been a fight for control that I had not said it. Realising my own anger, and coldness, I wept again. If he had anything he wished to say in return, or a gesture he meant to make, then he did not have the strength for it.

*　*　*

I dreamed that night that I was standing on the cliffs at Tintagel, and I was just a young girl once more. The dream was so vivid that I could feel the wind whipping against my face. I could taste the salt on my lips from the sea that crashed against the rocks, dark and beautiful, beneath the castle. It was a day in the middle of summer, but you would not have known it. In Tintagel the summers were always like this; stormy, and beautiful. There was rain in the air, and the threat of thunder, but no storm yet. But it would be soon. The rain would be heavy, and hard. I would long to stand out in it, and feel it melt through my clothes and against my skin in the hot, humid middle of the Cornish summer. But I would rush inside, as I always did, knowing that Elaine would scold me if I waited out for the rain and got wet.

I was dawdling. I knew I wanted to stay outside and watch the waves crash against the rocks, and feel the wildness and the power of nature all around me. I stood, staring out for another moment more. Strange; I knew it was a dream, for I was no longer young, but it felt so real.

I turned at last to go inside, and turned right into the arms of Uther, who was as he had been when he was a young man, wild and handsome. He pulled me to him in a kiss, and I melted into his arms. The kiss was how it had been the first time, all those years ago, only now I was experiencing it as a grown woman with all the knowledge of pleasure and none of the fear, and yet my young woman's body, and his, too, hard and muscular and lean. He had aged so badly, at the end, I had forgotten what a magnificent man he had been in his youth. And suddenly we were lying on the short, scrubby grass, and I could hear the thunder rumbling far away, and I shivered. But it was with delight, and anticipation, for Uther and I were tangled together, his hands in my hair, which was falling loose, our mouths pressed together. I felt his lips move down my neck, across my collarbone, and then, pulling down my dress, across my breasts and my nipples as I sighed. I prayed that I would not wake. I had missed the feel of his muscular arms around me, his skin under my hands. Suddenly, around us, the storm broke, and the rain pounded down, and I gasped – half with surprise, half with joy. But Uther did not notice the storm. He pushed back the skirts of my dress and thrust hard into me, and I gasped again, this time with pleasure. The world closed in, suddenly, and all I had were sensations. The rain, slightly warm against my lips and in my hair, and Uther, inside me, and the pleasure of my body gathering and tightening at the centre, making me hot and bright. The taste of the rain. The smell of the scrubby Cornish grass, and beneath that, the earth coming back to life under the rainfall. Uther's lips against my neck, the bare skin of his chest under my hand, the sound of my own breath – fast, hard, then gasping, as what had gathered within spread through me, filling me with light. I was afraid I would wake, but even then I did not, though it receded all into darkness, and a sleep as deep as death.

Chapter fifty

The next day, Merlin, who had haunted Uther's side like waiting death, came to my room, entering without a knock as I was braiding my hair through with a ribbon, trying to make myself look as presentable and queenly as possible for another day. I remembered, with an awful vividness, how he, as Melusine, used to plait my hair for me, and run his fingers through it. And I had let him rub my shoulders in the bath, and – I pushed the thought away. I greeted him coldly, without looking up from my hammered mirror.

"You and I, Igraine, must make a truce," Merlin said, evenly.

"There are no pacts between lions and men," I said, still not turned to face him. I tucked the last strand of hair into place. I was still beautiful, even though I was more than forty years old.

Merlin laughed. "Who is the lion, lady, and who the man? Who the noble Hector and who the brave Achilles? I must confess that I am neither. I do not think that you are, either. You have no more honesty in you than a snake. But you must heed me, for your son will need me if he is to find his way to the throne."

"What is the price?" I asked him, brushing my fingers across my cheeks, pushing the skin back a little, imagining once again my taut, youthful skin.

Merlin's face creased in mock disbelief. "Oh Lady Igraine, you are so cruel. Do you think that I seek only gain for myself?"

"I know it to be so, Merlin."

I had thought that he was playing games with me once more, but when I said that, in the mirror I saw his eyes flash with sudden anger, and I had an awful feeling at the pit of my stomach, like a wave of nausea. The room suddenly seemed to be blazing hot, and full of light, and I gasped, knowing that if I had the sense of it in my blood, the room would feel filled with all the sickening darkness of the Otherworld. His eyes fixed mine on the hammered surface and I felt myself frozen where I sat.

"You are a fool, Igraine. You think that I am greedy, and selfish. You are wrong. I am the instrument of Fate, and it works through me. But Fate always asks a price. It will have the son of King Uther Pendragon, and it will – I will, as its agent – set him so high that all kings will envy him, and long to have his fame. But Fate punishes those who try to escape it, Igraine. You have denied me before, and you have been punished. You should fear me, Lady. You are but a mortal woman, with nothing but your flesh. Some day the worms shall have you, and your beauty daily fades. You cannot fight me. I am the earth. I am the sea. I am the sky. Submit to me, and make your peace with Fate."

"If I am so little," I said, "then why should my compliance matter to you? If you are Fate, why should my disobedience be great enough to anger you? Bend me to your will if you have the power, Merlin, for I shall not bend myself."

"You would pit yourself against your son?" he hissed.

"No, Merlin," I said, flatly. I felt myself begin to tremble and I grasped the bone handle of my comb hard. "Nor will I oppose you for the sake of enmity. I want what you want, if it is true that you wish my son to be king. But I will not be your servant, as Uther has been."

Merlin paused, his black eyes running over my face in the reflection of the mirror, and a cruel smile spreading, pulling the blackened lips back from his ugly, skullish teeth. He leaned down beside me, his hands resting on the back of the chair where I sat, so that his face was beside mine on the hammered surface. For the moment, the image swam and rippled, as though someone on the other side had dropped a stone into a pond. A single black ant crawled out of Merlin's open mouth, across his cheek, and into the blackness of his hood.

"Uther is dead, Igraine."

I felt it hit me, like a punch to the chest, and it knocked the air from me. I closed my eyes, and I could hear my blood pounding, ringing in my ears. From far away I heard Merlin say, "I hid it from you. I had his body breathe as though he lived, but the life was gone from him days ago. I will keep it so, and you will keep it secret – his death, your son, my intentions – until I have found the boy, and brought him here. Do you understand?"

Through the stunned haze that surrounded me, I nodded. There was no power left in me now to resist. I felt a great, rushing wind run through the room as Merlin left, though it could only be the rush of Uther's loss. I had not had a chance to say goodbye.

Uther had been with me since I was fifteen years old. He had been in my dreams, he had followed me like my own ghost until I was his, and then he had become my whole life. I had lost everything, to be left only with him. He was everything. All pleasure, all pain. All happiness, all sorrow, all anger, all fear, all love, all hope, all redemption. He was the pillar of the world. And he was gone. I was a widowed queen without a son at court to save me, and I was alone. Alone with a witch as an enemy.

I have to leave, I thought. I have to go to Tintagel.

* * *

I gave Brastias the order, and he did not argue. Soon, Merlin would announce the news, and Britain would be without a High King. The kings of the border kingdoms would descend on Camelot, each hoping to be the first vulture to pick the corpse. I had no intention of waiting for them. Of becoming like Imogen. I knew what the world was. I had no intention of surviving only by committing myself as prisoner to a man's bed. I would wait for my son to rise, and I would stand with him. Until then, I had to disappear. I had resented Imogen and then I had pitied her, and now I only felt that she was my double, the mirror image of myself; someone I could have been, if I had been born into different circumstances. I, too, had been a daughter with no brothers.

I wrote to Morgan and to Morgawse. I wanted them to know I was safe. I could not pretend that my letter to Morgan was not more affectionate. I wished I could have been a better mother, but I did not have it in me at that moment to play at forgiving and forgetting with Morgawse.

I rode out with Brastias and a small garrison of knights as it fell dark. I went in men's clothes, cloaked and hooded, as though I were a merchant. It would be quicker, safer that way. We stopped at inns, which smelled of ale and men's sweat and the farmyard. But they were quiet and safe, and it was quicker than stopping with nobles who would need to be courted like spoiled little children and flattered that they were good hosts to the Queen of Britain.

I arrived at Tintagel just before the winter. It was cold and empty. Uther's soldiers had made it their home. I had expected them to make themselves free with the chambers that had been my fathers' and my sisters', and then mine and Gorlois', but out of some strange sense of duty or propriety, they had kept to the knights' quarters, and the family chambers were empty. They were dusty and dirty. The men grumbled when I asked them to find clean bedding, fresh straw for the beds, clean silk sheets, and wool blankets and furs for the winter cold, but they did it. Some of them seemed to recognise Brastias, and those who would not have listened to their queen listened to a seasoned knight, one who, I somewhat gathered, was famous for his prowess in battle. It was hard for me to think of it. I always thought of Brastias as a kind-hearted, somewhat shy, boy.

By the time everything was organised and I had new candles and a fire in the grate and decent bedding, it was already dark outside. Brastias had come to check that I had all I needed, and I thanked him, and nodded. He lingered, as though there was something else he wanted to say. He shuffled on his feet a little before he asked, and I saw the young boy once more.

"I suppose this means, Lady Igraine, that King Uther has died?"

"Merlin has forbidden me from speaking of that," I said gently, and he nodded. If any other man had forbidden me, I would have ignored it, alone with Brastias, but I was afraid that Merlin's words themselves were magic, and that his curses would find me if I spoke any of the words he had forbidden.

"Any news of your son?" he asked.

I shook my head. "He is still just a child. Merlin has pledged to find him, and bring him to the throne. Until then," I reached out and took his hand, "we bide our time, and see what will happen, from the safety of Tintagel Castle."

He nodded, and pressed my hand to his lips. I felt the awful temptation rise through me to clasp him to me, and drag him to the bed with me to forget my grief. He would not refuse me, I did not think. But I did not. His hand slipped from mine, and he turned towards the door. As his hand went to the latch I called out to him.

"Brastias," I said. He turned with an eagerness that betrayed that, as our hands had touched, he had had the same thought that I had. "Why don't you take the room below this one? Where the girls used to sleep. I would feel safer having you close."

He nodded. "Of course, Igraine."

I did not correct him.

Chapter fifty-one

The days passed, and I waited for news. There was a rumour that in the North some man was claiming to be Uther's son, but that came to nothing. Then, that a messenger had come from Emain Macha and been furious to find the Queen gone from Camelot. I heard, too, that Lot of Lothian had made sure that all men knew that he was closest to Uther's throne, sending letters patent to all the other kings, reminding them who his wife's stepfather had been.

There was word, too, of Merlin. That he had declared Uther dead to the men at Camelot, who had called him killer because of my flight, and threatened to tear him apart until he had struck three or four of them down with his magic. Then he had set Uther's great sword in a block of stone, and enchanted it with such a spell that only the rightful King of Britain could pull it out. Not Uther's son, but the rightful King of Britain. So were there other sons? Bastard boys begotten in war, or afterwards? I supposed there had to be, somewhere.

I dreamed of the boy I always dreamed of, who might or might not have been my son, running across a muddy field and past a church. As he passed the church he stopped, and ran back to look in, as though something inside had caught his attention. I could see his chest rising and falling hard from the run, his face flushed and a little grubby with mud and sweat. He was dressed in squire's clothes. I remembered what Viviane had said about the family she had given him to. He would have an older brother. He would not be first to fight, or be on his own. I dared not hope that what I saw was true.

He began walking slowly into the church, and as he did I saw inside, before the altar, a low block of stone with Uther's sword set up to the hilt in it. After glancing around, the boy ran forward and snatched it out as though it were only set in the earth, and ran off with it in his hand. It was only after he was gone that I saw the hole in the stone where the sword had been, and the thin line of little black ants that crawled out.

I woke with a strange sense that something great had changed, though I could not have said what. Surely, if that had been true, there would have been more ceremony? Someone to tell the boy that he was King of Britain?

* * *

Viviane came to Tintagel that day. I was glad to see her. I threw my arms around her as soon as she was back in my rooms, out from under the eyes of the men. Before them, I had to be cold, and steady, and queenly. Otherwise, I feared that they would not do all they could to protect me, and keep me safe from the kings who coveted Uther's throne.

"Is it true," I whispered, as soon as we were alone, "that Merlin has found my son?"

Viviane nodded.

"It is true. Arthur has drawn his father's sword from Merlin's enchanted stone, but it will be long yet before he is recognised as King."

"Arthur," I breathed. I had not known his name. "Will he be safe, Viviane, now Merlin has found him?"

She came over and took my hands in hers, giving me her comforting, motherly smile. She was always so motherly towards me, and the woad tattooed across her face – it made her seem ageless somehow. I remembered thinking that she seemed only a few years older than me, but now when I looked at her, she seemed younger. All of my life she had seemed the same age, and I could not place her. I had thought she must have been a young woman, truly, perhaps only twenty years old when she had stood behind Uther as Lady of Avalon, to raise him to Aurelianus' empty throne. Now, I was not so sure.

"He will be safe. As yet, I do not know if we were too cautious, too afraid of Merlin –"

"But you yourself –"

"I know, Igraine. I know what I have said of him. And yet, truly, I do not know. I never know if Merlin is one man or many men, or if he is something else entirely."

The distant look in her eyes was strange, and I crinkled my brow in confusion.

"What do you mean, Viviane?"

She sighed, shaking her head, as though shaking away memories. "Long ago, when I was just a girl at school in Avalon – I was born there, to the Lady of Avalon, so I grew there from a girl and was not harmed by the magic there as children born outside can be – there was also a boy there. Talesin. It seemed to me that he did not get older, for when I was a child, he was a young man, and when I was a young woman, he was a young man still. But I do not know any more if I imagined that, or if I pieced it together afterwards from suspicions, from the remnants of an ill-remembered childhood. Memory fails us, at times, Igraine, and even I, for all my skill in the magic arts, am weak in human matters, as we all are. But there was the young man Talesin, and he led me to believe that he was a student there as I was, with little knowledge of magic. I knew he had power beyond what I could know, and foolish and young as I was, I envied it. I was ambitious. My mother was Lady of Avalon, and I coveted the place for myself. It ought not to have belonged to a man, yet I knew that if Talesin's skill at the magic arts were greater than mine, then it was rightfully his. I sought to distract him. To learn his secrets. I never knew if he led me to my foolish plans, or if they were my own work, but I offered myself, and in return I gained all the knowledge I hoped for to make myself wise, and strong. He had a sister, too, I saw from time to time, who looked just like him; dark hair, dark eyes, slender and tall. Her name was –"

"Melusine."

"Melusine," Viviane agreed, with a nod that made me sure she knew and recognised what I had suffered, as I did for her. "Or I thought she was his sister. There was another, too, Silvestris, who is the man you know as Merlin, who used to live naked in the woods, and who has never aged a day. Others say that he gets younger each passing year, and was born at the end of days, and lives backwards. Others that he is mad. I do not think any of this is true, but truly he has lived for years in the deepest, darkest parts of the Otherworld where the dead are sealed within the trunks of trees, sleeping open-eyed like ghosts. He has drunk of the springs there, and tasted the fruit of the dead, and the asphodel flowers. He is the least like a man, and the one whom I most fear, for his magic is the blackest, and even I do not know all of his secrets.

"The last man who has borne the name Merlin is the prophet Ambrosius, who knows all the future, and all the past, and is a tall, thin man with a long, white beard. I think you have seen him too? Merlin also goes about in the shape of a child, but I do not know his name, or if he is another part of Merlin, or simply a shape he is able to assume.

"Truly, Igraine, I do not know if Merlin is one man with many faces, or several men and women who have bound themselves together with black magic into one, or even if they are all just Merlin Silvestris, and those whom he has bound to himself in black magic. I do not know what he wants, or if he acts on behalf of anyone but himself. I have heard him call himself the instrument of Fate, but I cannot say I trust his word.

"But Arthur will be safe. I know he will be safe, for it was not long ago that I saw Merlin, in the shape of the prophet Ambrosius, stand in Avalon's great chapel, and let the light of the future fill him. And he told me that Arthur would be the greatest King that Britain had known, would ever know, so he will not harm the boy. We should be wary, Igraine, but we need not be afraid." I nodded, but I was not entirely comforted. "Igraine, do not look so anxious." She squeezed my hands gently in hers. "I am instructing my apprentice, Nimue, in all the secrets I have learned from Merlin, and I hope that she will learn more from him in time. She is sworn and bound to protect your son with all the power she has. In truth, I had hoped to set such a task on Arthur's own sister, Morgan, but that is not her fate. She has a great gift for healing, and will be a great and powerful witch, but her place is in the world beyond Avalon."

"Morgan," I sighed, thinking of my little girl, grown to a quiet, serious young woman. I supposed that now she would be tattooed with woad. I longed to see her.

"She is well. She is a very clever girl. An excellent student. Now, Igraine, we must make ready, and ride to Camelot to be there in time to welcome your son. Would tomorrow be too soon?"

I shook my head. I could not bear to wait. I had to know if the child I had dreamed coming to manhood was my own child, or if I had imagined a stranger.

* * *

That night, a heavy snow fell. I had not realised how deep it had got into winter. It never really snowed at Tintagel, for we were right out on the sea, but I could see it, white on the horizon. When I gathered the men, the captain of the guard at Tintagel, a grizzled man in middle age called Rufus, with a grey beard cropped close to his face, said he could not allow us to ride out, because there was ice on the narrow path between Tintagel and the Cornish mainland. The last time it had snowed like this was the winter that Morgan was born.

"I am sorry, my Queen, but I would be little good as captain of the guard if I let either you or my men ride out there. You would fall, and break your necks, and kill your horses. If there truly is a King risen in Logrys, then it will make little difference if it is now or in the spring that you return to Camelot."

If I had not had Viviane beside me, I would have shouted at him and demanded it, but I did not. When I was alone with her, I asked if she could take us, by her magic, to Camelot, and she shook her head and said that she might bring the two of us safely over the patches of ice, but it would only do Arthur good if I came with all the state befitting a queen, and she said besides that she could not melt the ice and snow, for it would do the world no good for her to meddle in it so.

So we waited, and I spent my days with Viviane and Brastias, and my nights dreaming of Arthur. Arthur who now had a name. Who now had a sword, one that he took in and out of the stone Merlin had enchanted. And others cheered every time he did. Other men came and could not budge it from the stone, but again and again he put it in and took it out. I saw, too, the dark boy I had seen with him, fallen to his knees before Arthur, whom I suppose until that moment he had known only as his little brother, and a dark man beside him, who must have been the father who raised my son, whose face I could not see, for he, too, was bowed before the child who was suddenly his king. I saw Arthur again, in front of the kings of Ireland, and Gore, and of the borderlands south of Lothian, dressed in Uther's old red and gold surcoat with Merlin Silvestris at his side, pulling the sword from the stone in London's great cathedral. And even through the dream I could hear the roar of the crowd, cheering.

Were those dreams things that had already happened? Things that were going to happen? That were happening now? Word came slow and sparse to Cornwall, and the unusually heavy snows made it worse. Viviane came and went from Tintagel, to Avalon, to Camelot. She told me that she was needed in Avalon, with her apprentice Nimue, but she had heard that Arthur was accepted as King in Logrys. I had a letter from Morgan, long delayed by the snow, when the new year had already come, begging me to come to Camelot as soon as I could, because there was a king who claimed to be Uther's son. I could tell from the letter that Morgan was sorry for me because she suspected that this son of Uther's was with another woman. She said, too, that Morgawse had come to Camelot. I found that I was oddly pleased to know that Lot would be there. I did not like him, but he was a man who could be reasoned with. He was greedy enough to heed what I said to him, if he thought it would bring him advantage.

* * *

At last, after months of unbearable waiting, the snows were thawed enough, and the ice was gone from the path, and we could travel. The night before, I gathered my things carefully. I was nervous to see my son. What would he think of the mother who had handed him away to strangers? What would he know of his father? Would people have told him the story of how he had come to be conceived? I hoped not. I would not tell it to him. I would be a stranger to him. His real family were the mother and father who had raised him. The dark-haired boy who had been his companion as a child would be his brother, and Morgan and Morgawse not his sisters, but strangers, perhaps even rivals for his throne. Perhaps that was what Merlin had meant when he threatened to set my children against one another. Morgawse had perhaps a stronger claim to be heir of Britain than my lost son. She had four sons of her own, and was conceived within a lawful marriage. Her husband was a king. There would be those who would support Lot's desire to put one of his sons on the throne, rather than Uther's.

That night, when all was packed and ready for me to arrive in state, I sat up with Brastias in my public room, just the table and a candle between us, and the silence. Brastias looked once again through all the papers scattered across the table and sighed. I had brought up an old chest of charters from the vaults of Tintagel, but I did not know what I had been looking for, apart from distraction. I supposed part of me still cared that one of Morgawse's sons should inherit Tintagel, but there was nothing useful among what I had found. It was only grain laws, and lists of barons under the lordship of Tintagel.

I sighed, rubbing my eyes. It was late, but I was not sure if I could sleep.

"Brastias," I said softly, "how has it all come to this?"

If I traced back to the beginning all those years ago, I still could not see how it had all become such an awful mess. So much loss, and betrayal. I did not know how Uther and I had tangled so much, so many people, into our love, our fight for control, our – I was not sure what it had been.

"Some men believe in Fate," he said quietly, "but I do not. Some might say the will of God, but I am sorry to say that I don't believe in that either. Chance, perhaps. I suppose whatever men call it, it cannot be changed. But it will come to good, Igraine. Your son lives, and by all accounts is healthy and strong. He is accepted as King. All will be well. He will have sons, and the line will continue, and Britain will live in peace. We must all try to put aside the pain of our own lives, to remember that every sacrifice made for Arthur was one to bring peace to this land."

I nodded. I supposed he was right. The pain of our own lives. Yes, Brastias had suffered as well. Whether Gorlois had truly been his father, he had loved Gorlois like one, and lost him, and had been dragged this way and that by fate – or whatever it was – as I had been.

"Igraine." He reached across the table, and took my hand in his, and I felt a stirring of long-forgotten desire, but it was late for that. He was still young, and I was growing old, and now was not the time. So this was another pain that he wanted to speak of. But he was confused. There were young women for him to love. He was handsome. He cared too much for me, and he had confused duty with love. I drew my hand away.

"I am tired, Brastias. I will go to bed now."

He nodded, and I slipped out of the room. But I did not sleep. I lay awake playing over and over in my head what I would say to my son when I saw him at last.

Chapter fifty-two

I arrived with all of the splendour that I could muster from the poor stores at Tintagel – stores mostly bespoiled by Uther now sixteen years ago. I still had the white-gold crown of Cornwall that my mother had worn before me, and I had a cloak of lovely red-brown furs, and beneath that my dress of grey silk and silver thread. I knew that I looked like a queen. I wished that I had the crown of Logrys, but that had been left behind in Camelot in my hurry. Besides, it would not be long before that had to be given to someone else.

On the way, the possibility struck me that this boy might be an impostor. Someone conjured up from a backwater by Merlin to take the rightful place of my son. I would know when I saw him, but I would have to be prepared.

The hunting horns that announced a royal party sounded, so Camelot must have been peopled by those who knew well enough who I was, and the respect owed to me.

* * *

The first thing I saw as I rode through the gates was Morgan, and as soon as I set eyes on my daughter, I could think of nothing else. Hot and strong and blissful, the love rushed through me and I slipped from my horse and rushed over to wrap my arms around her. She was the very image of myself at that age, only her lovely pale skin was tattooed with woad. She was a wise woman now, a powerful woman of Avalon. A great and talented healer. And yet when I held her little, skinny body to mine she still felt like a little child, and her hair smelled the same: of the dust of books, and the clean smell beneath that of her skin. She was even taller than I was now. I kissed her on the cheek, and I took her hands in mine, and looked into the lovely grey eyes that were so like my own. I thought they looked unbearably beautiful on Morgan. She was the same as she had always been. Quiet, reserved, and perfect. Like a fawn, her slender limbs too long for her. I had missed her painfully.

"Morgan!" I could not contain a bright laugh to see her. It had been so long. Too long. Avalon had changed her, but she was still my little girl. My miracle child. "A proper woman of Avalon now. I am so proud. Your father, too, would have been proud." I kissed her on the forehead, and I saw her blush a little. I became aware that she was a woman grown, just turned eighteen, and did not want to be kissed by her mother.

"I hoped I would reach you before Christmas, but the snows near Wales were bad. Morgan, you are all grown."

I tucked a loose strand of her hair gently behind her ear. I wished that I had time to talk with her fully, to hear how the years had been to her, but I had to see this claimant as soon as possible, to know if he was my son. But first I had to tell her, and Morgawse, the truth. I wanted, too, to say it to Lot's face, so that he would understand that he could not challenge the new King.

"Your sister is here too?" I asked her. She nodded. "I must speak with you both, right away."

Men began calling for Morgawse, so obviously she was somewhere in the castle, even if she did not see fit to come out and greet her mother. Strange, that Lot did not come. He usually did not miss a chance to greet me and remind me that he was a great king to whom I owed some unspecified debt of gratitude. I turned over my shoulder to call to Brastias. "Take my bags to my room in the east tower. Send word to King Arthur that Igraine of Cornwall is here, and that I request an audience with him this afternoon."

Son or not, the new King of Britain would receive me like the queen I was, if he was to have my support. If he was a puppet of Merlin's, I would have him awed and afraid before he dared to challenge me. If he were my own son, then there would be time enough to lift the veil of queenship and be gentle with him.

I led Morgan up to the rooms that had been mine. I had not even thought that someone else might be installed in the queen's chambers, but I was right to assume so, because they were empty and dusty. I felt a prickle of annoyance. No one had cleaned them. So, Camelot was now a soldier's garrison, with hardly any women to prepare noble comforts.

The room was as I had left it, with a half-burned candle in the candlestick in the middle of the table. No one had come out to greet us properly. No knight of Arthur's. No sign of any formal greeting-party as befitted the visit of a queen. No sign, either, of the knights of Lothian.

"Where is Lot of Lothian?" I asked Morgan, who had come up with me. "Did he not come with Morgawse?"

Morgan, not meeting my eye, shook her head. There was something wrong there, then. I wondered if, visiting her sister, Morgan had had the misfortune to experience Lot's enthusiastic appetite for women. I hoped that he had not touched her. I was sure that if he had tried, she would have refused – she knew well enough what her maidenhood was worth, as a princess – but I hoped that he had not frightened her.

I shrugged off my cloak, hot from the ride and sweating slightly with nerves. What would my daughters make of my secret child? Would Morgan be upset when she heard how Uther had used me? I had long ceased to be. Morgawse would preen and gloat and say once more that she had always known Uther was a monster, and that would be hard to bear, but what if Morgan was frightened, or cried? I did not want to cause them suffering.

* * *

I was surprised that, when Morgawse came, she was pleased to see me, and cried out with joy, and rushed to embrace me. Still tense and defensive from our last argument about Uther, I held back. I knew I should have been calmer, more forgiving.

I was shocked once more, as I held her gently back from me, by how beautiful she was. She had not been a very pretty child, but now she was a stunning woman. Her eyes, blue, and bright and clear, were fringed with soft, thick lashes, and her skin was beautifully fair, and covered with pale gold freckles that gathered densely across the bridge of her nose and her chest. She had a necklace of amber beads about her neck – had I given them to her? – that were beautiful with her skin and red-gold hair; and gold at her ears, in her hair, gold rings on her fingers, and gold embroidered through her dress, which was close on her womanly form. She was enchanting. Dazzling. She smelled of wood smoke, and sandalwood from the east.

As she stepped back from our embrace, she carelessly threw off a white fur cloak that must have been worth more than all my clothes together. Truly, she did not appreciate in what luxury Lot's wealth kept her. Beneath, I noticed that the samite dress was taut over a stomach swollen with early pregnancy. Three months, perhaps four. So, she had reconciled a little with Lot. Perhaps I had imagined how bad our fights had been. Perhaps I had imagined what I had seen between her and Uther. He had denied it. And she was so lovely. So like Gorlois. So happy to see me. I put my hand gently to her cheek and she leaned into it – though she was a woman of twenty-seven – with all the wild, uninhibited affection of a child. I let my hand rest for a moment, thoughtfully, against the swell of Morgawse's stomach. I thought of my own child.

"You girls might want to sit down," I told them. They did not move. Morgawse drew back from me, and crossed her arms over her stomach. Morgan's hands closed over the back of the chair she stood behind, and her knuckles turned white. I knew what they were afraid of. That I was going to say that Uther's son meant them harm. Did they know him? How long had they been at Camelot with Arthur? I almost wavered, to ask them what Arthur was like, to try to guess if he truly was my son. I drew in a breath, closing my eyes, steadying myself. My daughters were women grown. They deserved to know the truth.

"There is something I have kept from you both. It was partly because of my own shame about the matter, partly because it was a dangerous time, and I wanted to protect you both from the knowledge of it. Just after your father died, a man came to me who I thought was your father. I didn't know he was dead, and I was sure it was he and, well – there was a child. A boy." I could see Morgan's mind working, behind her eyes, but Morgawse's face was still slack with incomprehension. I drew in another deep breath. I had to finish. It was not fair to make them guess. "That boy, that boy was Uther's son. Uther told me it had been he who had come to me in the shape of my husband. So, it is I. I am Arthur's mother."

Morgawse stepped back as though I had struck her. "No," she whispered. And then she began to scream in an awful, shrill voice, "No, no, no, Mother, no!"

Morgawse had always been selfish. This was not nearly so bad for her as it was for me.

"It's not that bad, Morgawse. I'm sorry I didn't tell you, but there's no need for histrionics."

An awful silence followed, and when I looked to Morgan, I realised that she was staring at me, and not at her sister, who had descended into whispering "No, no, no" to herself under her breath, as though deprived of her senses.

"Actually, Mother…"

But Morgan did not need to finish. I looked back to Morgawse's pregnant stomach. How long had they been in Camelot? Four months, by the account of Morgan's letter. Lot was ageing, and it had been eight years since Morgawse had brought a child of his to birth. I heard my blood rushing in my ears, and I felt a wave of cold disgust pass over me. I heard Merlin's voice. I will tear your precious family to pieces. I had never dreamed that he would achieve it so soon. Nor that he would know so well the weakness of my lustful, faithless daughter. How had Gorlois and I created such a creature between us as Morgawse? For all Gorlois' faults, he had always been dutiful.

"Morgawse. What have you done? Morgawse?"

I stepped towards Morgawse and, jolted from her whispering, Morgawse jumped back from me, as though she was afraid. She turned to me, and I saw the old anger and hate that I recognised flash in her eyes.

"You should have said something before. You should have said," she screamed.

"Morgawse, I didn't raise you to be a harlot, letting any man who asks you nicely into your bed. How was I supposed to expect this would happen? If you had been able to keep your legs together–"

"You married me to an awful old man, who was cruel to me, and rough with me, and who still forced himself on me when I had only just had his children and I was bleeding and begging him to stop. And you expect me to turn away one chance I get of kindness, of even a little bit of gentleness? Arthur is a king too, so I did not think there was any dishonour in it. You did not tell me."

Morgawse was savage in her anger. She did not care that I had made awful sacrifices to keep her safe, to find her the husband she disdained because he was not young and she did not understand his ways. And I had suffered from both my husbands. Gorlois, who had been kind, and whose pride I had allowed – and there were bastard children from her perfect father, I was sure of that. And Uther. Uther whom I had loved, whose love had seared me to the bone and left me empty. He had made me suffer, and I had made him suffer, and we had consumed each other. I had risked his anger again and again to make sure that she would be happy and safe. She dared to be ungrateful because her marriage was not the great romance she had dreamed of. She was a child. A selfish child.

I drew myself up, felt myself become cold.

"This is the duty of all wives, Morgawse. This is the way of things. How dare you speak to me as if I treated you ill in sending you to Lot. I saved your life when I sent you to him. He has been a good husband to you, given you many children and his protection to you and your family. I had hoped that he might keep us all safe now, but I see that cannot be hoped for, because of your foolishness. Many others have suffered as you have without thinking they deserve to indulge themselves with sin as their reward. And you have not just sinned in adultery, but with your own brother." I wished, painfully, in that moment, that Arthur was not my child, as I thought he was. I could bear the pain of disappointment that it was not really him, if it saved us from this horror. "You are disgusting, Morgawse." I turned to Morgan. "Morgan, is this too late to be undone?"

"No," Morgawse screamed. "No, don't ask her that. I won't do it. This is my child."

Morgan looked between us, pale beneath her woad.

"It could be done," she said very quietly, "but not without great danger to Morgawse."

"I won't do it," Morgawse said, stubbornly. Her face was set, and her eyes were shining with tears that she was too proud to let fall. Oh, I was sure that it was awful for her, but she had brought it upon herself. She was disgusting.

"Get out of my sight, Morgawse," I said, hard, and quiet, and cold.

Morgawse snatched up her cloak and swept out. She was not sorry. I could see that. She had been upset, had been angry at me for a moment, but now she was proud and stubborn, and she would not remedy her mistake. And now I would have to meet my son under the shadow of this abomination.

Chapter fifty-three

I knew it would be awful, and it would tarnish my first meeting with Arthur. I came with my daughters, Morgan quiet and tense, Morgawse sick and pale and hating me. As soon as I walked in the room, I knew that Arthur was my son. He was the boy I had seen in my dreams, but already he looked like a man. Tall; taller than Uther had been, but just as broad, with a sensitive face, my grey eyes. Uther's strong, masculine features, but a touch of softness that was, perhaps, only youth. He had the gold hair I had dreamed, but he was older. I had expected a boy. In Uther's coat and with the crown on his head – I noticed he had had himself crowned before I had come to agree to it – he looked grown. But I knew that he was only fifteen years old. My lost baby, my little boy. I wanted to throw my arms around him, but I could not. And Merlin was at his side with his ugly white and blue skull hidden in the hood of his robe, and his black eyes watching me. There were others in the room, but I barely saw them. Behind him, in a blur, the dark boy I had seen in my dreams, who must have been his brother. Behind that, others who faded into the background. All I saw was Arthur. I wanted to begin by telling him that I had loved him as a mother all these years. That I had missed him, and longed for him. That he had always been in my thoughts, and in my dreams. But he was already King, and the first thing was the truth.

I took in a deep breath, and began.

I watched Arthur's face fall, saw him struggle to catch his breath, lean on the table. This is how he will remember me, I thought, with sinking dread. Morgawse has tarnished this for us, for ever. And a mean little part of me wondered if this hadn't been her last revenge against me and Uther. It felt like a long silence after I had spoken, when Arthur was struggling under the weight of the revelation, before anyone spoke, but it was not. It was only a second. Only a second before one of the knights behind Arthur stood forward to blame me.

"You were dishonourable to keep this a secret!" he cried. "The suffering and peril this has caused my lord King Arthur as he fought to establish his kingdom. It is treason! Besides, how do we even know it is true?"

Merlin stood, slowly, a cruel smile spreading across his face. "I can vouch for the truth of this. It is I who brought the infant Arthur to Ector and his lady wife, and I who instructed Queen Igraine to keep her silence."

Ector. As I struggled against everything that had changed, everything that had happened, over Arthur's head, bowed in distress and defeat, my eyes met the eyes of a man I thought that I would never see again. Ector. His face was pale, too, with panic, with horror at what had come to pass. So, it was to Ector that my son had been given. With Ector and his Otherworld wife that Viviane had hidden Arthur. With Ector and the woman who bore her name. I remembered the abbess talking about a handsome knight, with two sons, one who is dark like the father, and the other who is fair like the mother, like two boys from a fairy tale. No one had suspected that Arthur was not Ector's own child. Where could Viviane have hidden my son where he would have been safer?

I reached forward and placed a hand on the table, just before Arthur's. I wanted to reach out and take his hands, but I was a stranger to him, and he would be afraid.

"I will return to you tomorrow, Arthur," I said, gently, "and I will tell you anything you desire to know. About me, about your father, about how things came to be this way."

Now was not the time. He was distraught, he was afraid. I knew he was afraid of me, too, otherwise why would he have received me in the privacy of his council-chamber, but with all his knights, and wearing Uther's coat and crown? We had been afraid of each other. I had come to him the same way. Each fearing the power of the other would tear them down. A new king. A widowed queen. Natural enemies.

* * *

309

I went back to my room, alone, to wait. To pray to every god I knew that there would be some way to save my son. To save all my children from this. From the fate Merlin had promised to them.

I stood at my window, staring down at the garden beneath. I was not sure what I was looking for. Whatever it was, I did not see it. Some comfort, some hope, some familiar face. As proud as I was of Morgan, her woaded face made her different, marked her as belonging to a world beyond what I could understand. Morgawse had also become something, someone beyond my understanding. Arthur was a stranger, Merlin an enemy, and Brastias – I could hardly call him to me now. What kind of comfort could we offer one another that would not tear the both of us apart? The time for that was long past, long lost, and the thought now left me cold and clammy with an unpleasant shame. I did not want that.

The sun was sinking towards the horizon, and in the early spring light, its golden glow was pale, and weak, and the sky was not a lovely deep red but a strange, cold purple. I wanted to close my eyes and open them again in Tintagel, and find it was all an awful dream. But it was not an awful dream. It was Merlin's victory. *I will tear your precious family to pieces.* He had begun. He had known and he had not stopped Arthur. Arthur had not stopped himself. He had not known that Morgawse was his sister, but he had known that she was another man's wife.

"Igraine." I heard my name softly, and turned to see Ector, standing warily in the doorway. I found myself glad that he had come. He looked at once entirely different and entirely the same as I remembered him. Still handsome, his thick hair still mostly dark, still kind-faced, still gentle, but the days were long gone when he wore gold armour and rich silk. He had a tatty old surcoat of black sewn with gold thread. It was tight across his shoulders and dusty, as though he had hidden it away for years and had only just put it on once more because Arthur was King.

"Come in, Ector," I said, gently. I wanted him to stay. I supposed I wanted to hear more about Arthur, about how he had been as a boy.

Ector closed the door behind himself, but he did not come towards me. He leaned back against it. He looked awfully nervous.

"Forgive me, Queen Igraine," he said, gazing down at his feet. "I know I must be the last person you would like to see, at this moment."

"Why do you say that?"

Ector shook his head, rubbing his forehead with the heel of one hand. "If it were not enough, that long, long ago I did you a great wrong when I was nothing more than a foolish boy – the Lady of Avalon entrusts your son to me, and this befalls him. My Lady, Queen Igraine, I swear…" He looked up at me then, and I could see the earnest desperation in his eyes, "I swear it that I loved him as if he were my own son. I suppose, it was as if he was. Viviane – my wife, Viviane – we had just lost a little baby girl when the Lady of Avalon came to Viviane with him, and she nursed Arthur as though he had been her own child, and we raised him beside Kay. Kay never knew that Arthur was not his own brother. People even said that Arthur looked like Viviane. We did not know who his parents were, only that it was our duty to keep him safe. I gave Arthur everything I could, all the love I had, but – I was only gone a brief time – I did not imagine –" He shook his head once more. "In truth, Igraine, if it had been either of them to do such a thing – I had feared it from Kay. And I was not enough. Not enough for them."

"What do you mean, Ector?" I asked, rushing over and taking his hands. He looked so sorrowful, so full of blame for himself that I could not bear it. Though I had not seen him since I was a girl, though I did not really know him, I felt that I did. Perhaps it was that, just now, we had suffered the same thing. The awful revelation that a child of ours, one we had loved and cared for and worried after, had done an awful thing, had been cast into danger by the fates.

He sighed heavily. "When Kay was ten years old, and Arthur seven, or thereabouts, Viviane grew ill suddenly, and died. I did all I could, but I could not be mother as well as father to those two boys. Kay became secretive, and then reckless. I supposed it was his way of grieving; looking for distraction. I did not know what to do. Then, when he was a few years older he became… involved – I had a half-brother, a fosterling in Avalon, about Kay's age. They were always close. I allowed it to continue, because I knew that Kay was still grieving for his mother, and I would not deny him comfort. I thought it would run its course, as these things often do between boys that age, but it did not. I was… forced to make an end of it myself. Kay was furious, obviously. He has always been so reckless. After that, it was women, girls, I don't know – he was always secretive about anything of that kind. Sometimes I wondered if it was to push me, to see if I would intervene. If either of them were to do something like this – and I have been so concerned for Kay in that regard, and Arthur among the tangled politics of court, I never thought to… Of course, with Arthur, there were always girls, but I was only afraid of little bastard children in the farmlands near Avalon, and that would not be such ill fortune for a king, I suppose, but nothing like this. I – Igraine, I cannot offer you any kind of adequate apology – I should have, there should have been some way to prevent –"

I hushed him gently, squeezing his hands gently in comfort. I felt the tears rising up in my throat. I should have been there for my son. I could have prevented this, if Merlin or the fates or whatever they were, were not set against me.

"Ector," I whispered, and I found myself leaning towards him, towards our shared suffering, lonely, and empty, and desperate for comfort. "I do not blame you for this. I know that you loved Arthur, and cared for him as though he were your own child."

Ector nodded. "I am sorry, too, that it was I. I know I must be the last person you wanted to raise –"

"No, Ector," I said gently, and I put my hand against his cheek. I was surprised to feel that it was damp, and a little hot. I had never seen a man cry before, I did not think. I felt my heart thud, hard, within me. "That was long ago. Besides, I knew where you had gone. I crept out, that night, into the courtyard, to see you. And Viviane was there, and she said you would be twice as cruel to abandon a woman you loved to marry one you did not. And she was right. You raised Arthur in a house full of love. That is more, Ector, than I could have offered him here, with Uther. Do not be sorry for anything. Some things cannot be changed."

Ector opened his mouth to reply, but he did not find the words. I closed my eyes as he put his hand to my cheek in return, and I leant into it, and slowly, slowly, forwards into him until my forehead rested on his, and we stood for a moment, leaning in to one another. I drew in a long, slow breath. I had been foolish to forget that there was someone else in the castle who was feeling what I was feeling.

Slowly, I softened towards the heat of his body, and I felt a spark of desire run through me, that I had not expected to feel, filling my cold body with life. I whispered Ector's name, but I did not know what I was about to say, for suddenly he grasped hold of me and kissed me. I sighed into it. Oh, if he could have kissed me like that thirty years ago. No wonder Viviane had chased him from Avalon to Tintagel. I felt the familiar delicious weakness spread down my spine, and I melted into his touch. His lips were soft, and gentle, yet also passionate. His hair, as I ran my hands into it, was still thick, although it was touched through with grey at the temples. I had expected, too, that he would be hesitant and courteous as a lover, as Gorlois had been, for he had shown me the same careful respect in public, but he was not. He was confident and passionate in his kisses, and in the touch of his hands as they unwound the plait of my hair and ran through it. He must have learned to be so from years with a wife whom he truly loved, and who had loved him without reserve. It must have been blissful. He drew away then, just a little, just as I was flushed and sighing with sudden delight. I leant towards him, hungry for more, and he drew back a little more, though his hands were now running down to the lacing at the back of my dress, pulling it undone, and hot with frustration and longing, I grasped him hard by the front of his tatty old coat and pulled him up against me. I heard him groan low in his throat. He picked me up suddenly, and I was surprised to feel the strength of him. Though he was a prince, he had been forced to become a knight, and was thick with muscle from battle. He lifted me, and turned us round to press me up against the door. I wasted no time in freeing him from his dusty old coat, and his shirt. Beneath his shirt was more thick, dark hair. Soft, inviting, almost velvety; not coarse like either of my husbands' had been. I ran my hands over him, feeling the heat of his skin, the shape of his muscle. He was pulling the dress down from my shoulders, his lips eagerly following. He caught me by the thighs and lifted me up against the door. I closed my eyes, and leant my head back as his lips pressed against my neck, lost in the intoxicating bliss of sensation. I did not want to think. I did not want to remember. Neither did he. Perhaps it was nothing more than desperation, and in the cold light of the morning it would leave us both regretful and empty, but in that moment it wiped everything else out, and it was all I needed.

Chapter fifty-four

Half-awake, I was aware that there was a man in the bed beside me. A naked man. I could feel his skin against mine, beneath the covers. Still half-asleep, lazy, and filling slowly with a warm desire that was half-borne of remembered pleasure, I reached out my hand beneath the covers and felt warm, thick, inviting hair, and hot, waking skin, and I heard the man beside me groan, and wake, and pull me into his arms.

"Ector," I whispered, "I do not want to wake from this dream."

He groaned beside me, in mixed relief and reluctance that our small escape would end.

"No, I do not either. But I think that we must, the both of us."

He turned, then, and propped himself up on his elbow, resting his head on his hand. I reached out a hand, and let my fingers rest lightly against his chest. I could feel the heat of his body, and so close, I was tempted again to run my hand through the hair there, and sink into it once more.

"I… I was glad of this comfort, Ector. But I do not think that–"

He nodded, taking my hand in his, and pressing it softly to his lips.

"No, I do not think it would be wise for us to… meet again, in this way."

I found myself smiling, though I was not sure why. Perhaps it was because it was simple. We had had pleasure and comfort and relief, and there was no lie, no fight for power, no confusion, or tangle. He would leave, and I would continue, and it would be just a sweet memory.

"I should leave," he said, reluctantly, leaning over to kiss me one last time. He meant it to be brief, but he lingered for a moment, and I held tight to the feel of his soft lips against mine.

He dressed carefully, and I sat up in the bed, propped about by my pillows. He came by one last time to kiss me, gentle and brief, and said goodbye. It was early still, the sun not yet fully up, and I hoped that no one would notice him. Somehow, I felt as if anyone knew our secret, it would steal a piece of it, make it into something illicit, something unpleasant or tawdry, and it had not been. It had not been love, or marriage, or anything the world outside considered noble, but it had been pleasure, and comfort, the sharing of sorrow, and the easing of pain, and these were virtues that the world did ill not to praise.

* * *

By the time I had dressed and made ready and gone to see my daughters, I found with a jolt of guilt that they had already gone. Ridden to Lothian, the servants said. Did they both hate me so much, now, that they had gone without saying goodbye?

But there was no time for that. No time to pause and reflect. Affairs were in disarray still from Uther's death. I made enquiries within the castle, and it seemed that Arthur had done a good enough job of rallying men to him, and convincing them that he was indeed Uther's true heir, but this was not enough. There were charters to witness, claims to settle. All the dull affairs of state. And all to be done as soon as possible by a fifteen-year-old boy reeling from a series of disorientating revelations.

I was glad that Ector was there when I met with Arthur in council again. Arthur was afraid of me, I could tell. I was the Queen of Britain to him, not a mother, not a person he could know. I did my best to be kind but I also had to be firm, because I knew best what ought to be done. The older knights and the old councillors of Uther supported me, and Merlin stood there dark and silent and did not speak against me. I liked, too, to have Ector there for my own sake. To, for a moment, close my eyes and imagine his lips against my cheek, and then my mouth, and his hands gripping my body. It was a secret, it was mine, and it protected me from the world outside. All the sweeter, too, knowing that it would not be tarnished by more encounters, the growth of jealousy and possession, of failed expectations. Brief, and perfect.

And then, at long last, after fifteen years, I was alone with my son. I had dreamed of this moment. Of him. Truly, though, he was not the same boy I had seen. He was weighed down, now, with what had befallen him. He looked older even than the day before; something about his face, the way he held himself. Grown. Aware that he was a man with responsibilities now, rather than a boy. He stood the other side of the table, and in the low light of the candle, which was burning down to nothing, his profile was picked out in soft, orange light. Like my own, I supposed, for I looked at him and wondered at how much he looked like Morgan. They had known each other, I supposed, as children, and yet neither of them had realised they were brother and sister. It was the same long, straight nose, the same intense, thoughtful expression. Was that mine? It must have been. They did not share a father. And like Uther he was tall and broad, but where Uther had been rough-looking, his looks combined with mine had made our son masculine but handsome. I could see that. He must have been charming, too, and practised with women to convince a woman of Morgawse's age and experience that he was more than a boy.

"Arthur," I began tentatively, and he looked up at me, his grey eyes wary, nervous. "I said I would answer any question you had, about me, or your father, or how –"

"Is it true," he asked, quietly, still half-turned away from me, but his eyes fixed on mine, "what you said about how I was – King Uther – my father, I – that he…?"

"That he came to me in disguise? Yes, Arthur, that is true."

He nodded, looking down at his feet. He seemed upset to hear it, but he was a man grown, and he had fathered a child. He had to begin to see the world as an adult.

"Why did you give me away? Was it because…?"

"No, Arthur," I said, gently. I knew that women often did so, if they had not wished the child, and the conception had been violent and unpleasant. Queens did not have that luxury. "It was to keep you safe."

I wanted to say more. To warn him about Merlin, but I did not have the words for it. I wondered if Merlin had some enchantment on me that stopped my voice and held me silent, or if it was only my own weakness, my own fear.

Arthur nodded once more. "I should send someone. To call my sisters back. To bring them here. It isn't safe in Lothian for them. I should send Lancelot, and Bors and –"

So, he could not bear to say Morgawse's name. I wanted them back as badly as he did – worse. They were my daughters, and they had ridden off without a goodbye, into danger. But it was too late.

"No, Arthur. That cannot be done. It is too late for that. They will reach Lothian. Lot will learn that it is not his child, and we will brace for war. It would have come sooner or later, Arthur. Lot is an ambitious man who thinks that the throne of Britain would suit him or one of his sons better than it suited your father, or you."

Arthur nodded, but he did not look convinced. He was thinking about his child, and his sister. He was deep in it, weighed down with it, heavy. I had wanted to talk about childhood and what kind of life he had known. I had wanted to tell him I saw him in my dreams. That I had thought of him every day. But he had no room in his thoughts for that.

"So," he said quietly, "there will be war, already."

"There will, Arthur. But you will not lose."

He did not answer. I knew what he was thinking. He was thinking: you do not know that. I did not. But Viviane and Merlin had seen great things for Arthur, and I had nothing to put faith in apart from them and their Otherworld secrets.

"I will live under this my whole life," Arthur said softly to himself. He would not have said that if he remembered who I was, there with him. I felt a wave of sickening panic rush through my body. He would, indeed, have to live under the shadow of his bastard child by incest if he did not act. I had tried. Morgan and Morgawse had refused. I had to press for it now, if it was to be done.

Arthur was leaning down hard against the table, as though he needed it to keep himself upright, his head hanging down between his shoulders, which were tensed, stiff. He was being slowly destroyed by this; I could see that in every fibre of his body. I had to do this. I had to be strong. This was what a mother did. This was what a queen did.

"Arthur," I said softly, my voice steady and calm. I was pleased with that. I felt as though I were made up of a thousand tiny shards of glass, all held together with nothing more than a gossamer-thin film of desperation, and if I let go for a moment, I would fall apart. "Arthur, now we must not panic. We must not give up hope. These are the times that kings and queens must put away all sentiment, must steel themselves for those things that are necessary. This will be the hardest thing you ever do, Arthur, but it must be done."

I could feel myself shaking, every nerve in my body, the bile rising up my throat. Merlin had promised me this moment, and I had bought it for myself in the desperate risk I had taken to ensure Arthur's safety. I did not regret it. This was the price; I knew it, I paid it. There was nothing more to it than that. Now Arthur would do as I had done. We were strong, and we would prevail.

Slowly, Arthur looked up at me, with those grey eyes that I recognised as my own.

"What, lady?" he asked in a choked half-whisper.

"You must give the command that once the child is born, that it be found, and killed."

The silence rang between us, and for a moment Arthur did not react, as though he had not heard. I wondered if I ought to repeat what I had said; I wondered if it were, in fact, that I had not dared to say it, it was so appalling. But as I opened my mouth to speak again, Arthur began shaking his head, and saying, "No, no, I cannot, I cannot –"

"Arthur," I said more firmly, feeling stronger, feeling the shards within me fuse and grow strong to a hard, unyielding spire of glass. I remembered all the ruthless sacrifices I had made for him, and for his sisters, and for Uther as his Queen. "Now is the time that you must do what must be done. For your people. If you shy back now, then you are no fit man to be King. Arthur…" I stepped forward, and fired by my boldness, I took his face in my hands, as if we had been the close mother and son I had always wished we had been. "I have done things that would make men hate me. I have done things that have made me hate myself. I gave you into the hands of a stranger to save your life. I would do them all again, because they were necessary. They were my duty, they were what was required. Do you understand? It is not always easy. It is not always pleasant. But you must act like a king now, and you must be strong."

I pressed my lips against his forehead, and I felt him tremble, but just a second, before he nodded. How much more would I have liked to wrap my arms around him, and hold him against my bosom as though he were truly still a child, to smooth his hair, to whisper to

317

him that all would be well. But that was lost to me. I held him at arm's length by the shoulders, staring at him hard.

"You are strong enough for this, Arthur," I said.

Arthur nodded slowly once more, "Yes, my lady Queen," he replied. I would have given anything, in that moment, to have him call me Mother.

"Give the order, Arthur. When Morgan comes back to Camelot, and she will come, learn – if you can – from her, what day your child was born, and send your soldiers north in plain armour to kill the children born on that day. It is the only way, Arthur. The only way."

He nodded, rubbing his face with his hands.

Very, very, softly, I said, "You will survive this, Arthur."

But I was not sure if what I said was true.

Chapter fifty-five

I was glad that it was not urgent, not pressing that Arthur act now. I think it would have broken him. Merlin came to me soon after that. To gloat, I think. He did not say anything, but when he smiled, I could hear him say: *I will tear your precious family to pieces. I will set your daughters to war with one another.* Well, they would be now. Morgan would not stay in Lothian. I was sure of that. Her place was with Avalon, and Avalon was with Arthur.

Merlin needed me to keep the affairs of state in order. Arthur had not been raised to a life of politics, and even though the father who raised him had, he had not taught it to Arthur, or to his son. The older brother – rather, Ector's son – Kay was a strange, quiet boy. His smile was Ector's smile, though. Handsome, charming. He had a relaxed, easy way about him, and he and Arthur seemed to care deeply for one another. I was glad that Arthur had had a brother.

Arthur was receptive to my lessons in statecraft, but reserved. He never treated me as a mother, only as a queen. He paid dutiful attention as best he could. He was not studious like Morgan or me. He was impetuous like his father; impulsive, driven by wild flashes of emotion. He needed to learn to control that. I thought that perhaps he ought to look for a wife. A man with war looming on his horizon – even if it had not been openly declared yet, it was coming – could make good use of a new ally. I did not know, in truth, if my blood would be enough to get the King of the Vale, the Kings in Emain Macha and all the kingdoms of Wales behind Arthur. Lot had money, and there were those who still called Arthur a bastard child of

Uther's. Those who questioned his legitimacy. Those who had not seen Merlin's magic trick with the sword. Those who thought Lot of Lothian would be a more profitable overlord. I had seen how men chose to believe that which profited them the most.

Still, Arthur learned. He cared, deeply, about being a good king. He had a burning sense of duty about him. I encouraged him to hide it. It was a virtue, but if men knew it, then they would try to use it against him. He grew better. Stronger. More like a king. He had it in him, in his blood and in his bones. My guidance was enough to bring it out.

* * *

At the end of spring, Viviane came back from Avalon. If I had known what was to come then I would have rushed from the dais where I sat beside Arthur and thrown my arms around her, but I did not. I smiled at her, and raised a hand in greeting. I had missed her. She was the last thing in the world I had left like a friend. Viviane had been by my side since I was little more than a girl.

She stood at the side of the room, and I noticed that she had a sword belted about her waist – which I thought was strange – but I said nothing. Often the workings of Avalon were mysterious to me. I wondered if she had come to call a knight to bring Morgan back from Lothian. It was time she came back, now. I pushed away the fear that Lot might try to keep her as a hostage. No time for such things now.

Arthur stood beside me. The hall got to its feet, and a quiet fell. This was the time when Arthur sat in justice to hear the petty complaints of his men. A man came forward, a young man, a knight – by his dress, tall and slender – but scarred already from battle, down his cheek. He bowed before Arthur.

"Speak your name, sir, and what it is you request."

Arthur had learned the voice of a king, and he sounded firm but gentle.

"My lord, King Arthur, my name is Sir Balan. My brother resides in your prison, and I have a statute sealed and signed by your father, King Uther Pendragon, promising his release by this date."

Arthur held out his hand for the parchment. I saw him squint at it. He still could not read as well as other noblemen his age, and I knew that he did not read in Latin. Uther had not either, but I had signed and sealed the charter in his name and I knew what it concerned.

"What was your brother imprisoned for, sir?" Arthur asked.

"He stood accused of murder, my Lord."

A murmur went round the room. It was common for knights to kill those beneath them in station with impunity, but for a knight to be convicted of murder, he must have killed one of his own rank, and off the battlefield.

I took the paper from Arthur, and glanced over it.

"He has served his time, Arthur," I said. "It does a king well to keep to his own law."

"Let him be brought here, then," Arthur declared loudly. The young knight looked pleased, and relieved. I wondered if the brother in prison in the castle had been some petty enemy of Uther's. I could not remember the trial.

They brought him up while the hall buzzed with fervent excitement to see a knight prisoner. I was sure that the peasant-folk were thrilled at the thought of seeing a nobleman brought low. If he had been clean, not bound with chains, his beard shaved and his hair clipped, I supposed he would have looked very like his brother. He was young. Perhaps a little older than the brother, perhaps the same. I wondered if he had been kept down in the dark. Certainly he was thin, his bones protruding at the collarbone, the shackles loose on his wrists and ankles. He was covered with dirt; his skin was dark with it. When his brother saw him, he started towards him, his face puckering with upset and concern, but shied back when the gaolers holding the prisoner knight leered threateningly at him. The man looked as though he had been treated like an animal. That was no honourable condition for a knight to be held in, even as prisoner.

"Are you Sir Balin?" Arthur asked.

The man nodded and his chains rattled.

Arthur glanced down at the paper, pretending to be able to read it.

"My father King Uther's records state that today is the day you might be released. Do you repent you of your crimes?"

Balin nodded fervently. His eyes looked a little wild, and there was unpleasant white scum from his saliva around his mouth and in the straggling ends of his beard.

"Release him," Arthur said. The gaolers unlocked his shackles and turned their backs and left. Balin collapsed into his brother's arms. Awfully, before the gathered crowd, in the silence, I could hear the brother sobbing. It was too raw, too shameful. If I, a woman, had held myself tight and secret and careful all those years in public, surely those two men could manage it. Though it was the brother crying, he hushed Balin, and drew him to the side of the room.

In the silence that followed, Viviane stood forward and Arthur inclined his head in deference to her. I thought it was well that a king in Camelot was still wise enough to bow to the lady of Avalon. There were powers beyond this world, after all.

"My lord King Arthur," she said, her voice clear and bright, filling the room. "I come to Camelot with a quest. The quest belongs to the man that can draw this sword from its scabbard."

There was another discontented murmur around the room. It was forbidden to draw a weapon in the King's hall, but the Lady of Avalon had brought it. Had she come, knowing that Arthur needed distraction? What was it for? What was so important now, now that my son was only just king, now that Britain was once again going to be plunged into darkness, and civil war?

The knights were already jostling to try. I noticed that the only ones who did not thrust themselves forward were Kay, and a dark-haired young man standing with him, who was talking to him in a whisper. Kay was smiling and nodding. I wondered with a jolt if this was the young man that Ector had spoken of, with whom Kay had been more friendly than was decent. A fosterling in Avalon. He must have been the boy that Viviane fostered. Yes, he was about that age, and Ban's son. I did not see how I had not pieced it together before. How strange, though. How perverse.

There was a scuffle around Viviane, and men crying out, and I glanced away from the two men whispering together, back to the centre of the hall. The prisoner-knight Balin was standing with the sword drawn and in his hands, and men were shouting.

"Silence," Arthur shouted, and they fell still.

"It cannot be you," Viviane said quietly. But her voice carried, low and dangerous. "Return my sword to me at once."

Balin shook his head with a kind of wild fervour. I could see how years in Uther's dungeon would make a man mad. Balin looked mad. He did not rave, or babble, but he had it in his eyes. The madness of a desperate man with nothing to lose.

"Give me my sword," Viviane insisted.

"I drew it," he replied, his voice rasping, long unused. "It is mine."

"You are not fit," Viviane barked. She turned to Arthur. "My lord Arthur this man was in prison for the murder of my own mother. My own mother. He is not fit for this quest, he –"

Viviane could not finish, for Balin had lifted and brought down the sword in his hands, and it sliced clean through her neck. There was an awful moment of silence, stillness, as though the blow had been so clean that no one had noticed, and Viviane's mouth opened in a reflex of horror before she crumpled to the floor in a pool of blood. There were screams, and people running about, but I only heard them from far away. Arthur beside me was on his feet, shouting, incandescent with anger. It was the anger of a man, the anger of a king, and I ought to have been proud, but it did not register with me. It was all distant to me. I could hear a rushing in my ears, and a coldness at my core. Why? Why was it so senseless? So meaningless? Of all people, that Viviane could be so fragile, so human, so weak as to be ruled by flesh and blood and bone when she had all the power of Avalon behind her. It was a terrifying thought. Viviane. I wanted to cry out, but there was no point. Who would hear me?

We left, swiftly. What was to be done? I gave orders to that Viviane's body should be taken away quickly to Avalon where they would bury her in the manner that was most fitting to their own customs.

Arthur was shaken, shocked, but not worse than I was. Viviane had been like the White Goddess herself to me: mother, protectoress, guide. But she was now, too, the angel of death, the taker of blood. I was a grown woman, but now that she was gone, I felt lost.

* * *

The next day, Merlin came to my rooms when I was alone, and he was different. A little cowed, perhaps, by Viviane's death. It was impossible to tell whether this was because he had cared for her, or because it had reminded him that even the men and women of Avalon were made of flesh and blood, and weak as any other to the sword. But he was uncharacteristically tender and sentimental when he came. No, no, it was not quite that. Though, for once he did not come to me as an enemy; for a moment we were fellows, in the loss of Viviane.

He sat beside me at the little table in my council room. We talked a little about Viviane. He assured me that she had been buried in Avalon, and rested there with all those who had been Lady of Avalon before her. He said that her apprentice Nimue, though she was only seventeen years old, had assumed her place.

"It is just all so meaningless," I sighed. "The sword, that knight – for it to end that way, for Viviane to – it's unbearable."

Merlin shook his head slowly, thoughtfully. "It is not so meaningless as you think, Igraine. We are all bound together. Viviane coming here with the sword. That was for you, and Arthur. It is the

Cup of the Blood of the World that Viviane coveted. That was the quest she hoped to send her chosen knight on."

I looked back, blank. The Cup of the Blood of the World. What did that mean?

"You know it by another name, perhaps. The Grail."

The Grail.

Merlin reached forward and put his hand over my eyes, and I felt a sickening lurch in the pit of my stomach. But then I saw Viviane standing before me once more, and she was with Merlin, and they were arguing.

* * *

"Now is not the time, Viviane," Merlin said, his words reaching me dulled, blurred as though in a dream, or through water, and I saw as though through a mist. They were in Avalon, she pacing, he still.

"But it must be now. I feel it." She turned over her shoulder and called out, "Send for Nimue."

Merlin shook his head. "It is too soon. There will be a child, conceived in magic, who will be raised to seek the Grail."

Viviane crossed her arms over her chest. "Your way is not the only way, Merlin. There is more than one destiny. Not every point of the promised future must be achieved by deception and rape."

Merlin shook his head once more. "I tell you only what I see, Viviane."

"No, Merlin," she snapped. "You tell me only what suits you."

At that point, the girl came in, small-boned, white-haired, like an angel. She had big, blue eyes and a delicate, perfect face, that was all the lovelier for its blue-green woad. She folded her hands neatly before herself, and looked between Viviane and Merlin.

"The time has come, Nimue," Viviane began. "The time for what I have spoken to you of. If I should fail, it falls to you to take up the task yourself."

The girl nodded, and said, softly, "You shall not fail, lady."

I was not sure if I imagined it, or if the young girl's eyes flickered over to Merlin in an accusatory manner, as though she imagined that Merlin might be the cause of such failure if it came to pass.

And then I heard Merlin's ugly rasping voice in my head. Viviane was wrong. Now was not the time. She had seen shadows and dreams, and shadows of dreams, and thinking she saw the truth, she rushed at it. Long ago, her hands had failed to save the life of a young boy's mother, and as so often happens, when we show the common men our skill in magic, if our magic fails to save, they say that it has murdered.

So this young boy said, and he hunted out Viviane's old mother and killed her in revenge. Uther had the man thrown into prison in the dungeons. He should have had him executed, but I suspect he was sympathetic to the man's youth, to his prejudice and fear.

Viviane would never forget that face. But that man, Balin, he is also part of the destiny of the Cup of the Blood of the World.

I saw him then, the young man, with the stolen sword in his hand, walking from a dense wood out to a long, wide lake. And in the middle of the lake was a small boat, and in the boat sat a man in the clothes of a prince. I saw that man there again, many years later, his beard long and grizzled with grey, and his legs maimed and twisted, and I knew I looked on the Drowned God and the Maimed King in one, and that the fabric of the world was being torn at as we all tried to fight against our fate.

"He will see the cup." Merlin spoke again, and I saw the knight running through a castle, past plates and cups and dishes of all kinds, a spear in his hand. "But he will not know it. He will strike the King of the Wasted Land, and then he will die at the hand of the man he loves most in the world."

The images faded around me as Merlin drew back his hand.

"Viviane was afraid." The realness of his voice after the dreams and the visions, after the strange half-submerged feeling his magic gave me, surprised me. "She acted too soon. She was afraid for Arthur's sake, for the destiny that he has brought on himself. Those like you and Viviane who try to meddle, you refuse to learn that those who challenge Fate can only suffer. It cannot be changed. I am glad that the new Lady of Avalon, Nimue, is wise enough to see that."

There was a strange tone to his voice, a hint of weakness. So even Merlin, who was so beyond flesh and blood, was weak to a beautiful young girl. I should have known that even the great Merlin would have the weakness of all men. Well, I would mourn Viviane, and I would comfort Arthur, and then when the war was over I would turn to Nimue. We would destroy him.

Chapter fifty-six

For the moment, I did nothing. There was nothing to be done. Better to wait, and strike at the right moment. Besides, Arthur needed me to take care of the day-to-day affairs of state. He had not been raised to be King, and no one had told him what to do. He was a steady, careful pupil, but he was preoccupied and anxious, dogged by the sin he felt had stained him. I was surprised to find that Arthur was a deeply sincere Christian. It seemed strange to me, when Uther had tolerated God and Christ, and openly paid his tribute to the gods of the land and the sky. I knew what it was to trust in the Virgin Mother, and pray to Christ, but they were not my only gods. I had played the part of a Christian queen, because that was what was expected of me. Ector was a genuinely pious man, but the other son, the boy Kay, I hardly ever saw him in the church, and when I did he was staring off, bored, or fiddling or fidgeting like a child. He and Arthur had the kind of easy boisterousness of brothers everywhere but at church, where Arthur would sit beside Kay silent as a saint, while Kay picked at the carvings on the pew, or tapped his fingers on it, restless and inattentive. I was glad that Arthur was a Christian man. It would be easier for him. Except for his new knowledge of sin. I could see that it consumed him. I was consumed too, but with worry for Morgan, and even for Morgawse, though I knew she little deserved my concern. I had not had any news from them at all.

At last a message came from Morgan. But it was not to me, it was to Kay. I wondered why she would be writing to him, but I supposed she dared not write to Arthur about her sister's child, and Kay was closest to him. She was coming back, she said. The rumours of war had become unignorable, and it seemed that Lot intended to avenge his wounded honour in the most unequivocal way possible. He wanted to kill Arthur.

Arthur glanced over the letter once, crumpled it and threw it into the fire. It was a beautiful late summer day and the sky was clear, but it was beginning to get dark, and the light that slanted low through the windows was red as blood.

"Every effort must be made to bring Morgan back safely," I said.

Arthur nodded, staring into the flames. We were in the council room, and it was really too small for a fire, and the air felt thick and cloying.

"You can't send an army up there – what are you going to do?"

Arthur shook his head. I pushed down my rising irritation.

"We should send Lancelot." Kay spoke softly from the other side of the room. I did not turn to him. "He will be quick, able to defend her on the road. He'll know ways to get there and back without running into Lothian's knights. That's the only way to be sure she will be safe."

Arthur shrugged in uninterested agreement.

"See it done then," I said.

There was a long quiet in which the logs in the fire cracked, and I felt the heat of the flames grow uncomfortably hot against my face. Arthur was a step closer, and still staring into them, but he did not feel them. "When she returns," Arthur asked quietly, "then war begins, doesn't it?"

"It does, Arthur." I turned away, towards where Kay stood on the other side of the room, leaning against the wall with his arms crossed over his chest, his face unreadable.

I supposed this was more than Arthur could ever have imagined. He had thought himself the son of a simple farmer, a boy who might aspire to become a knight, with his brother as his squire, and now that brother was King and the world was different and confusing. Ector beside his son did not bother to hide his open concern. I wished I could have spoken with him alone, but I was glad to have him there, with his careful, gentle ways, and the real love he had for Arthur. I was not glad for the presence of his half-brother Bors, who was a soldier to the core, and seemed pleased at the thought of war. He was the man who had treated me roughly when I had come to tell them all who I was to Arthur, and I resented him. He was a pig-headed churl, and insisted on calling Ector's son Guy, pronounced in the French manner, which made both Ector and Kay wince. He was too much of a narrow-minded French fool to realise that the Celtic names of the British peoples were not just some offshoot of those of his own language. I supposed, when I had been a little girl I had been Ygerna, but I now went by the name that those outside of Cornwall found easier to say.

"What is to be done?" Arthur asked, looking up at me, his big grey eyes wide and lost. I wanted to hug him to my breast, but he was King and he could not plead like a lost little boy forever. He had drawn Uther's sword. He had fathered a child. He had been playing at adult games without considering the consequences.

Bors, ever with a mind on war, replied. "It seems to me, my lord Arthur, that we ought to make sure of the allegiances of those kingdoms that could take Lothian's side in this quarrel. Emain Macha will stay out of this, so we need not concern ourselves with them, unless we can make a marriage with them that will encourage them to fight on our side. Cornwall is ours, so we need not worry on that account. The King of the Vale will not go against Lothian, for his lands border on theirs. Of those who could fight for either side, I would say that we must try to get Wales or Brittany on our side."

"You will not have the Bretons," I replied, bitterly. "They are proud and, besides, the sister of the Breton Queen is married to Lot's brother."

"There is a princess in Carhais who is near to Arthur's age," Bors replied. "It is said in the French court that the girl is a great beauty." He glanced at Arthur, who did not look interested at all.

"That is hardly relevant to war," I said, shortly. Did he think that he could convince Arthur to press the Bretons for allegiance simply by appealing to his desire? We did not need them, anyway. They were a rabble. We wanted the Irish, Máel's family in Emain Macha, though the link was almost lost there, or the Welsh. There were those in Rheged castle who still remembered Gorlois, I thought.

"The Bretons have the Hundred Knights of Carhais. There are those who think that they are still savages, more a tribe than a kingdom, but that is no longer true. Leodegrance has raised an army of great warriors and he preens them and trains them. If we get that princess, we get that army."

"What of the princes in Carhais? I have an unmarried daughter. If Morgan were to choose –"

Bors gave a rough laugh. "Forgive me, Queen Igraine, but we do not have the leisure for your daughter to choose a husband she prefers. All the princes of Carhais are already wed to women from their own country. If we are to have the Bretons, then it must be the girl."

Arthur shook his head. "I do not want to be wed."

A look passed between Ector and Bors. Arthur was young, and truly I could see why he would not wish it, after what had passed between him and Morgawse, but it would not be long before he would have to take a wife.

"Give me leave, lady, to write to the son of my old companion, King Ywain, in Gore. If the son, Uriens, is like the father was, he would be a good match for your daughter, Morgan, and we would have all of Wales fighting at our side," Ector suggested, gently.

Wales, I thought. And had Uriens not been a young knight when I had seen him last? I nodded. Still, afterwards I could not help feeling that I had betrayed Morgan somehow, though I did not see what else we could have done.

* * *

Uriens came from Gore, and he was older than I remembered, with a gruff, soldierly way, and he didn't remember who I was, or know who Gorlois had been. His father Ywain would have known. I was worried for Morgan, gentle and shy, with such a rough man, but she was as I was, and I had been something like happy with Uther, who had been such a man.

They were in a hurry, because news had come that Lot's forces were gathering on the borders of Northumbria, and that the Bretons and the Irish – who we had assumed would stay out of it – were packing their ships with soldiers and supplies and planning to fight at Lot's side. It was all agreed before Morgan even arrived. I felt awful, and sad for her, but I knew there was no choice for us, for Britain.

She looked terrified. I supposed that she had been at school with the women of Avalon, and though she was nineteen years old, it would all be new to her, and frightening. I was disappointed to see that Uriens did not seem to be a gentle or sensitive man, and I was afraid that he would be rough with her. I kissed her on the forehead and hugged her to me, when she was dressed and ready for the wedding. She was so beautiful. More beautiful than I had ever been. Tall and willowy and slender as I was, but with Gorlois' gentle smile, and marked all over with the gorgeous woad of Avalon. I wished that her training in Avalon could have kept her safe from this.

* * *

After the wedding, they went right away to Rheged castle, to ready the armies, and I barely got to see my beloved Morgan at all. I felt the ache of it, that my sight of her had been so brief, and now all was so dominated by the war that Merlin had promised me, with one of my daughters on each side.

When she left, I asked Arthur if he had given the order that I had advised him to, and sent the men to Lothian to kill the child. He said that Morgan had told him that the child was a boy, his son, and he had nodded, and said that he had said the words. He looked broken, and heavy with regret, but it was all the more important if his bastard child was a boy for all trace of him to be gone.

When I asked the men, none of them had dared to carry out such an awful request, for they had been afraid it was spoken in anger, or upset. I commanded them to do it, on pain of death, and stood and watched as the small band of men in unmarked armour rode away. And I prayed that they would succeed in their task.

I did not know how Arthur would survive this. How he would come out of it being the King he needed to be, if he persisted in sighing and mourning for what he had done. Yes, it had been awful. Yes, the child and everything about its birth and death an abomination, but he was a boy, and he had all of his life ahead of him. He walked around his own castle under a heaviness that all could see.

That was no way to live as King. He was not yet sixteen years old. This could not be the end of him.

"He needs to be distracted," I said to Ector.

He nodded silently.

* * *

Some of the noblemen who had come to pledge to the war in Arthur's cause had brought their daughters. I knew what they wanted. They wanted Arthur to marry one of them. But he would not. He was High King of Britain, and it would be one of the princesses of Britain or the continent for him, not some nobleman's daughter. Still, it presented an opportunity for him to be distracted. Some were young, and beautiful. I hoped that his taste was not all for grown women Morgawse's age. A young girl would be good for him. She would, besides, be neither experienced nor cynical enough to try to manipulate him and turn the situation to her advantage.

It did not take long for me to spot a suitable girl. She was the daughter of one of Arthur's liege lords, some man named Bors, as they all seemed to be those days, who held some lands in the North. Important country in a war fought against Lothian. His daughter was tall and slender with thick pale-gold hair wound in a plait down her back. I supposed that she was about Arthur's age, or a little younger. Fourteen, fifteen, something like that. She had big, blue eyes, wide with innocence, and pale gold freckles just across the bridge of her nose. She was very beautiful. I saw her first talking with Kay. He stood leaning against the wall beside her, giving her a glimpse of his charming smile, leaning down to whisper something in her ear. Well, he could have his sport with someone else. Arthur needed a good, noble girl his own age to distract him. Kay would be satisfied with anyone, from what I had heard from his father. There were plenty of handsome young knights in the hall, many of whom, I was sure, would not pass up the offer. Kay was a charming, good-looking boy. He would find someone else.

I slipped into the chair beside her father, smoothing down the skirts of my dress as though distracted, and without looking at him, I said, quietly, "How well, my lord, would you like to be grandfather to the son of the King of Britain?"

I could feel him turn to look at me. Perhaps he was shocked.

"My lady…" he stammered. "It would be an honour. But my daughter, Lionors, she is a girl of virtue. I –"

"I can ensure no scandal falls on her, and the appropriate recognition is given, my lord," I interrupted. "Give only your consent, and I shall ensure the favour of the King falls on her."

He gazed over at his daughter. Kay's fingers were brushing against the plait of her hair where it lay on her shoulder, and he stiffened beside me. I almost made some comment, as I saw her smile at him in return, about how she did not seem all that virtuous in her intention, but I checked myself. I did not want to offend the old man.

"As I said, Lady Igraine, I would be honoured," he answered tersely. So, he wanted me to walk over now and pull Lionors from Kay's charms. I was willing.

I felt his eyes follow me as I did not go over, but slipped back into my seat at Arthur's side. He was staring down at his plate, lost in some deep, awful thought. I wanted to put my hand on his shoulder, to kiss the top of his head. But he would not have welcomed that from me. I drew in a breath, and collected myself. This must be done. I had been thrown about between men for the sake of the land, the future of the kingdom. This was no different, no worse. It was more than a girl of her station might reasonably hope for.

"Lionors," I called, across the hall, and she jumped back from Kay, blushing a little. Good, she knew that she should not have been so taken in by a man who was barely more than a common soldier. "Won't you come and sit with me?"

Flustered, she curtseyed. "Of course, Queen Igraine."

She rushed to my side, and I gave her a gentle smile. She did not need to suffer on account of it. I would take care of her. There was nothing for her to be afraid of.

I did not introduce her to Arthur, though I did sit her the other side of me, and turn my back to him. I asked her about herself, complimented her pretty dress and hair, and from over my shoulder, I knew that Arthur was looking at her. I knew that he caught her eye, because suddenly she blushed, dark, and gazed down at her hands, twisting together in her lap. I felt a little rush of triumph. There was far more in her look than there had been in her casual flirting with Kay. I supposed she might have been a little dazzled by Arthur, in his father's old red and gold surcoat, with the crown on his head, when from far away he would have seemed small, and hunched with the weight of his new kingship.

At the end of the evening I kissed her on the cheek, and bade her come and attend on me the next day. I kissed Arthur on the cheek as well. He seemed to barely feel it. He did not respond. I supposed it was the kiss of someone who was barely more than a stranger, and meant little to him, after all.

Chapter fifty-seven

News came that Lot's army had marched into Northumbria, and Arthur's amassed forces prepared to move. The night before the army marched out, all the men in Camelot were feasting and drinking for the last time. I stood back and watched it all with detached disgust. They were all the same. Animals, compelled by hunger and fear and lust. I watched as Lionors slid into Arthur's lap, and Arthur, drunk, wrapped his arms around her, and kissed her, letting the cup of wine fall from his hand, and, spilling, roll away under his father's great high table. It had been even easier than I thought it would be. But then, I should have known. Men were simple, women were simple. If two wanted the same thing – or thought they did – then it was easy to throw them together. Ector, beside me, watching with the same remove, the same distaste, sighed. His own son by blood was also tangled up with a girl, limbs wound with limbs, his hands in her dark hair, her body pressed against his. She was a servant, from her clothes, but it hardly mattered for him, and I think Ector was just glad that Kay was not publicly entwined with a boy.

I watched as Arthur took Lionors by the hand and led her from the feast and up to the King's rooms he now occupied as his own. And I knew he would not treat that great King's bed with the sanctity his father had done, sharing it only with his wife. He had already had Morgawse in it, I was sure of that. Had he taken her by the hand and led her up there, just the same? Or had she already known the way? What if she had slipped up those stairs many dark nights when I was asleep in my own chamber? I could picture her, her cloak sliding from her shoulders, her usually careless hands suddenly ready to be set to purpose. Uther stripped to his shirt, holding the door open, the moonlight catching only his profile. Morgawse, with one sly look over her shoulder, disappearing inside. How did I know, now, that she had not done so? How did I know, now, what she was capable of?

* * *

I waited in the courtyard the next day for Arthur to come and greet his gathered army, to give them orders. I supposed I wrongly assumed that he had a plan, for Uther had always been so assured, and Arthur looked so like him at times; so like him and yet so entirely different. Gentle where Uther was rough, hesitant where Uther was sure. I had taught him to manage his household, but I was no battle-general. I was expecting a king, but I had a frightened boy.

I looked for him around the castle, but I knew where he was. In his chamber. Hiding. I knocked on the door. There was no answer. I sighed. I knew he was in there. He had been drinking too much, carousing too much, feeling too sorry for himself. It was time that he stopped. War had been declared throughout Britain, and he was going to have to become a man all at once. And a king. There would be time for mercy later, for enjoyment. Perhaps even time for us to get to know one another. Right now, he needed to put on Uther's armour, get on his horse, and lead his army north.

"Arthur," I called. No response again. I flicked open the latch. It wasn't bolted. Good. I didn't want to have to embarrass him by calling for one of the knights to throw their shoulder against the door. I wished, fleetingly, that I had not left Brastias behind to hold Tintagel.

It was dark and stuffy in the room, and it smelled of wine. The morning light, which was already bright outside, since it was still just about summer and approaching prime, filled the room with an oppressive orange light through the shutters and the heavy brocade cloth Arthur had stuffed over them to keep it out. I wondered, distantly, if Morgawse – who had never seemed, even as child, to want to wake before full light – was still up to the same tricks in Lothian.

I wrenched open the shutters and light flooded into the room that used to be the room I shared with Uther. Arthur hadn't bothered to draw the bed-curtains closed – had he had bed-curtains in Ector's house? I did not know – and as the light reached him he rolled onto his front, and groaned, and wrapped his arms around his head. There was a shape beside him in the bed, and I recognised the light gold hair of Lionors. That was something, I supposed.

"Arthur, wake up," I said, sharply.

Shocked by the sound of my voice, the voice of someone unfamiliar, Arthur jerked awake. When he saw me standing at the foot of the bed, my arms crossed over my chest, he blushed, dark. So, he was still a child, still embarrassed at being found with this woman or that. And what if I had wandered in to Camelot to find him still in bed with Morgawse? The pair of them were so fond of sleeping in, I might well have done, if I had arrived earlier in the day.

"Queen Igraine…" he said, groggily, and I feel it prickle against my skin, that in his sleepy waking state he reverted to the most formal tone of address, and neither of us could even pretend we were more than strangers.

"It is almost prime, Arthur. The men are restless, they want to ride north."

Lionors, beside him, was stirring awake, and I could see the dark flush of shame on her neck and cheeks as well. She gathered a handful of the covers close to her chest, shrinking away. I did not look at her. I did not come here to embarrass her. I wanted her to continue to distract Arthur.

"Come down to the council chamber, Arthur," I said gently, adding, "Once you are dressed."

* * *

Ector was there before me, and Kay, lounging against the wall as though the whole thing bored him, though I was sure it did not. I had heard things. Rumours. Arguments between Arthur and Kay that had been overheard, when Morgawse was staying in Camelot. I had the distinct impression that Kay was more worried for the boy – the man – who had been his little brother than he would like to show. But he was proud as well, wounded that Arthur had not listened to him. I could not make him out, Kay. He was not really like Ector at all, nor was he very much like the little glimpse of Viviane that I had seen. Perhaps in a different time, in a different place, he would have had her wicked joy. Now, he was quiet and tense, and affecting an air of disinterest.

Arthur arrived still blushing, still flustered, Uther's old surcoat over his shirt and breeches in an attempt to fill his father's place. He did not fill it out so full as Uther had, but he was young yet, and if he survived this war then it would make him strong. It was my intention that, above all else, Arthur would survive.

"What is to be done, my lord Arthur?" Bors, the dull half-brother of Ector asked. Though he always insisted he was French, I noticed that his voice had the rough tones of Northern England. Ector, too, had lost that French purr that he had had when he arrived at Tintagel all those years ago. Well, he had been a young man when he came to Britain, and had lived more than half his life here. Bors, I suspected, had not been raised in Ban's great castle. Why else would the son of a king command only the place of a knight at Arthur's court? Acknowledged son, yes, but legitimate? I was not so sure.

Arthur shook his head. "We must ride north. Beyond this…"

He glanced warily at me, as though he expected me to scold him.

"First," I began, "we must consider our allies. My castellan in Cornwall has a small garrison, half of whom we will send, but Cornwall is not a military country; it can defend itself for siege, but it cannot make open war, and we have little to give to Camelot in the way of men, or horses, or weapons. We have Wales, led from Uriens in Rheged castle. And we have Avalon."

A murmur went around the small party of knights gathered in the room, half approving, half disapproving. Witches, I heard among the whispering.

"But the Lady of Avalon is dead," Percival, the stern, quiet knight objected.

"Another will have risen to take her place," I replied, dismissive.

"They are just an island of women," Bors cut in.

I turned to look him in the eye. "If you do not fear them, Bors, I invite you to challenge their power, see how well you fare."

He shrank back, afraid even of me, of my vague threat.

Merlin, who somehow I had not noticed, stepped forward then. Had he come in another shape? Bors jumped when he noticed him, but Arthur did not, as if he had been aware of Merlin all along. I saw the way he looked at him. With absolute trust. Merlin had led him to the sword that made him King. There was no thought in his head that Merlin might have anything to gain from it.

"Avalon will stand with the rightful king of Britain, and there has never been a war fought in Britain where the side favoured by the Lady of Avalon did not win." He turned to Arthur. "The lady Viviane was by your father's side when he conquered Britain, and you will be kept safe by her successor, and by your sword, and by its scabbard."

Arthur nodded, looking dazed, touching his hand to the hilt in a gesture of automatic comfort.

"There is," Merlin continued, "a way to make victory more secure. Marry Isolde of Ireland. Then the Irish will fight for us, and not for Lot."

"They ought to fight for us anyway," I said, peevishly. "My sister was the wife of one of their princes, and gave him two sons."

"But they will not," Merlin replied smoothly, "because Lot has more gold than we have, and he is experienced and skilled on the battlefield, and he has five sons. All that stands in my lord Arthur's favour – if you will forgive me, my liege – is that he is Uther's rightful heir, and he has Avalon behind him."

I knew that Merlin was right. I glanced at Arthur, questioningly. A look had passed between him and Kay.

"I do not want to marry, not before the war is over."

Does he think he is being noble? Perhaps he was. Still, it would be wiser for him to leave a son behind that wasn't inside his sister, before he plunged into the battle.

"Very well," Arthur continued, gathering himself, and I saw a flash of his father's cold, military determination cross his face. "Do we set out immediately? If we are faster, then we catch King Lot by surprise. But is it wise to make the troops march in this heat?"

At last, he was thinking like a solider. Like a leader. Like a king. I felt relief flood through my body. Perhaps he would grow quickly into the role after all.

Ector shook his head. "It will tire them." He pulled the map on the table towards him, and began drawing imaginary lines with his fingers. Long ago, he must have learned from the Latin books of Caesar's campaigns, and Livy's histories, and Tacitus' account of the German wars, how to plot strategy. That was what they taught princelings in France. Why had he not taught Arthur? Or his own son? Had he thought it would never be necessary for either of them? Or had he just been too blank with grief at the loss of his wife? "We can march tonight, from when dusk falls to darkness, to this woodland here. Camp overnight. Set off before it gets light and, if we are lucky, we will reach the woodland here." He pointed on the map. "Further north the wood thins out, and there's more moorland, but hopefully it will be colder by then. We should be able to march the troops to the Northumbrian border in a week and a half. Uriens will be waiting there with his army. We won't be there before the Lothians, but we will be there before they expect us."

A week and a half. They'd have to march like the Roman legions to get there that fast, just on mornings and dusk-to-darkness to avoid the heat. But I did not say anything.

The plans were drawn up, detailed and agreed. I did not say that I was planning to ride with them. I thought they might try to stop me. Bors would object, great oaf that he was. Merlin might not like it. I planned to write to Avalon, to whoever was lady there – Nimue, most probably – that night. When everyone else dispersed to pack their belongings, I did as well, but as I closed the door behind me, I heard Arthur's voice, and I lingered.

"Do you remember what day it is today, Kay?" he asked, quietly.

"Of course I remember," Kay snapped.

"I should like to go to see our mother if we –"

"Our mother? You just saw your mother."

"She's not my mother. Not really. It's not fair for you to –"

"Funny," Kay replied, bitterly, "that you say that now. You were quick to remind me that we were of different blood when I was telling you not to go to bed with the Queen of Lothian. Quick to remind me that you were a king, and you could do as you pleased."

"Kay –"

"No, don't, Arthur. It's fine."

"I wasn't going to apologise," Arthur said, tersely.

"I know you weren't," Kay said. "I just wanted to pretend to myself that you are even a little bit sorry about all of this."

"Kay," Arthur began, and there was an awful tone of pleading in his voice, "I don't want to fight with you about this. Not today. I regret all of it. Can't we just – I want to go to Amesbury. Can't we just ride there, and see her, see the tomb?"

Kay gave a rough laugh. "Through the armies waiting for us? I wish we could, Arthur."

"I wish it could all be undone," Arthur said, very softly, and I felt it strike me at the core. He didn't want me. Or to be King. Or to be Uther's son.

"Well, it cannot, Arthur. But some things don't have to change." Kay's voice softened, just a little. "I will… always be here."

"I know, Kay."

But they did not know. No man's life was certain in war, and Kay, as well-meaning as he was, could no more promise to live than I could, or Arthur, or any other man or woman. They meant everything to each other, as brothers ought, as my surviving sister never had to me, and I felt the raw burn of jealousy. She is not my mother, Arthur said. I never would be to him. The bright-eyed fairy woman whose death he had mourned was the only mother he would ever hold in his heart. I had made the sacrifices of a mother, not she. But it could not be changed.

Chapter fifty-eight

Once the army was on the move, Arthur suddenly seemed to come into himself. I supposed that it was in his blood. Uther had never liked politics or negotiations either. He wanted to fight. I could see it in Arthur's eyes. As soon as he was astride his horse and on the road with Kay beside him bearing his father's banner, the blue-green dragon, he sat tall in the saddle, and he was calm and intense. It came over him like a spell, and as he leant over the map in the evening with Ector, he nodded in careful attention – attention I was sure he had never paid to his books – and approached it all with the calm intensity of a natural warrior. I felt a thrill to see it. To imagine what a fine king my son would become. Finer than his father. Arthur had everything that Uther had had, and he had time to learn more.

One evening, as we crossed the Pennine hills, I found myself alone with Arthur. He had been focussed and assured in the council meeting, but we expected to clash with the enemy on the next day, and I could tell that he was nervous. The thought struck me that he had never killed a man before. What cause would he have had for that? He was well-trained. I could see that from the way he held a sword, but he was not yet seventeen years old, and he had grown up under Uther's peace.

"What was my father like?" he asked, softly, staring out of the open flap of his tent at the camp surrounding us, slowly falling dark as fires were extinguished and the men began to sleep. "In battle?"

"He was fearsome, Arthur. I never saw him – but I know. Men talk about such things. But he was not a merciful man. He was a great man, but he was a harsh man. Unyielding. A time will come when you will need to show mercy in this war. If you do not, it will be too great, too absolute. It will destroy Britain if you clash with five of its kings until they are all dead."

Arthur nodded, saying nothing for a long time.

"But King Lot of Lothian… he is an old man?" Arthur asked, hopefully.

What had Morgawse been telling him? Of course, Lot was older than Arthur, older than Morgawse, but he was in his fifties, still strong. He was by no means an old man, not like Leodegrance in Carhais who walked bent over his stick, and whose hair was almost all grey.

"Lot of Lothian is one of the most ruthless and experienced killers in Britain. He has five strong sons, three of whom are of age to be riding to battle beside him." I felt a stab of fear at the thought of my grandsons. I prayed that Morgawse had been sensible enough to keep them in Lothian. I felt, too, an unpleasant spasm of guilt, and to my surprise, longing, for Morgawse. How she must feel, alone in Lothian castle. How she would feel if her sons were among the armies of Lot. I pushed the thought away. She had decided upon her own fate. "You must leave him to someone else, Arthur." I turned to face him, and he met my gaze. "This is not a point of honour, or valour. He will take pleasure in cutting you down. You must not get near him. You must survive. There is no honour in the death of a king that would plunge a kingdom into an awful war."

"But… that is not brave," Arthur said, simply.

"No, Arthur. It is braver not to care what men think. It is braver to live and face the mess you have made, and heal Britain. There is nothing brave about rushing into the arms of death."

"But I might not –"

"You would, Arthur. You would not survive coming sword-to-sword with Lot. This is a boy's dream. Leave that to another man. One with less to lose."

Arthur nodded, but I could tell he was not happy. Such was the way with boys who had never seen war. Their heads were filled with stories about brave knights risking everything for this lady or that. But he had to forget that. Besides, Morgawse was not his lady. I wondered if he was thinking of his sister, far to the north. I wondered what they had whispered together. I wondered if she had said anything to him about me, about his father. I did not ask. If she had, I did not want to know.

* * *

At first, I was afraid for Arthur out on the battlefield. He was untried, untested. I had heard him boasting, as boys did, that no other boy had been able to best him in any of the mock-fighting tournaments. That meant nothing in war. It was the highborn who won the tournaments. It was the ruthless who won at war.

But Arthur was ruthless. I had not expected it. He was usually so mild, but out on the battlefield he had the wild intensity I had seen when he had been talking the business of war with Ector, and it only increased. As Arthur found he had a talent for battle, he found also that he had a taste for bloodshed. I encouraged it. In the evenings, as winter drew nearer and we gathered together in one tent around the fire, I told tales of Uther's days at war. The only questioning eyes were Ector's, and I knew he would not challenge me. He knew how important it was that Arthur believed in his own strength.

But Arthur did have talent on the battlefield. So, it seemed, did Kay. Before winter fully set in, Kay had slain the King of the Vale in battle, after the King of the Vale had caught Arthur by surprise, and slashed him across the chest, cracking the steel breastplate like a nut. Kay had killed him, and brought Arthur back on his own horse. Arthur was covered in blood, and I had been scared for his life, but hardly any of it was his. There was a wound, a cut across his chest, and Nimue, the new Lady of Avalon, appeared silently in his tent like a ghost, and healed it tight and sound so that the infection could not get in. I remembered her lovely face, her quiet way. I resolved even more firmly to seek her help against Merlin. I was glad, besides, that Avalon was still watching over us, over Arthur.

* * *

The winter was hard. Arthur send half the troops back to Camelot with Kay, worried that they would not survive the cold and

338

the hunger. He stayed with the rest of the army, in the castle of Lionors' father. That was another advantage that the Lothians had. They were used to the cold. But the Bretons were not. I thought of Melita and her sons in their light leather armour. Did they borrow furs from the northern armies, or just shiver in their tents? It suddenly occurred to me that there was one ally we had not sought, either of us: the French. They would have gone with Arthur, for Ector's sake. Or perhaps they would not have done – for Ector's sake.

I thought of my daughters when midwinter and Christmas came and I could not enjoy even the meagre festivities. I thought of Morgan, alone in Rheged castle. She was with child as well, I had heard. Had she written to me, or had Uriens told me? I could not remember. It was all a blur. But she would be there, pregnant and alone. I thought of Morgawse as well, though I did not want to. Thinking of Morgawse made me feel an unpleasant mix of heavy with guilt and hot with anger. But also hollow with pity. She would be alone. She would have had her son taken from her, and killed. Would her sons with Lot stand by their mother, or would they all side with their father and his wounded pride? I remembered suddenly, vividly, the energetic, outgoing, grubby little girl who stole honeycombs from the kitchen in Tintagel, and got them tangled in her red-gold hair. Who at seven could throw one of the boys' practice spears and hit a mark none of the boys could manage, but who couldn't eat her dinner without spilling it down herself. Who wriggled and complained when asked to learn her Latin letters, but who listened rapt to her father's tales in Welsh Gaelic as though she understood every single word, when I knew it was as unfamiliar to her as it was to me. I had loved that little girl as intensely – more intensely – than my own life. When had it changed? When her father died, I supposed, and she had blamed me. I wondered if she believed that I had plotted the murder with Uther. But then I remembered how she had grown. Beautiful, and sly with it. Shrewd, bitter, willing to use her loveliness as a weapon to punish me and Uther. Punish me for everything she blamed me for. I glanced over at Arthur, who seemed as merry as the rest of his men. When we had only just pitched camp in the summer, I had overheard him and Kay talking about her. Arthur had said, I still dream sometimes, that I am… with her. When I do, I wake retching, and I think I can taste her perfume in my mouth, and it's choking me. This ought to have comforted me, that Arthur was disgusted with the thought of Morgawse, and what had passed between them, but somehow, it had made me feel an empty sense of dread in the pit of my stomach that, try as I might, I could not explain.

It was not until the first green shoots of spring began to show that Arthur's army clashed with the full amassed force of Lot and all his allies. There were more than I had thought, too. Not just the Bretons, and the Irish, and those left from the Vale, but Saracen mercenaries who rode huge, dark horses and swung nasty-looking crescent-shaped swords, hooked like scythes. But they were no match for Arthur's forces. Though we were fewer, Arthur had grown into an inspiring leader. He did not talk much. He was no battlefield speech-giver like Julius Caesar from the history books – although who knew how much of that was written long after, perhaps Caesar himself had been silent as Arthur on the battlefield – but the men saw the fearless way he threw himself into battle, and said that he was the very image of Uther. As I watched, day by day, Arthur leading back his band of closest knights, all unharmed, and Lot's maimed army limping back to its camp, I realised not only was Arthur winning, but his army was slaughtering the enemy. It wasn't just warfare. It was massacre. I had feared for their lives, for all of us, but the men who fought for Lot fought for money. The men who fought for Arthur fought for Britain, for the banner of Uther the Dragonking.

Still, among the enemy were those I cared about. One of the legions of Lot's army was led by one who carried Lot's shield, the two-headed gryphon, but who was not Lot, and sat on his horse towering head and shoulders over the other men. He could have been none but one of my grandsons. I could not tell if it was Gawain or Aggravain. I prayed that whoever it was would not be among the dead, counted each day. I began to climb up the tall hill overlooking the plain where the forces were now meeting, each trying to push the other back. We were in Lothian now, Arthur having swept Lot's forces from Northumbria, and it was bare, and rocky. It was hard to fight in, but from the crest of the hill, it was easy for me to see.

On one of those early spring days, I saw the Breton princes set upon Arthur, all three of them – or were they four? I could not remember – and from far away I saw a tangle of horses, and red hair. Someone went down, but it was not Arthur. A knight of his? One of the Breton princes? I could smell blood and steel on the air, along with the new smell of snowdrops and young grass. Disconcerting. Then, as if from nowhere, the Breton queen rode in at the head of a pack of mounted – what were they? I could hardly call the Breton soldiers knights… warriors? Ector, Uriens and Arthur were all tangled up with them, but I saw the queen's horse go down, and the men –

Arthur's men, for the Breton princes had disappeared under the hooves of the horses as surely as if they had melted away – swarmed over her like so many ugly black ants. I felt my stomach clench with revulsion. Slaughter. I had already turned my back when I heard the trumpets calling Lot's crippled army to retreat.

Chapter fifty-nine

I could hear shouting outside the tent. Men arguing. Arthur's voice. He shouldn't have been squabbling with his men.

But as they came in through the door, I could see what it was about. I had thought I saw Melita, Queen of the Bretons, fall in battle and get swarmed over by a pack of knights. I thought Arthur had ignored my words, or forgotten them, the ones about mercy. He had not. Arthur had not, for he seemed to be arguing with Uriens, who had his hand clamped around the back of the neck of the Breton queen who had been dragged bruised and broken from the battlefield, about her fate. I felt a spasm of dislike for my daughter's new husband, and regret that she, the dearest and most delicate of all my children, should have been the one to end with so rough a spouse. Ector and Bors stood, too, at the back of the tent, but it seemed that whatever argument had been beginning outside the tent had been stilled by my presence, a reminder that Arthur was King, and I Queen, and though Uriens was the older and more experienced solider, it was Arthur and I who would make the final call.

I straightened a little, ready to speak, to give an order, to rebuke them for squabbling, but I caught Melita's eye, and I felt myself hesitate. So proud, so wild, so stubborn her gaze, even now with her arms tied behind her back, her cheek swelling from a blow she had not taken in battle, a line of blood threading her lip, too, and darkening the inside of one nostril. Someone had struck her for the amusement of degrading a queen when they had her captured. It was sickening. And worst of all, as I stood there, I could not help but imagine myself in her place. A defeated queen with a man's hand around the back of my neck. I knew what it was to watch an enemy, a victor, ride through my castle gates and know that I had no protection left. I knew the fragile dignity of a conquered queen. And yet, I was not her. She was wild, I prudent. I had given Morgawse at twelve years old to a man who had promised the pair of us violence and only the most precarious of protections, to keep her safe. Melita had thrown herself into his war because she was too proud to even consider pledging her only daughter to the honour of the throne of Britain. Though I was sure it was not only that. Not only about ancient, magic blood, but more about pride, and customs, and foreignness. They didn't like our ways. They hadn't liked our King.

"What is your will, Arthur?" I asked, steadily. I noticed some of the men shifting uneasily on their feet in the corner of my vision. I heard what people said. Queen Regent, they said. He's too old to be listening to the old queen now; he's not a boy anymore. Perhaps. But while my son still wanted to hear, I would still speak.

Arthur's mouth opened, but he did not speak. Kay rushed in through the open tent flap, spattered with blood across his armour, his helm thrown off, his face flushed, his thick, dark hair plastered to his forehead with sweat and dirt. His dark eyes shone with the last of the battlefield fervour. Arthur turned to him as though they were alone, and threw his arms around him. I could see Kay's chest still rising and falling hard. He didn't seem to feel whatever wound it was leaking blood from the shoulder joint in his black platemail. He was relieved to be alive.

"Arthur," I persisted. I felt the awful burn of guilt to be calling him away from the joy and comfort of his brother, alive and in his embrace, but this had to be dealt with. Slowly, he drew away from Kay. I could see that his eyes were shining. Had Kay gone down in that huge melee in the battle and I not seen? I had not been looking out for him. Ector, beside me, was quiet and watchful. "You must decide what is to be done with the prisoner. We may ransom her, but we do not need gold, and Carhais does not have much gold to give. It would, therefore, be wiser to exchange her."

"For whom?" Arthur asked, his face blank with defeat in the face of diplomacy. His skill was in warfare, not here. "They have no prisoners of ours."

I shook my head. "They do not." I looked uneasily between Ector and Arthur once more. "But there is one there for whom we might make an exchange of the Queen, to end this war. A princess, about your age."

Arthur didn't catch on, but Kay did, and whispered in his ear. Arthur nodded, slowly.

"But would it be sure? I can't – I don't... Is it not better to end this thing decisively?"

He still doesn't want to marry, I thought. He is only just seventeen years old. He wants to live the life he planned for, working Ector's farm and groping the dairymaids.

"Peace is better than ever more war, Arthur," I said. "Peace is always better."

"The Bretons will not agree to it," Merlin said, with a self-satisfied sneer. I jumped when he spoke, despite myself, for I had not noticed him leaking into the tent like a bad smell, always there, always hanging close to Arthur. Of course, Merlin would object to this. It would win Arthur a wife with the magic blood of Maev the witch-queen of Cruachan, as the girl's father told it, and that would give him some protection against Merlin's magic. How much, I could not be sure, but Merlin's discouragement of the match only made me sure it would do Arthur good.

"We should make the offer," I pressed.

Uriens, whom I had forgotten, and whom I disliked more and more every time he spoke, said, "Who shall do that? None of us speaks Breton."

"Do you understand me?" I said to Melita, in French. She did not respond, but I saw her eyes flicker over to me, though she tried to hide it. So, she did not speak English, but she spoke French. That was well enough. I had learned it as a girl, from Erec and Enid, and from my books.

"Leave me with her," I commanded. The men looked between themselves, but when Arthur did not question me, with a slight murmur of discontent, even Merlin left without objection. I felt Ector's eyes brush over me, and I pushed back the momentary distraction, the desire to reach out and take his hand in public, to press my mouth to his and demand comfort, relief, oblivion. Let me be a woman, and not a queen. Love me as though you love me. I pushed it away. It lingered for a moment – his beard, thick and soft against my lips, his hands closing tight around my thighs, the heat of his mouth – and then it passed away, engulfed by what had to be done.

Uriens gave Melita a final, cruel shove forwards as he left, and she stumbled. I almost jumped forward to catch her, but I could not have risked such a show of sympathy in front of the men, and I needed to be alone with her, to talk her into seeing sense. I was glad that she was steady on her feet, even though her hands were bound. I did not think I could have borne to see such a proud queen landing face-down in the mud, without imagining myself in her place.

"Do you want to live, Melita?" I asked her, flatly.

She did not pretend she did not understand my French. Neither of us could be bothered with the pretence.

"Death is better than dishonour," she replied. She was wrong.

"What about your daughter?" I asked, pointedly. "What is better for her? Your dishonour, or your death?"

Melita spat at my feet. I raised my eyebrows in cool nonchalance. I supposed she thought I was some kind of palace prissy who would be intimidated by her. Everyone else seemed to think so. They were wrong. I knew more about war and suffering, bloodshed and lies than most of the men combined. And I knew more than Melita. She must have been naïve indeed to believe so in honour.

"What will happen to Carhais, to your girl, if you die, Melita?"

"You treat girls like cattle here. I will not trade her."

I sighed heavily. "I am sure you will not believe me, Melita, but I want to help you. Wouldn't it be better if the war ended sooner, with your daughter as Queen of Britain, than years later with her and your people starving to death in Carhais?"

She gave a rough laugh. "You want to marry her to your brute of a son? You would have him take her to his bed with the blood of her brothers still on his hands?"

I took a step closer. She stank of sweat and blood. "She would not be the first bride touched with blood."

"Your son lays his dirty hands on her, she will slit his throat while he sleeps," she hissed, leaning in towards me, her teeth bared like an animal. "We will not surrender. Not to you. Not to your boy."

"You must surrender, if you want to survive. If you want your daughter to survive." She was stubborn, pig-headed, ignorant. No desire to save herself or her family. I drew myself back, felt myself becoming cold, detached, dispassionate. I no longer imagined myself in her place. I would never have been so proud, so stupid.

"I will never surrender.

"Well, then I cannot help you," I said.

Uriens came in when I called him, and dragged her away.

* * *

By the time full summer came, I had returned to Camelot with the small band of men Arthur sent back there, led by Kay. I was tired of the front lines, of the pavilions, of listening to the men at night shouting, drinking and whoring. I was tired of watching the camp-followers in the morning, bedraggled and diseased and exhausted, creeping back to their group of low tents on the edge of the camp. It was hard to think of them as women, the same as I was. They were pathetic and dirty, and the thought of it made me feel awful, and hollow and vulnerable. I warned Arthur in no uncertain terms to stay away from them. He was King; there would always be a plentiful supply of clean, noble women, eager to meet his every need. Let the men take their chances with the whores. He had seemed alarmed that I would talk about it so openly, but what good would it have done to wait until it was too late? But I didn't like, either, thinking of him alone, dreaming of Morgawse. I had Lionors sent back to her father's castle, which was near enough Arthur's camp. She was glad, thought it an honour. I supposed I was growing cold, and manipulative. But perhaps I had always been that way. People talked so much about it, said so many different things, I could no longer quite remember for sure if I had spent fifteen years playing some awful game of chase with Uther, if Gorlois had been part of it all, or if I had been some kind of silly, naive girl. I could not really believe that I had been. I did not want to believe that I had been foolish. Better to believe that I had been cruel.

Back at Camelot there was much to attend to. The castle had been neglected without either its Seneschal or its Queen. Provisions had been pillaged through in the winter, and though it was getting towards the end of summer, there was hardly anything in the stores. I found, to my surprise, that when he wasn't chasing all the young men and women in the castle, Kay was calm and serious and competent as a seneschal. He considered all of my suggestions, and followed most of them. He was young, and of much lower birth than I, and yet I found myself impressed that he did not blindly follow me simply because I was his Queen. He would think carefully about each decision, and nod thoughtfully, and carry it out immediately. Or sometimes he would suggest something, often something better. I remembered Brastias' blind obedience. Brastias, back in Tintagel. I wrote to him, and he to me, but I missed him still. My one constant friend. Perhaps more, if things had turned out differently.

Arthur's victory was near. That much was obvious from Camelot. Men were coming, wanting to pledge. Kay took their pledges, and promised them a proper greeting from their King when they joined their army. If men were coming from the fields and the small towns, that meant that word was spreading, and Arthur's victory was considered far and wide to be a foregone conclusion. That was good. That meant he was safe.

I took advantage of the fact that Merlin was at Arthur's side in the war-camp to the north, and I began making arrangements for Arthur's marriage. Yes, he was young, but it was never too soon for a king to have an heir. I wrote to Emain Macha, and to the Lady of Avalon. I wrote to Carhais as well, though I had had no word from Rheged castle, where they had taken the Queen. Or perhaps I had, and Kay had hidden it from me. He looked at me strangely sometimes, as though he were worried about me. As though he did not think that I had been at the centre of a war before. Or perhaps he was afraid of me, since he knew what I had ordered for Arthur's son with Morgawse. I could not tell.

* * *

Emain Macha sent its princess Isolde, and Kay and I received her with as much grandeur as Camelot could spare, as autumn deepened into winter. There was game, and wine, and the girl did not seem to notice that she was the only one with the apple pie, or the little bowl of plums. She was young, but she was lovely. Big, blue eyes like pools, a slender frame. The white-gold hair that Máel and his brothers had had. She must have been the daughter of one of his older brothers or half-brothers. I wondered what had happened to Elaine's sons. I knew Mark was greedy for Tintagel, having nothing of his own, but I knew nothing of my younger nephew. I pushed away the pang of sorrow and longing, and focussed on the girl in front of me.

"How do you like Camelot, Isolde?" I asked brightly. I noticed Kay pause with his spoon of broth halfway to his mouth, his eyes fixing on her from across the table. I felt a bristle of annoyance. His consideration was not meant to count.

She smiled a big, open smile with her soft pink mouth.

"I like it very much, Lady Igraine."

"Good," I said. "And how old are you, Isolde?"

Isolde thought for a moment, as though the answer were not something at the forefront of her mind.

"I shall be twelve, this spring."

I heard Kay choke on his broth, and I ignored it. She was tall, so I had thought she was a little older. Still, more years of childbearing.

The conversation was pleasant. Isolde was sweet, and gentle. That was clear enough. But I couldn't make up my mind as to whether she would be a good match for Arthur. They were both young, true, and Isolde, though she was charming, would be little help as a queen, so I would have to stay in Camelot to make sure that Arthur had enough guidance that did not come directly from Merlin. But I couldn't be sure there were any other sensible options.

* * *

"It will be no good, Lady Igraine," Kay objected, the next time I met in council with the important men still left in Camelot – which at this point was only myself, Kay and a serious young man named Percival. "She is too young, and she is simple."

346

"It is not for you to decide," I said sharply.

Kay sighed. "No, forgive me. But could Arthur not marry some woman from Avalon? Someone with knowledge of the magic arts? Knowledge of healing?"

I shook my head. I had asked as much from Nimue, and she had claimed there were none there of suitable birth or status. Or the right age. Older women. Women in their thirties. I supposed he could have an older wife, and then take a younger one once her time for childbearing was past, but people didn't like that. Mess. Complication. Second marriages. People had held it against me. Against Uther, for taking the wife of another man.

When Arthur returned for Christmas, secure enough that victory was almost complete, he shook his head in horror when I suggested Isolde.

"Twelve?" he said. "She's just a child. I would... I would hurt her. No, Lady Igraine. I cannot marry a child."

What else did I expect from a boy who at fifteen had, of all the women in Camelot, desired above all one who was almost thirty years of age? I sighed. It was always men – would always be men – who had the freedom to make that choice.

Chapter sixty

War was over by the end of spring. Gawain surrendered to Arthur when Lot was killed, and the armies surrendered with him. The news came when Kay and I were in the council chamber with Percival, whom often I forgot, because he was so quiet. I read the letter with my heart hammering. Arthur was safe. My grandsons were all safe. I could not have been more relieved.

And yet, that night, I dreamed awful dreams. I dreamed of the Bretons, cut down in battle again. I saw it, as if I had been beside them on the field. The first prince – was it Conan? Felix? I did not remember – jumped right from his horse onto Arthur's sword without realising it. He died with his sword arm still raised, and blood trickling from his mouth, red as his hair. He had been twice Arthur's age, but he was half his size. Small, slight. Wiry but, in the end, weak. They hadn't come in steel platemail, and the swords of Arthur's men were cutting through their ranks like scythes through corn. The second prince screamed an awful, painful scream and his horse reared over Arthur, who stabbed up through the beast's chest, and man and horse fell, and tangled together. Someone else finished that prince off, but Arthur was off his horse and spattered with blood by the time the third one – was it the youngest? The one I had seen flirting with his aunt? – threw himself at him. It was painful, how easy it was. A swipe across the neck, and the prince crumpled like a doll. Arthur stared down, frozen, at the heap at his feet. Pausing long enough for the mother to leap from her horse on to him, knocking him off his feet and onto the pile of bloodied, mangled bodies. But it was too late. Hands were closing around her arms, Uriens, Ector, other knights whose names I did not now, and dragging her away. The killing went on. Slaughter. And every time Arthur's sword cut the skin of one of the men, instead of blood, I saw thousands and thousands of tiny black ants swarm out, all over the field, all over the bodies of the Breton princes I had known, all over the bodies of Lot's dead knights. Over the shield of my grandson Gawain as he raised it into the air and roared like a bear, calling the knights back to him. I felt my stomach turn, and I was afraid to open my mouth, lest the little ants swarm out of there, as well.

Suddenly, through my dream, as though he spoke at my ear, I heard Merlin speak.

"The gods curse those who kill for the sake of killing, Arthur. There will be no mercy for you, if you will never have done."

And I heard Arthur reply, low and quiet with resignation, "I cannot. I cannot."

But the war was over. I reminded myself of that when I woke. I wrote once more to Nimue in Avalon, and I wrote to Leodegrance in Carhais. I had not liked him, but perhaps he would be willing to be reasonable now. It was worth presenting Arthur with more than a single princess whom he did not want. There was no reply.

I worried a lot about Morgan, about her child. I had not heard from her. Uriens was unfriendly, unkind and quiet. I had thought he would be like his father Ywain. What kind of mother had raised him to make him so different? Or perhaps I had not understood Ywain at all, and though he had been charming in public perhaps he had been harsh and cold with his son. It did not comfort me much, though, to think that Uriens himself might have suffered at the hands of a cruel father, since Morgan was suffering at his hands. Or perhaps she was not. What had people thought about me and Uther? That he was making me suffer? We had made each other suffer. I had refused to be sorry for marrying Gorlois, and Uther had refused to be sorry for killing him. Perhaps it was the same for Morgan and her husband. I wanted to believe that she had a little of what I had had. But then, I had known Uther a long time, loved him a long time. Uriens and Morgan had married as strangers.

When Arthur returned, I stood in the courtyard to greet him. I felt my body tense with the urge to run out and throw my arms around him, press his face against my breast, smell his hair, hold him as though he had been my son since he was a child. But he would have shied away, or called me madam, or worse, Queen Igraine, and that was worse than not offering myself at all. So I stood, with the crown on my head and, though it was full summer, the rich fur cloak of the Queen of Logrys – that last, I think, I had seen Imogen wear – to greet him not as my son, but as a king.

He rode through the gates on his horse, still dirtied, still even a little bloodied from the battle, on a huge grey horse that was armoured, too, and with his great sword at his side, but his helm thrown off and his gold hair glinting in the sun, almost as bright as the polished metal of his armour. He looked glorious, like some creature sent down from heaven. Beside him, one whom I had not expected, on a white horse – small enough, perhaps, to be a pony, though I did not see how such a little creature could have kept up with the men's warhorses – sat Nimue, her white-gold hair encircled with a white-gold circlet marked with the five-pointed star of Avalon, her childlike body wrapped in a flowing robe of pale blue. Such a strange creature. A beautiful creature, but strange. She had been there, then, at the last. I knew that she was older than Arthur, of an age with Morgan, and yet she looked like a child among those men. So delicate. So small. I was not fooled. I had tasted the power of Avalon. Of Viviane, who could bring a man back to life with the touch of her hands.

At Arthur's other side came Merlin, his face hidden from the touch of the sun in his black cowl. But I could feel his black, beady eyes on me, on my skin, on my heart, stripping me down to my blood and my bones.

"Arthur!" Kay cried beside me, forgetting all formality, all proper behaviour, running forward across the courtyard as Arthur slipped from his horse and the two collided together in an embrace of desperate relief, Kay in his fine surcoat of black and gold, Arthur in his armour, burning from the sun, and dirty from the ride.

"Welcome home, Arthur, King of Britain," I interrupted their brotherly whispering. At the reminder of who he was, Arthur stepped back, and looked up, and nodded with a new solemnity. Oh yes, he knew now what war meant. What kingship meant. The killing, the slaughter that forged a kingdom. Blood spilled. He had tangled with the bodies of the dead on the battlefield every time he fell. He had come back each evening spattered with the blood of men he did not know, that he could not tell apart from his own. He was truly a king now.

I saw that Melita was not with them. So there was to be no trade. No bargain. Someone, somewhere, had given the order for her to be executed. What an end for a warrior queen. Whoever had made that judgement had done so unwisely. It was always better to be merciful to those who could no longer do you harm.

I knew that Arthur wanted to feast and drink with his men, wanted to be with his foster-brother, but I called him to council with me.

Out of his armour, and cleaned and dressed in Uther's old surcoat, he looked his age again. Just seventeen years old. He filled out the surcoat now, having grown thick in the shoulders from swinging the sword and bearing the armour on his back, but his face was still the gentle face of a man just out of boyhood, and he still had that bright, innocent smile – though I saw it a little less now than I had before the war had begun, or perhaps it was tinged with something different. Some new experience.

"Arthur, now that war is over, peace must be consolidated as soon as possible. Do you know what this means?"

"I think so." Arthur nodded, not looking at me. He was staring off into the half-distance. In the evening half-light, with the low orange of the candlelight filling my council chamber he looked even younger than he was. Slightly lost. I wanted to put my hand against his cheek. This man who was not afraid of war was afraid of marriage. Of course he was. What wife would love a husband who told her that he had fathered a child with his sister? But whatever wife he chose would not have to know. The child was gone.

"Arthur." I stepped forward, put a hand against his shoulder, and he jumped around. I saw his muscles tense as though he were preparing to fight, some impulse of the battlefield still in him. But, after a moment, he sighed and relaxed. "This is chance for you to begin again. A foreign girl who will know nothing of the past. Morgawse is far away in Lothian." Arthur flinched when I said her name. "And the child is gone. It can all be forgotten."

Arthur looked at me properly at last, then, his eyes bright with distress. "You do not know, Lady Igraine?"

"Do not know what?" I felt my stomach drop within me.

"Someone warned Morgawse. She still has the child – my son. She still has my son."

I hushed him gently. I wanted to draw him into my arms, but as I stepped towards him, he shied back, and I pretended as though I were reaching for a chair to draw out and sit down in. It must have been Morgan who had warned Morgawse. I wished that she had not, but I could not blame her for loving her sister.

"Did you bring Lionors back with you?" I asked.

Arthur shook his head, looking away again. He was ashamed of himself. So, he had grown tired of her.

"That is for the best, Arthur. Your father kept — well, I lived much of my life as his wife with another woman at court with whom I knew he spent his nights, and it would be all for the best since you will be marrying some girl from far away who does not already — well, she will have no reason to be forgiving. It is better that way."

Arthur looked up at me in disbelief. "My father...?"

"Oh, don't seem so surprised, Arthur. It is common enough for kings," I said, bitterly.

Arthur's face hardened. I did not expect it. He was angry. Angry with me. "Did you even love my father at all? What kind of man was he? What kind of child am I? I have heard what they say, you know. About how — is that why you were rid of me? To keep me away from him?"

"Do not mistake me, Arthur," I said, more sharply than I meant to. "I loved your father. But he was not an easy man to love."

There was a tense moment of silence. That implacable stare — was it Uther's or mine?

"Arthur..." I weakened, I stood, I tried to put my arms around him, but he pushed me away, striding across the room. Sulky, angry. Like his sister. "Arthur, try to understand. It was as I said it was. I had to, to keep you safe. Uther had enemies. It was not through any fault of yours. And I did. I did love your father. He was not a kind man. He was a harsh man. But he was a good king, and I did love him. I loved you too, all those years, though you were far away, and you did not know it. When you are married, it will be permitted for you to have other women. Expected, perhaps. Some for political reasons. Rich widows that might marry someone else, and be a threat to you. Or if your wife cannot give you a child, and she herself is too politically useful to divorce. Don't think about love. Don't imagine the parents who raised you, and hope for that. You are the King, and that is not for you. But always remember that you can have any woman you desire. Oh, I know it sounds harsh, but at least you are not a woman, Arthur. Not a princess. Then you would marry a stranger, and have only him for the rest of your life."

"This is what is expected of me?" Arthur said, thickly.

"This is what is required of you," I replied.

There was a long, quiet pause.

"Who should it be?" Arthur asked softly. He looked back up at me, turning over his shoulder, and I could see that he was lost. Battle was easy for him, politics was hard. Perhaps he should marry a woman who was trained in the art of politics. He should marry one who could help him to rule. One who had been raised to be strong, rather than deferential. A woman a little older, perhaps. If there could not be a woman from Avalon, then Arthur could have the next best thing.

"Send to Carhais, say that you will have the Princess Guinevere as your wife. They will refuse, but they have no grounds to. Instruct your messenger to insist. Their knights are still in Britain, and their Queen and princes are dead. You have the power to insist upon it. She is a little older, perhaps, than is usual for a bride, but from what I have heard the girl has been steward in all but name in her father's kingdom during the war, and she will know how to rule. Have them send her right away."

"Won't she hate me? If I demand –"

I shook my head. "It is a conqueror's right to demand, Arthur. She will know that." I thought of Aurelie, pressing herself against Uther, the things she had said about Breton women and men who won in war. I hoped it was true. I suspected it was not. I had heard, too, that the girl ran around Carhais like the virgin goddess Diana herself, hunting and refusing to be tamed. And I remembered what Melita had said: Your son lays his dirty hands on her, she will slit his throat while he sleeps. But if she did not, she would be able to give him guidance a girl like Isolde could not. "Even if she does hate you, if she is like her mother, she will be a good queen to you. Useful. Strong."

"How old is she?" he asked.

I shrugged. "Morgan's age, or thereabouts."

Arthur nodded thoughtfully. I was glad that he had not seen Isolde. He was easily attracted by pretty girls, and I could not imagine a girl more lovely than Isolde. The Breton girl would not be so neat, so feminine, so enticing, but she would be a better queen. If she was as I expected her to be. I hoped that she was. I was going against Merlin once more, and I hoped that it would be worth it, for Arthur's sake.

Chapter sixty-one

So arrangements were made. Messengers were sent. In the end, I wrote the letter to Leodegrance. I remembered everything he had said to me, long ago, and I knew he would remember my words, and he would know he had lost. I wondered if the girl would come angry, and bearing a grudge. If she knew that it had been Arthur himself who killed two of her brothers, and allowed – I had learned – Uriens to execute her mother. I hoped that she did not. Did they shield their girls from the horrors of war in Carhais, as they did with us in Logrys? I did not know which men Uther had killed. I had even shied away from Brastias' tale, in the end, of how he had come to kill Gorlois.

I packed up my things, for I would no longer be Camelot's Queen. I moved into rooms the other side of the castle, prepared that after Arthur was married I would go to Tintagel, back to my home at last, to Brastias, to the rocks and the sea. That would be the end for me. The end of my time as Queen, which had lasted so long. It felt as though it had been unbearably long.

Arthur was nervous and Merlin angry as the news came that Leodegrance had agreed to the marriage and was sending his daughter over the sea to Arthur. Arthur was nervous, too, because Morgawse would come down with her sons from Lothian, and he would have to face her as he married his new wife. I thought about warning him not to tell his bride, but then I thought perhaps it was better for her to know. I had not enjoyed hearing of Uther's crimes after I had given him my trust, and my love.

I wanted to know when my daughters would arrive. I wanted to see Morgan – painfully, overwhelmingly – and I did want to see Morgawse. I was not sure how I would feel when I did, but I wanted to see her nonetheless. I went to Arthur's council chamber, because I thought that Ector would be there, and he would know, but when I opened the door, it was Arthur and Kay in there, and they jumped to their feet as they heard me come in. Kay's hand found the hilt of his sword, and Arthur drew his, with a flash of steel in the candlelight, so close that it almost cut my face. I jumped back, my heart hammering in my chest, but I could see that they were more afraid than I was. Kay, pale even to his lips, and Arthur, his eyes wide enough that I could see white all the way round the grey irises, both catching their breath, both tensed. I had surprised them. A noise in the night, an unexpected visitor. They were still tensed for war, Arthur more than Kay. Or perhaps he was just the better fighter, the faster to his sword.

Slowly, embarrassed, Arthur lowered his sword.

"Forgive me, Lady Igraine, I was startled, I –"

Had Uther ever been like that? No. War had washed off him like the seas off the stone beneath Tintagel Castle. I looked between them, Arthur and Kay. Boys, still, beneath it all. And afraid.

"War is long over, Arthur," I said, sternly, though it was only a few weeks, "and you are about to invite a foreign princess into your home. Any sign of weakness –"

Arthur nodded, sliding the sword into its scabbard, looking down, ashamed.

"There is nothing… at night, is there, Arthur? You don't wake, or – or scream?"

Arthur shook his head, and I was relieved. I had seen some, heard them. Those who saw war and could not forget. Arthur could not be married to the Breton girl if there were anything that she might tell Leodegrance that might prompt him to attack. Not that he had any of his forces left. But still, always better to be careful.

"That is well, Arthur." I put a hand gently on his shoulder. "Try to forget. It is the only way."

I turned to leave, and Kay called after me, "What was it that you came here for, lady?"

I turned back. "Oh, I wanted to know when my daughters might arrive."

Arthur rubbed his face, sinking a little at the thought of Morgawse returning to Camelot.

"Morgan will come tomorrow. We did not send for Morgawse," Kay said, warily.

I thought about scolding them, telling them that as a vassal queen she had a right to be there, but I did not. Knowing Morgawse, she would come anyway.

As it was, I found, when I stood at my window and watched Morgawse ride into Camelot with Gareth and Gaheris, her two youngest sons by Lot, at her side, and the infant I had tried to have slain held against her breast, wrapped in swathes of fabric to keep him warm, I could not go down. I wanted to. I wanted to be the kind, forgiving mother. I wanted to offer her my love freely. How could I, when I had condemned her son to death? When I would never know whether or not she had seduced my husband? I wanted to be more. I wanted to be better. But I could not. I watched her, small and far away, disappear in the castle, and I did not go to her. It was too late.

I supposed, then, that since she had come only with her youngest, that my two eldest grandsons Gawain and Aggravain were in the castle already. Had sworn into being Arthur's knights on the battlefield. Why hadn't I known that? Men were neglecting to tell me things already. This was Arthur's kingdom now. Not Uther's, not mine. He would have a new queen. I was old. I would be expected to fade gracefully into the background and disappear. It wasn't my business if Gawain had come back with Arthur's army when they pledged, though he was my flesh and blood. Not to them, not to the men. Blood meant something different to us women. It meant childbirth, and faith, and belonging. To the men, it meant war, and conquering. And that was more important than the blood I shared with the twin grandsons whom I had watched being dragged into the world.

And Morgan – Morgan must have arrived after that, late in the night, for in the morning when I steeled myself to speak with Morgawse, going with the intention of asking how she had fared, how her sons were, I found Morgan there as well, in her nightclothes. Something about it irritated me, seeing the two of them like that, huddled together in Morgawse's bedroom as though they were little girls. It was getting towards prime, as well, and Morgan was not dressed. That seemed more like something Morgawse would do. Morgawse who had brought her bastard child with her, no thought to Arthur or his new wife. Perhaps it was an act of deliberate defiance. Perhaps it was an act of motherly love. Either way, she should not have done it, but she was angry when I was terse with her, and she seemed to consider herself Morgan's champion, jumping in to remind me what a cruel mother I was for giving her sister away in marriage as well. Some part of me did not doubt that Morgan had good reason to hide from Uriens with her sister, but I had never hidden, and I was sure that without Morgawse's influence, Morgan could have found a way to be happy. Morgawse filled her head with stories of how cruel Lot was, which, while based in truth, were selective and exaggerated. There had been times when I had seen Morgawse and Lot entwined in passionate kisses, or Lot in moments of uncharacteristic tenderness, kissing her hand or stroking her hair. Yes, she had been young, but this was just another way of punishing me. Trying to make Morgan, too, believe that I was a heartless mother. So I left before long, and I felt heavy and cold. But I had tasks to turn myself to, duties to complete, and it would not be long before Arthur's bride came to her new home.

* * *

I stood at the edge of the courtyard to watch them ride in. I didn't wear my crown, or rich clothes, or jewels. I wanted to see the girl – the woman – without her noticing me. For she would be a woman. Almost twenty years old. It was lucky that Arthur did not look his age. Some men at seventeen still looked like little boys. I wondered what the Breton princess would make of him. I remembered her only as a little girl, of two or three years old, striding around with all the strange confidence of an outgoing child. Like Morgawse had been. It struck me again that as a child she had reminded me of Morgawse. Would she be like my daughter now? Wilful, stubborn and sulky? I hoped not, for Arthur's sake. No, she would be like her mother. Harsh and proud. He needed that. He was gentle, when he was not on the battlefield, and he needed someone with a hard head for politics. Would they have taught her that? Did they teach girls that in Carhais? No one had taught me. It was too late to worry about that now. She would, at least, bear him children. Her mother had had three sons. I had pushed Arthur in the right direction. I was sure of it. I was sure.

I was shaken from my thoughts by the sound of hooves, and I looked up to see Kay at the head of the party, and Arthur behind him on the same horse, a strange, wild grin on his face, his arms wrapped around Kay's waist. Right behind them, the reins of the huge warhorse she rode on clasped confidently in one little white hand, came the princess Guinevere. Even from across the courtyard, the sight of her made me catch my breath. Red, red hair, dark as Gorlois' and Morgawse's red hair was fair, wild and loose, thick red curls of it that tumbled around her, and against which her white face, proud and set, was all the more striking. No mistaking that she was a foreign girl, sat astride the horse like a man, her hair loose, a dress of thin, plain silk – dark green, lovely against her pale skin – that was too obviously either old or borrowed in place of the leather armour she would, like her mother, have been accustomed to wearing. Too tight, too plain for a British princess, the fabric too thin. No jewels, no furs against the chill of the late summer evening. Hitched up to her knees, as well. She slipped from the saddle of her horse – was it not the huge grey horse that Kay had ridden out on? – and jumped to the ground with all the fearless recklessness of one long-accustomed to leaping in and out of the saddle. I would have called someone to lift me down from a horse so tall, and I thought myself a good rider. But the horse was still for her, and calm, as horses were for Kay. There it was, then: the precious magic blood Leodegrance had been so unwilling to share.

"Exquisite, don't you think?" Merlin sneered beside me. I had not seen him, but I held back the impulse to jump in surprise, not wanting to give him the satisfaction. I did not look at him.

"What a prize," he continued. "You were once such a prize, though I suppose that memory is a little faded, now."

It was not. I still remembered standing outside the keep at Tintagel, staring down the narrow path at the men in armour coming through my gates, realising that they were not Gorlois' men, and Morgan in my arms snuggling against me, away from the cold wind, and Morgawse running down the path and into Uther's hands. But I would not give that away to Merlin. I wanted him to think now that I did not care. I shrugged.

"It was different."

"Oh, yes, Lady Igraine, it was." I did not look at him, but I knew he was giving me his unpleasant skullish smile. "For you had wanted Uther all along, and your son and this girl are strangers. But you were afraid. I remember that, Igraine. And she is not. There is only one reason that girls in her situation are not afraid."

It was true. She did not look afraid, down from the horse, and now running her hand down its muzzle as though it were one of the women's ponies, trained to be petted and fussed by silly girls who wanted one as a toy, rather than for war. But the horse was still, and even nuzzled its nose into her hand. She had a strange look on her face; focussed, as though the horse were the most engrossing thing in the world.

"Girls like her, they are not afraid, because they are plotting how they will get home. We two, we should have insisted that Arthur marry Isolde."

I was half-ignoring Merlin. If he had only come to be troublesome then I was not going to pay him attention. But I did remember Aurelie, how she had played Uther in the hope of getting home. That option was not open to Guinevere. She could not offer Arthur the same thing in exchange without binding herself to him. I wondered if, still, she would consider it. I would send a servant to search her things, take away anything she might use to do Arthur harm. I wondered, too, if she were already married, back in Carhais. Certainly, Leodegrance had said that she was bound with one of her own people. What if he was trying to deceive us? But they had been at war the past two years. Not even Leodegrance was stubborn enough to waste a valuable diplomatic token like a daughter at such a time, I did not think. Well, in a few days we would know, I supposed.

It was then that I noticed Arthur, standing holding the reins of the horse Kay was unbuckling the saddle from – though he did not need to, for the horse was obedient and still under Kay's touch. He was gazing over his shoulder at the woman who was to be his wife, a thoughtful half-smile on his face that felt somehow dangerous. I watched his eyes follow her hand as she absently brushed it across her brow and into her red hair, pushing back a handful of it. He looked as though he were coming under some kind of spell, and she was utterly oblivious, ignoring him. She did not seem to know who he was.

She turned away from the horse and called something in Breton to the women she had brought with her, and they gathered to her, three of them, one tall and dark, one little like a bird, almost a head smaller than the princess, and one fair. Arthur stepped out into her path to say something to her – I could not hear what – and her eyes flickered over him in detached disdain. She thought he was just some knight, then. She inclined her head a little in acknowledgement, but she did not reply. By then Ector had come across the courtyard to greet her, and she followed him inside, up to the rooms that were no longer my own. I felt a heaviness in the pit of my stomach. This, truly, was the end of my time as Queen.

Chapter sixty-two

When I was sure that the small party was gone, I went out across the courtyard to Kay, who was unsaddling the rest of the horses. Arthur, Gawain, and Percival – the others who had ridden to Dover to meet her – were gone, and I was partly glad of it. It would be harder to talk plainly with Arthur there.

"Kay," I said, gently, and he looked up from what he was doing.

"Queen Igraine." He turned to me, dropping the buckle he had been fiddling at, and gazing past me, off where the Breton princess has gone. "So, I suppose you have seen the future Queen of Britain."

"Kay… are you sure she is the girl we were promised? Is she…?"

Kay seemed to know what I meant, for he nodded before I had finished and said, in a strange voice that I could not read, "She is the heir to Carhais, all right. That is for sure."

I nodded thoughtfully. "Good. She looks like her mother, but it was best to be sure."

Kay nodded, still gazing off where the women had gone, as though deep in some thought, and he ran a hand through his hair, which stuck up from the sweat of the ride. Suddenly, vividly, I saw his father at his age, how I remembered him from all those years ago. With the dirt of the ride on him, a little dark stubble across his chin, Kay looked less boyish, and very like his father. It was the thoughtful look, as well.

"Thank you, Kay," I said, and he jumped as though he had been lost somewhere else. What had he been thinking about? Surely not the wife his brother was about to take. But I was still thinking about her.

* * *

I wandered through the castle, feeling at a loss. My rooms were now someone else's, my place here transitory rather than permanent, my role now in question. Until tomorrow I would be Queen, and then afterwards – what? Queen Mother? Queen of Tintagel?

I found myself tracing the way automatically back to my rooms, and just as I was about to turn around, back to where I was now staying, I ran into the dark Breton woman who had come with Princess Guinevere, and I realised that I knew her. When she had been a young girl, she had come with the Bretons as the princess' nurse. She gave a nod of deference when she saw me, but said nothing. I wanted to say something. To tell her that I remembered her. To ask if she remembered me. But I did not, and she rushed past me to fetch something or other. She was still lovely, and looked younger than was possible, given that it was seventeen years ago that I had seen her last, and she had been grown then. White skin, black hair, a sprightly, brisk manner. She could have been half my age, when I knew she was only ten years younger or so. I wondered if she and the Breton prince had still been lovers when Arthur had cut him down on the battlefield. If I had been my daughter Morgawse, and bold, I would have stopped her, and asked. But I just watched her disappear. I wondered what they were thinking, here in the home of their old enemy.

I supposed that I ought to talk to Arthur. There would be certain things expected of him tomorrow, when he was married, and he needed to know what those were. When I arrived at his council chamber, I could already hear people talking inside. Arthur, Kay and Ector. It sounded casual, jovial even. Well, I supposed it was easy for them. They were men. They were not waiting to be given away into the hands of an enemy, or remembering what it was like to be deprived of the choice. Why was it so raw? I had thought I had forgotten it all, all the horror that had come with my marriage to Uther. But I could not think of Guinevere, going to sleep in the unfamiliar room, trying not to imagine what the next day would bring, without feeling as though it were happening over again – as it had been for me in those awful days after Uther rode through the gates of Tintagel Castle.

I pushed open the door to see Arthur sat in a chair, his legs stretched out before him, a big, boyish grin across his face. Kay lounged against the table opposite him, an amused half-smile on to match. Only Ector seemed to be suitably serious, sitting against the table like his son, but his arms folded over his chest, his look distant and thoughtful.

Arthur checked himself a little when he saw me, stopped grinning quite so widely, and Kay glanced at me warily as I shut the door behind me.

"Is everything prepared for tomorrow?" I asked them. Ector nodded, but did not look up at me. "Good. Now, Arthur, there will be a lot expected of you tomorrow. The right vassal lords will need to be made to feel important, to be given a special seat, or an honoured role. I can take care of most of it, but you have to –"

Arthur wasn't listening. When he noticed that I had stopped talking, and was staring at him, he blushed a little. I crossed my arms over my chest, annoyed. This wasn't some silly game, some love-match. She wasn't going to be like Lionors; he wouldn't be able to get rid of her if he changed his mind, or got tired of her.

"This is serious, Arthur," I said sharply. "If anything goes wrong, with the ceremony, with the feast, with the princess, then you might have another war on your hands."

Arthur did not look cowed. He was too excited. He put his hands behind his head and leaned back in his chair, still smiling.

"I find that I am eager to be married after all," he said, smiling at Kay, who smiled back in return, a small, thoughtful smile, and gazed down at his feet.

I felt my blood run cold. Arthur did not really understand. Not how this would be for the princess. She would be dressed up in foreign clothes, shoved down the aisle of the church and into his hands, and she would be his property. It did not matter that he seemed to be smitten with the sight of her. It did not matter that she was brave and proud. She would be afraid. I had been afraid with Gorlois, and that had been my own choice. She was little more than a prisoner.

I glanced at Ector, and he looked back at me. I drew in a deep breath. I supposed it was better coming from me, but Ector was

Arthur's parent more than I was. I knew he needed to hear a woman's voice about this, but we were strangers and Ector was his father.

"She is very beautiful, Arthur," I said, carefully. It was not the right word, for she was not, but there was no word for what it was about her that I wanted to describe. She was hard to look away from, wild, the colours of her bright – green, and white, and red. The small, strong body, the bold way she spoke, the careless way she moved. It was inviting, though I could not have said exactly why. She was not doing it on purpose. I could see that. She was not doing it for him. He would have to see that. He would have to be gentle. Persuasive.

"Yes," Arthur replied, smiling more broadly, tipping back a little in his chair. He had Uther's easy, confident movements. "She is, isn't she?"

I could feel Ector looking at me. What did he expect me to say? This was his responsibility as much as it was mine. But I tried again, taking a step forward, and sitting on the edge of the table, facing Arthur. I had all of the impulses of my motherhood in me, and I felt them strongly looking at him. He was rash, too eager, too inexperienced. I wanted to hold him tight, and tell him that I would take care of everything, but I had no right to do that, because I had not raised him. He is my son, and I felt it deep as my bones to look at him, but I was not a mother to him.

"Arthur," Ector began carefully, stepping forward into the small circle of the candlelight. "You will be careful, won't you… tomorrow night?"

So Ector had the same thought I had, the same fears.

"What do you mean?" Arthur asked, a little aggression edging into his voice. With the candle throwing shadows across his face and his brow creased a little in annoyance, he could not have looked more like Uther.

"Arthur," Ector sighed again, "she is a princess. She will not have –" he gave a little cough, though I did not know why he was being quite so coy about it – "known a man before. She will be shy."

"She didn't seem shy," Arthur said, crossing his feet in front of him, and looking down at the toes of his boots for a moment. When he looked up at us again, I became afraid that nothing we could say to him would make any difference. He was lost in it already, the wildness of his desire. "You didn't see the way she spoke to Kay, or the way she hitched up her skirts and jumped up onto his horse. She wasn't shy about riding like a man astride the horse. Or letting us all have a good look at her ankles –"

"Arthur." Ector's tone had descended into that of fatherly scolding. "You know that is not what I mean. You are used to women –" he gave another little cough and glanced at me, as though afraid I might scold him for talking about it – "who have gone to your bed of their own choosing. Guinevere is a princess, and is here because she must be. Do not forget that. For kings and queens, it is about duty, not about love. She will go to this as her duty. She might be afraid. She might be silent, or worse, cry. It is different, Arthur, when there is no desire –"

"How would you know?" Arthur demanded, his cheeks flushed with annoyance. "You married for love. Besides, I am a handsome man, and young and strong. Why do you not believe that she would desire me as I desire her?"

"If only every woman desired every man who thought himself handsome," I said, before I could stop myself. The words sounded harsh and unkind as they came out, but I had not meant to scold. I had not burned with physical desire for Gorlois, but I had loved him. But I, too, had chosen him. It had been my desire to choose sensibly, without my mind being clouded with other thoughts.

Arthur was staring at me. He looked hurt. I sighed, and stepped forward, and took his hand. "Arthur," I said gently, "I do not mean to suggest that you are not a man any woman would be grateful to have as her husband. You are. You are kind and gentle, and brave and strong. But only be wary at first. She is a foreign girl, come here alone, into the heartland of the people who were until now her enemy. Our language is not her language. Our ways are not her ways. She might be lonely, and afraid. Just be careful."

"I am not an animal," Arthur said, snatching his hand back, a tone of sulkiness creeping into his voice. "I can control myself."

"Can you, Arthur?" I said, more sharply than I meant to. We both knew what I was talking about, and he drew back from me, hurt.

I did not see how he and Morgawse had not guessed that they were of one blood. They were the same; impulsive, passionate, and stubborn. Sure of themselves, sure they were right. Brave, but reckless.

Arthur crossed his arms over his chest. "What do you mean by that?"

I shook my head, pressing the heel of my hand into my forehead. "Nothing, Arthur. Nothing."

Arthur stood, pulling Uther's old surcoat off the back of his chair and shrugging it on. It fitted him well. Of course it did.

"I'm going to bed," he said, but as he left he gestured at Kay with his head to follow him, and Kay – whom I had all but forgotten was in the room with us, as he had stood back, watchful and silent – followed him out.

I sighed out a deep breath of frustration as Arthur shut the door hard behind him, and Ector came and put his hand on my shoulder. I leaned into the touch. It had been a long time since I had felt any comfort, any kind human touch. I missed my daughters, I missed the husbands I had known. Merlin had taken so much from me when he had taken Arthur from me as a baby. But I would pay him back. That would come.

"Igraine," Ector sighed, and I felt his lips against my forehead, and I leaned against him. I knew he was trying to be comforting, but I was not sure what comfort there was. "I am sure that it will all be well."

I felt him take my face in his hands and I looked up at him. Even with his hair threaded with grey at the temples, and the lines of care on his face, he was still handsome. I remembered the moment of desperate comfort we had shared. I was not sure that it would all be well. I had grown to love Gorlois, but only because he had been gentle, and it had been my choice. I did not want my son to offer his wife the kind of marriage I had had with Uther. Wild with passion, but painful.

"We know what these Breton people are like, Ector," I said softly, even as I felt his thumb brush gently along my cheek. "They are proud. If he harms her – even by accident –"

Ector hushed me gently, and I felt his lips brush against mine, the softness of his beard, the tenderness of his kiss. If he could have kissed me like that thirty years ago, when I had come to tell him my father had given our marriage his blessing, then we might have lived as King and Queen in France. We might have had beautiful, noble children. Neither of us would have had to have made such painful sacrifices, to have lost loved ones.

"Ector." I sighed his name as I felt his hands run gently up my arms and he drew me closer against him. I felt myself melt towards him, into the gentleness of his touch, the warmth of comfort. My mouth opened under his, and the touch of his tongue against mine was soft, and sensual and intoxicating. I did not have time to question myself over what I was doing; I simply gave myself to it, to the animal comfort of it, and I was glad of it. I slid my hands up into his hair, which was thick and soft still, and I pulled him closer as his arms wrapped around me, holding me tight. How had we both grown so old so fast? I could feel the years on me; the heaviness, the regret. But what was there to regret? It had all been decided for me, so long ago, by Merlin. But if only Ector could have loved me all those years ago. I did not ask if he loved me now. He did not love me, and I did not love him. Comfort and desire had their own value, their own goodness, but they were not love, and I would not pretend that they were.

As I felt one of his hands slide into my hair, and his fingers firm and pleasant against rub against my scalp, I sighed into him, my hands tightening on the front of his surcoat, and then finding the buttons, and slipping them undone. I could feel my heart beginning to race, my mind beginning to cloud with it. I had been lonely a long time, and I remembered how blissful the comfort we had shared had been before, and I longed for it.

Then, suddenly, the door flew open, and I heard Kay's voice say, "Father –", beginning some mundane question, some trivial comment, before he realised what he was seeing, and fell silent.

Ector stepped away from me. I could see the flush of shame on his cheeks, and he hesitated in front of his son, unsure of whether or not to explain himself.

There was no need to, though, for Kay simply shrugged, said, "Never mind," and turned and left, slamming the door behind him.

Ector sighed, leaning back against the table, rubbing his face in his hands.

"Do you think he will tell Arthur?" I asked quietly. I tried not to think too hard about the fact that I was asking Ector about my own son, as if he were a stranger.

Ector shook his head, not lifting his hands away from his face.

"I don't know," he said, thickly. "Probably not tonight."

There was no reason for it to be wrong. We were both widowed, both noble. Still, I could not imagine Arthur being pleased. No, not at all.

Ector dropped his hands, but gazed off after Kay.

"Perhaps I should go after him," he said, absently.

I almost told him not to, but what business was it of mine? Ector still belonged to the wife that he had lost years ago. He wasn't going to put me, or himself, before their son. I was as irrelevant to Ector as I was to my own son. A relic of times past. A woman almost faded into nothingness.

Chapter sixty-three

There were arrangements to be made, and these fell to me. The Breton princess did not have jewels or fine things to be married in, so I sent ones of my own for her to wear. I did not want her to look like a prisoner. I remembered how it had felt to be at Uther's mercy, unsure of my place, those few weeks before we had been married. I didn't want her to have to feel that way. I didn't want her to begin with Arthur without, at least, all of the outward trappings of queenship. There were other things to be ordered as well – food, musicians, lodgings for the large retinue she had brought with her. Most of these things had to be organised through Kay, since he was Seneschal. He was attentive, but he would not meet my eye. I did not care. It was beneath my interest.

* * *

I sat in the chapel, at the front, and I watched as the princess came in, dressed in the dress I had had brought to her, and the old jewels of mine. She looked entirely different from how she had when she had ridden through Camelot's gates the evening before – wild, and in the ill-fitting dress of rough silk. Her ladies had plaited up and pinned back her wild red hair into a knot at the back of her head that was neater than I could have imagined such curly hair could have been forced into. With the hair pulled back from her face she looked older, and certainly, though youthful, her face had the set seriousness of a grown woman and a queen, rather than the wild, almost girlish way she had appeared on the horse. The loveliness of her face was all the more obvious, too. The rich green of her dress brought out the green of her eyes, like her father's, bright and intense, the whiteness of her skin, her high cheekbones, her proud, lovely features. Everything that Isolde had not been. No softness, no gentleness. And her gaze, impassive. I supposed it was the kind of look a man wore as he prepared himself to ride into battle. As she approached the altar where Arthur stood, I saw her eyes catch on him and recognition, and then anger, flash in them. She had not managed to hide that, though as far as I could tell she had hidden every other emotion. She remembered him from the night before. I saw her jaw clench when she took the hand he offered her. I did not blame her. He had been childish, wanting to peek at her without her knowing.

Still, she did not object, and said the words and did as she was bid during the ceremony. At the end, Arthur grasped hold of her tight, and kissed her with an eagerness that she did not return, though she did not push him away. I saw his arm slide around her waist as the men cheered, but her hands pressed against his arms, as though she were trying to hold him away. If she felt anything other than blank panic, then it did not show on her face. If she said anything to Arthur, then it was eaten up by the roar of the crowd congratulating their King.

* * *

I followed the trail of people out to the feast, looking for Morgan and Morgawse in the crowd. I saw Morgawse, with Gawain and Gareth and Gaheris by her side, fussing at Gareth, the youngest, but I did not see Morgan. Gareth, of all my grandsons, was the only one who truly reminded me of Gorlois. Gawain and Aggravain had their mother's russet colouring, but both had something of Lot's sly look about them, Aggravain more than his brother. It was only Gareth that smiled the bright open smile that I had almost forgotten, who made me wish that Gorlois had given me a son. There must have been some of Lot in him, but he was all his mother's child to look at him. All Gorlois' grandson. Morgawse didn't see me, and I hung back. I wanted to go to her, to offer her a little comfort, for I knew, I knew that she suffered. But after all she had done, after all I had done, it would be too little, and she would reject it, so I watched as they left, and I followed, and I saw them find Morgan and Aggravain in the courtyard, and Morgawse fuss away with Gareth, probably taking him to his bed before the feasting began. Perhaps setting him to watch her youngest child, Arthur's son, while they were there. I was glad she did not intend to bring him to the feast.

Around me, I could hear the chatter of the crowd. Women saying the Queen was beautiful, men not saying it, and if their wives said it to them, agreeing with all the same wordless noise of men who dare not say too much, dare not agree too strongly.

"So," I heard Merlin wheedling beside me, "it is done. There is another queen in Britain now."

I sighed. "I was long ago weary of being Britain's Queen."

Merlin clicked his tongue in a mix of disapproval and amusement. "Dowagerhood will not suit you, Igraine. You think you are tired, but you will not like it when your son listens better to what that creature whispers to him in the night than what you say in council, or all his wise councillors."

I turned to Merlin, an eyebrow raised. "Are you afraid of that?"

"A little," Merlin said, with an unpleasant smile that made me feel sure that he was not afraid of anything. "A beautiful woman is a dangerous thing to a king, Igraine. You yourself know this all too well. How women who have the power to make men also have the power to break them."

"It is you who are the breaker of men, Merlin," I said, staring back out across the courtyard.

"If you think that," Merlin sneered, "then you are more of a fool than I thought you were."

* * *

I waited to enter the feast until Arthur and his new wife were seated. I had the crown of Logrys still, and I intended to give it to her. I had it in my hands, but then at the last minute before I entered the hall, I put it on my head. This was the last time I would enter as a queen. I could hear people murmuring as I came in. What were they saying? That I was old? That I was faded? That they remembered my wedding to King Uther? I did not remember. It was a blur, a dark, half-lost memory.

I came up to the high table, and greeted Arthur with a kiss. I was close enough then to see Guinevere properly. I could see that her whole body was tensed. She was afraid, but afraid like an animal, ready to strike. She was in a hostile place. She was a captive. Suddenly, I was back in Tintagel, standing before Uther at the high table as he pulled off his armour and his men settled into my hall. But this was worse for her. Her home was across the sea. We were not even speaking her language. I had expected the harshness of the mother, the set face, the unrelenting nature. Perhaps that was there, but up close, she looked like a terrified girl. I greeted her formally, lifted the crown from my head, and placed it on hers. As I did, I leaned down and whispered, "It will get easier."

I thought I saw her nod, just a little, in recognition. I wondered how much she knew, how much her father had told her, for he had known me. He knew what I had lost, and now he knew that I knew what he had lost, to have his daughter far away. Had I not warned him? He had not listened.

I slipped into the seat beside her, and watched as Merlin came to bow before them, and then Morgan, whom Arthur stood to kiss warmly on the cheek, and Morgawse whom he greeted awkwardly, only with a nod. I saw Guinevere take all of it in; the warmth to one sister, the coldness to another. Then lord after lord, knight after knight, until even I – who was used to it – was weary. Guinevere's hand was wrapped tight against the stem of her goblet, so tight that her knuckles were turning white, but she showed no other sign of feeling it; she was staring out impassively at the tide of people who passed before her to greet her as their Queen. I stopped watching the men coming up, and I looked over at Morgan, who sat tensely beside her husband. Should I have done more? Intervened? Did I truly know what was a normal level of violence between a man and his wife, after Uther? After everything? She looked so unhappy beside him, and he so unpleasant. How different he was from his gentle father, as I had known him. Morgawse, beside her sister, her sons to her right, was already tipping back her goblet of wine, and I felt my stomach clench with vicarious embarrassment. She would be drunk soon. I hoped that she did not say anything. I remembered how she had shouted at Uther, the day we were married. Beside her, Aggravain caught my eye, and I could see that he was wary, too. She was lucky to have a son like him; wise, careful, and devoted to her. She must have been a good mother, despite what I thought of her, for all her sons loved her with an absolute devotion. One I had not inspired in her, or Morgan. Or Arthur. I had done all that I could.

"Lady Guinevere." I put my hand gently on her arm, and she jumped, as though she had been lost in some deep thought, somewhere else. "Was your journey long?"

It was boring conversation, small talk, but since Arthur was laughing and joking with Kay and Gawain rather than trying to make conversation with his new wife – though he was happy to let his arm lie around the back of her chair in a lazy gesture of ownership already – I thought that I had better try.

Her little red mouth gave a slight twitch, that might have been the beginning of a smile, had she not been so tense. "Not long. Perhaps a couple of days. But this is the furthest I have ever been from my home."

Her voice was lovely; low and rich, and thick with the beautiful accent of the Bretons. It was like the tones of the Welsh; soft, and almost singing. I wondered how we sounded to her. I supposed to her and to Gorlois we must have sounded rough and unpleasant. I wished I had learned the old language of my people in Cornwall. My father had not thought it necessary for us to learn. The language of the peasants, he had said. Better to learn Latin and French. Perhaps it would not have been so different from hers. The way she said 'home' was somehow heartbreaking, as though she felt the loss of Carhais worse than anything else. Perhaps I imagined it, only, because of how I had felt about Tintagel. I had a sudden powerful feeling that she would have loved Tintagel Castle, its wildness, out by the sea.

"I knew your father," I offered, hopeful of a little more conversation from her. She had relaxed enough, at least, to lift her cup of wine to her lips rather than just gripping it tight where it sat on the table.

She nodded. "He spoke of you, a little," she said absently. Her eyes glossed over the unfamiliar faces around her. She hadn't eaten any of the food on the plate that she shared with Arthur.

"He did not come with you?" I offered. I had not seen him there.

She shook her head. "He is old, and there is much to attend to in Carhais." I thought she had finished, but she spread her palm out flat against the embroidered cloth on the table and stared down at it. "But I did bring this table from my home."

How had I not noticed that it was different? I had been staring too hard at her, remembering too much of my own weddings. The table we were sat around was circular, far larger than anything of the like in Logrys. What a strange thing to bring. I wondered if Arthur had asked for it. It seemed like a strange thing to want, but I said nothing. Their customs were different. Perhaps a table was a traditional bride-gift among the Bretons.

I was distracted, then, by Ector slipping into the seat beside me. I felt Kay's eyes gaze over us, but I ignored both of them, until Ector spoke.

"Arthur looks happy," he said quietly, without looking over at him, picking up his cup and lifting it to his lips.

I made a noncommittal sound of agreement, and glanced back to Arthur. He was watching his new wife, who was not looking at him, but at the cup of wine that she lifted to her lips and drained. His eyes followed her every movement, lingered on her lips as she brushed the back of her hand against them. She was a little flushed already, but it only made her look more alluring. Even I wanted to reach over and touch her cheek; was it as soft as it looked? Arthur put a hand over hers, where it held the cup, to fill it again for her. She didn't look up at him. She was staring at the hand, closed over hers, that was twice the size of her own. I knew what she was thinking, and I pushed the thought away.

"That is well, Ector," I said, comfortingly. If Kay had not been sat across from us, I would have put my hand on top of his. As it was, I smiled gently at him. He still looked uncomfortable, anxious. He still, I supposed, felt responsible for whatever his sons did. No. Arthur was not his son. Still, he was Arthur's father. He had raised him, and Arthur had never known anyone else.

Across the table, Morgawse was emptying what must have been a fourth or a fifth goblet of wine, and holding up the empty cup for another. I saw Aggravain take it from her hand and fill it deliberately only half-full, but that would not stop Morgawse making a spectacle of herself, only slow her down. I noticed that Arthur did not look at her, at all. He was looking at his wife, who was making polite but strained-looking conversation with Uriens across the table. I had thought that she was withdrawn and reticent with me, but she only nodded, or answered yes or no to what he said.

I did not realise how late it had already got until the servants came and cleared the meat and vegetables away and brought the little sweet cakes. I had barely eaten anything, having watched Morgawse get increasingly drunk, Morgan get increasingly uncomfortable beside her husband, who was also getting drunk, and Guinevere beside me not eating, not talking at all anymore, and slowly and tensely drinking. Already, Arthur was standing, thanking his guests, his men, and offering his hand to his bride. Slowly, she looked up from her cup, where she had been staring at the dark, glassy surface of the wine, to him, her face set once more, as it had been when she walked into the chapel, and slipped her hand into his. I felt my stomach clench, and pushed away the thought of what waited for her, at the hands of my own son. Perhaps it would be as it had been for me, and for Uther.

The men around the table began to cheer, my grandsons among them, and began to chant: Arthur the Conqueror. I saw Morgan wrinkle up her nose in distaste as her husband began shouting it as well. Kay was suddenly behind Morgan, whispering in her ear, and I felt a stab of fear – what was he saying to her? – but they were not looking at me, they were gazing off after where Arthur had gone.

Then, from across the table, I heard Uriens, loud and drunk, begin to speak.

"You know, they say that red-headed women like her –" he jabbed his finger clumsily off after where Arthur had gone, and then turned to Morgan beside him, his eyes only half-focussed on her – "and your sister Morgawse here…" He lost his thread for a moment, narrowing his eyes unpleasantly at Morgawse, as though he were measuring how far he could push it. He had not noticed Aggravain, sober beside his mother, watching him. "They say that red-headed women love to be fucked by a man."

"Be quiet, Uriens," Morgan hissed. She tensed in her seat, her face set with pain, and I wished that I could have stridden over there and ordered him to be silent.

"I bet that Breton girl squirms like an eel when Arthur fucks her tonight. Oh, of course she looks angry, but it's the angry ones that want it, really. Except Morgan of course. You're always angry, aren't you? And you never want to be fucked. Funny, isn't it, how the King fucks all the best women, and leaves me with you? You're hard and dry as an old twig, aren't you, Morgan?"

Ector's hand closed around my wrist. I think he knew I was thinking of going over, shouting at Uriens. But what would I do? I was just an old woman. Perhaps he would have struck me, and then I could not ignore what kind of man I had given my daughter to. I hoped, with a sudden flash of white hot anger, that he would die. That he would fall asleep drunk, and choke on his vomit and die. Lot had never been that bad. Had never publicly humiliated Morgawse, hadn't even harmed her, as far as I could see, when she had had another man's child. Morgan's husband was a disgusting brute. I wished I was a man with the power to destroy him. As it was, as I glanced out of the corner of my eye to see Aggravain about to stand from his chair. I hoped that it was to knock Uriens out. Was this how people had spoken about me the night I married Uther? When they said I had wanted it, I was a witch who had seduced him, had used Gorlois in my game to have them both? Were men really so foolish about women?

Uriens leaned past Morgan, towards Morgawse, who was so drunk now that she sat with her eyes closed, noticing nothing. "All you red women love the feel of a man, don't you?"

Gawain's fist banged hard on the table and he went to stand, but Aggravain held him back. Perhaps he wanted the pleasure for himself, perhaps he wanted to avoid an open brawl on the night of his King's wedding.

Aggravain's voice was low with threat, but it reached me across the table nonetheless. "Be careful what you say, Uriens. Our mother is your sister by marriage now, so any shame you say to her is shame upon yourself. Besides, do not think because our father is dead that Lothian has lost its strength, and will not crush those who dishonour Lot's blood. You are drunk, sir, and have been foolish. But remember this; the next time you insult the sons of Lot or our lady mother, who is Queen of a realm ten times the strength of yours in arms, will be the last time."

It seemed to settle down, in the wake of Aggravain's threat. I stood to leave, and Ector stood with me. As I turned, I caught Kay's eye, and his look was tense, judgemental, even though he had no right. I caught Morgan's eye, too, and in it saw the mute appeal for help. But there was none I could give her. Not here. Not in public.

Out in the courtyard, I turned to Ector.

"What should we do? Set someone to watch?"

I had told him what Mclita had said to me, the threats she had made about her daughter. I tried not to picture Arthur seizing her by the hair, the way that Uther had done with me, and her drawing some knife from somewhere and stabbing it into his neck.

Ector nodded. "I will set Kay to it."

An uneasy silence fell between us. I had hoped that we might find some mutual forgetting, but perhaps that chance was missed.

"He is angry with you?" I asked, softly.

Ector sighed. "He is confused. There were never any other women – after his mother. And you are Arthur's mother. He is young – it pains him to think that his father is not perfect, that his father is capable of the same ill judgement he is. No – I do not mean to suggest –"

I hushed him, put a hand against his arm.

"I understand."

I left Ector to set the watch. I did not want to go back into the hall and face my daughters. Being wife to a king had damaged all of us, and I had just sold another woman into that life. Late at night, silently, Morgan slipped into my room, wriggled beneath the covers with me as she had done when she was only a little thing of two or three, and I kissed the top of her head and wrapped my arms around her. And I did not ask why she had come, because I knew, and if I could keep her safe from that even a short time, then I would.

Chapter sixty-four

The next morning, when it was time for mass, I watched Arthur's new wife in the chapel, though I was not sure what I was looking for. Some sign of happiness, some sign of unhappiness. I wondered what I would have looked like to anyone watching me the morning after I married Uther. She sat beside Arthur, tense and careful, her hair wound tightly away as it had been before, her hands folded in her lap. Had he pulled that knot of hair loose, and clasped her to him with the same kind of passion that I had known from his father? Or had he been wary, and careful? I wondered, obliquely, if he had wanted her to slap him across the face, as Uther had wanted me to do. If he liked that. If it ran in his blood. I did not know him at all, really, did not know what he might be like. I supposed it was something that it was impossible for a mother to imagine. She was gazing down at her folded hands, and she looked as though her mind was far away. Beside her, Arthur sat with his head bent, his eyes closed, and his lips moving in time with the words of the prayers. I should have been praying as well. Then I noticed her glance at him, with his eyes closed, lost in the devotion of a good Christian, and I realised that she was not praying because she did not know the words. She is a pagan, I thought. Why did Arthur not consider that before he chose her as a wife? Why did I not consider that? The Bretons were slow to put aside their ancient gods for Christ, and I had heard men call Leodegrance a witch, and I had heard him speak stubbornly of the old worship, but I had not pieced it all together. Had not thought what it might mean for me, for my son, for this.

When the service was over, I watched how Arthur put his arm around her waist as they stood. I could not tell if she welcomed it or not.

* * *

It was a few days later that I had occasion to speak with her again. There was much to be put in order, and I was reluctant to leave it to anyone else. I had spent a wonderful few days with my grandsons, who seemed – at least – not to have been infected with their mother's disappointment in me. I could not believe how much they had grown. Gawain, who was tall now as Gorlois had been, even told me that he had two sons of his own already – with some servant in Lothian, but children of his own nonetheless. My daughters were both still in the castle, but seemed to have made themselves scarce for whatever reason, Morgawse hiding with her bastard child, probably, and Morgan secreting herself away from her husband. She did not slip into my room again, and I suspected that she was sleeping side-by-side with her sister as though they were little girls once more.

But I could not indulge myself with family joys forever. I needed to be sure that Arthur was attending to things in the kingdom, despite the distractions of a new wife, and all the hunts and feasts and celebrations that came along with that, and so I went to find him in his council chamber. But it was not his voice that I heard when I approached, but hers, unmistakable with its thick Breton accent.

"No," I heard her say, firmly. "No, Kay. What good is the gift of the Hundred Knights if they are not properly equipped? And you cannot keep them all here. A hundred armed men all longing to fight? No. Split them into quarters and garrison them at places where your borders are weak. North – here, along the old Roman wall. And to the west, anywhere on the Welsh marches that seems vulnerable. Perhaps the Cornish border."

I pushed the door open fully, and saw her stood at the great round table, moved now from its place in the great hall, a map, its edges curling, laid out in front of her, her finger pressed assertively at the last spot she had indicated, which looked to be a few miles south of the old Roman city of Isca. Kay, standing across from her, had his arms crossed thoughtfully over his chest, and his bottom lip between his teeth. She was right, of course. And she knew a lot about Britain. She looked up as she heard me come in, and gave a nervous nod of deference, all of that self-possession and command I had overheard melting away.

"Queen Igraine," she said. Her accent was very strong; pretty, but obvious. Kay's eyes on me were steady, and without the due respect.

"I am making preparations to return to Tintagel Castle once everything is settled here," I told her, ignoring Kay. "If they are ready and you can spare them, I would like to take some of your knights."

She nodded, looking back down at the map. Was she shy? Was that why she did not talk now? She had had plenty to say to Kay.

I opened my mouth to ask another question about the knights, hoping to induce her to speak more to me, when Arthur charged into the room through the open door and, without even pausing to see what we were discussing, wrapped his arms around her from behind so enthusiastically that he lifted her off her feet. She tensed as he nuzzled his face into her neck. I was not sure if it was that she found him unpleasant, or if she was conscious that I was there.

"I thought I would find you here – occupied with something boring," Arthur said thickly, his mouth half-full of her hair.

"It isn't boring," she protested, her voice a little stern.

"What if I could occupy you with one of a queen's far less boring duties?" He slid his hands up from around her waist as though he were going to press his hands against her breasts with Kay right there, but she spoke sharply, in time to stop him.

"Your lady mother, Queen Igraine, has come to tell us she plans to return to Tintagel."

Arthur jumped back from his wife, blushing. No, he had not noticed I was there. All he had seen from the stairs was the red hair, the white neck, the possibility of handling his wife like a common whore in front of the foster-brother who seemed to see no problem with it.

"Your wife has been kind enough to offer me twenty-five of her hundred knights, to help keep Cornwall fully garrisoned."

Arthur nodded, still too flustered to speak.

I turned to Kay, imperious. "Give the order that that number be prepared for me. I should like to know they have left before prime tomorrow."

Kay nodded, and I left. As I did, I heard Arthur say something to Kay in low tones, and Kay laughed. I wondered what Guinevere thought of the pair of them, or of Arthur. Before he strode in and seized her, she had made quite a good figure of a queen. Harsher, perhaps, than I would have been in her tone, but not some fool who would be no use. And did she enjoy being handled like that by him? She gave no obvious sign that she did, but also no sign that she did not. Perhaps it was all for the good. The sooner they had their own child, the better. I knew how ill things grew in a land with no heir. I had lived through it twice.

* * *

After that, I sought out Nimue. I had been watching her while she was at court. The way she spoke to Arthur – leaning close to listen to him while he did not seem to notice at all, speaking his name softly, putting a hand on his arm to get his attention – and the way that Merlin had, in turn, spoken of her made me hope that between us I could make one final effort to protect my son for sure. I watched one evening, barely a week after Arthur's marriage, as those of us who were closest to the throne ate in Arthur's public room where Guinevere's bride-table had been brought. Arthur was completely absorbed with Guinevere, one arm around the back of her chair, his eyes barely straying from her face. She was talking – quiet, reserved, in short careful sentences, but talking nonetheless – with Ector across from her about what provisions had finally been made for her knights, and arranging for messages to be sent back to her father in Carhais. She had an infant nephew there, it seemed, and wanted to make sure that everything would be provided for him. That her father, in his grief and loneliness, would not neglect the next generation now that his daughter was gone. But Arthur was not listening, he was only looking. Even as she was speaking, his hand moved from the back of the chair to the back of her neck, toyed at the hair, threatening to spill loose the knot of curls. Nimue was watching him with something less than detachment and different from disapproval. She put a hand against Arthur's arm, and he drew away, leaned down obediently so that she could whisper something to him, but his eyes were already drifting back to his wife. When we all departed, I lingered, hoping to speak with Nimue alone, but she was caught up in conversation with one of the knights. Out in the stairway, Guinevere was still talking to Ector, but, as I passed, Arthur, from half a flight up the stairs, called out to her, and she bid goodnight to Ector to follow him. Nimue passed me just as Guinevere reached Arthur on the stairs and he pulled her against him in a possessive kiss, one arm around her waist, drawing her with him up to his bedchamber. Nimue watched, her mouth a tense little knot, and I was sure that my suspicions were well-founded.

* * *

I called her to me the next day, and she came. I had half-expected her to be as elusive as Merlin.

"You are Lady of Avalon now, in Viviane's place?" I asked.

Nimue nodded.

"And you care for my son?"

"He is Avalon's chosen King. He is Britain's rightful King." She was tense, irritated. There was no need for her to deny it.

"Would you do anything necessary to keep him safe?"

"Anything." Her eyes burned, and the intensity of her reply betrayed what she had been so adamant to dismiss. Had women longed for Uther like this, while he had been mine? If they had, he would not have left them longing. I wondered if – once the burning passion of the new had died down in Arthur – he would be the same.

"Merlin has promised an evil destiny, and is resolved not to save him. He says it is my doing, because I would not commit Arthur into his hands as a child, but it may well be his own ambition. Merlin has a weakness for you –"

"I know it," she said sharply. "And he has spoken to me of such things. But Merlin wants, most of all, for Britain to remain as it is. Not overrun with Saxons or Romans. Not completely in thrall to the Christians. He knows Arthur is the rightful King."

"He has made threats to me," I said.

Nimue nodded. "I know that as well. He has promised me great learning – great magic that might be used to keep Arthur safe. To safe him from this bad destiny that Merlin claims was caused by the begetting of his sister's child."

"Merlin must die," I said, simply. I knew in my heart there would be no safety for my son until he was gone. Nimue was silent a long time. "Can it be done?"

I expected there to be a fight, a battle of wills, but Nimue nodded, as though it were something she were already long consigned to. She would betray her teacher, and kill him. But had she not been Viviane's pupil? Perhaps in part. Or something like Viviane's own daughter. But real power – that which had been forbidden in Avalon under Viviane – I knew well enough how that only came from Merlin.

376

"I will do it," Nimue said, softly. When she looked up at me then, I could see in the cold blue of her eyes that I was dealing with a woman very like myself. Calm, and ruthless. She looked so like a child, but she was nothing like a child. "I am certain that I can destroy Merlin. The rest… I do not know." She shook her head. "It all depends on how much Merlin has told us about himself is true. If he is only the voice of fate… then it cannot be changed. Some spirit of good luck protects Morgawse's child, for there are others besides you who have tried to have him killed, but still he lives. Killing innocent children is not the answer. But perhaps… if I could have all of Merlin's knowledge from him. Perhaps I could. The Cup of the Blood of the World…"

I had heard of that before. When Viviane had been slaughtered in Arthur's hall by the mad knight-prisoner. It boded ill. It sounded like superstition and dreams, like shadows and false lights from the lands of fairies.

"That seemed a lot to me like one of Merlin's dreams," I said.

Nimue shook her head, and said nothing more.

* * *

That night I dreamed I was walking through Camelot, up the narrow stairs in the King's tower. And Uther was in the council chamber. And he put his arms around me and kissed me with the same youthful passion with which I had seen Arthur kiss his wife. And he turned me around in his arms, and rushed me up the stairs to his bedchamber. But when I flung open the door, Morgawse was spread out across the bed, naked but for a heavy string of amber beads and the thick swathes of her loosened red-gold hair. And suddenly I was not myself, but Guinevere, and I turned over my shoulder to see it was Arthur behind me, staring at his sister with the same drunk-eyed look I had seen him turn on his wife. When I woke I felt awful, as though I had not slept at all.

Chapter sixty-five

After another week or so had passed, Morgan went back to Rheged, and I said goodbye to her, holding in my sorrow. She deserved more than that. So gentle, so wise, so good. She was so precious to me. And I had hoped so dearly that she would be happy with her husband. I did not know where Morgawse was – skulking somewhere, or perhaps returned to Lothian. Her sons were occupied now, training every day, and riding out to make sure Arthur's peace was ever secure, and it was time for me to return to Tintagel.

I said goodbye to Ector, first. He was quiet, awkward. I had hoped for one more moment alone, one last taste of comfort, but he was afraid, now, of his son's judgement, and I understood. He did kiss me, briefly, softly, but that was all. It had, in the end, been only an illusion.

Arthur and his Queen said goodbye with all of the formality of rulers, but I longed to hold him as my son. I had waited so long, I had been so careful, but in that moment I held him to me and kissed the top of his head like he was just a boy. To my surprise, he returned my embrace warmly, if not with the same intensity of familial love with which I gave it. I was relieved. Guinevere accepted my kiss on her cheek with the same even look she always wore.

* * *

I wondered about them. Their happiness. Arthur seemed completely enamoured of her, but I had never seen her fully return his affections. I might have wondered forever if I had not forgotten my cloak up in my room and rushed back to get it before we finally departed for my old home. I was hurrying down the stairs out to the courtyard when the sound of soft voices around the corner stopped me where I was. After a moment, I realised that the man's voice I could hear was Arthur's. I supposed that I should have announced myself, and walked casually by, but I was filled with a mother's urge to see my son as he was when he was not on his best behaviour for Lady Igraine, to see him how I had never been able to see him growing up as a child. Then I heard a woman's laugh, and with a stab of annoyance I thought, He is just married; surely he is not at his old games already. But when I peered around the corner, I saw that the woman Arthur was with was his wife. He had her pressed up against the wall, his big hands around her waist almost covering her narrow ribcage entirely, and under his hands her chest was rising and falling fast. I wondered for a moment if she were afraid, but then I saw her eyes, fluttering half-closed, and the flush against the white skin on her neck, and high on her cheeks. Her hands gripped his arms as though at once she was trying to pull him towards her and push him away. Arthur leaned closer, and as he brushed his nose down against hers, her face followed his, leaning towards him, her red lips parting, just a little, in anticipation of a kiss. He kissed her, but just a little, and she sighed quietly, leaning a little towards him, and he gave a little more, but just a little before he leaned away, and she followed him. Arthur was young, and I was surprised to see him tease her like that, surprised that my young son knew that what a woman wanted was not all roughness all at once. But I remembered all that Ector had said about him, how it had been a worry of his that Arthur might get many illegitimate children before the time ever came for him to be made King. But I did not think that what I was seeing were the acts of a lecherous man. Those men were greedy and wanted only what was their own pleasure. This was something else.

Finally, though, as though he could bear his own teasing no longer, Arthur kissed her hard, pressing her up against the wall. She wriggled with delight, running her hands up into his hair and twining them there. I could see the gold rings on her fingers glinting against his gold hair. He drew away just a little, but I could see that his hands had slid around to her back, and were drawing her against him now, and that he too was a little flushed, a little lost in his desire.

"Arthur," she whispered, as he pressed his mouth to hers once more, and whatever else she was going to say was lost. Her hands slid down, across his shoulders, to close in fists around the front of his surcoat, and she pulled him closer.

"Arthur, take me to bed," she murmured, her accent thick and gorgeous, and he laughed softly.

"My love, it is the middle of the day, and I have many other duties –"

This time, when he leaned down to kiss her, she drew away, and he sighed in frustration, leaning in towards her once more as, smiling, she still held back from him. I had seen the power shift between them, and where before she had been following him, now he was following her.

She opened her mouth as though she was going to say something in reply, but then, with a low groan of abandon, Arthur wrapped his arms tight around her, and kissed her wildly. She held his face gently in her hands, and it looked for a moment as though Arthur was going to pick her up and carry her away as she wished it. But then, from out in the courtyard, I heard men calling for him, and so did he. With a low groan of frustration, Arthur unwound his arms from her, and kissed her once more, softly this time.

"I must go," he said, reluctantly, and she nodded, brushing her fingertips down his cheek. He made as though to leave, but then darted back to kiss her once more before he left.

And after all, were they happy, when at the start it had all seemed so distant, the possibility that they might grow to love one another? I watched Guinevere pat her hand across her hair, checking it was all in place, and smooth down her dress, smiling to herself.

She turned, and walked up towards me. I was half-worried that she would know I had seen them, and would be angry, or embarrassed, but when she saw me she gave that slight reserved smile I had seen her give in public, and I realised with a jolt that she was entirely different when she was alone with Arthur. I had just heard her laugh, when now all of a sudden she seemed tense, and wary and withdrawn. She did not seem to be unhappy. I half-heard her voice in my head once more – Arthur, take me to bed – and that woman seemed worlds away from this careful, queenly woman who was the one I had seen before in public and who was suddenly facing me now. I found that I was pleased, and I wondered, suddenly, if I were not the same. I had heard people say of me that I was cold, and unyielding, and yet I thought myself to be warm, and sensitive and kind. Perhaps this was the lot of all queens.

Guinevere nodded in gentle respect, and said, "Lady Igraine, are you well? Do you have everything you need for your journey? I do hope you will return soon."

* * *

I did not truly appreciate how much I had missed Tintagel until I saw my home rising over the horizon. I felt it in my blood and my bones. This was where I belonged. Brastias stood where I had once stood to watch Uther ride as conqueror through my gates, and he raised a hand to greet me as my horse picked its way up the narrow, rocky path.

"Your son," he asked gently, as he offered me his hand to help me down off the horse, "what was he like?"

I thought for a moment. "He was exactly how I imagined he would be. He will be a good king, I'm sure."

Brastias nodded.

* * *

My room was just the same. I stood at the window and watched the sea crashing white against the rocks below. There was a heavy raincloud far away on the horizon, but the sky was a clear, pale blue all around Tintagel. I stood staring out for as long as I could, because I knew I was not alone.

As though I felt nothing, as though I sensed nothing, I sighed, bored, and slipped into the seat before my mirror. The once-beautiful surface was rusting at the edges. There had been no queen here, and no one had polished it. I picked up my comb, but froze halfway lifting it to my hair as I at last caught the eye of a dark young man standing behind me.

"Vanity is a great sin, even for a great beauty," he said.

"You must be vain yourself, Merlin, to take a shape like that."

His lips twitched into a half-smile.

"You must think this shape is pleasing, to accuse me of being vain in taking it."

"Tell me what you want here, Merlin, so that I can get some food. I've ridden many miles today."

"You are dying, Igraine," Merlin said, and I remembered when he had stood beside me at the mirror and told me that Uther was dead, and it had felt like a blow to the chest. I felt nothing. So I was dying. My children were grown, and I was ageing. I knew my time was done. And in the mirror now, I saw him shift beside me, melt in the rippling image on the polished silver, to the skull-faced Silvestris, on to Ambrosius, and then from the old white-haired man back into the young man who might or might not have been Melusine's brother. He reached out, and drew the loose hair back from my neck on one side.

"What a queen you might have made for me, Igraine, if I had chosen to set myself on the throne instead of Uther. That was all that made me think Uther was more than a dumb brute, that it was you on whom he set his heart. And I could have had you, and we could have ruled Britain by the old ways, side by side. I entertained the thought, once or twice. You were a rare beauty in your youth. Not like those women men now commonly claim to be so. Arthur's Queen, who is nothing more than a savage, hot in the blood, and wild. Morgawse, who, like the lovely sirens, lures men close only to drown them. No," he leaned a little closer, "you are cold to the core, Igraine. And you are far more lovely."

His fingertips brushed down my neck.

"Not so lovely as Nimue," I said, carefully.

Merlin stiffened, but did not draw back. "No, not so lovely." Suddenly intent on revenge, for he had not expected me to have guessed his secrets, he let a finger slide across my cheek, half-threatening, and down across my lower lip. "Did you ever wonder, Igraine, before you knew, who it was who had come to you in your husband's shape, and given you that son? Did you fear that it had been the witch at Uther's side, slipping inside you, whispering those words: Tell me you want me."

Was I surprised that Merlin spied on everything and everyone? No, I was not. I was disgusted, but only dimly. It was not beyond what I had expected of him.

"How you must have longed for a woman to be so with you," I said, wryly, picking up my little bottle of perfume, and dabbing it against my wrists. "I cannot imagine that even in that young shape of yours you have much success with seduction. How appropriate that a man with every power in the world still does not have the power to make a woman love him. You think you can possess us, but you cannot. You think one day Nimue will recognise your power, or finally appreciate your devotion, but she will not. Uther became mine, not yours, the moment I returned his love. Arthur became Guinevere's, not yours, the moment he felt real love for her. I see, now, why you would have preferred Isolde. Someone pretty and distracting, but for whom Arthur could not have felt real love. You were a fool, perhaps, to set Uther to winning me."

"I was not," Merlin said, straightening up behind me. "For you made him the King he was."

"The King you wish you had been."

"My days are not yet done, Igraine."

"I know."

We stared at each other on the polished surface for a long moment. I could feel my heartbeat through every part of my body. I could feel the animal instincts in my blood telling me to run or strike a blow, but I did nothing. Merlin had come to gloat, but I was sure now that he meant Arthur harm, and I knew, as deep as my bones, that I would destroy him.

Chapter sixty-six

"He will do it," I said, quiet with dread.

Nimue nodded. She was far away, her pale eyes unfocussed, her hands wound together so tight that even in the cold light of the full moon mirrored in the calm seas outside, I could see they were white under the woad. She had received my letter, calling her here, telling her that Merlin had threatened Arthur.

"If we hesitate now," I pushed her, "then all is lost."

Nimue said nothing, still stared, as though there was something before her that she could not tear her eyes away from. Perhaps some vision of the future she could not bear.

"How sure are you," she said at last, "that this is what he intends?"

"Sure enough."

I could have hesitated. I could have shown mercy. I could have said, I know nothing of such things, or Merlin has always threatened me, but never done me or Arthur harm, but if I had said these things then Nimue would have let him live, and while he lived Arthur was not safe. I was sure enough of that. I was sure, too, if I impressed upon Nimue the danger to Arthur personally, then she would lose some of that careful control, and she would give herself to me in this. I needed Merlin gone. Of all the sacrifices I had made for my children this was the least; I already hated Merlin.

"He is in love with you."

Nimue looked up sharply, her cheeks flushing, her eyes widening. I had meant Merlin. She thought I had meant someone else.

"Merlin is in love with you. You have nothing to fear from him. I will see it done with you. We will see it done."

* * *

It felt like months, but it was only a few days before Nimue returned, set to her purpose. She had something in her hands, wrapped in a cloth that was sooty and blackened from a forge. She smelled of iron and ash. She did not bother to greet me, or to ask if I still had my heart set on Merlin's death.

"You must take this, Igraine – take it, quickly – and when Merlin returns, you must stab him with it, as close as you can to the heart. Do you understand me?"

She held out the sooty package to me, and I nodded and stepped forward. Her lips were blue, as though she were freezing cold, and her hands were shaking. I unwrapped the package in her hands. It was what looked like an ordinary dagger. It was beautifully made, its hilt set with gems like Arthur's sword, but ordinary. When I took it from her hands, though, Nimue gasped as though relieved from a great pain, and colour rushed back to her face.

"What is it?" I asked. Holding the knife, I myself felt nothing.

"It is made with iron ore, mined in the Otherworld."

The common folk said that fairies hated iron, that it poisoned them and made them weak. But Merlin and Nimue were no fairies.

"How can you be sure that he will die?" I asked.

Nimue looked at me, her gaze steady and empty.

"I am not."

We went through it together, step by step, like two generals preparing for war. There was a cave down at the foot of the cliffs, in sight of the castle, where Nimue would set two of her women to watch for us and ensure we were safe – or safe enough – but far enough that the ordinary folk would not hear our voices, or any other noises that might come. Nimue had written to Merlin, promised to meet him there at the hour of low tide. We talked quietly, practically.

Where I would stand. Did I know how to use a knife? Not really, but neither did Nimue. I had seen it done. The knife itself had more strength than I had. More strength than any man. My life, my hopes, all my faith were with Nimue, and I did not doubt her. I knew too well the power of one in love with one they cannot have. There might come a time, too, when Arthur would be less dazzled by his new wife, and would be happy to take the Lady of Avalon into his bed and into his counsel. I had hated Imogen, but she had done Uther good, and she had not been half so clever as Nimue.

* * *

I could taste salt on my lips from the sea-spray. It filled the air at the entrance to the cave. My lungs ached, and it was hard to breathe in the damp air. I was sure this was the sickness Merlin had seen, and it was tightening its grip on me fast. Couldn't Nimue have lured Merlin to some comfortable room somewhere? Though that was one temptation Merlin did not seem to have succumbed to – a love of fine things.

"Merlin?" I called, glancing behind me at Nimue, who was already melting into the shadows. I knew she was there, but she was somehow indistinguishable from the rock. I turned back to the depths. There was a shape there. A man's shape. Tall, and when he stepped forward and the light caught his hair, fair. Arthur. When he saw me, a wry, oddly familiar smile curled at his lips.

"Igraine – I was expecting someone else."

"You were expecting Nimue," I answered, breathlessly.

I felt, as I had before when he had threatened me at Uther's death, that wave of sickening heat pass over my skin. This time, I was not afraid.

Before me, he became Uther, and the smile more hungry, more animal. "I have had two women at once before," he said, "and it was a delight to both of them, as well as to me."

Despite myself, I flushed.

"What have you come here to do, Igraine?" He took two confident strides towards me, and slid his arm around my waist. His hand slid just a palm's breadth above where I had Nimue's dagger hidden, and I caught my breath. This, it seemed, was just the reaction Merlin was hoping for. He slid his other hand into my hair and pulled me into a kiss. It was not convincing; it was only an illusion, and beneath was the sickly smell of Otherworld herbs on Merlin's skin, and his leathery lips. I pushed him back and, to my surprise, my hands were on Morgawse's shoulders.

This was different. Her familiar smell – sandalwood, wood smoke, honey – filled my nostrils. This was more than an illusion. Her big blue eyes blinked up at me, the thick pale lashes fluttering.

"Are you here to kill me, Mother?" she whispered, pleadingly, pressing her front teeth into her plump lower lip. "Or are you going to take my child? Take my child and save Arthur – the only child of yours you ever truly loved. That's right, isn't it? I know you didn't love my father. But you loved Uther, didn't you? Did you think I was too young to see what was right in front of me? But I learned enough watching one seducer; I made sure that that love you thought worth my father's death was tainted and broken. It was easy; I just copied you."

"Morgawse, stop," I gasped. Where was Nimue? Could she not stop this?"

"That's right, Mother. I was on my knees sucking my stepfather's cock from the moment we arrived in Camelot."

I slapped her – slapped him – hard. She did not stop.

"But that's just what I knew. And I first learned that from my own dear father. Oh, you didn't know why he loved me so much better than you? They both loved me better than you. You're just a jealous, dried-up old bitch."

I slapped her again, and I found the strength to do it harder. This time, the force of my blow changed the creature before me from one daughter into the other, and Morgan stood before me, fifteen years old, her face unmarked with woad. She held a hand to her cheek, which was red where I had struck her, and pursed her lips, rubbing at it.

"You're a fool, Mother," she said, in that neat little voice of hers. "You were watching Morgawse so closely, you didn't see what was right in front of you." She looked up at me, then. "It was me, all along. But not like you think. We were lovers. Uther loved me. It started when I was about fifteen. The age, I suppose, you were, when you let him rub himself all over you like a dog in season in Aurelianus' courtyard. Used to say I reminded him of the way you used to be, the way you ought to have been. Virginal." Morgan laughed, and the sound was harsh. "Well, the first time. He used to come to the abbey, and we would fuck right there among the nuns."

"You're a liar," I hissed, and this time I had a little more clarity. Morgawse – that I could be stretched to believe – but he did not know Morgan at all.

I had the presence, this time, to draw the dagger, and I thrust it hard into his chest.

I had never stabbed a man before, never committed any act of physical violence greater than a slap. I had expected the blade to snag on bone and muscle and sinew, to have to force it through his ribs and into his chest, but it sank into his skin as though it were butter. And the moment it did, Morgan became Arthur, blood pouring from his wounded chest, and I screamed.

"Nimue –" I turned over my shoulder, but I could not see her. "Nimue – what have I done?"

I knelt beside him where he had fallen, scrabbled around, my panicked hands tugging at the dagger, but although it had slid in without any resistance, it was now somehow wedged firm.

"Arthur –"

His eyes were falling closed, and he was coughing blood up out of his lungs. I did not care that this was, perhaps, just another trick of Merlin's. It was bad enough that he would make me watch my son die. I wrenched at the knife again, and it came loose, but Arthur still lay against the stone, his breath rattling. I knelt beside him, taking his hand in mine.

"Arthur," I breathed, reaching out to smooth the hair back from his brow, and as I did, he shifted again, became Gorlois, his face bruised and swollen.

"You did this to me," he hissed.

I jumped back. "I did not."

He thrust an accusing finger at my chest. "You did this to me," he screamed. And at last I heard the rasping tones of Merlin's voice, and the illusions around me were shattered. I fell on him, thrusting the knife in again as hard as I could. This time, it found its mark.

There was no blood on the knife as I stepped back with it still clutched in my hand. Somehow, I had not expected it. I had not, either, expected Merlin to die when killed. Instead, he lay at my feet on the rock, his eyes wide, his breath coming in panicked gasps, and his shapes flickering between those I knew as his own: Talesin, Melusine, Ambrosius, Silvestris, the shape of a little boy.

"Is this it?" I asked Nimue, as I felt her come to stand beside me. "Is he dead?"

Nimue shook her head. "I do not know that he can be killed. But now he is weak I can begin my work, and when I am ready I will shut him in the earth, in the rock, and he will not be free in my lifetime. Perhaps he will never be free. Arthur will be safe."

* * *

That night I had strange and awful dreams; dreams in which I stood in my room in Tintagel, and through the door limped a man who was sometimes Uther, sometimes Arthur, sometimes Gorlois. And he took my face in his hands, and he said, over and over again,

Give me the child, bring me the boy, and I will take all your pain away.

And I said, Who? Who do you want?

And Arthur took hold of me hard by the arms, and his hands were smeared with blood, and he said, Blood must be paid with blood, Mother. Sin must be paid with sin.

And I knew they were talking about Morgawse's child. Somewhere in the world, somewhere perhaps beneath the earth, Merlin was dying, and because I had struck the blow he was drawing me down to him. I could smell the salt of the sea, the damp earth, iron.

I know what you are, Igraine, Uther's voice said, close against my ear. And his arms wrapped around my waist, and his lips pressed against my neck, and I surrendered to the touch. I can take away your pain. I can restore him to you, if you only set me free.

Uther's voice, but another's words. Even deep asleep, I was not Merlin's fool. I never had been.

Chapter sixty-seven

"Igraine."

I started. I had been sitting in the window seat, trying not to re-live again and again plunging the dagger into Morgan, and finding my hands smeared with Arthur's blood. I was less and less sure of what I had done, less and less sure that I had not harmed my children, and less and less sure that Nimue would ever be able to contain Merlin.

Brastias stood in the doorway. Gone at last was that boyish look of adoration. I was an old woman now, and thin and frail and sick. That morning, it had taken me hours to feel strong enough to stand. I could not have basked in the admiration of men forever.

"What is it, Brastias?"

"Morgawse has arrived."

I nodded, and he left. I supposed he thought I was angry, or disappointed. Certainly, she hadn't done the polite thing and written ahead to say that she wanted to stay, but Morgawse was never one to respect the codes of etiquette the rest of us relied on, and this was her home as much as it was mine. I found, in fact, that I was glad that she had come. I wanted to see her. With Merlin's final curse to me – with what I had done, with what I had seemed to see as he flicked through shapes trying to escape me – raw in my mind, I wanted to make some kind of peace with my daughter.

I remembered how she had been when she was little – the bright, open smile that was her father's, the ready laugh, the boundless curiosity for new experience – but more than that I remembered how much I had loved her. Those first few months when it had been just the two of us. She had been all the world to me, and she had been so perfect. I could not, in fact, remember a time before her father was killed, despite how she had been – loud and wilful and indulged by Gorlois – that I had not thought she was perfect. It had all begun when he died, and she had blamed me.

And perhaps I had not been as understanding as I should have been. She had been a child, deprived of her father. Whatever she was now, I had had a hand in making her that way. She was my flesh, my blood, my bone. She had suffered with me being wrenched from Tintagel Castle all those years ago. And instead of holding tight to one another, we had somehow been torn asunder. Whether it was her, or Uther, or me, I did not know, but it was done. I would not mend it with one conversation, but I was dying, and I would do what I could.

* * *

Morgawse didn't come to see me until the next morning. I was tired from my illness, and she took a long time to stable her horses and unpack her things. As always, travelling with too much, fussing too much about everything. When she did come, I felt stronger than I had for those last few days, after a night of deep sleep, sitting in the window seat wrapped in my blankets and staring down at my beloved rocks below. When she came, Morgawse entered warily. Though she was almost thirty years old, when she came in, she peeped around the door like a nervous child.

"Mother?"

I turned fully in my seat. Here, here in our home, in Tintagel, she looked different once again. Beautiful, yes. Covered in jewels and wrapped in samite and furs, yes. But her beauty did not seem so gaudy in the cool light of the Cornish morning. The clear blue eyes, the red-gold hair – Gorlois' features. Rustic. Wholesome. The soft, sweet features of a pretty dairymaid, wrapped up in queen's clothing.

I opened my mouth to greet her, but it was early and I had not spoken yet, and I was overtaken by hacking coughs that made my eyes water. Morgawse was over to me in three great bounding strides, seemingly completely unencumbered by all those layers of fabric, and she slapped me hard at the back. I felt the air rush back into my lungs, and patted her hand in thanks. Swiftly, Morgawse withdrew her hands, as though she were afraid I would scold her. Perhaps she had felt the bones of my spine against them, and was disgusted by my illness. If that were so, I could not look at her and see awful pity. I fixed my eyes on the rocks below.

"Merlin says I am dying."

I heard Morgawse's breath catch. I hoped she was not going to cry. I would not hold myself together if she cried.

"Is there nothing he can do?" she asked, softly.

I shook my head. "Nothing I am prepared to allow. I'm ready to go."

"Mother, no," Morgawse cried, stepping towards me. I knew she wanted to wrap her arms around me, to bury her face in my hair and sob as she had done when she was a little girl. I couldn't bear that. I couldn't bear to be reminded how cold we had become to one another, how only my death could make her bear to long for her mother's embrace once more. And she would feel my brittle bones and my weak breath, and she would feel sorry for me. I was her mother; I did not want that. I did not want her to remember me weak and shattering to pieces in her arms. I did not want to cry. I did not want her to see me break. I held up my arms, shooing her away from me. I could not bear her fuss.

But she did sit beside me on the window seat when I drew up my knees and tapped the cushion beside me. She was so lovely. Unbearably lovely. There was something perfect about the way her plump lips rested together as she looked out at the rocks below, the way her thick eyelashes, which were visibly reddish even in the cool morning light, fluttered as she gazed away, lost in some thought. My child, my beautiful child. And even if I had been angry with her for blaming me, I knew what kind of man I had given her to. I had done it to save her, but I had no delusions about Lot. He had expected her to be as much of a wife to him as a grown woman when she was only twelve years old, and by the time she turned fifteen she had three little sons to care for alone in the North, far from her sister and mother. I would have been angry. I wanted to believe that Morgawse and I were different, but ultimately we were the same; hadn't I, in some part, enjoyed Brastias' enduring infatuation with me? I certainly missed it now it was gone. The same way she enjoyed the looks and affections of men. Hadn't I felt anger like hers? Anger at Gorlois for abandoning us to Uther's mercy. Anger at Merlin. Anger at her.

I opened my mouth to speak, to tell her how lovely she was, how I was proud of those things I could be proud of – that she was a good mother, that she was strong – but drawing in my breath made me cough again, and when I took my hand away from my mouth, it was spattered with blood. It made me think of Uther. Morgawse must have reached out to steady me as I coughed, for her hand was still on my shoulder.

I was on my knees – I pushed Merlin's words away. Only lies. I would make things right.

"Morgawse," I began warily, "I am glad you are here, because I wanted to feel that things were… right between us. Since I do not have long."

"Mother –"

I shook my head, waved away her fussing. "Please, just listen, Morgawse." Reluctantly, she nodded. Her eyes were bright on me with some inexpressible emotion. "I made sure that that love you thought worth my father's death was tainted and broken," she said.

"I know that you never forgave me for being happy with Uther." She opened her mouth once more to speak, and I held up a hand for her silence. I could feel my heart racing, my blood rushing.

"No – Morgawse, please. I know that you did not. I know, too, that you think your marriage was some kind of punishment. I married your father for love, and that only led to sorrow. I was young, and wealthy. I was the heir to this castle, and he was a young knight, the youngest brother of three. I should have married a greater man, with land of his own. But I married for love. I married him because he was strong, and brave, and full of wild idealism. I married him for love of all those things that brought about his death; those qualities that he has given to you. I didn't want that for you. I wanted you to marry someone who would be powerful enough to protect you. Someone who would temper your wildness.

"But, also, I wanted you to be happy. I supposed that I mistakenly thought that since I had found happiness in the embraces of my new husband, that you might find the same. Find some comfort, some protection. Maybe I underestimated how much you missed your father. You think I am a bad mother to you, an unkind mother, but I did what I hoped would make you happy. But –"

I had something else to say. Something kind. Some pathetic plea for forgiveness. But then I thought of Lot. I thought of his hand closing around my arm, of him grasping hold of me in a dark corridor of Camelot and demanding I play the whore for him, which I agreed to only in order to save her. And Uther had punished me for that, and Lot had accused me of playing games with him.

She could not have known as a girl of not yet twelve, but even when she was an adult woman, she had never reflected on those awful days between her father's death and her marriage, never thought what it must have cost me to save her life, what I must have suffered because she could not keep her mouth shut.

And yes she had been unhappy then, but afterwards she had been happy. I had seen her with Lot, after Gaheris was born, with her arms wound around his neck, and he with his hands burrowed somewhere under her cloak, and she wriggling with pleasure at the touch. And still she insisted that I was selfish and cruel, and still she never cared if I had suffered. She had not even once acknowledged that Gorlois' death had pained me at all. It had never crossed her mind that the loss of her father was a loss I might have borne with her. Instead, she made me her enemy. She blamed me for it all. She chose to hate me. I drew in a breath, steeling myself to demand the truth I needed.

"Instead you learned from the love of your husband not happiness, but control. I never saw a woman learn so fast what effect her looks had on men. I suppose that no one expected you to be beautiful, since you looked like your father, but you grew so, and you learned to use it to punish me for being happy after your father's death, and to punish your husband for being someone else's choice. No, Morgawse, please let me finish. Before I die, I have to hear you speak the truth. All those awful things you said about Uther – I know that you made them up to punish me for being happy with him. I saw you, too, flirting with him in front of your husband, whispering with him. Perhaps that was for me as well. But you must understand, I was young when your father died, I did not want my life to be over. I had to find a way to be happy. Morgawse, forgive me, and tell me the truth, so that I can forgive you."

I held out my hand to her, and Morgawse recoiled. There was an awful look in her eye, like the look of the hind when it knows the bratchets have its scent. Wild panic, animal desperation. She licked her lips slowly. She wound her hands together in her lap. I had waved her away before, but if she had pulled me into her arms then, I would have given up every restraint and wept into her embrace.

"I know that you chose my husband with care, and that you only wanted me to be safe."

I waited for her to say more. Her look was glassy, distant. There was something awful concealed there. She did not want to share truths with me. She did not want to confess or forgive.

I reached out and took her hand. It was soft, slightly warm. Slightly damp. She was nervous. Suddenly, I remembered walking into my audience room and seeing her guiltily sprawled among the cushions. She had never explained herself to me. She had never offered any kind of excuse. Because there was none. She had seduced Arthur deliberately, because she hated Lot, and because she had done the same with his father before him. Lot and Uther had hated each other so deeply; what a perfect revenge for her on the husband she resented to seduce his enemies, both father and son.

"And the rest, Morgawse?" I asked, in barely more than a whisper. I was not sure if I wanted to know the truth.

Morgawse looked away from me, pulled her hand back, shook her head.

I pushed aside the tangle of voices in my head that threatened to cloud out my thoughts. I had to know.

"You did go to bed with him, didn't you?"

Morgawse closed her eyes. I felt an awful wave of nausea pass through me. I had suspected it, of course, but seeing it confirmed like this right before me tore through every memory I had of Uther. One guilty tear rolled down her cheek. When did it begin? As soon as we were in Camelot? Before she married Lot? Or in the years after, when she grew beautiful?

I was so panicked at the thought that I almost missed that she was shaking her head. A rush of desperate relief went through me.

"Well, then you made it up?" I cried.

Morgawse did not move, only continued to shake her head, her eyes screwed shut, the tears falling more steadily now. So this was what it would be; silence, and tears. She could not even look me in the eye. Anger brought me to my feet, filled me with strength I thought was long gone, and I found myself pacing the room. I turned back to her, wild with desperation.

"Morgawse, why can't you tell the truth even now? I want things to be right between us."

She wrapped her arms around her knees and rested her forehead on them. Oh, I had seen that gesture before. When I had walked in on her with Uther. Guilt. Shame. Regret, perhaps. But her regret meant nothing to me if she would not repent.

Faithless bitch. I was her mother. Her mother.

She had played the whore for my husband, and then for her own brother, and she could not even look me in the eye now, now I was dying, and tell me the truth. And what of Merlin's words in her shape? What of his words about Gorlois? He had spoiled her. No, she had spoiled everyone and everything. Now I would leave this world, my memory of Uther forever tainted by her selfishness and greed. And in all this she was determined to hate me. I did not deserve that. I left.

Chapter sixty-eight

I did not know how I had the strength in me for it, but my anger took me up to the battlements of Tintagel. I did not think I had stood here since Morgawse was a little child. I gasped the air into my lungs, I gripped the cold stone battlements hard. I knew what Uther had wanted with her, I knew. All his talk of the old ways, his long obsession with proving himself as powerful as any of the old Kings of all Britain. First Morgawse's father had resisted him, then I had married her to a man who had tried time and again to throw Uther's sovereignty off him, or to take it for himself.

Every woman was her husband's weakest spot, the first point of attack in a bid for political power. I understood that. I had let Uther into Tintagel, I had sealed Gorlois' fate when we had kissed in the corridor. But Morgawse had done what she had done consciously. She had played Lot and Uther and me off against one another. She had wanted to punish me. Perhaps I deserved it. Perhaps. I knew Lot; I knew that he had the capacity to be cruel.

* * *

When I came down from the battlements, damp from the mist, shivering with cold, struggling with wheezing breaths, it was to find Brastias loitering in my bedroom, a distinct look of guilty unease on his face. Perhaps he had overheard me arguing with Morgawse. He did not meet my eye. Perhaps she had even been talking to him, trying to draw him into sympathy with her. Perhaps he believed her. Perhaps it was all true. Even if it were not, Morgawse was still right about her father. I had killed him. But no more than he had killed himself.

"Come here, come, sit beside me."

I patted the window seat cushion and gave Brastias the warmest look I could muster. He had been my friend all these years. If I were dying, I would say goodbye peacefully to him, at least, even if I could not reach my daughter.

Brastias sat reluctantly, and still would not meet my eye. Perhaps he was frightened by my coming death. I was not. I had lived too long in the world to fear leaving it. Whatever was beyond would, at least, be less ambiguous.

I reached out and took his hand.

"You have been a faithful servant all these years, Brastias," I said softly. I patted his hand, then folded it between the two of my own. "To think you were a boy of fifteen when you first came here. It has been twenty-five years – twenty-five? Something like that. Half a lifetime, Brastias, that you have been by my side."

I sighed, and leant my head against his shoulder. Slowly, he put his arm around me. I was relieved, at least, that that glimmer I had seen in his eye had been passing, for now he held me gently and carefully like the old lady I was. I closed my eyes, and I felt his hand smooth down my hair.

"I'm not ready for you to go," Brastias said thickly, after a long time.

I hushed him, sitting up, and took his face in my hands. I was surprised to see that he had tears in his eyes, and his face was splotched with red. I brushed his cheeks with my thumbs.

"It is already done, Brastias." I almost said: *those the White Goddess has claimed cannot be saved*, but I thought better of it. It would only be remembered and then ascribed to some deathbed mania. No man in Britain believed that Igraine, most Christian of queens, might have remembered the gods who watched over her as a girl.

He leaned his forehead against my temple, and I leant into him. I would not have thought, twenty-five years ago, that it would be me and Brastias at the last, clinging together like children. I would have thought it would have been one of my daughters beside me. Or Gorlois, the pair of us grown old together. I supposed I would not have been surprised if I had looked into my future and seen Uther by my side. But Brastias? We do not remark enough upon the presence of our friends.

"I need to know," he whispered, after we had sat in silence like that for a long time. "I need to know whether – if circumstances had been different – my birth, your station, the accidents of time –"

I shushed him.

"Brastias." I squeezed his hand in my own. "You are only saying this because you know I am dying."

I did not want to humour him. It was a useless game to play when no chance, no fate, no circumstance could have kept me and Uther apart. He would never have rested until we were together. I did not even think death would have stopped him.

"I have done things, Igraine. Things of which I am so deeply ashamed. I —"

I stopped him once more. "I am not your confessor, Brastias. We have all sinned." I turned in my seat to look up at him, to put my hand to his cheek. "Whatever your sins, you have been a good friend to me, Brastias. Take care of Tintagel Castle after I am gone, make sure it ends in the care of one of Morgawse's sons. Promise me this."

Brastias nodded, promised with a cracking voice, took my wrist in his hand, and pressed his lips against my palm. He was trembling.

"I need to know," he breathed again. "I need to hear you say it, before it is too late, Igraine. If things had been different — if we had made it to Tintagel that time we tried to run away — if there had been no Gorlois, no Uther —" He drew in a gasping breath and I felt my stomach sink. "Igraine, all of these years I have —"

I put my fingers to his lips, stopped him, stilled him to silence. I leant my forehead against his temple, and he wrapped his arms around me and pulled me to him.

"It would not have made any difference, Brastias," I sighed.

"But that night when you — when we —"

I shook my head, and Brastias took my face in his hands.

"One reckless accident made in anger, Brastias, does not erase a lifetime of real love. You care for me, and you have cared for my daughters. You have protected us all. I am dying, and that makes you believe things that are fantasy and illusion. You are strong. You will survive without me. You have survived this long. You are my friend, Brastias, and that is stronger, steadier and safer than either of the husbands I have known. You love me and I love you, but like a brother, like a sister. Don't torture yourself with false ideas of our past, just because I am dying."

Brastias did not speak again, but he pressed his lips to my forehead, and wrapped his arms around me, and wept. He did not ask me again to pretend that I had been in love with him. I held him tight. I was not sure he believed my words about friendship, but I believed them, and I had said them as much for myself as for him.

When it was growing dark outside, I drew away from him.

"Call Nimue to me please, Brastias. Tell her I'm ready."

* * *

395

Nimue came with the moon. I did not ask if she had finally bound Merlin to the earth, for I could see in her eyes that she had not.

"Are you close?" I asked.

She nodded.

"I'm ready," I began, "but I want to know. I want to know, will my children be safe? Will they be happy?"

Nimue slid into the window seat behind me, and folded my hand between both of hers.

"Soon I will succeed in binding Merlin, then we can be sure. But you know I will do all that is in my power to protect all three of them."

"I know," I sighed. "Show me – will you? Show me how it ends." Nimue put her hand gently over my eyes, and I saw Arthur, approaching middle age, with his beautiful wife beside him, lovely still, though her red hair was faded to copper and there were gentle crinkles of many smiles in the corner of her eyes. He put his arm around her and kissed her softly, just as a young girl ran up to them both, with bright gold curls falling loose from her hair and fierce, grey eyes. She looked for all the world like my sister Elaine, but for the sharp proud nose and the little red mouth that were unmistakably Guinevere's. Behind her ran up a wild young boy who bumped into the back of her legs and fell down. He had thick, red hair cut short, and a stubborn little face that wrinkled up as though he were about to cry. But he did not, and Guinevere bent down to lift her little son back up to his feet and kiss him on the cheek. There was another girl close behind – a girl still, not one halfway to womanhood like the one I had seen first – whose long red hair was still loose, and who still wore the clothes of a child, but whose thoughtful expression and grey eyes reminded me strongly of Morgan, preternaturally adult, and careful. So Arthur would have children, a little family. Into the image before my eyes came Viviane's fosterling, Lancelot, and from the way he slid his arm around the eldest daughter's waist, and the way she leaned towards him in easy affection, I realised that Arthur had married his eldest child to his dear old friend. And though I could not hear the words they said, I could see all of their lips moving in happy, easy conversation, and I felt painfully glad.

The picture before me shifted, and I saw Morgan and Morgawse together, ageing too. Morgan, with her hair threaded thick with grey at the temples, could have – but for her woad – been the image of myself in the mirror, and she sat beside Morgawse holding a book open across both of their laps. Morgawse was dressed plainly and simply, with none of the gaudy jewels and rich silks I had seen her in before, and her hair was tied modestly back. They leant fondly together, as they had always done when they were small. Morgawse looked up as though she had heard a noise, and Gawain, a man in middle age himself, walked in with two young men who must have been his sons, for they bore all his russet looks and broad frame, and they kissed their grandmother and great aunt on the cheek, and sat down with them. In as well came two lovely young girls with Morgan's – and I supposed my own – dark, elegant looks; just a few years apart in age they looked, and as close as Morgan and Morgawse were. The place I saw, I thought, was Lothian castle, so Morgan and Morgawse would be together, and happy, and calm and safe.

I wanted to know more, to see more, and images flashed past me, fast. Morgawse, not much older than I had last seen her, married to a steady, sensible looking man who looked on her with genuine affection, rather than greed for her good looks. Morgan in Avalon, standing in one of their sacred pagan groves hand in hand with Arthur's own foster-brother, and joined in pagan marriage there by the Lady of Avalon herself. Then faster and faster they came, all of my children, and their children, together in Camelot's great hall. Arthur's little son grown and dressed in the armour of a knight, my grandsons Gareth and Gaheris married to a lovely pair of sisters and happy in their homes, and all merry and full of love and goodness.

Nimue did not lift her hand away. I knew what this meant. I did not ask for her to take me to Avalon again, I simply sighed. "So it was worth it."

And she knew what I meant. She knew that I was asking if every sacrifice I had made had been worth it, everything I had suffered, every drop of my own blood I had fought to the death with Merlin over, and softly, softly, she whispered, "Yes, Igraine, it was."

* * *

As the images darkened around me, became different in quality, sharper, colder, I saw one last moment, of Arthur standing face to face with his son. But wait – not the son I had seen before. Not the red-haired boy, but one older, one who could not be much more than fifteen years younger than Arthur himself. Had Arthur and Guinevere had a son right away? Was that what I had seen? He was so like Arthur, made entirely in Arthur's image. Tall, and strong.

But something was strange. Arthur was not an old man, only approaching middle age, yet it was his son who wore Uther's old red and gold coat, and the way that he and Arthur stood to face each other was aggressive, and hostile. Arthur's face was tense, and drawn.

I could feel myself weakening, sinking, and I could not work out what it was about that single moment that made me feel so strange. Not until I saw, across the bridge of Arthur's son's nose, a line of pale gold freckles. So like Morgawse, I thought, as I slipped away. So like Morgawse.

To discover more great books like
Igraine by Lavinia Collins visit:
thebookfolks.com

Printed in Great Britain
by Amazon